## "You can take care of yourself, right? Never need any help."

"I wouldn't say that." Frankie opened her door and got out.

Hank swore and, throwing the pickup into Park, got out and went after her. "Frankie, wait."

She stopped and turned back to him.

"I don't know what your story is, but I do know this," he said. "You have closed yourself off for some reason. I recognize the signs because I've done it for the past three years. In your case, I suspect some man's to blame, the one who keeps calling. One question. Is he dangerous?"

She started to step away, but he grabbed her arm and pulled her back around to face him again.

"I'm fine. There is nothing to worry about."

He shook his head but let go of her arm. "You are one stubborn woman."

He couldn't help but smile because there was a strength and independence in her that he admired.

He'd never known a woman quite like her...

# THE COWBOY'S MISSION

New York Times Bestselling Author

## B.J. DANIELS

Previously published as *Iron Will* and *Cowboy's Redemption*

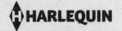

ISBN-13: 978-1-335-42729-8

The Cowboy's Mission

Copyright © 2022 by Harlequin Enterprises ULC

Iron Will
First published in 2019. This edition published in 2022.
Copyright © 2019 by Barbara Heinlein

Cowboy's Redemption
First published in 2018. This edition published in 2022.
Copyright © 2018 by Barbara Heinlein

Recycling programs
for this product may
not exist in your area.

For questions and comments about the quality of this book,
please contact us at CustomerService@Harlequin.com.

Harlequin Enterprises ULC
22 Adelaide St. West, 41st Floor
Toronto, Ontario M5H 4E3, Canada
www.Harlequin.com

Printed in U.S.A.

# CONTENTS

**B.J. Daniels** is a *New York Times* and *USA TODAY* bestselling author. She wrote her first book after a career as an award-winning newspaper journalist and author of thirty-seven published short stories. She lives in Montana with her husband, Parker, and three springer spaniels. When not writing, she quilts, boats and plays tennis. Contact her at bjdaniels.com, on Facebook or on Twitter, @bjdanielsauthor.

## Books by B.J. Daniels

### Harlequin Intrigue

#### Cardwell Ranch: Montana Legacy

*Steel Resolve*
*Iron Will*
*Ambush before Sunrise*
*Double Action Deputy*
*Trouble in Big Timber*
*Cold Case at Cardwell Ranch*

#### Whitehorse, Montana: The Clementine Sisters

*Hard Rustler*
*Rogue Gunslinger*
*Rugged Defender*

### HQN

#### Montana Justice

*Restless Hearts*
*Heartbreaker*
*Heart of Gold*

Visit the Author Profile page
at Harlequin.com for more titles.

# IRON WILL

This one is for Paula Morrison,
who believes like I do that if one schlep bag is a
great idea, then let's make a dozen. Thanks for
making Quilting by the Border quilt club so fun.

# Chapter One

Hank Savage squinted into the sun glaring off the dirty windshield of his pickup as his family ranch came into view. He slowed the truck to a stop, resting one sun-browned arm over the top of the steering wheel as he took in the Cardwell Ranch.

The ranch with all its log-and-stone structures didn't appear to have changed in the least. Nor had the two-story house where he'd grown up. Memories flooded him of hours spent on the back of a horse, of building forts in the woods around the creek, of the family sitting around the large table in the kitchen in the mornings, the sun pouring in, the sound of laughter. He saw and felt everything he'd given up, everything he'd run from, everything he'd lost.

"Been a while?" asked the sultry, dark-haired woman in the passenger seat.

He nodded despite the lump in his throat, shoved back his Stetson and wondered what the hell he was doing back here. This was a bad idea, probably his worst ever.

"Having second thoughts?" He'd warned her about

his big family, but she'd said she could handle it. He wasn't all that sure even he could handle it. He prided himself on being fearless about most things. Give him a bull that hadn't been ridden and he wouldn't hesitate to climb right on. Same with his job as a lineman. He'd faced gale winds hanging from a pole to get the power back on, braved getting fried more times than he liked to remember.

But coming back here, facing the past? He'd never been more afraid. He knew it was just a matter of time before he saw Naomi—just as he had in his dreams, in his nightmares. She was here, right where he'd left her, waiting for him as she had been for three long years. Waiting for him to come back and make things right.

He looked over at Frankie. "You sure about this?"

She sat up straighter to gaze at the ranch and him, took a breath and let it out. "I am if you are. After all, this was your idea."

Like she had to remind him. "Then I suggest you slide over here." He patted the seat between them and she moved over, cuddling against him as he put his free arm around her. She felt small and fragile, certainly not ready for what he suspected they would be facing. For a moment, he almost changed his mind. It wasn't too late. He didn't have the right to involve her.

"It's going to be okay," she said and nuzzled his neck where his dark hair curled at his collar. "Trust me."

He pulled her closer and let his foot up off the brake. The pickup began to roll toward the ranch. It wasn't that he didn't trust Frankie. He just knew that it was only a matter of time before Naomi came to him pleading with him to do what he should have done three years ago. He felt a shiver even though the summer day was unseasonably warm.

*I'm here.*

## Chapter Two

"Looking out that window isn't going to make him show up any sooner," Marshal Hud Savage said to his wife.

"I can't help being excited. It's been three years." Dana Cardwell Savage knew she didn't need to tell him how long it had been. Hud had missed his oldest son as much or more than she had. But finally Hank was coming home—and bringing someone with him. "Do you think it's because he's met someone that he's coming back?"

Hud put a large hand on her shoulder. "Let's not jump to any conclusions, okay? We won't know anything until he gets here. I just don't want to see you get your hopes up."

Her hopes were already up, so there was no mitigating that. Family had always been the most important thing to her. Having her sons all fly the nest had been heartbreak, especially Hank, especially under the circumstances.

She told herself not to think about that. Nothing was going to spoil this day. Her oldest son was coming home after all this time. That had to be good news. And he was bringing someone. She hoped that meant Hank was moving on from Naomi.

"Is that his pickup?" she cried as a black truck came into view. She felt goose bumps pop up on her arms. "I think that's him."

"Try not to cry and make a fuss," her husband said even as tears blurred her eyes. "Let them at least get into the yard," he said as she rushed to the front door and threw it open. "Why do I bother?" he mumbled behind her.

FRANKIE KNEW THE sixty-two-year-old woman who rushed out on the porch had to be Dana Cardwell Savage. Hank had told her about his family. She thought about the softness that came into his voice when he talked about his mother. She'd heard about Dana's strength and determination, but she could also see it in the way she stood hugging herself in her excitement and her curiosity.

Hank had warned her that him bringing home a woman would cause a stir. Frankie could see his mother peering inside the pickup, trying to imagine what woman had stolen her son's heart. She felt a small stab of guilt but quickly pushed it away as a man appeared behind Dana.

Marshal Hud Savage. She'd also heard a lot about him. When Hank had mentioned his dad, she'd seen the change not just in his tone, but his entire body. The trouble between the two ran deep. While Dana was excited, holding nothing back, Frankie could see that Hud was reserved. He had to worry that this wouldn't be a happy homecoming considering the way he'd left things with his oldest son.

Hank's arm tensed around her as he parked and cut the engine. She had the feeling that he didn't want to let her go. He finally eased his hold on her, then gave her a gentle squeeze. "We can do this, right? Ready?"

"As I will ever be," she said, and he opened his door. The moment he did, Dana rushed down the steps to throw her arms around her son. Tears streamed down her face unchecked. She hugged him, closing her eyes, breathing him in as if she'd thought she might never see him again.

Frankie felt her love for Hank at heart level. She slowly slid under the steering wheel and stepped down. Hud, she noticed, had descended the stairs, but stopped at the bottom, waiting, unsure of the reception he was going to get. Feeling for him, she walked around mother and son to address him.

"Hi, I'm Frankie. Francesca, but everyone calls me Frankie." She held out her hand, and the marshal accepted it in his large one as his gaze took her measure. She took his as well. Hud Savage was scared that this visit wasn't an olive branch. Scared that his son was still too angry with him. Probably more scared that he was going to let down his wife by spoiling this reunion.

"It's nice to meet you," the marshal said, his voice rough with what she suspected was emotion. A lot was riding on what would happen during this visit, she thought, and Hud didn't know the half of it.

"Frankie," Hank said behind her. His voice broke. "I want you to meet my mom, Dana."

She turned and came face-to-face with the ranch woman. Dana had been a beauty in her day; anyone could see that. But even in her sixties, she was still very attractive with her salt-and-pepper dark hair and soft, gentle features. She was also a force to be reckoned with. Dana eyed her like a mama bear, one who was sizing her up for the position of daughter-in-law.

Whatever Dana saw and thought of her, the next thing Frankie knew, she was being crushed in the woman's arms. "It is so wonderful to meet you," Dana was saying tearfully.

Behind her, Frankie heard Hud say hello to his son.

"Dad," Hank said with little enthusiasm, and then Dana was ushering them all into the house, telling her son that she'd baked his favorite cookies and made his favorite meal.

Frankie felt herself swept up in all of it as she told herself this would work out—even against her better judgment.

"HANK SEEMS GOOD, doesn't he," Dana said later that night when the two of them were in bed. She'd told herself that things had gone well and that once Hank was home for a while, they would get even better. She hadn't been able to ignore the tension between her son and husband. It made her heart ache because she had no idea how to fix the problem.

"He seems fine." Hud didn't look up from the crime novel he was reading.

"Frankie is pretty, isn't she."

"Uh-huh."

"She's not what I expected. Not really Hank's type, don't you think?"

Hud glanced over at her. "It's been three years since we've seen him. We have no idea what his type is. He probably doesn't know either. He's still young. I thought Naomi wasn't his type." He went back to his book.

"He's thirty-three, not all that young if he wants to have a family," she said. "It's just that Frankie isn't anything like Naomi."

"Maybe that's the attraction."

She heard what he didn't say in his tone. *Maybe that's a blessing.* Hud had never thought Naomi was right for Hank. "I suppose it might be why he's attracted to her. I just never thought he'd get over Naomi."

Hud reached over and, putting down his book, turned out his bedside light. "Good night," he said pointedly.

She took the hint and switched off her own lamp as her husband rolled over, turning his back to her. Within minutes he would be sound asleep, snoring lightly, while she lay awake worrying. The worst part was that she couldn't put her finger on what made her anxious about Hank coming home now and bringing a young woman.

"He wants to move on, put Naomi and all that ugliness behind him, don't you think?" She glanced over at Hud's broad back, but knew he wasn't going to answer because he didn't have the answer any more than she did.

She was just glad that Hank was home for however long he planned to stay and that he wasn't alone anymore. "As long as he's happy…" Hud began to snore softly. She sighed and closed her eyes, silently mouthing her usual nightly prayers that her family all be safe and happy, and thanking God for bringing Hank home.

"IT'S BEAUTIFUL HERE," Frankie said as she stood on the guest cabin deck overlooking the rest of the ranch in the starlight. The cabin was stuck back high against the mountain looking down on the ranch and the Gallatin River as it wound past. "I feel like I can see forever. Are those lights the town?" she asked as Hank joined her.

"Big Sky, Montana," he said with little enthusiasm.

She turned to him. "How do you think it went?"

He shook his head. "I'm just thankful that my mother listened to me and didn't have the whole family over tonight. But maybe it would have been less uncomfortable if they'd all been there. Tomorrow you'll meet my sister, Mary, and her fiancé, Chase."

"There's your uncle Jordan and aunt Stacy."

"And a bunch of my mother's cousins and their families," he said with a sigh.

She couldn't imagine having all that family. Her father had left when she was three. Her mother had married several times, but the marriages didn't last. Her mother had died in a car accident right after she'd graduated from high school, but they'd never been close. The only real family she'd ever felt she had was an uncle who'd become her mentor after college, but he was gone now too.

"You could just tell them the truth," she said quietly after a moment. She envied Hank his family, and felt lying to them was a mistake.

He shook his head. "This is difficult enough." He

turned to go back inside. "You can have the first bed-room. I'll take the other one." With that, he went inside and closed the door.

Frankie stood on the deck, the summer night a fragrant blend of pine and water. There was just enough starlight that she caught glimpses of it shining off the surface of the river snaking through the canyon. Steep, rocky cliffs reflected the lights of the town, while the mountains rose up into the midnight-blue star-filled canopy.

She felt in awe of this ranch and his family. How could Hank have ever left it behind? But the answer seemed to be on the breeze as if everything about this place was inhabited by one woman. Naomi. She was what had brought Hank home. She was also why Frankie was here.

## Chapter Three

Hank rose before the sun and made his way down the mountainside to the corral. He'd missed the smell of saddle leather and horseflesh. He was breathing it in when he heard someone approaching from behind him.

He'd always been keenly aware of his environment. Growing up in Montana on a ranch, he'd learned at a young age to watch out for things that could hurt you— let alone kill you—in the wild. That instinct had only intensified in the years he'd been gone as if he felt a darkness trailing him, one that he could no longer ignore.

"You're up early," he said to his father without turning around as Hud came up behind him.

"I could say the same about you. I thought you and I should talk."

"Isn't that what we did at dinner last night?" Hank asked sarcastically. His father hadn't said ten words. Instead his mother had filled in the awkward silences.

"I'm glad you came back," Hud said.

He turned finally to look at his father. The sun glowed behind the mountain peaks to the east, rimming them with a bright orange glow. He studied his father in the dim light. They were now both about the same height, both with broad shoulders and slim hips. Both stubborn to a fault. Both never backing down from a fight. He stared at the marshal, still angry with him after all these years.

"I'm not staying long."

Hud nodded. "That's too bad. Your mother will be disappointed. So am I. Son—"

"There really isn't anything to talk about, is there? We said everything we had to say three years ago. What would be the point of rehashing it?"

"I stand by what I did."

Hank laughed. "I'd be shocked if you didn't." He shook his head. "It must be wonderful to know that you're always right."

"I'm not always right. I just do the best I can with the information and evidence I have."

"Well, you're wrong this time," he said and turned back to the horses. One of the mares had come up to have her muzzle rubbed. Behind him, he heard his father head back toward the house and felt some of the tension in his chest release even as he cursed under his breath.

DANA HAD INSISTED on making them breakfast. After a stack of silver-dollar-sized pancakes swimming in butter and huckleberry syrup, a slab of ham, two eggs over easy and a tall glass of orange juice, Frankie sat back smiling. She couldn't remember the last time she'd eaten so much or liked it more.

No matter what happened on this visit to the ranch, she planned to enjoy herself as much as was possible.

"I thought dinner was amazing," she told Dana. Hank's favorite meal turned out to be roast beef, mashed potatoes, carrots and peas and homemade rolls. "But this breakfast... It was so delicious. I never eat like this."

"I can tell by your figure," her host said, beaming. Clearly Dana equated food with love as she looked to her son to see if he'd enjoyed it. He'd cleaned his plate, which seemed to make her even happier. "So, what do you two have planned today?"

"I thought I'd show Frankie around Big Sky," Hank said.

"Well, it's certainly changed since you were here," his mother said. "I think you'll be surprised. Will you two be back for lunch? Your father still comes home every day at twelve."

"I think we'll get something in town, but thanks, Mom. Thanks for everything."

Tears filled her eyes and her voice broke when she spoke. "I'm just glad to have you home. Now, plan on being here for supper. Your dad's doing steaks on the grill and some of the family is stopping by. Not everyone. We don't want to overwhelm Frankie."

"I appreciate that," he said.

Frankie offered to help with the dishes, but Dana shooed them out, telling them to have a fun day.

Fun was the last thing on the agenda, she thought as she left with Hank.

HANK HAD BEEN restless all morning, but he'd known that he couldn't get away from the house without having one of his mother's breakfasts. The last thing he wanted to do was hurt her feelings. It would be bad enough when she learned the truth.

Pushing that thought away, he concentrated on his driving as he headed downriver. He'd grown up with the Gallatin River in his backyard. He hadn't thought much about it until Frankie was doing her research and asked him, "Did you know that the Gallatin River begins in the northwest corner of Yellowstone National Park to travel one hundred and twenty miles through the Gallatin Canyon past Big Sky to join the Jefferson and Madison Rivers to form the Missouri River?"

That she found this so fascinating had surprised him. "I did know that," he told her and found himself studying her with renewed interest. The river had been part of his playground, although he'd been taught to have a healthy respect for it because of the current, the deep holes and the slippery rocks.

Now as he drove along the edge of the Gallatin as it cut through the rocky cliffs of the canyon, he caught glimpses of the clear green water rushing over granite boulders on its way to the Gulf of Mexico and felt a shiver because he'd learned just how deadly it could be.

A few miles up the road, he slowed to turn onto a dirt road that wound through the tall pines. Dust rose behind the pickup. He put down his window and breathed in the familiar scents. They made his heart ache.

Ahead, he could see the cliffs over the top of the

pines. He parked in the shade of the trees and sat for a moment, bracing himself.

"This is the place?" Frankie whispered, her gaze on the cliff that could be seen over the top of the pines.

He didn't answer as he climbed out. He heard her exit the pickup but she didn't follow him as he walked down through the thick pines toward the river, knowing he needed a few minutes alone.

An eerie silence filled the air. When he'd first gotten out of the truck, he'd heard a squirrel chatting in a nearby tree, a meadowlark calling from the tall grass, hoppers buzzing as they rose with each step.

But now that he was almost to the spot, there was no sound except the gentle lap of the water on the rocks. As he came out of the pines, he felt her—just as he always had. Naomi. It was as if her soul had been stranded here in this very spot where she'd died.

His knees went weak and he had to sit down on one of the large boulders along the shore. He put his head in his hands, unaware of time passing. Unaware of anything but his pain.

Like coming out of a daze, he lifted his head and looked across the river to the deep pool beneath the cliff. Sunlight glittered off the clear emerald surface. His heart in his throat, he lifted his gaze to the rock ledge high above the water. Lover's Leap. That was what it was called.

His gaze shifted to the trail from the bridge downriver. It was barely visible through the tall summer grass and the pines, but he knew that kids still traveled along it to the ledge over the water. The trick, though, was to jump out far enough. Otherwise...

A shaft of sun cut through the pine boughs that hung out over the water, nearly blinding him. He closed his eyes again as he felt Naomi pleading with him to find out the truth. He could feel her arguing that he knew her. He knew she was terrified of heights. She would never have gone up there. Especially alone. Especially at night. Why would she traverse the treacherous trail to get to the rock ledge to begin with—let alone jump?

It had made no sense.

Not unless she hadn't jumped to her death. Not unless she'd been pushed.

Hank opened his eyes and looked up through the shaft of sunlight to see a figure moving along the narrow trail toward the rock ledge high on the cliff. His throat went dry as shock ricocheted through him. He started to call to her even as he knew it was his mind playing tricks on him. It wasn't Naomi.

He opened his mouth, but no sound came out and he stared frozen in fear as he recognized the slim figure. Frankie. She'd walked downriver to the bridge and, after climbing up the trail, was now headed for the ledge.

HUD HEAVED HIMSELF into his office chair, angry at himself on more levels than he wanted to contemplate. He swore as he unlocked the bottom drawer of his desk and pulled out the file. That he'd kept it for three years in the locked drawer where he could look at it periodically was bad enough. That he was getting it out now and going over it as he'd done so many times over those years made it even worse.

He knew there was nothing new in the file. He could practically recite the report by heart. Nothing had changed. So why was he pulling it out now? What good would it do to go over it again? None.

But he kept thinking about Hank and his stubborn insistence that Naomi hadn't committed suicide. He didn't need a psychiatrist to tell him that suicide was the most perverse of deaths. Those left behind had to deal with the guilt and live with the questions that haunted them. Why hadn't they known? Why hadn't they helped? Why had she killed herself? Was it because of them? It was the why that he knew his son couldn't accept.

Why would a beautiful young woman like Naomi Hill kill herself? It made no sense.

Hud opened the file. Was it possible there was something he'd missed? He knew that wasn't the case and yet he began to go over it, remembering the call he'd gotten that morning from the fisherman who'd found her body in the rocks beneath Lover's Leap.

There had been little doubt about what had happened. Her blouse had caught on a rock on the ledge, leaving a scrap of it fluttering in the wind. The conclusion that she'd either accidentally fallen or jumped was later changed to suicide after more information had come in about Naomi's state of mind in the days before her death.

Add to that the coroner's report. Cause of death: skull crushed when victim struck the rocks below the cliff after either falling or jumping headfirst.

But his son Hank had never accepted it and had never forgiven his father for not investigating her death longer, more thoroughly. Hank had believed that Naomi hadn't fallen or jumped. He was determined that she'd been murdered.

Unfortunately, the evidence said otherwise, and Hud was a lawman who believed in facts—not conjecture or emotion. He still did and that was the problem, wasn't it?

# Chapter Four

Hank felt dizzy and sick to his stomach as he watched Frankie make her way out to the edge of the cliff along the narrow ledge. She had her cell phone in her hand. He realized she was taking photos of the trail, the distance to the rocks and water below as well as the jagged rocky ledge's edge.

As she stepped closer to the edge, he heard a chunk of rock break off. It plummeted to the boulders below, and his heart fell with it. The rock shattered into pieces before dropping into the water pooling around the boulders, making ripples that lapped at the shore.

He felt his stomach roil. "Get down from there," he called up to her, his voice breaking. "Please." He couldn't watch. Sitting down again, he hung his head to keep from retching. It took a few minutes before his stomach settled and the need to vomit passed. When he looked up, Frankie was no longer balanced on the ledge.

His gaze shot to the rocks below, his pulse leaping with the horrible fear that filled him. There was no body on the rocks. No sign of Frankie. He put his head back down and took deep breaths. He didn't know how long he stayed like that before he heard the crunch of pine needles behind him.

"I'm sorry," Frankie said. "I should have known that would upset you."

He swore and started to get to his feet unsteadily. She held out a hand and he took it, letting her help him up. "I'm usually not like this."

She smiled. "You think I don't know that?"

"You should have told me you were going up there," he said.

"You would have tried to stop me," she said and pulled out her phone. "I needed to see it." She looked up from her screen. "Have you been up there?"

"Not since Naomi died, no."

She frowned, cocking her head. "You've jumped from there."

"When I was young and stupid."

Nodding, Frankie said, "You have to push off the cliff wall, throw your body out to miss the rocks and to land in the pool. Daring thing to do."

"Helps if you're young, stupid and with other dumb kids who dare you," he said. "And before you ask, yes, Naomi knew I'd jumped off the ledge. She was terrified of heights. She couldn't get three feet off the ground without having vertigo. It's why I know she didn't climb up there on her own. Someone made her."

"Sometimes people do things to try to overcome fears," Frankie said and shrugged.

"Naomi didn't. She was terrified of so many things. Like horses. I tried to teach her to ride." He shook his head. "I'm telling you, she wouldn't have climbed up there unless there was a gun to her head. Even if she'd wanted to kill herself, she wouldn't have chosen that ledge as her swan song."

With that, he turned and started toward the truck, wishing he'd never come back here. He'd known it would be hard, but he hadn't expected it to nearly incapacitate him. Had he thought Naomi would be gone? Her soul released? Not as long as her death was still a mystery.

Frankie didn't speak again until they were headed back toward Big Sky. "At some point you're going to have to tell me why your father doesn't believe it was murder."

"I'll do one better. I'll get a copy of the case file. In the meantime, I'll show you Big Sky. I'm not ready for my parents to know the truth yet."

She nodded and leaned back as if to enjoy the trip. "I timed how long it took me to walk up the trail from the bridge to the ledge. Eleven minutes. How long do you think it would have taken Naomi?"

"Is this relevant?"

"It might be." She turned to look at him then. "You said the coroner established a time of death because of Naomi's broken wristwatch that was believed to have smashed on the rocks. We need to examine the time sequence. She left you at the ranch, right? The drive to the cliff took us ten minutes. She could have beat that because at that time of the evening in early fall and off season, there wouldn't have been as much traffic, right?"

He nodded.

"So if she left the ranch and went straight to the bridge—"

"She didn't. She met her killer at some point along the way. Maybe she stopped for gas or… I don't know. Picked up a hitchhiker."

Frankie shot him a surprised look. "From what you've told me about Naomi, she wouldn't have stopped for a hitchhiker."

"It would have had to be someone she knew. Can we stop talking about this for just a little while?" He hated the pleading in his voice. "Let me show you around Big Sky, maybe drive up to Mountain Village."

She nodded and looked toward the town as he slowed for the turn. "So Big Sky was started by Montana native and NBC news co-anchorman Chet Huntley. I read it is the second-largest ski resort in the country by acreage." She gazed at Lone Mountain. "That peak alone stands at over eleven thousand feet."

He glanced over at her and chuckled. "You're like a walking encyclopedia. Do you always learn all these facts when you're…working?"

"Sure," she said, smiling. "I find it interesting. Like this canyon. There is so much history here. I've been trying to imagine this road when it was dirt and Yellowstone Park only accessible from here by horses and wagons or stagecoaches."

"I never took you for a history buff," he said.

She shrugged. "There's a lot you don't know about me."

He didn't doubt that, he thought as he studied her out of the corner of his eye. She continued to surprise him. She was so fearless. So different from Naomi. Just the thought of her up on that ledge— He shoved that thought away as he drove into the lower part of Big Sky known as Meadow Village. His mother was right. Big Sky had changed so much he hardly recognized the small resort town with all its restaurants and fancy shops along with miles of condos. He turned up the road to Mountain Village, where the ski resort was located, enjoying showing Frankie around. It kept his mind off Naomi.

"So you met the woman Hank brought home?"

Dana looked up at her sister, Stacy. They were in the ranch house kitchen, where Dana was taking cookies out of the oven. "I thought you might have run into them this morning before they took off for some sightseeing."

Her sister shook her head. Older than Dana, Stacy had been the wild one, putting several marriages under her belt at a young age. But she'd settled down after she'd had her daughter, Ella, and had moved back to the ranch to live in one of the new cabins up on the mountainside.

"I stopped over at their cabin this morning to see if they needed anything," Stacy said now, avoiding her gaze.

Dana put her hands on her hips. She knew her sister so well. *"What?"*

Stacy looked up in surprise. "Nothing to get in a tizzy over, just something strange."

"Such as?"

"I don't want to be talking out of turn, but I noticed

that they slept in separate bedrooms last night." Her sister snapped her lips shut as if the words had just sneaked out.

Dana frowned as she put another pan of cookie dough into the oven and, closing the door, set the timer. Hadn't she felt something between Hank and Frankie? Something not quite right? "They must have had a disagreement. I'm sure it is difficult for both of them being here after what happened with Naomi. That's bound to cause some tension between them."

"Probably. So, you like her?"

"I do. She's nothing like Naomi."

"What does that mean?" Stacy asked.

"There's nothing timid about her. She's more self-assured, seems more…independent. I was only around her for a little while. It's just an impression I got. You remember how Naomi was."

Her sister's right brow shot up. "You mean scared of everything?"

Dana had been so surprised the first time Hank had brought Naomi home and the young woman had no interest in learning to ride a horse.

*I would be terrified to get on one*, she'd said.

*Naomi isn't…outdoorsy*, was the way Hank had described her. That had been putting it mildly. Dana couldn't imagine the woman living here. As it turned out, living at Cardwell Ranch was the last thing Naomi had in mind.

"Frankie looks as if she can handle herself. I saw Hank gazing at her during dinner. He seems intrigued by her."

"I can't wait to meet her," Stacy said now.

"Why don't you come to dinner? Mary's going to be here, and Chase. Jordan and Liza are coming as well. I thought that was enough for one night." Her daughter and fiancé would keep things light. Her brother and his wife would be a good start as far as introducing Frankie to the family.

"Great. I'll come down early and help with the preparations," her sister said. "I'm sorry I mentioned anything about their sleeping arrangements. I'm sure it's nothing."

FRANKIE LOOKED OUT at the mountain ranges as she finished the lunch Hank had bought them up at the mountain resort. This was more like a vacation, something she hadn't had in years. She would have felt guilty except for the fact that technically she *was* working. She looked at the cowboy across the table from her, remembering the day he'd walked into her office in Lost Creek outside of Moscow, Idaho.

"Why now?" Frankie had asked him after he'd wanted to hire her to find out what had really happened to his girlfriend. "It's been three years, right? That makes it a cold case. I can't imagine there is anything to find." She'd seen that her words had upset him and had quickly lifted both hands in surrender. "I'm not saying it's impossible to solve a case that old…" She tried not to say the words *next to impossible*.

She'd talked him into sitting down, calming down and telling her about the crime. Turned out that the marshal—Hank's father—had sided with the coroner that the woman's death had been a suicide. She'd doubted this could get worse because it was clear to her that Hank Savage had been madly in love with the victim. Talk about wearing blinders. Of course he didn't want to believe the woman he loved had taken a nosedive off a cliff.

"I thought I could accept it, get over it," Hank had said. "I can't. I won't. I have to know the truth. I know this is going to sound crazy, but I can feel Naomi pleading with me to find her murderer."

It didn't sound crazy as much as it sounded like wishful thinking. If this woman had killed herself, then he blamed himself.

Her phone had rung. She'd checked to see who was calling and declined the call. But Hank could tell that the call had upset her.

"Look, if you need to take that…" he'd said.

"No." The last thing she wanted to do was take the call. What had her upset was that if she didn't answer one of the calls from the man soon, he would be breaking down her door. "So, what is it you want me to do?"

Hank had spelled it out for her.

She'd stared at him in disbelief. "You want me to go to Big Sky with you."

"I know it's a lot to ask and this might not be a good time for you."

He had no idea how good a time it was for her to leave town. "I can tell this is important for you. I can't make you any promises, but I'll come out and look into the incident." She'd pulled out her standard contract and slid it across the table with a pen.

Hank hadn't even bothered to read it. He'd withdrawn his wallet. "Here's five hundred dollars. I'll pay all your expenses and a five-thousand-dollar bonus if you solve this case—along with your regular fee," he'd said, pushing the signed contract back across the table to her. As the same caller had rung her again, Hank had asked, "When can you leave?"

"Now's good," she'd said.

## Chapter Five

Frankie had tried to relax during dinner later that night at the main ranch house, but it was difficult. She now understood at least the problem between Hank and his father. From what she could gather, the marshal was also angry with his son. Hank had refused to accept his father's conclusion about Naomi's death. The same conclusion the coroner had come up with as well.

Hank thought his father had taken the easy way out. But Frankie had been around Hud Savage only a matter of hours and she knew at gut level that he wasn't a man who took the easy way out. He believed clear to his soul that Naomi Hill had killed herself.

During dinner, Hank had said little. Dana's sister, Stacy, had joined them, along with Dana's daughter, Mary, and her fiancé, Chase, and Dana's brother, Jordan, and wife, Liza. Hank had been polite enough to his family, but she could tell he was struggling after going to the spot where Naomi had died.

She'd put a hand on his thigh to try to get him to relax and he'd flinched. The reaction hadn't gone unnoticed by his mother and aunt Stacy. Frankie had smiled and snuggled against him. If he hoped to keep their secret longer, he needed to be more attentive. After all, it was his idea that they pretend to be involved in a relationship. That way Frankie could look into Naomi's death without Hank going head-to-head with his father.

When she'd snuggled against him, he'd felt the nudge and responded, putting an arm around her and pulling her close. She'd whispered in his ear, "Easy, sweetie."

Nodding, he'd laughed, and she'd leaned toward him to kiss him on the lips. It had been a quick kiss meant to alleviate any doubt as to what was going on. The kiss had taken him by surprise. He'd stared into her eyes for a long moment, then smiled.

When Frankie had looked up, she'd seen there was relief on his mother's face. His mother had bought it. The aunt, not so much. But that was all right. The longer they could keep their ruse going, the better. Otherwise it would be war between father and son. They both wanted to avoid that since it hadn't done any good three years ago. Frankie doubted it would now.

"Cake?" Dana asked now, getting to her feet.

"I would love a piece," Frankie said. "Let me help you." She picked up her plate and Hank's to take them into the kitchen against his mother's protests. "You outdid yourself with dinner," she said as she put the dishes where the woman suggested.

Taking advantage of the two of them being alone with the door closed, Dana turned to her—just as Frankie had known she would. "I'm not being nosy, honestly. Is everything all right between you and Hank?"

She smiled as she leaned into the kitchen counter.

She loved this kitchen with the warm yellow color, the photographs of family on the walls, the clichéd saying carved in the wood plaque hanging over the door. There was a feeling of permanency in this kitchen, in this house, this ranch. As if no matter what happened beyond that door, this place would weather the storm because it had survived other storms.

"It's hard on him being back here because of Naomi," Frankie said.

"Of course it is," Dana said on a relieved breath. "But he has you to help him through it."

She smiled and nodded. "I'm here for him and he knows it. Though it has put him on edge. But not to worry. I'll stand by him."

Tears filled the older woman's eyes as she quickly stepped to Frankie and threw her arms around her. "I can't tell you how happy I am that Hank has you."

She hadn't thought her generic words would cause such a response but she hugged Dana back, enjoying for a moment the warm hug from this genuine, open woman.

Dana stepped back, wiping her tears as Stacy and Jordan's wife, Liza, came in with the rest of the dirty dishes and leftover food. "We best get that cake out there or we'll have a riot on our hands," Dana said. "If you take the cake, I'll take the forks and dessert plates."

"I'M SORRY," HANK SAID when they reached their cabin and were finally alone again. Dinner had been unbearable, but he knew he should have played along better than he had. "You were great."

"Thanks. Your mother was worried we were having trouble. I assured her that coming back here is hard on you because of Naomi. Your family is nice," she said. "They obviously love you."

He groaned. He hated lying to his mother most of all. "That's what makes this so hard. I wanted to burst out with the truth at dinner tonight." He could feel her gaze on him.

"Why didn't you?"

Hank shook his head. He thought about Frankie's kiss, her nuzzling against him. He'd known it would be necessary if they hoped to pass themselves off as a couple, but he hadn't been ready for it. The kiss had taken him by surprise. And an even bigger surprise had been his body's reaction to it, to her.

He turned away, glad it was late so they could go to bed soon. "I think I'm going to take a walk. Will you be all right here by yourself?"

She laughed. "I should think so since I'm trained in self-defense and I have a license to carry a firearm. You've never asked, but I'm an excellent shot."

"You have a gun?" He knew he shouldn't have been surprised and yet he was. She seemed too much like the girl next door to do the job she did. Slim, athletic, obviously in great shape, she just kept surprising him as to how good she was at this.

If anyone could find out the truth about Naomi, he thought it might be her.

AFTER HANK LEFT, Frankie pulled out her phone and looked again at the photographs she'd taken earlier from the ledge along the cliff. Standing up there being buffeted by the wind, her feet on the rocky ledge, she'd tried to imagine what Naomi had been thinking. If she'd had time to think.

Hank was so sure that she'd been murdered. It was such a strange way to murder someone. Also, she suspected there were other reasons his father believed it was suicide. The killer would have had to drag her up that trail from the bridge and then force her across the ledge. Dangerous, since if the woman was that terrified of heights, she would have grabbed on to her killer for dear life.

How had the killer kept her from pulling him down with her? It had been a male killer, hadn't it? That was what Frankie had imagined. Unless the couple hadn't gone up to the ledge with murder in mind.

Frankie rubbed her temples. People often did the thing you least expected them to do. Which brought her back to suicide. What if Hank was wrong? What if suicide was the only conclusion to be reached after this charade with his family? Would he finally be able to accept it?

The door opened and he came in on a warm summer night gust of mountain air. For a moment he was silhouetted, his broad shoulders filling the doorway. Then he stepped into the light, his handsome face twisted in grief. Her heart ached for him. She couldn't imagine the kind of undying love he'd felt for Naomi. Even after three years, he was still grieving. She wondered at the size of Hank's heart.

"I'd like to talk to Naomi's mother in the morning,"

she said, turning away from such raw pain. "Lillian Brandt, right?"

"Right." His voice sounded hoarse.

"It would help if you told me about the things that were going on with Naomi before her death, the things that made the coroner and your father believe it was a suicide." When he didn't answer, she turned. He was still standing just inside the door, his Stetson in the fingers of his left hand, his head down. She was startled for a moment and almost stepped to him to put her arms around him.

"There's something I haven't told you." He cleared his throat and looked up at her. "Naomi and I had a fight that night before she left the ranch." He swallowed.

She could see that this was going to take a while and motioned to the chairs as she turned and went into the small kitchen. Opening the refrigerator, she called over her shoulder, "Beer?" She pulled out two bottles even though she hadn't heard his answer and returned to the small living area.

He'd taken a seat, balancing on the edge, nervously turning the brim of his hat in his fingers. When she held out a beer, he took it and tossed his hat aside. Twisting off the cap, Frankie sat in the chair opposite him. She took a sip of the beer. It was icy cold and tasted wonderful. It seemed to soothe her and chase away her earlier thoughts when she'd seen Hank standing in the doorway.

She put her feet up on the well-used wooden coffee table, knowing her boots wouldn't be the first ones that had rested there. She wanted to provide an air of companionship to make it easier for him to tell her the truth. She'd learned this from her former cop uncle who'd been her mentor when she'd first started out.

"What did you fight about?" she asked as Hank picked at the label on his beer bottle with his thumb without taking a drink.

"It was stupid." He let out a bitter laugh as he lifted his head to meet her gaze. "I wasn't ready to get married and Naomi was." His voice broke again as he said, "She told me I was killing her."

Frankie took a drink of her beer before asking, "How long had you been going out?" It gave Hank a moment to collect himself.

He took a sip of his beer. "Since after college. We met on a blind date. She'd been working as an elementary school teacher, but said she'd rather be a mother and homemaker." He looked away. "I think that's what she wanted more than anything. Even more than me."

She heard something in his voice, in his words. "You didn't question that she loved you, did you?"

"No." He said it too quickly and then shook his head. "I did that night. I questioned a lot of things. She seemed so...so wrong for me. I mean, there was nothing about the ranch that she liked. Not the horses, the dust, the work. I'd majored in ranch management. I'd planned to come home after college and help my folks with the place."

"And that's what you were doing."

He nodded. "But Naomi didn't want to stay here. She didn't like the canyon or living on my folks' place. She wanted a home in a subdivision down in Bozeman. In what she called 'civilization with sidewalks.'" He shook his head. "I had no idea sidewalks meant that much to her before that night. She wanted everything I didn't."

"What did she expect you to do for a living in Bozeman?"

"Her stepfather had offered me a job. He was a Realtor and he said he'd teach me the business." Hank took a long pull on his beer. "But I was a rancher. This is where I'd grown up. This is what I knew how to do and what I..."

"What you loved."

His blue eyes shone as they locked with hers. She saw that his pain was much deeper than even she'd thought. If Naomi had committed suicide, then he blamed himself because of the fight. He'd denied her what she wanted most, a different version of him.

"So she left hurt and angry," Frankie said. "Did she indicate where she was going? I'm assuming the two of you were living together here at the ranch."

"She said she was going to spend the night at her best friend Carrie White's apartment in Meadow Village here at Big Sky and that she needed time to think about all of this." He swallowed again. "I let her go without trying to fix it."

"It sounds like it wasn't an easy fix," Frankie commented and finished her beer. Getting up, she tilted the bottle in offer. Hank seemed to realize he still had a half-full bottle and quickly downed the rest. She took both empties to the kitchen and came back with two more.

Handing him one, she asked, "You tried to call her

that night or the next morning?" As she asked the question, she knew where his parents would have stood on the marriage and Naomi issue. They wouldn't want to tarnish their son's relationship because of their opinions about his choice for a partner, but they also wouldn't want him marrying a woman who was clearly not a good match for him. One who took him off the ranch and the things he loved.

"That night, I was in no mood to discuss it further, so I waited and called her the next morning." He opened his beer and took a long pull. "Maybe if I'd called not long after she left—"

"What had you planned to say?" she asked, simply curious. It was a moot point now. Nor had his plans had anything to do with what happened to Naomi. By then, she was dead.

"I was going to tell her that I'd do whatever she wanted." He let out a long sigh and tipped the beer bottle to his lips. "But when she didn't answer, I changed my mind. I realized it wasn't going to work." His voice broke again. "I loved her, but she wanted to make me over, and I couldn't be the man she wanted me to be." His eyes narrowed. "You can dress me up, but underneath I'm still just a cowboy."

"Did you leave her a message on her phone?"

He nodded and looked away, his blue eyes glittering with tears. "I told her goodbye, but by then it would have been too late." His handsome face twisted in pain.

Frankie sat for a moment, considering everything he'd told her. "Was her cell phone found on her body or in her car?"

He shook his head. "Who knows what she did with it. The phone could have gone into the river. My father had his deputies search for it, but it was never found." His voice broke. "Maybe I did drive her to suicide," he said and took a drink as if to steady himself.

"I'm going to give you my professional opinion, for what it's worth," she said, knowing he wasn't going to like it. "I don't believe she killed herself. She knew that you loved her. She was just blowing off some steam when she headed for her friend's house. Did her friend see her at all?"

He shook his head.

"So she didn't go there. That would explain the discrepancy in the time she left you and when her watch was broken. Is there somewhere else she might have gone? Another friend's place? A male friend's?"

His eyes widened in surprise. "A male friend's? Why would you even ask about—"

"Because I know people. She was counting on you to change and do what she wanted, but after four years? She would have realized it was a losing battle and had someone else waiting in the wings."

He slammed down his beer bottle and shoved to his feet. "You make her sound like she was—"

"A woman determined to get married, have kids, stay home and raise them while her husband had a good job that allowed all her dreams to come true?"

"She wasn't—she—" He seemed at a loss for words.

"Hey, Hank. Naomi was a beautiful woman who had her own dreams." He had showed her a photograph of Naomi. Blonde, green-eyed, a natural beauty.

Ignoring a strange feeling of jealousy, Frankie got to her feet and finished her beer before she spoke. She realized that she'd probably been too honest with him. But someone needed to be, she told herself. It wasn't just the beer talking. Or that sudden stab of jealousy when she'd thought of Naomi.

In truth, she was annoyed at him because she knew that if he'd reached Naomi on the phone that night, he would have buckled under. He would have done whatever she wanted, including marrying her. On some level, he would have been miserable and resented her the rest of his life, but being the man he was, he would have made the best of it. Naomi dying had saved him and he didn't even realize it.

"We need to find the other man," Frankie said as she took her bottle to the recycling bin before turning toward the bedroom.

Hank let out a curse. "You're wrong. You're dead wrong. I don't know why I—"

She cut off the rest of his words as she closed the bedroom door. She knew he was angry and probably ready to fire her. All she could hope was that he would cool down by the morning and would trust that she knew what she was talking about. Oh, she'd known women like Naomi all her life—including her very own mother, who chewed up men and spit them out one after another as they disappointed her. That was the problem with trying to make over a man.

HANK COULDN'T SLEEP. He lay in the second bedroom, staring up at the ceiling, cursing the fact that he'd brought Frankie here. What had he been thinking? This had to be the stupidest idea he'd ever come up with. Clearly, she didn't get it. She hadn't known Naomi.

Another man?

He thought about storming into her bedroom, telling her to pack her stuff and taking her back to Idaho tonight. Instead, he tossed and turned, getting more angry by the hour. He would fire her. First thing in the morning, he'd do just that.

Who did she think she was, judging Naomi like that? Naomi was sweet, gentle, maybe a little too timid… He rolled over and glared at the bedroom door. Another man in the wings! The thought made him so angry he could snap off nails with his teeth.

As his blood pressure finally began to drop somewhere around midnight, he found himself wondering if Naomi's friend Carrie knew more than she'd originally told him. If there had been another man—

He gave that thought a hard shove away. Naomi had loved him. Only him. She'd wanted the best for him. He rolled over again. She thought she knew what was best for him. He kicked at the blanket tangled around his legs. Maybe if she had lived she would have realized that what was best for him, for them, was staying on the ranch, letting him do what he knew and loved. Sidewalks were overrated.

Staring up at the ceiling, he felt the weight of her death press against his chest so hard that for a moment he couldn't breathe.

*You don't want to let yourself believe that she committed suicide because you feel guilty about the argu-*

*ment you had with her before she left the ranch*, his
father had said. *Son, believe me, it took more than some
silly argument for her to do what she did. We often don't
know those closest to us or what drives them to do what
they do. This wasn't your fault.*

Hank groaned, remembering his father's words three
years ago. Could he be wrong about a lot of things? He
heard the bedroom door open. He could see Frankie
silhouetted in the doorway.

"If there is another man, then it would prove that
she didn't commit suicide," the PI said. The bedroom
door closed.

He glared at it for a long moment. Even if Frankie
had gone back to her bedroom and locked the door,
he knew he could kick it down if he wanted to. But as
Frankie's words registered, he pulled the blanket up
over him and closed his eyes, exhausted from all of
this. If there had been another man, then he would be
right about her being murdered.

Was that supposed to give him comfort?

# Chapter Six

"I told my mother that we were having breakfast in town," Hank said when Frankie came out of the bedroom fully dressed and showered the next morning. He had his jacket on and smelled of the outdoors, which she figured meant he'd walked down to the main house to talk to his mother.

"I'm going to take a shower," he said now. "If you want to talk to Naomi's mother, we need to catch her before she goes to work." With that, he turned and went back into his bedroom.

Frankie smiled after him. He was still angry but he hadn't fired her. Yet.

She went into the kitchen and made herself toast. Hank didn't take long in the shower. He appeared minutes later, dressed in jeans and a Western shirt, his dark, unruly hair still damp at his collar as he stuffed on his Stetson and headed for the door. She followed, smiling to herself. It could be a long day, but she was glad she was still employed for numerous reasons, number one among them, she wanted to know now more than ever what had happened to Naomi Hill.

Lillian Brandt lived in a large condo complex set back against a mountainside overlooking Meadow Village. She'd married a real-estate agent after being a single mother for years, from what Hank had told her. Big Sky was booming and had been for years, so Lillian had apparently risen in economic stature after her marriage compared to the way she'd lived before Naomi died.

From her research, Frankie knew that Big Sky, Montana, once a ranching area, had been nothing more than a sagebrush-filled meadow below Lone Mountain. Then Chet Huntley and some developers had started the resort. Since then, the sagebrush had been plowed up to make a town as the ski resort on the mountain had grown.

But every resort needed workers, and while million-dollar houses had been built, there were few places for moderate-income workers to live that they could afford. The majority commuted from Gallatin Gateway, Four Corners, Belgrade and Bozeman—all towns forty miles or more to the north.

Lillian was younger than Frankie had expected. Naomi had been four years younger than Hank. Frankie estimated that Lillian must have had her daughter while in her late teens.

"Hank?" The woman's pale green eyes widened in surprise. "Are you back?"

"For a while," he said and introduced Frankie. "Do you have a minute? We won't take much of your time."

Lillian looked from him to Frankie and back before she stepped aside to let them enter the condo. It was bright and spacious with no clutter. It could have been one of the models that real-estate agents showed prospective clients. "I was just about to leave to go to the office." She worked for her husband as a secretary.

"I just need to ask you a few questions," he said as she motioned for them to take a seat.

"Questions?" she asked as she moved some of the pillows on the couch to make room for them.

"About Naomi's death."

The woman stopped what she was doing to stare at him. "Hank, it's been three years. Why would you dig all of it back up again?"

"Because he doesn't believe she killed herself," Frankie said and supplied her business card. "I didn't know your daughter, but I've heard a lot about her. I'm sorry for your loss, ma'am." Then she asked if it would be okay if Mrs. Brandt would answer a few questions about her daughter. "She was twenty-six, right? Hank said she was ready to get married."

Lillian slumped into one of the chairs that she'd freed of designer pillows and motioned them onto the couch. "It's all she wanted. Marriage, a family."

"Where was she working at the time of her death?" Frankie asked.

"At the grocery store, but I can't see what that—"

She could feel Hank's gaze on her. "Is that where she met her friend Carrie?"

Lillian nodded. Her gaze went to Hank. "Why are you—"

"I'm curious," Frankie said, drawing the woman's attention back again. "Was there anyone else in her life?"

"You mean friends?"

"Yes, possibly a male friend," Frankie said.

The woman blinked before shooting a look at Hank. "She was in love with Hank."

"But she had to have other friends."

Lillian fiddled with the piping along the edge of the chair arm. "Of course she had other friends. She made friends easily."

"I'm sure she did. She was so beautiful," Frankie said.

The woman nodded, her eyes shiny. "She got asked out a lot all through school."

"Do you remember their names?"

Lillian looked at Hank. "She was faithful to you. If that's what this is about—"

"It's not," Hank assured her.

"We just thought they might be able to fill in some of the blanks so Hank can better understand what happened to Naomi. He's having a very hard time moving on," Frankie said.

The woman looked at Hank, sympathy in her gaze. "Of course. I just remember her mentioning one in particular. His name was—" she seemed to think for a moment "—River." She waved her hand wistfully. "Blame it on Montana, these odd names."

"You probably don't remember River's last name," Frankie said.

"No, but Carrie might. She knew him too." Lillian looked at her watch. "I really have to go. I'm sorry."

"No," Frankie said, getting to her feet. "You've been a great help."

"Yes," Hank agreed with much less enthusiasm. "Thank you for taking the time."

"It's good to see you," the woman said to him and patted his cheek. "I hope you can find some peace."

"Me too," he said as he shared a last hug with Mrs. Brandt before leaving.

HANK CLIMBED BEHIND the wheel, his heart hammering in his chest. "You aren't going to give up on your other man theory, are you?"

"No, and you shouldn't either," Frankie said from the passenger seat.

He finally turned his head to look at her. Gritting his teeth, he said, "You think she was cheating on me? Wouldn't that give me a motive for murder?"

"I don't think she was cheating. I said she had someone waiting in the wings. Big Sky is a small town. I suspect that if she'd been cheating on you, you would have heard."

"Thanks. You just keep making me feel better all the time."

"I didn't realize that my job was to make you feel better. I thought it was to find a killer."

He let out a bark of a laugh. "You are something, you know that?"

"It's been mentioned to me. I'm hungry. Are you going to feed me before or after we visit Naomi's best friend, Carrie?"

"I'm not sure I can do this on an empty stomach, so I guess it's going to be before," he said as he started the pickup's engine.

"Over breakfast, you can tell me about Carrie," she said as she buckled up.

"I don't know what you want me to tell you about her," he grumbled, wishing he'd gone with his instincts last night and stormed into her bedroom and fired her. Even if he'd had to kick down the door.

"Start by telling me why you didn't like her."

He shot her a look as he pulled away from the condo complex. "What makes you think…?" He swore under his breath. "Don't you want to meet her and decide on your own?"

"Oh, I will. But I'm curious about your relationship with her."

Hank let out a curse as he drove toward a local café off the beaten path. The place served Mexican breakfasts, and he had a feeling Frankie liked things hot. She certainly got him hot under his collar.

It wasn't until they were seated and had ordered— he'd been right about her liking spicy food—that he sat back and studied the woman sitting across from him.

"What?" she asked, seeming to squirm a little under his intent gaze.

"Just that you know everything about me—"

"Not everything."

"—and I know nothing about you," he finished.

"That's because this isn't about me," she said and straightened her silverware. He'd never seen her nervous before. But then again, he'd never asked her anything personal about herself.

"You jumped at this case rather fast," he said, still studying her. She wasn't the only one who noticed things about people. "I suspect it was to avoid who-ever that was who kept calling you." He saw that he'd hit a nerve. "Angry client? Old boyfriend?" He grinned. "Old boyfriend."

"You're barking up the wrong tree."

"Am I? I don't think so." He took her measure for the first time since he'd hired her. She was a very attrac-tive woman. Right now her long, dark hair was pulled back into a low ponytail. Sans makeup, she'd also played down the violet eyes. And yet there was something sexy and, yes, even sultry about her. Naomi wouldn't leave the house without her makeup on.

That thought reminded him of all the times he'd stood around waiting for her to get ready to go out.

This morning Frankie was more serious, more pro-fessional, more hands-off. Definitely low-maintenance in a simple T-shirt and jeans. Nothing too tight. Noth-ing too revealing.

And yet last night at dinner when she'd snuggled against him, he'd felt her full curves. Nothing could hide her long legs. Right now, he could imagine her contours given that she was slim and her T-shirt did little to hide the curve of her backside.

"Why isn't a woman who looks like you married?" he asked, truly surprised.

"Who says I'm not?"

He glanced at her left hand. "No ring."

She smiled and looked away for a moment. "Isn't it possible I'm just not wearing mine right now?"

Hank considered that as the waitress brought their

breakfasts. "*Are* you married?" he asked as the waitress left again.

"No. Now, are you going to tell me why you didn't like Naomi's best friend or are you going to keep stalling?"

## Chapter Seven

Johnny Joe "J.J." Whitaker tried the number again. Frankie hadn't been picking up, but now all his calls were going to voice mail. Did she really think he would quit calling? The woman didn't know him very well if she did. That was what made him so angry. She *should* know him by now. He wasn't giving up.

He left another threatening message. "Frankie, you call me or you're going to be sorry. You know I make good on my threats, sweetheart. Call me or you'll wish you had."

He hung up and paced the floor until he couldn't take it anymore. She had to have gotten his messages. She had to know what would happen if she ignored him.

He slammed his fist down on the table, and the empty beer bottles from last night rattled. One toppled over, rolled across the table and would have fallen to the floor if he hadn't caught it.

"Frankie, you bitch!" he screamed, grabbing the neck of the bottle. He brought the bottle down on the edge of the table.

The bottom end of the bottle broke off, leaving a lethal jagged edge below the neck in his hand. He held it up in the light and imagined what the sharp glass could do to a person's flesh. Frankie thought he was dangerous?

He laughed. Maybe it was time to show her just how dangerous he could be.


CARRIE WHITE HAD gotten married not long after Naomi died, Hank told her on the way over to the woman's house. She had been about Naomi's age, and they'd met at the grocery store where Naomi had worked. Carrie had worked at one of the art shops in town. They became friends.

"Was she a bad influence?" Frankie asked.

Hank shrugged. "I don't know."

"How was Carrie with men?"

"She always had one or two she was stringing along, hoping one of them would pop the question."

Frankie laughed. "Is this why you didn't like her?"

"I never said I didn't like her. I just didn't think she was good for Naomi. You have to understand. Naomi was raised by her mother. Her father left when she was six. It devastated her. Lillian had to go to work and raise her alone without any more education than a high school diploma."

"So they didn't have much money?"

"Or anything else. Naomi wanted more and I don't blame her for that."

"Also Naomi didn't want to end up like her," Frankie supposed.

"She wanted a husband, a family, some stability. When

her mother started dating the real-estate agent, she wanted that for us."

"Seems pretty stable at the ranch," Frankie said.

"I would have been working for my parents. Naomi couldn't see how I would ever get ahead since even if they left me the ranch, I still have a sister, Mary, and two younger brothers, Brick and Angus. I could see her point. She wanted her own place, her own life, that wasn't tied up with my family's."

Frankie held her tongue. The more she found out about Naomi, the more she could see how she would not have been in the right place emotionally to be involved in a serious relationship. But she was having these thoughts because the more she learned about Hank, the more she liked him.

"So Carrie encouraged her how?"

Hank seemed to give that some thought as he pulled up in front of a small house in a subdivision in Meadow Village. "Carrie encouraged her to dump me and find someone else, someone more…acceptable. Carrie married a local insurance salesman who wears a three-piece suit most days unless he's selling to out-of-staters, and then he busts out his Stetson and boots."

Frankie got the picture. She opened her door, anxious to meet Carrie White and see what she thought of her for herself. She heard Hank get out but could tell that he wasn't looking forward to this.

At the front door, Frankie rang the bell. She could hear the sound of small running feet, then a shriek of laughter followed by someone young bursting into tears.

"Knock it off!" yelled an adult female voice.

She could hear someone coming to the door. It sounded as if the person was dragging one of the crying children because now there appeared to be at least two in tears just on the other side of the door.

"Naomi's dream life?" she said under her breath to Hank.

The woman who opened the door with a toddler on one arm and another hanging off her pants leg looked harried and near tears herself. Carrie was short, dark-haired and still carrying some of her baby weight. She frowned at them and said, "Whatever you're offering, I'm not inter—" Her voice suddenly broke off at the sight of Hank. Her jaw literally dropped.

"Fortunately, we aren't selling anything," Frankie said.

"We'd just like a minute of your time," Hank said as the din died down. The squalling child hanging off Carrie's leg was now staring at them, just like the toddler on her hip. "Mind if we come in?"

The woman shot a look at Frankie, then shrugged and shoved open the screen door. "Let me just put them down for their morning naps. Have a seat," she said over her shoulder as she disappeared down a hallway.

The living room looked like a toy manufacturing company had exploded and most of the toys had landed here in pieces. Against one wall by the door was a row of hooks. Frankie noticed there were a half-dozen sizes of coats hanging there.

They waded through the toys, cleaning off a space on the couch to sit down. In the other room they could hear cajoling and more crying, but pretty soon, Carrie returned.

Frankie could see that she'd brushed her hair and put on a little makeup in a rush and changed her sweatshirt for one that didn't have spit-up on it. The woman was making an effort to look as if everything was fine. Clearly the attempt was for Hank's benefit.

"It's so good to see you," Carrie said to him, still looking surprised that he'd somehow ended up on her couch.

Frankie guessed that things had not been good between Carrie and Hank after Naomi's death. It seemed Carrie regretted that.

"How have you been?" she asked as she cleared toys off a chair and sat down. She looked exhausted and the day was early.

"All right," he said. "We need to ask you some questions."

The woman stiffened a little. She must have thought this was a social call. "Questions about what?"

"I understand you didn't see or hear from Naomi the night she died," Frankie said. Carrie looked at her and then at Hank.

He said, "This is Frankie, a private investigator. She's helping me find out what happened that night."

The woman turned again to her, curiosity in her gaze, but she didn't ask about their relationship. "I've told you everything I know," she said to Hank before turning back to Frankie. "I didn't hear from her or see her. I told the marshal the same thing."

"Were you planning to?"

The question seemed to take Carrie off guard. "I can't…" She frowned.

"Hadn't your best friend told you that she was going to push marriage that night and if Hank didn't come around…"

The woman's eyes widened. "I wouldn't say she was pushing marriage exactly. It had been four years! How long does it take for a man to make up his mind?" She slid a look at Hank and flushed a little with embarrassment.

"How long did it take your husband?"

Carrie ran a hand through her short hair. "Six months."

Frankie eyed her, remembering the coats hanging on the hooks by the door. "Were you pregnant?"

The woman shot to her feet, her gaze ricocheting back to Hank. "I don't know what this is about, but—"

"She was your best friend. You knew her better than anyone," Frankie said, also getting to her feet. "She would have told you if there was someone else she was interested in. I'm guessing she planned to come back to your place that night if things didn't go well. Unless you weren't such good friends."

Carrie crossed her arms. "She was my *best* friend."

"Then she would have told you about River."

That caught the woman flat-footed. She blinked, looked at Hank again and back to Frankie. "It was Hank's own fault. He kept dragging his feet."

She nodded. "So Naomi must have called to tell you she was on her way."

Carrie shook her head. "I told you. I didn't see her. I

didn't hear from her. When I didn't, I just assumed everything went well. Until I got the call the next morning from her mother."

Frankie thought the woman was telling the truth. But Naomi would have called someone she trusted. Someone she could pour her heart out to since she left the ranch upset. "Where can we find River?"

HANK SWORE AS he climbed into his pickup. "I don't want to go see River Dean," he said as Frankie slid into the passenger seat.

"After Naomi left you, she would have gone to one of two places. Carrie's to cry on her shoulder. Or someone else's shoulder. If the man waiting in the wings was River Dean, then that's where she probably went. Which means he might have been the last person to see her alive. If he turned her down as well, maybe she did lose all hope and make that fatal leap from the cliff. You ready to accept that and call it a day?"

Without looking at her, Hank jerked off his Stetson to rake a hand through his hair. "You scare me."

"She wanted to get married and have babies and a man who came home at five thirty every weekday night and took off his tie as she gave him a cocktail and a kiss and they laughed about the funny things the kids had done that day. It's a fantasy a lot of people have."

He stared at her. "But not you."

She shrugged.

"Because you know the fantasy doesn't exist," he said, wanting to reach over and brush back a lock of dark hair that had escaped from her ponytail and now curled across her cheek.

"I'm practical, but even I still believe in love and happy-ever-after."

Surprised, he did reach over and push back the lock of hair. His fingertips brushed her cheek. He felt a tingle run up his arm. Frankie caught his hand and held it for a moment before letting it go. He could see that he'd invaded her space and it had surprised her. It hadn't pleased her.

"You said you wanted the truth," she reminded him, as if his touching her had been an attempt to change the subject. "Have you changed your mind?"

RIVER DEAN OWNED a white-water rafting company that operated downriver closer to what was known as the Mad Mile and House Rock, an area known for thrills and spills.

Frankie could still feel where Hank's fingertips had brushed her cheek. She wanted to reach up and rub the spot. But she resisted just as she had the shudder she'd felt at his sudden touch.

Hank got out of the pickup and stopped in front of a makeshift-looking building with a sign that read WHITE-WATER RAFTING.

The door was open, and inside she could see racks of life jackets hanging from the wall. A motorcycle was parked to one side of the building. Someone was definitely here since there was also a huge stack of rafts in the pine trees, only some of them still chained to a tree. It was early in the day, so she figured business picked up later.

All she could think was that Naomi was foolish enough to trade ranch life for this? A seasonal business determined by the weather and tourists passing through? But maybe three years ago, River Dean had appeared to have better options. And if not, there was always Naomi's stepfather and the real-estate business.

Hank stood waiting for her, staring at the river through the pines. She felt the weight of her cell phone and her past. She'd turned off her phone earlier, but now she pulled it out and checked to see that she had a dozen calls from the same number. No big surprise. She didn't even consider checking voice mail since she knew what she'd find. He'd go by the office and her apartment—if he hadn't already. He would know that she'd left town. She told herself he wouldn't be able to find her even if he tried. Unfortunately, he would try, and if he got lucky somehow...

"You ready?" Hank said beside her.

She pocketed her phone. "Ready as *you* are."

He chuckled at that and started toward the open door of the white-water rafting business. She followed.

The moment she walked in she spotted River Dean. She'd known men like him in Idaho. Good-looking ski bums, mountain bikers, river rafters. Big Sky resembled any resort area with its young men who liked to play.

River Dean was tanned and athletically built with shaggy, sexy blond hair and a million-dollar smile. She saw quickly how a woman would have been attracted to him. It wasn't until she approached him that she could tell his age was closer to forty than thirty. There were lines around his eyes from hours on the water in sunshine.

Hank had stopped just inside the door and was staring at River as if he wanted to rip his throat out.

"You must be River," she said, stepping in front of Hank. River appeared to be alone. She got the feeling that he'd just sent some employees out with a couple of rafts full of adventure seekers.

"Wanting a trip down the river?" he asked, grinning at her and then Hank. His grin faded a little as if he recognized the cowboy rancher Naomi had been dating.

"More interested in your relationship with Naomi Hill," Frankie said.

"You a…cop?" he asked, eyeing her up and down.

"Something like that. Naomi came to see you that night, the night she died."

River shook his head. "I don't know who you are, but I'm not answering any more of your questions."

"Would you prefer to talk to the sheriff?" Frankie snapped.

"No, but…"

"We're just trying to find out what happened to her. I know she came to see you. She was upset. She needed someone to talk to. Someone sympathetic to her problem."

River rubbed the back of his neck for a moment as he looked toward the open door and the highway outside. She could tell he was wishing a customer would stop by right now.

"We know you knew her," Hank said, taking a threatening step forward.

River was shaking his head. "It wasn't like that. I was way too old for her. We were just friends. And I swear I know nothing about what happened to her."

"But she did stop by that night," Frankie repeated.

The river guide groaned. "She stopped by, but I was busy."

"Busy?" Hank said.

"With another woman." Frankie nodded since she'd already guessed that was what must have happened. "Did you two argue?"

"No." He held up his hands. "I told her we could talk the next day. She realized what was going on and left. That was it," River said.

Hank swore. "But you didn't go to the sheriff with that information even though you might have been the last person to see her alive."

"I wasn't why she jumped," River snapped. "If you're looking for someone to blame, look in the mirror, man. You're the one who was making her so unhappy."

Frankie could see that Hank wanted to reach across the counter and thump the man. She stepped between them again. "Tell me what was said that night."

River shook his head. "It was three years ago. I don't remember word for word. She surprised me. She'd never come by before without calling."

Behind her, Frankie heard Hank groan. River heard it too and looked worried. Both men were strong and in good shape, but Hank was a big cowboy. In a fight, she had no doubt that the cowboy would win.

"It's like I just told you. She was upset before she saw what was going on. I told her she had to leave and that we'd talk the next day. She was crying, but she seemed okay when she left."

"This was at your place? Where was that?"

"I was staying in those old cabins near Soldiers' Chapel. Most of them have been torn down since then."

"Did you see her leave?" Frankie asked. "Could she have left with anyone?"

River shook his head and looked sheepish. "Like I said. I thought she was all right. I figured she was looking for a shoulder to cry on over her boyfriend and that she'd just find someone else to talk to that night."

"Was there someone you thought she might go to?" she asked.

River hesitated only a moment before he said, "Her friend Carrie maybe? I don't know."

## Chapter Eight

"You should have let me hit him," Hank said as he slipped behind the wheel and slammed the door harder than he'd meant to.

"Violence is never the answer."

He shot her a look. "You read that in a fortune cookie?" He couldn't help himself. He couldn't remember the last time he was this angry.

He saw Frankie's expression and swore under his breath. "Yes, I'd prefer to blame River Dean rather than the dead woman I was in love with. You have a problem with that?"

She said nothing, as if waiting for his anger to pass. His father had warned him that digging into Naomi's death would only make him feel worse. He really hated it when his father was right—and Hud didn't even know that was what he was doing.

He drove back to the ranch, his temper cooled as he turned into the place.

"I had no idea about what was going on with Naomi," he said, stating the obvious. "You must think me a fool."

Frankie graced him with a patient smile as he drove

down the road to the ranch house. "She loved you, but you both wanted different things. Love doesn't always overcome everything."

"Don't be nice to me," he said gruffly, making her laugh. Her cell phone rang. She checked it as if surprised that she'd left it on and quickly turned it off again.

"You're going to have to talk to him sometime," Hank said, studying her.

"Is there anyone else you want to go see?"

He shook his head, aware that she'd circumvented his comment as he parked at the foot of the trail that led to their cabin on the mountainside. "I need to be alone for a while, Frankie. Is that all right?"

"Don't worry about me."

He smiled at her. "You can take care of yourself, right? Never need any help."

"I wouldn't say that." She opened her door and got out.

He swore and, after throwing the pickup into Park, got out and went after her. "Frankie, wait."

She stopped and turned back to him.

"I don't know what your story is, but I do know this," he said. "You have closed yourself off for some reason. I recognize the signs because I've done it for the past three years. In your case, I suspect some man's to blame, the one who keeps calling. One question. Is he dangerous?"

She started to step away, but he reached for her arm and pulled her back around to face him again. "I'm fine. There is nothing to worry about."

He shook his head but let go of her arm. "You are one stubborn woman." He couldn't help but smile because there was a strength and independence in her that he admired. He'd never known a woman quite like her. She couldn't have been more different from Naomi, who he'd always felt needed taking care of. Just the thought of Naomi and what he'd learned about her before she died was like a bucket of ice water poured over him. He took a step away, needing space right now, just like he'd told her.

"I'll see you later." With that, he turned to his pickup and drove off, looking back only once to see Frankie standing in the ranch yard, a worried expression on her face.

"Nothing to worry about, huh?" he said under his breath.

As FRANKIE TURNED toward their cabin on the mountain, she saw movement in the main house and knew that their little scene had been witnessed. They didn't appear to be a loving couple. She didn't know how much longer they could continue this ruse before someone brought it up.

But this was the way Hank wanted it. At least for the time being. She felt guilty, especially about his mother. Dana wanted her son to move on from Naomi's death and find some happiness. Frankie wasn't sure that was ever going to happen.

She hated to admit it to herself, but the moment Hank had told her about the problems they'd been having, she'd nailed the kind of young woman Naomi had been.

The weight of her cell phone in her pocket seemed to mock her. She was good at figuring out *other* people, but not so good when it came to her own life.

"Frankie!" She turned at the sound of Dana's voice. The older woman was standing on the ranch house porch, waving at her. "Want a cup of coffee? I have cookies."

She couldn't help but laugh as she started for the main house. Dana wanted to talk and she was using cookies as a bribe. Frankie called her on it the moment she reached the porch.

"You've found me out," Dana said with a laugh. "I'll stoop to just about anything when it comes to my son."

"I understand completely," she said, climbing the steps to the porch. "Hank is a special young man."

"Yes, I think he is," the woman said as she shoved open the screen door. "I thought we could talk."

Frankie chuckled. "I had a feeling." She stepped inside, taking in again the Western-style living room with its stone fireplace, wood floors, and Native American rugs adjacent to the warm and cozy kitchen. She liked it here, actually felt at home, which was unusual for her. She often didn't feel at home at her own place.

"I never asked," Dana said as she filled two mugs with coffee, handed one to Frankie and put a plate of cookies on the table. "How did you two meet?" She motioned her into a chair.

*Hank hired me to pretend to be his girlfriend.* "At a bar." It was the simplest answer she could come up with. She wondered why she and Hank hadn't covered this part. They should have guessed at least his mother would ask.

"Really? That surprises me. I've never known Hank to be interested in the bar scene and he isn't much of a drinker, is he?" Dana let out an embarrassed laugh. "I have to keep reminding myself that he's been gone three years. Maybe I don't really know my son anymore."

Frankie chuckled and shook her head. "Hank only came into the bar to pick up some dinner. Apparently it had been a long day at work and he'd heard that we served the best burgers in Idaho. I just happened to be working that night, and since it was slow, we got to talking. A few days later, he tracked me down because I was only filling in at the bar. A friend of mine owns it. Anyway, Hank asked me out and the rest is history."

It was pure fiction, but it was what she saw Dana needed to hear. Hank was no bar hound. Still, she felt guilty even making up such a story. It would have been so much easier to tell the truth. But her client had been adamant about them keeping the secret as long as they could.

Dana took a sip of her coffee and then asked, "So when not helping a friend, what do you do?"

"I'm a glorified secretary for a boss who makes me work long hours." That at least felt like the truth a lot of days. "Seriously, I love my job and my boss is okay most of the time. But I spend a lot of time doing paperwork."

"Oh my, well, you must be good at it. I'm terrible at it. That's why it is such a blessing that our Mary stayed around and does all of the accounting for the ranch."

"These cookies are delicious," Frankie said, taking

a bite of one. "I would love your recipe." The diversion worked as she'd hoped. Dana hopped up to get her recipe file and began to write down the ingredients and explain that the trick was not to overbake them.

"So you cook," Dana said, kicking the conversation off into their favorite recipes. Frankie had no trouble talking food since she did cook and she had wonderful recipes that her grandmother had left her.

FRUSTRATED AND ANGRY at himself and Naomi, Hank drove out of the ranch, not sure where he was going. All he knew was that he wanted to be alone for a while.

But as he turned onto the highway, he knew exactly where he was headed. Back to the river. Back to the cliff and the ledge where she'd jumped. Back to that deep, dark, cold pool and the rocks where her body had been found.

He knew there was nothing to find there and yet he couldn't stay away. It was one of the reasons he'd left after Naomi died. That and his grief, his unhappiness, his anger at his father.

After pulling off the road, he wound back into the pines and parked. For a moment he sat behind the wheel, looking out at the cliff through the trees. What did he hope to find here? Shaking his head, he climbed out and walked through the pines to the rocky shore of the river. Afternoon sunlight poured down through the boughs, making the surface of the river shimmer.

A cool breeze ruffled his hair as he sat down on a large rock. Shadows played on the cliff across from him. When he looked up at the ledge, just for a moment he thought he saw Naomi in her favorite pale yellow dress, the fabric fluttering in the wind as she fell.

He blinked and felt his eyes burn with tears. Frankie was right. He and Naomi had wanted different things. They hadn't been right for each other, but realizing that didn't seem to help. He couldn't shake this feeling he'd had for three years. It was as if she was trying to reach him from the grave, pleading with him that he find her killer.

Hank pulled off his Stetson and raked a hand through his hair. Was it just guilt for not marrying her, not taking the job with her stepfather, not giving up the ranch for her? Or was it true? Had she been murdered?

He reminded himself that this was why he was back here. Why he'd gone to Frankie to begin with and talked her into this charade. He realized, as he put his hat back on to shade his eyes from the summer sun, he trusted Frankie to find out the truth. Look how much she'd discovered so far. He told himself it was a matter of time. If they could just keep their...relationship secret...

At the sound of a twig breaking behind him, Hank swung around, startled since he'd thought he was alone. Through the pines he saw a flash of color as someone took off at a run.

He jumped to his feet, but had to work his way back through the rocks, so he couldn't move as fast. By the time he reached the pines, whoever it had been was gone. He told himself it was probably just a kid who was as startled as he was to see that there was someone at this spot.

But as he stood, trying to catch his breath, he knew it

hadn't been a kid. The person had been wearing a light color. The same pale yellow as Naomi's favorite dress or just his imagination? He'd almost convinced himself that he'd seen a ghost until, in the distance, he heard the sound of a vehicle engine rev and then die away.

## Chapter Nine

After her visit with Dana, Frankie realized that she and Hank had to move faster. His mother was no fool. Frankie could tell that she was worried.

"Is there a vehicle I could borrow?" Frankie asked after their coffee and cookies chat.

"Of course." Dana had moved to some hooks near the door and pulled down a set of keys. "These are to that blue pickup out there. You're welcome to use it anytime you like. Hank should have thought of that. Where did he go, anyway?"

"He had some errands to run and I didn't want to go along. I told him I would be fine exploring. I think I'll go into town and run a few errands of my own." She gave the woman what she hoped was a reassuring smile and took the keys and the pickup to head into town.

Frankie felt an urgency to finish this. It wasn't just because their pretense was going to be found out sooner rather than later. Nor was it because she'd left a lot of things unfinished back in Idaho, though true. It was being here, pretending to be in love with Hank, pretending that there was a chance that she could be part of this amazing family at some time in the future.

That, she knew, was the real problem. Hank was the kind of man who grew on a woman. But with his family, she'd felt instant love and acceptance. She didn't want to hurt these people any longer. That meant solving this case and getting out of here.

At the local grocery store, she found the manager in the back. She'd assumed that after three years, the managers would have changed from when Naomi had worked here. She was wrong.

Roy Danbrook was a tall, skinny man of about fifty with dark hair and eyes. He rose from his chair, looked around his incredibly small office as if surprised how small it really was and then invited her in. She took the plastic chair he offered her, feeling as if being in the cramped place was a little too intimate. But this wouldn't take long.

"I'm inquiring about a former worker of yours, Naomi Hill," she said, ready to lie about her credentials if necessary.

Roy frowned and she realized he probably didn't even remember Naomi after all this time. The turnover in resort towns had to be huge.

"Naomi," he said and nodded. "You mentioned something about an insurance claim?"

She nodded. She'd flashed him her PI credentials, but he'd barely looked at them. "I need to know what kind of employee she was."

He seemed to think for a moment. "Sweet, very polite with customers…" She felt a *but* coming. "But I had no choice but to let her go under the circumstances."

This came as a surprise. Did Hank know Naomi had been fired? "The circumstances?" That could cover a lot of things.

The manager looked away for a moment, clearly uncomfortable with speaking of past employees, or of the dead? "The stealing." He shook his head.

"The stealing?" All she could think of was groceries.

"Unfortunately, she couldn't keep her hand out of the till. Then there was the drinking, coming in still drunk, coming in late or not coming in at all. I liked her mother, so I tried to help the girl." He shook his head. "Finally, I had to let her go, you understand."

Frankie blinked. He couldn't be talking about the same Naomi Hank had been involved with. "We're talking about Naomi Hill, the one who—"

"Jumped off the cliff and killed herself. Yes."

Stealing? Drinking? Partying? Blowing off work? She tried to figure out how that went with the image Hank had painted of Naomi, but the two didn't fit.

A thought struck her. "She wasn't doing all this alone, right? There had to be someone she hung out with that might be able to give me some insight into her character."

He nodded. "Tamara Baker."

"Is she still around?"

"She works at the Silver Spur Bar." She didn't have to ask him what he thought of Tamara. He glanced at the clock on the wall. "She should be coming to work about now. If she is able to." He shook his head. "I hope this has helped you. I find it most disturbing to revisit it."

"You have been a great help, thank you." She got to her feet, feeling unsteady from the shock of what she'd learned. Sweet, timid little Naomi. Frankie couldn't wait to talk to her friend Tamara.

WHEN HUD CAME home for lunch, as he always did, Dana had sandwiches made and a fresh pot of coffee ready. She hadn't planned to say anything until he'd finished eating.

"What is it?" her husband demanded. "You look as if you're about to pop. Spit it out."

She hurriedly sat down with him and took half of a sandwich onto her plate. Broaching this subject was difficult. They'd discussed Hank on occasion but it never ended well. Sometimes her husband could be so mule-headed stubborn.

"It's Hank."

"Of course it is," Hud said with a curse.

"Something's wrong."

Her husband shook his head as he took a bite of his lunch, clearly just wanting to eat and get out of there.

"This relationship with Frankie, it just doesn't feel… real."

"You have talked about nothing else but your hopes and prayers for Hank to move on, get over Naomi, make a life for himself. Now that he's doing it—"

"I don't believe he's doing it. Maybe coming back here was the worst thing he could do. I can tell it's putting a strain on him and Frankie. Earlier, I saw them… They aren't as loving toward each other as they should be."

Hud groaned as he finished his sandwich and reached for a cookie, which he dunked angrily into his coffee mug. "What would you like *me* to do about it?"

"Why is it we can't talk about Hank without you getting angry?" she demanded. They hardly ever argued, but when it came to the kids, she was like a mama bear, even with Hud. "I want to know more about Frankie." She said the words that had been rolling around in her mind since she'd first met the woman.

"You don't like her."

"No, I do. That's the problem. She seems so right for Hank."

Hud raked a hand through his hair before settling his gaze on her. "What am I missing here?"

"That's just it. I like her so much, I have to be sure this isn't— I mean, that she's not— Can't you just do some checking on her to relieve my mind so I can—"

"No." He stood up so abruptly that the dishes on the table rattled, startling her. "Absolutely not. Have you forgotten that the trouble began between my son and me when I did a background check on Naomi?"

"Because he was so in love with her. It was his first real crush. I asked you to make sure that she was all right for him because he seemed blind to her…"

"Blind to the fact that she didn't want what he wanted more than anything? That she would never have been happy with Hank if he settled here? She wanted marriage so badly that it was all she talked about. That she was pressuring our son and I could see that he felt backed against a wall?" Hud demanded. "Yes. Those were all good reasons. Along with the fact that I sensed a weakness in her. A fragility…"

"You questioned her mental stability, not to mention she'd been arrested for shoplifting."

He nodded, looking sick. "Something I never told our son. As it turned out, maybe I should have. I was right about her, which gives me no satisfaction." He raised his head to meet her gaze. His eyes shone. "I lost my son. I'm not sure I will get him back because of everything that happened. I can't make that mistake again." He reached for his Stetson on the wall hook where he put it each time he entered the kitchen. "Thank you for lunch." With that, he left.

Dana looked after him, fighting tears. She couldn't help the knot of fear inside her. Something was wrong, but she had no idea what to do about it.

TAMARA BAKER WAS indeed behind the bar at the Silver Spur. The place was empty, a janitor was just finishing up in the restroom, and the smell of industrial-strength cleanser permeated the air.

"Tamara Baker?" Frankie asked as she took a barstool.

"Who wants to know?" asked the brunette behind the bar. She had a smoker's rough voice and a hard-lived face that belied her real age. Frankie estimated she was in her midthirties, definitely older than Naomi.

"You knew Naomi Hill."

Tamara's eyes narrowed to slits. "You a reporter?"

Frankie laughed. "Not hardly. I heard that you and Naomi used to party together."

"That's no secret." That was what she thought. "But if you aren't with the press, then—"

Frankie gave her the same story she had Roy, only Tamara wasn't quite as gullible. When Frankie flashed her credentials, the bartender grabbed them, taking them over into the light from the back bar to study them.

"You're a PI? No kidding?"

"No kidding. I was hoping you could tell me about Naomi. Other people I've spoken with have painted a completely different picture of her compared to the stories I've heard about the two of you." She was exaggerating, but the fib worked.

Tamara laughed. "Want something to drink?" she asked as she poured herself one.

"I'd take a cola."

"I knew a different side of Naomi," the woman said after taking a pull of her drink. "She let her freak flag fly when she was with me."

"How did you two meet?"

"At the grocery store. She helped me out sometimes when I didn't have enough money to feed my kids." Tamara shrugged. "I tried to pay her back by showing her a good time here at the bar."

Frankie understood perfectly. Naomi would steal out of the till at the grocery store for Tamara, and Tamara would ply her with free drinks here at the bar. "What about men?"

"*Men?* What about them?"

"Did this wild side of her also include men?"

Tamara finished her drink and washed out the glass. "Naomi wasn't interested. She had this rancher she said she was going to marry. She flirted a little, but she was saving herself for marriage. She had this idea that once she was married, everything would come up roses." The bartender laughed.

"You doubted it?"

"I've seen women come through here thinking that marriage was going to cure whatever ailed them," Tamara said. "I've been there. What about you?" she asked, glancing at Frankie's left hand. "You married?"

She shook her head. "You must have been surprised when you heard that Naomi dove off the cliff and killed herself."

The woman snorted. "I figured it was just a matter of time. She was living a double life. It was bound to catch up with her."

"You mean between the bar and the cowboy?"

Tamara looked away for a moment as if she thought someone might be listening. "Naomi had a lot more going on than anyone knew."

"Such as?"

The front door opened, sending a shaft of bright summer sun streaming across the floor like a laser in their direction. A man entered, the door closing behind him, pitching them back into cool darkness.

"Hey, Darrel," she called to the man as he limped to the bar. "What ya havin'?" The bartender got a beer for the man and hung around talking to him quietly for a few minutes.

Frankie saw the man glance in her direction. He was

about her age with sandy-blond hair, not bad-looking, but there was something about him that made her look away. He seemed to be suddenly focusing on her a little too intensely. She wondered what Tamara had told him about her.

When the bartender came back down the bar, Frankie asked, "You didn't happen to see Naomi that night, the night she died, did you?"

"Me?" She shook her head. "I was working until closing. It's my usual shift. You can ask anyone."

Frankie noticed that the woman now seemed nervous and kept glancing down the bar at the man she'd called Darrel.

As she straightened the shirt she was wearing, Tamara asked, "Can I get you anything else?" She didn't sound all that enthusiastic about it.

"You said Naomi was into other things. Like what?"

"I was just shooting my mouth off. You can't pay any attention to me. If I can't get you anything else, I really need to do some stocking up." She tilted her head toward the man at the end of the bar. She lowered her voice. "You know, want to look good in front of the customers."

"Sure." She could tell that was all she was going to get out of Tamara. But she wondered what it was about the man at the end of the bar that made her nervous.

As she left, she found herself still trying to piece together what she'd learned about the woman known as Naomi Hill. The pieces didn't fit. She tried to imagine what Naomi could have been involved in that would get her murdered—if that had been the case.

More and more, though, Frankie believed that the woman had come unhinged when she'd seen her planned life with Hank crumbling, and it had driven her to do the one thing that terrified her more than her so-called double life.

HANK KNEW HE couldn't put it off any longer. He swung by his father's office, knowing the man was a creature of habit. Marshal Hudson Savage went home every day for lunch. And every day, his wife would have a meal ready. Hank used to find it sweet. Then his father went back to his office. If nothing was happening, he would do paperwork for an hour or so before he would go out on patrol.

He found his father sitting behind his desk. The marshal looked up in surprise to see Hank standing in the doorway. "Come on in," he said, as if he knew this wasn't a personal visit. "Close the door."

Hank did just that, but he didn't take the chair his father offered him. "I want a copy of Naomi's file." Hud started to shake his head. "Don't tell me I can't have it. She'd dead. The case is closed. Pretend I'm a reporter and give me a copy."

His father sighed as he leaned back in his chair, gazing at him with an intensity that used to scare him when he was a boy and in trouble. "Your mother and I had hoped—"

"I know what you'd hoped," he interrupted. "Don't read too much into my wanting a copy of the file."

"What am I supposed not to read into it? That you still haven't moved on?"

Hank said nothing.

"What's the deal with you and Frankie?" the marshal asked, no longer sounding like his father. "Are you in love with her?"

"Seriously? Mother put you up to this?"

"We're concerned."

Hank laughed. "Just like you were concerned when I was in love with Naomi."

"Are you in love with Frankie?"

"Who wouldn't be? She's a beautiful, smart, talented woman. Now, if we're through with the interrogation, I still want that file. Let's say I need it to get closure."

"Is that what it is?"

He gave his father an impatient look.

The marshal leaned forward, picked up a manila envelope from his desk and held it out to him.

Hank stared at it without taking the envelope from him for a moment. "What is this?"

"A copy of Naomi's file."

"How—"

"How did I know that you would be asking for it?" His father asked the question for him as he cocked his head. Hank noticed his father's hair more graying than he remembered. "Maybe I know you better than you think."

Hank took the envelope from him. "Is everything in here?"

"Everything, including my notes. Will there be anything else?"

He shook his head, feeling as if there was something more he should say. "Thank you."

His father gave him a nod. His desk phone rang.

Hank opened the door, looking back as his father picked up the phone and said, "Marshal Savage." He let the door close behind him and left.

# Chapter Ten

J.J. went by Frankie's apartment and banged on the door until the neighbor opened a window and yelled out.

"I'm going to call the cops."

"Call the cops. Where's Frankie?"

"The woman who lives in that apartment? She packed up and left with some man a few days ago."

"What?" He described Frankie to the man since it was clear the fool didn't know what he was talking about.

"That's her," the man said. "I know my own neighbor. She left with a cowboy—that's all I can tell you. She's not home, so please let me get some sleep."

He thought he might lose his mind. Where could she have gone? He'd been by her office. It was locked up tight. He told himself she was on a case. But why wouldn't she answer her phone? Why wouldn't she call him back? She knew what a mistake that would be once he got his hands on her.

He'd called her number, left more messages, and still she hadn't gotten back to him. What if she'd left for good?

She wouldn't do that. She was just trying to teach him a lesson, playing hard to get. Once he saw her again, he'd teach *her* a lesson she wouldn't soon forget. No one pulled this kind of crap on him. Especially some woman.

He knew there was only one thing to do. Track her down and make her pay.

After all, he had the resources. He just hadn't wanted to use them. He'd hoped that Frankie would have come to her senses and realized she couldn't get away from him. But she had.

And now he was going after her.

FRANKIE FOUND HANK poring over papers on the small table in their cabin.

Hank looked up, surprised as she came in the door, as if he'd forgotten all about her. "Where have *you* been?"

"I've been working. You all right?"

He nodded. "I stopped by the marshal's office and got a copy of Naomi's file."

"Your dad gave it to you?" She couldn't help being surprised.

"He'd already made a copy for me." He grunted. "He says he knows me better than I think he does. You're probably right about them seeing through us. Mom said you took one of the pickups into town. I'm sorry I didn't think to give you keys for a vehicle."

"It was fine," she said, pulling out a chair at the table and sitting down. "I had coffee and cookies with your mother before I left."

He raised a brow. "How did that go?"

"She quizzed me about us, about me. She wanted to know how we met. We should have come up with something beforehand. I had to wing it." She told him the story she'd given to his mother.

Hank nodded. "Sorry about that, but it sounds like you covered it."

"We had a nice visit. I don't like lying to her, though. She's going to be hurt."

"I know." He got to his feet. "You hungry? I haven't had lunch."

"Me either."

"I know a place up the canyon, the Corral. They used to make great burgers. Want to give it a try?"

She smiled as her stomach rumbled loudly.

It was one of those beautiful summer days. Frankie breathed it in as Hank drove them through the canyon. Sunlight glimmered off the pines and the clear green of the river as the road and river wound together through cliffs and meadows.

Frankie sat back and enjoyed the ride. She'd decided she would tell Hank later what she'd learned so as not to spoil his lunch. It could wait, and right now she was enjoying just the two of them on this amazing day. Even Hank seemed more relaxed than she'd seen him. He turned on the radio, and as a country song came on from a local station, they both burst into song. Frankie had grown up on the old country classics, so she knew all the words.

They laughed as the song ended and fell into a companionable silence as the news came on and Hank turned off the radio.

"You said you were working while I was gone—"

"We can talk about it later."

He shot her a look before going back to his driving, as if he knew it wasn't going to be good news. Not far up the road he turned into the Corral. The place had originally been built in 1947. It had changed from when Hank was a boy, but it still served great burgers and fries. Now you could also get buffalo as well as beef and sweet potato fries or regular. The booths had been replaced with log furniture and yet he still felt as at home here as he had as a boy when his grandfather used to play guitar in a band here.

After they ordered, Hank said, "I like your hair." He reached over and caught a long lock between his thumb and finger. "Do you ever wear it down?"

She eyed him suspiciously.

"What? I can't compliment you? You said we needed to act like lovers."

"Lovers?" She broke into a smile. "Something happen I don't know about?"

He let go of her hair and glanced toward the bar. "Before I went down to my father's office for a copy of Naomi's file, I stopped by the river again where she died. There was someone else there. I heard them behind me and when I turned around they ran. I caught only a glimpse of fabric through the trees and then I heard a car engine start up and the vehicle leave."

FRANKIE COULD SEE that the incident had spooked him. She wasn't sure why, though. Nothing about it sounded sinister. "Who do you think it was?"

He shook his head. "I thought I caught a glimpse of Naomi up on the ledge, wearing this pale yellow dress she loved."

"Was anyone up on the ledge?"

He shook his head. "But there was someone behind me. Someone wearing a light-colored garment running through the trees."

"You thought it was Naomi?"

"Naomi is dead. She can't step on a twig and break it directly behind me and startle me." He picked up his napkin and rearranged his silverware. "I'm not losing it."

"I know you're not. You saw someone. But that doesn't mean it had anything to do with Naomi. Unless you think you were followed."

He shook his head. "Why would someone follow me?"

She shrugged. Clearly neither of them knew. He realized that she was right. It was just someone who was looking for a spot on the river. He'd probably startled them more than they had him.

"But then again," Frankie said, "if you're right and Naomi was murdered, then her murderer is still out there."

"If you're trying to scare me—"

"What you have to figure out is why anyone would want to kill Naomi in the first place. I have some thoughts that I'll share on the way back to the ranch. But in the meantime—"

"Just a minute. You learned something?"

Fortunately, their burgers and fries came just then.

They'd both gone for beef, regular fries and colas. Hank looked down at the food, then at her. She picked up a fry and dragged it through a squirt of ketchup she'd poured onto her plate before taking a bite.

"I can't remember the last time I had a burger and fries," she said with enthusiasm. Picking up the burger, she took a juicy hot bite and made a *hmmm* sound that had him smiling.

He could see that she didn't want to talk about what she'd found out. Not now. He decided to let it go until after their lunch because it was a beautiful day and he was sitting here with a beautiful woman. "Did I just see you put mayo on your burger?"

"You have a problem with that?" she joked.

He reached for the side of mayo she'd ordered. "Not if you share. I guess it's just one more thing we have in common."

"We have something in common?"

Hank met her gaze. "Maybe more than you realize." He took a bite of his burger and they ate as if it might be their last meal.

HANK COULDN'T REMEMBER the last time he'd enjoyed a meal more—or his dining companion. Frankie was funnier than he'd expected her to be. The more time he spent around her, the more he liked her. She'd definitely been the right choice when he'd gone looking for a private investigator.

He'd asked around and was told he couldn't beat Frankie Brewster. At that point, he'd thought Frankie was male. It wasn't until he saw her that he knew how to come back to the ranch without drawing attention to his reason for returning. So far, it seemed to be working, even if his parents were suspicious of their relationship. Let them worry about that instead of his real reason for bringing her home.

"Okay, let's hear it," he said as they left the Corral and headed the five miles back toward Big Sky and the ranch.

She started to say something when she glanced in her side mirror. "Do you know the driver of that truck behind us?"

He glanced in his rearview mirror and saw a large gold older-model truck behind them. As he watched, he saw that the truck was gaining speed on them. "No, why?"

"I saw it behind us earlier on the way to the Corral."

"You think whoever is driving it is following us?" The idea sounded ludicrous until he reminded himself of the person he'd seen by the river earlier— and the reason he was home. She was right. If Naomi had been murdered, then her killer was still out there.

Looking in the rearview again, he saw that the truck was coming up way too fast. The canyon road was winding with tight curves and few straightaways, and yet the driver of the truck acted as if he planned to pass—and soon—given the speed he was traveling.

"Hank, I have a bad feeling," Frankie said as the driver of the truck closed the distance.

He had the same bad feeling. Earlier there'd been more traffic, especially close to Big Sky, but other than a few semis passing by, they seemed to be the only two vehicles on this stretch of the highway right now.

Hank looked for a place to pull off and let the truck pass. Maybe it was a driver who didn't know this canyon and how dangerous it could be. Or maybe— The front of the truck filled his rearview mirror.

"He's going to ram us," he cried. "Brace yourself."

The driver of the truck slammed into the back of them. Hank fought to keep the pickup on the road. This section of highway was bordered on one side by cliffs and the river on the other. Fortunately, there was a guardrail along the river, but up ahead there was a spot where the guardrail was broken apart from a previous accident and hadn't been replaced yet.

All thoughts of the driver of the truck behind them being new to the area dissolved. Whoever was at that wheel knew exactly what he was doing. Hank knew going faster wasn't going to help. He couldn't outrun the truck.

"He's going to try to knock us into the river at this next curve," he told Frankie as the bumper of the truck banged into them again and he had to fight the wheel to keep from wrecking. "There is nothing I can do, so I have a bad feeling we will be swimming soon."

As he came around the curve, the trucker did exactly what he'd anticipated he would do. Hank tried to stay on the highway, but the truck was too large, the driver going too fast. The large truck smashed into the side of his pickup, forcing them off the road. Fortunately, Hank saw that the riverbank wasn't steep. Rather than let the trucker roll the pickup off into the river, he turned the wheel sharply toward the water and yelled, "Hang on!" and hoped for the best as the pickup left the highway and plunged into the Gallatin River.

## Chapter Eleven

"I was just at the grocery store," Dana said without preamble when her husband answered his phone at the marshal's office. "I overheard the manager talking to one of his employees about Naomi."

"Dana, I'm right in the middle of—"

"Roy said that a woman named Francesca Brewster with some insurance company had come in and was asking questions about Naomi and her death. Why would Frankie be asking about Naomi's death?"

"Maybe she's curious," her husband said after a moment. "After all, Naomi was Hank's former girlfriend. Frankie probably wants to know what happened to her and I doubt Hank is very forthcoming. Hell, he still thinks she was murdered."

"I'm worried. You know how I felt about Naomi and I'm afraid Hank did too. Now it's like he doesn't trust me. I have no idea how he feels about Frankie."

"He brought her home with him. That should tell you something."

"It would if they were getting along. Stacy said they aren't sleeping in the same bed and earlier I saw them having another argument. If she's asking people questions about Naomi—"

"I think you're making too much out of this."

"We don't know anything about her."

"Dana—"

"He's our son, Hud. I don't want to see him make a terrible—"

"There is nothing we can do about it. If either of us says anything..." He swore. "Honey, we have to let him make his own mistakes. We both tried to warn him about Naomi and look where that left us."

"It's just that I don't think he can take another woman breaking his heart." She hated how close to tears she sounded.

"He's a grown man. He can take care of himself. Give him a little credit. Maybe Frankie is exactly what he needs."

IT HAPPENED SO FAST, Frankie didn't have time to react. One minute they were on the highway, the next in the river. The pickup plunged into the water, the front smashing into the rocks. Water rushed around them and began to come in through the cracks, building up quickly at her side window.

"We have to get out of here," Hank yelled over the roar of the river and the sound of water as it began to fill the cab.

She saw him try to open his door and fail against the weight of water. Her door was facing upstream, so she knew there was no opening it. She unhooked her seat belt, only then aware of her deflated airbag in her lap.

Water was rising quickly. Hank was right. They had to brave the river because if they stayed in the pickup much longer—

Next to her, Hank had unsnapped his seat belt and was trying to get his side window to slide down, but it didn't appear to be working. He moved over and leaned back against her. "Get ready," he said. "Once I kick out the window…" He didn't need to tell her what would happen. She could see the water rushing over the cab of the pickup and forming an eddy on his side of the truck.

Hank reared back and kicked. The glass turned into a white spiderweb. He kicked again and the window disappeared out into the river. Cold water rushed in. Hank grabbed her hand. "Hang on," he said as the cab filled faster.

She held on as if her life depended on it. It did. For a moment, the force of the water rushing in wouldn't let them escape. But Hank kicked off the side of the pickup, dragging her with him. For a few moments, which felt like an eternity, she saw and felt nothing but water all around her. Her chest ached from holding her breath. She needed air, would have done anything for one small intake of oxygen. Hank never let go of her hand, or her his, even as the river tried to pull them apart.

And then, gloriously, they surfaced, and she gasped for breath. Nothing had ever felt so good as she took air into her lungs. As Hank pulled her toward shore, she looked back, surprised by how far downriver they'd surfaced. The truck cab was completely submerged in the water. She coughed and gasped for air as she stumbled up onto the rocks.

Hank pulled her to him, rubbing her arms as if to take away the chill. She hadn't realized how hard she was trembling until his strong body wrapped around her. She leaned into him, taking comfort in his warmth as what had just happened finally hit her. Someone had tried to kill them—and she'd lost her purse as well as her gun.

On the highway, vehicles had stopped. People were calling to them. Someone said they'd phoned for help and that the marshal was on his way.

DRENCHED TO THE skin and still shivering from the cold water and the close call, Hank climbed into the back of his father's patrol SUV with Frankie. His father had given them blankets, which they'd wrapped up in. Still he put his arm around her, holding her close to share his body heat. He still couldn't believe what had happened and was just thankful they were both alive.

He'd gotten her into this. So of course he felt responsible for her. But he knew it was more than that as he pulled her closer. He wasn't sure when it had happened but they felt like friends. Almost dying did that to a person, he thought.

He became aware of how her wet clothes clung to her, revealing curves he'd always known were there but hadn't seen before. The fact that he could think about that now told him that he was definitely alive—and typically male.

"Why would someone want to force you off the road?" his father asked after he'd told him what had happened.

He heard the disbelief in his father's tone. He'd been
here before. Hud hadn't believed that Naomi was murdered. He didn't believe that someone had just tried to
kill them. "Believe whatever you like," he snapped.
"But this was no accident. The truck crashed into us
twice before it forced me off the road. It wasn't a case
of road rage. Frankie had seen it behind us on the way
to the Corral. The driver must have followed us and
waited until we came out."

"Okay, son. I've called for a wrecker. I'll have your
truck taken to the lab. Hopefully there will be some
paint from the other truck on it that will help us track
down the make and model, along with the description
you've already given me of the driver. Even if the driver
wasn't trying to kill the two of you, he left the scene
of an accident. I've put a BOLO out. Later, after the
two of you get a shower and warm clothes on, I'll take
your statements."

Hank rested his head on the top of Frankie's as she
leaned into his chest and tried not to let his father get
to him. The man always had to be Marshal Hudson
Savage, all business. The show-me-the-evidence lawman. Just for once, Hank would have liked him to believe his own son.

He drew Frankie closer and closed his eyes, just
thankful to be alive. Thankful he hadn't gotten her
killed. And more aware than ever of the woman in his
arms.

FRANKIE FELT AS if she was in shock. After they were
dropped off at their cabin, Hank led her into the bath-

room and turned on the shower. *It's probably hypothermia,* she thought, since she'd felt fine in Hank's arms, but the moment he'd let her go, she'd begun to shake again.

The mirror in the bathroom quickly steamed over. "Get in with your clothes on." She looked at him as if he'd lost his mind. "Seriously," he said and, opening the glass shower door, pushed her toward the warm water streaming down from the showerhead. "Just toss your wet clothes on the floor of the shower. I'll take care of them later. I'll use the other shower. You need to get warm and dry as quickly as possible. Trust me."

Trust him? She looked into his handsome face and had to smile. Surprising herself, she did as he suggested and stepped into the walk-in shower, clothes and all. She did trust him. More than he knew. The warm water felt so good as it soaked her clothing and took away the cold. With trembling fingers, she began to peel off the wet garments to let the warm water get to her bare skin.

She felt something heavy in her jeans pocket. Her cell phone. She pulled it out and reached out to lay it next to the sink. At least she wouldn't have to worry about getting any more calls she didn't want to take since she could see that the screen was fogged over, the phone no doubt dead.

Worse, earlier, she'd put her gun into her purse. She could only hope that her purse had stayed in the pickup. Otherwise, it had washed downriver.

A shiver moved through her and she stepped back into the shower. But she knew that it would take more than warm water to stop her from shaking. Someone had tried to kill them. She thought about the truck that had forced them off the highway and into the river. She'd only glimpsed the driver. A man. A large angry man.

*It wasn't him*, she told herself. It couldn't have been. Where would he have gotten a truck like that and how would he—

Unless he had somehow tracked her to Big Sky. She glanced at her phone and felt her heart drop. Tracking her phone would have been child's play for anyone who knew how. Especially for a cop.

She leaned against the shower wall, suddenly weak with fear. The last thing she wanted was her past catching up with her here. She told herself that she was only running scared. He hadn't found her. The man in the truck hadn't been him. All of this was about Naomi— not about her.

Refusing to give in to her fears that she might have been responsible for almost getting Hank killed, she concentrated on the feel of the warm water cascading down her body. As she turned her face up to the spray, she assured herself that she was fine. Hank was fine. Better than fine. She thought of how he'd held on to her until they were both safe on shore and then hugged her in his arms, sharing his warmth, protecting her, taking care of her even when he had to be as cold as she was.

She felt her nipples pucker to aching tips at the memory of his hard body against hers. It had been so long since she'd felt desire for a man. It spiked through her, turning her molten at her center at just the thought of

Hank in the other shower, warm water running down his naked body.

Frankie shut off the water and, stepping over her wet clothes, reached for a towel. Hank was her employer. Nothing more. She was reacting to him like this only because they'd just shared a near-death experience.

But even as she thought it, Frankie knew it was much more than that. She'd never met anyone like Hank. His capacity to love astounded her. Look how he'd mourned Naomi's death for three long years and still refused to give up on finding out the truth. Frankie couldn't imagine a man loving her like that.

She toweled herself dry and pulled on the robe she saw that Hank had left for her. After drawing it around her, she pulled up the collar and smelled the freshly washed scent. Hugging herself, she realized she was crying softly. She'd never been so happy to be alive.

Frankie quickly wiped her tears and busied herself wringing out her clothes and hanging them in the shower to dry. Then, bracing herself, she tied the robe tightly around her and stepped out of the bathroom.

HUD RETURNED TO his office. He quickly checked to make sure that a deputy and a highway patrol officer were taking care of traffic while the wrecker retrieved Hank's pickup from the river.

He realized he was still shaken. He didn't want to believe that the driver of the truck who'd run them off the road had been trying to kill them. But the driver had forced them off the road where the guardrail was missing—as if he knew exactly where to dump them

into the river. That made the driver a local and that was
what worried Hud.

Hank believed this had something to do with Naomi's death. But Hud had seen Frankie's face in the
rearview mirror. She'd just been through a terrifying
experience, no doubt about it. Yet he'd seen a fear in her
eyes long after she'd been safe and warm in the back
of his patrol SUV.

Swearing under his breath, he turned on his computer, his fingers hovering over the keys for a moment
as he considered what he was about to do. He ticked off
the reasons he had to do this. Hank's unexpected return. His son bringing a woman home after three years.
Francesca "Frankie" Brewster, someone they'd never
heard about before. The two were allegedly a couple,
but their behavior was in question by Dana, who was
good at these things. Add to that, Frankie had been
asking around about Naomi's death. Throw in the "accident" that ended up with them in the river and what
did it give you?

With a curse, he put his fingertips on the computer
keys and typed Francesca "Frankie" Brewster, Lost
Creek, Idaho.

What popped up on the screen made him release the
breath he'd been holding. He sat back, staring at the
screen. What the hell? Frankie Brewster Investigations?

It took him only another minute to find out that she
was a licensed private investigator in the state of Idaho
and had been in business for four years. Her name came
up in articles in the local paper. She'd actually solved a
few cases that had made the news.

He sat back again, berating himself for looking and, at the same time, wondering what he was going to do now with the information. Just because she was a PI didn't mean that she and Hank weren't really a couple. In fact, Hud thought that might be what attracted his son to her to begin with. So why make waves?

If he said anything to Hank, his son would be furious. He would know that his father did it again, checked up on Frankie—just as he had with Naomi. Only with Frankie there was no sign that she'd ever been arrested or put under mental evaluation, at least.

"That's a plus," he said to himself and turned off the computer to rub the back of his neck and mentally kick himself. "Frankie's investigating Naomi's death," he said to himself, realizing that was what was going on. His son thought he could pull a fast one, bring Frankie home, pretend to be an item, and all the time the two were digging into Naomi's death.

He swore under his breath. Was it possible that someone was getting nervous? Was that why that truck had forced them off the road? To warn them to stop? But if that was the case…

Hud picked up the phone and called the lab. "I want information on the vehicle that forced that pickup off the road ASAP. Call me at home when you get it."

In all his years in law enforcement, he'd never felt this unsettled. What if Hank had been right all along and Naomi had been murdered? Enter Frankie, and the next thing he knew, his son and the PI were run off the highway and into the river. A little too coincidental to suit him.

With a sigh, he knew what he had to do. He had to stop them from investigating even if it meant making his son mad at him again. Hank had to let him look into it. Even as he thought it, Hud knew hell would freeze over before his son would trust him to do that. There would be no stopping Frankie and Hank if they were doing what he suspected they were.

He thought of all the mistakes he'd made with his oldest son. As he got to his feet, he just prayed that he wasn't about to make an even bigger one. But he had to stop the two of them before they ended up dead.

HANK CAME OUT of the bathroom only moments after Frankie. He'd stood under the warm spray for a long time. His emotions were all over the place. The trucker running them off the road proved what he'd been saying all along, didn't it?

So why didn't he feel more satisfaction? He'd been right. But as he stood letting the water cascade over his body, all he'd been able to think about was Frankie. He kept picturing her soaking wet, her clothes clinging to every curve. The memory had him aching.

He had turned the shower to cold and tried to get a handle on his feelings. Shivering again, he'd turned off the shower and had stood for a moment, still flooded with a desire like none he'd ever felt. He'd loved Naomi but she hadn't stirred this kind of passion in him. Was that another reason he hadn't wanted to rush into marriage?

Shaking his head, he'd stepped out of the shower and grabbed a towel to roughly dry himself off. He didn't want to be feeling these yearnings toward Frankie, not when he'd come home to set things right with Naomi. He told himself that he would keep her at a distance. But try as he might, he still felt an aching need at even the memory of her in his arms in the back of the patrol SUV.

He'd hung up his wet clothes and pulled on one of the guest robes that his mother supplied to the cabins. He promised himself that he would keep his mind on the investigation. If he was right, then they had rattled Naomi's killer. They were getting close. Maybe too close, he'd thought as he'd stepped out of the bedroom.

At the sight of Frankie standing there, his bare feet faltered on the wood floor. Her long, dark hair was down, hanging below her shoulders to the tips of her breasts beneath the robe. Her face was flushed, as was her neck and throat. Water droplets still clung to her eyelashes, making her eyes appear even larger, the violet a darker purple.

She looked stunning. When their gazes met, he saw a need in her that matched his own and felt all his resolve to keep her at arm's length evaporate before his eyes. He closed the distance between them without a word, without a thought. She didn't move, her gaze locked with his, a vein in her slim neck throbbing as he approached.

He took a lock of her long hair in his fingers. It felt silken even wet. She still hadn't moved. Still hadn't broken eye contact. His heart pounded as he brushed her hair back on one side before leaning in to kiss that spot on her neck where her blood pulsed. The throbbing beat quickened beneath his lips and it was as if he could feel his own heart drumming wildly to the same beat.

It had been so long since he'd felt like this. As his lips traveled down her neck into the hollow at her shoulder, she leaned back, giving him access. He heard her sharp intake of breath as he stroked her tender flesh with the tip of his tongue. From the hollow at her shoulder, it would have been too easy to dip down to the opening of her robe and swell of her breasts he could see rising and falling with each of her breaths.

He lifted his head again to look into her eyes before he cupped the back of her neck and drew her into a kiss, dragging her body against his. Desire raced along his veins to the riotous pounding of his heart. She looped her arms around his neck as he deepened the kiss and pulled her even closer until their bodies were molded together, almost as one. He could feel her breasts straining against the robe. He wanted desperately to lay open her robe and press his skin to hers. He wanted her naked body beneath his more than he wanted his next breath.

Reaching down, he pulled the sash of her robe. It fell away. He untied his own. As their robes opened, he pushed the fabric aside. He heard a gasp escape her lips as their warm, naked bodies came together. He felt her hard nipples press against his chest. Desire shot through him.

The knock at the door startled them both. "Hank? Frankie? I need to talk to you." Another knock and then the knob turned slowly.

They burst apart, both frantically retying their robes

as the marshal stuck his head in the door. "Sorry. I…" He started to close the door.

"It's all right," Hank said. His voice sounded hoarse with emotion and need even to his ears. He shot a look at Frankie and saw that she was as shaken as he was. If only he had thought to lock the door. If only his father had picked any time but now to stop by.

And yet, now that he'd cooled down some, he knew it was for the best. He had enough problems without jumping into bed with Frankie—as much as he would have loved to do just that. But life was complicated enough as it was. A part of him was still in love with Naomi. He wasn't sure he'd ever get over her—and he had a feeling that Frankie knew that.

"Did you find out something about the truck that ran us off the road?" Frankie asked, her voice breaking.

They shared a look. Both of them struggling not to laugh at the irony of the situation. He wondered if she felt as disappointed as he did—and maybe just as relieved. Their relationship was complicated enough without this. And, he reminded himself, there was that man who kept calling her, the one Frankie didn't want to talk to. The one he suspected was her lover, past or present. Whoever the man was, Frankie hadn't dealt with him, he thought as his father stepped into the cabin, Stetson in hand and a sheepish, amused and yet curious look on his face.

HUD LOOKED FROM his son to Frankie. Both were flushed and not just from their showers. He hadn't known what he was going to say, but after walking in on what he'd just seen, he surprised himself.

"I've decided to reopen Naomi's case," he said as the two hurriedly moved away from each other like teenagers caught necking on the couch. Dana had thought they weren't lovers. If he hadn't come along when he did, they would have been. Maybe his wife was wrong about the two of them. Maybe he was too.

"Why would you reopen the case?" Hank asked as Frankie straightened her robe.

"I'm going to get dressed," she said. "If you'll excuse me." She hurried off toward the bedroom.

"I'm sorry," Hud said. "Clearly I interrupted something."

His son waved a hand through the air. "I thought you didn't believe that Naomi was murdered?"

"I'm still not sure I do. But after what happened today, I want to take another look."

Hank shook his head, mumbling under his breath as he turned toward the kitchen. "I'm going to get dressed and have a beer. You want one?"

He glanced at his watch. He was off the clock. Normally he would pass because he wasn't in the habit of drinking before dinner, but today he'd make an exception. "I would love one." That apparently had taken Hank by surprise, because he felt his son studying him as Hank returned in jeans and a Western shirt with two bottles of beer.

As Hank handed him one and twisted off the top on his own, he said, "Thank Mom for stocking our refrigerator."

"You know your mother. She wanted you and Frankie to be…comfortable up here." Earlier, he'd come up to the cabin, planning to bust them, exposing Frankie as a PI and their relationship as a fraud. But seeing them together, he'd changed his mind and was glad of it. He could eat a little crow with his son.

Anyway, what would it hurt to reopen the case unofficially? He still had misgivings about Hank's accident earlier today. Maybe all it had been was road rage. Either way, he was determined to track down the truck—and driver.

Frankie came out of the bedroom dressed in a baggy shirt and jeans, her feet still bare. Without asking her, Hank handed her his untouched beer and went into the kitchen to get another one.

Hud stood for a moment, he and Frankie somewhat uneasy in each other's presence. He was sure that his son had given the PI an earful about him. He'd lost Hank's respect because of Naomi's case. He'd thought he wouldn't get another chance to redeem himself. Maybe this would be it.

Hud took a chair while Frankie curled up on the couch, leaving the chair opposite him open. Hank, though, appeared too restless or stubborn to sit. He stood sipping his beer.

"Any word on the truck that put us in the river?" Frankie asked into the dead silence that followed.

"Not yet. I've asked that it be moved to priority one," he said. "I also have law enforcement in the canyon watching for the truck. It will turn up." He sounded more confident than he felt. He needed that truck and its driver. He needed to find out what had happened earlier and why—and not just to show his son that he knew what he was doing. If Hank was right and the driver of that truck was somehow connected to Naomi's death... well, then he needed to find Naomi's killer—before his son and Frankie did.

"If I was wrong, I'll make it right," he told his son, who nodded, though grudgingly. As he finished his beer, his cell phone rang. "That will be your mother. Don't tell her about this," he said, holding up his empty bottle. "We'll both be in trouble," he joked, then sobered. "Dinner isn't for a while. But I also would play down what happened earlier in the river during the meal. You know your mother."

Hank smiled. "I certainly do." Hud saw him glance at Frankie. A look passed between them, one he couldn't read, but he could feel the heat of it. He really wished his timing had been better earlier.

FRANKIE WAS STILL shaken from those moments with Hank before the marshal had arrived. She'd come so close to opening herself up to him, to baring not just her naked body, but her soul. She couldn't let that happen again. She reminded herself that their relationship was fake. He was her employer. He was still in love with the memory of Naomi.

That last part especially, she couldn't let herself forget. Not to mention the fact that she had her own baggage he knew nothing about. With luck, he never would. Once she was finished with this job, she would return to Idaho. Who knew what Hank would do.

Clearly, he loved the ranch and wanted to be part of the family's ranching operation. Would what they discovered free him from the past? Free him from Naomi enough that he could return?

"We have time for a horseback ride," Hank said out of the blue as the marshal left. "It's time you saw the ranch. You do ride, don't you?"

"I grew up in Montana before I moved to Idaho," she said. "It's been years since I've ridden, but I do know the front of the horse from the back."

"Good enough," Hank said. "Come on."

Frankie got the feeling that he didn't want to be alone with her in their cabin for fear of what would happen between them. She felt relieved but also a little disappointed, which made her angry with herself. Had she learned nothing when it came to men?

They walked down to the barn, where Hank saddled them a couple of horses. She stood in the sunlight that hung over Lone Mountain and watched him. She liked the way he used his hands and how gentle he was with the horses. There were many sides to this handsome cowboy, she thought as he patted her horse's neck and said, "Buttercup, you be nice to Frankie, now."

He handed her the reins. "Buttercup said she'll be nice. You need to do the same. No cursing her if she tries to brush you off under a pine tree." He turned to take the reins of the other horse.

"Wait," Frankie cried. "Will she do that?"

He shrugged as he swung up into the saddle and laughed. "Let's hope not." He looked good up there, so self-assured, so at home. He spurred his horse forward. "Also, Buttercup's got a crush on Romeo here, so she'll probably just follow him and behave. But you never know with a female." He trotted out of the barn, then reined in to wait for her.

She started to give Buttercup a nudge, but the mare was already moving after Romeo and Hank.

They rode up into the mountains through towering pines. The last of the summer air was warm on her back. She settled into the saddle, feeling more comfortable than she'd expected to be. Part of that was knowing that she was in good hands with both Buttercup and Hank.

Frankie stole a glance at him, seeing him really relax for the first time since she'd met him. He had his head tilted back, his gaze on the tops of the mountains as if soaking them into his memory for safekeeping. Was he sorry he'd left? It didn't really matter, she realized. He couldn't come back here—not with Naomi's ghost running rampant in his heart and mind. Until he knew what had happened to her, Frankie doubted he would ever find peace.

In that moment, she resolved to find out the truth no matter what it was. She wanted to free this man from his obvious torment. But even as she thought it, she wondered if he would ever really be free of Naomi and his feelings for the dead woman.

"Wait until you see this," Hank said and rode on a little ahead to where the pines opened into a large meadow. She could see aspens, their leaves already starting to turn gold and rust and red even though summer wasn't technically over. This part of Montana didn't pay much attention to the calendar.

As she rode out into the meadow, she was hit with the smells of drying leaves and grasses. It made her feel a little melancholy. Seasons ended like everything else, but she hated to feel time passing. It wouldn't be long before they would be returning to Idaho and their lives there. That thought brought back the darkness that had been plaguing her for the past few months. She was going to have to deal with her past. She only wished she knew how.

Hank had ridden ahead across the meadow. She saw that he'd reined in his horse and was waiting for her at the edge. Buttercup broke into a trot across the meadow and then a gallop. Frankie surprised herself by feeling as if she wasn't going to fall off.

She reined in next to Hank. He was grinning at her and she realized she had a broad smile on her face. "I like Buttercup."

"I thought you might. She's a sweetheart. Except for when she tries to brush you off under a pine tree." His grin broadened.

"You really are an awful tease," she said as he came over to help her off her horse.

"You think so?" he said as he grabbed her by her waist and lifted her down to stand within inches of him. Their gazes met.

Frankie felt desire shoot like a rocket through her. She'd thought she'd put the fire out, but it had only been smoldering just below the surface. She wanted the kiss as much as her next breath.

He drew her closer. "What is it about you that is driving me crazy?" he asked in a hoarse whisper.

She shook her head, never breaking her gaze with his. "I could ask you the same thing."

He chuckled. "I want to kiss you."

She cocked her head at him. "So what's stopping you?"

"I've already had my heart broken once. I'm not sure I'm up to having it stomped on just yet," he said, but he didn't let her go. Nor did he break eye contact.

"You think I'm a heartbreaker?" she said, surprised how breathy she sounded. It was as if the high altitude of the mountaintop had stolen all her oxygen.

He grinned. "I know you are and yet..." He pulled her to him so quickly that she gasped before his mouth dropped to hers.

The kiss was a stunner, all heat. His tongue teased hers as he deepened it, holding her so tightly against him that she felt as if their bodies had fused in the heat.

He let her go just as quickly and stepped away, shaking his head. "We should get back, but first you should see the view. My mother is bound to ask you at dinner what you thought of it."

She was still looking at the handsome cowboy as she swayed under the onslaught of emotions she didn't believe she'd ever felt before. "The view?" she said on a ragged breath.

Hank laughed and took her hand. "It's this way." He led her to the edge of the mountaintop, still holding her hand in his large warm one. "What do you think?"

She thought that, for a while, they'd both forgotten Naomi. "I've never enjoyed a horseback ride more in my life," she said, her gaze on the amazing view of mountains that seemed to go on forever.

He gently squeezed her hand. "It is pretty amazing, isn't it?"

## Chapter Twelve

Dinner was a blur of people and laughter and talk as more relatives and friends gathered around the large dining room table, including Dana's best friend, Hilde, and her family. Fortunately, most of it was going on around Frankie, and all she had to do was smile and laugh at the appropriate times. She avoided looking at Hank, but in the middle of the meal, she felt his thigh brush against hers. She felt his gaze on her. When he placed his hand on her thigh, she wasn't able to control the shiver of desire that rocketed through her. She moved her leg and tried to still her galloping pulse. Getting her body to unrespond to his touch wasn't as easy.

Once the meal was over, she and Hank walked back up to their cabin. For a long way, neither said a word. It was still plenty light out.

"Are you all right?" Hank asked over the evening sounds around them. She could hear the hum of the river as it flowed past, the chatter of a squirrel in the distance and the cry of a hawk as it caught a thermal and soared above them.

"Fine. You?"

He stopped walking. "Damn it, Frankie. You can't pretend that the kiss didn't happen. That things haven't changed."

She stopped walking as well and turned to face him. Was he serious? They were pretending to be in a relationship and had almost consummated it. Worse, it was all she could think about. And maybe even worse than that, she wanted it desperately. "It hasn't changed anything."

He made a disbelieving face. She wanted to touch the rough stubble on his jaw, remembering the feel of it earlier when he'd kissed her. Not to mention the memory of their naked bodies molded together for those few moments was so sharp that it cut her to the core. "Don't get me wrong. I wanted you more than my next breath. I still do. But—"

"But?" he demanded.

"But you're my employer and this is a job. For a moment we let ourselves forget that."

"So that's the way we're going to play it?" he asked, sounding upset and as disappointed as she felt.

"Let's not forget why we're here. You're still in love with the memory of Naomi after three years of mourning her death. Let's find out who killed her—if she really was murdered—and then…" She didn't know what came after.

"Do you doubt Naomi was murdered after what happened when we left the Corral?" he demanded.

She thought there could be another explanation, though not one she felt she could share with him until she knew for sure. She still wanted to believe that no one knew where she was, especially the man who'd left her dozens of threatening messages on her phone.

Choosing her words carefully, she said, "Based on that and what I've learned about Naomi, I think there is a very good chance that she was murdered."

He stared at her for a moment. "That's right. You haven't told me what you learned about her today." He started walking again as if bracing himself for the worst. "So let's hear it."

HANK LISTENED, GETTING angrier by the moment. They'd reached the cabin by the time she'd finished. "This woman, Tamara Baker, is lying. Naomi hated the taste of booze."

"Tamara insinuated that Naomi was into something more than booze. Not men. But something more dangerous."

"Like what? Money laundering? Drugs? Prostitution?" He swore. "Stop looking at me like that. Go ahead, roll your eyes. You think I didn't know my own girlfriend?"

"Why would Tamara lie?"

"I have no idea. But she's wrong and so is Roy at the grocery store. Naomi wouldn't steal. He's thinking of the wrong girl. Naomi sure as heck didn't get fired. She was one of his best workers. She showed me the bonus she got for..." His voice trailed off. "I can't remember what it was for, but I saw the money."

Frankie said nothing, which only made him even angrier. He shoved open the door to the cabin, let her go in first and stormed in behind her. "What if it's all a lie to cover up something else?" He knew he was reaching. He couldn't imagine why these people would make up stories about Naomi.

She shrugged. "I only told you what I'd learned. Maybe she had another life when she wasn't with you."

He shook his head and began pacing, angry and frustrated. "You didn't know her. She was afraid of everything. She was...innocent."

"All right, maybe that's how she got involved in something she didn't know how to get out of."

He stopped pacing. "Like what?"

"She had a boyfriend before you, right?"

"Butch Clark. Randall 'Butch' Clark. But she hadn't seen him in years."

"I want to talk to him. Alone," she added before he could say he was going with her.

"Why? I just told you that she hadn't seen him in years."

She said nothing for a moment, making him swear again. "Just let me follow this lead. I'll go in the morning. Any idea where I can find him?"

"His father owns the hardware store. He'd probably know." He felt sick in the pit of his stomach as he recalled something. "He was at Naomi's funeral. I recognized him."

"So you knew him?"

He shook his head. "Naomi pointed him out once when we first started dating. He didn't seem like her type. I asked her about him, but she didn't want to talk about him, saying he was her past."

Frankie nodded knowingly and he caught a familiar glint in her eye.

"I don't even want to know what you're thinking right now," he said with a groan.

She shrugged. "Naomi had a past. That's all."

He cocked his head at her, waiting.

"That she didn't want to talk about," she added. "Happy?"

"You are so sure she had some deep dark secret. I might remind you that you have a past you don't want to talk about."

"True, but you and I aren't dating."

"We're supposed to be," he said, stepping toward her. "I don't see that as being so unbelievable given what almost happened earlier. How about I fire you, end this employer-employee relationship, and we quit pretending this isn't real?"

FRANKIE LOOKED INTO Hank's blue eyes and felt a shiver of desire ripple through her. It would have been so easy to take this to the next level—and quickly, given the sparks that arced between them. Common sense warned her not to let this happen. But the wild side of her had wanted him almost from the first time he'd walked into her office. The chemistry had been there as if undercover, sizzling just below the surface.

Any woman in her right mind would have wanted this handsome, strong, sexy cowboy. She doubted Hank even knew just how appealing he was. Naomi had held his sensuality at arm's length, using herself as a weapon to get him to the altar. Frankie could see that the wild side of Hank wanted out as badly as she wanted to unleash it.

He stopped directly in front of her, so close she could smell the musky outdoor male scent of him. She felt her pulse leap, her heart pounding as she waited for him to take her in his arms.

Instead, he touched her cheek with the rough tips of his fingers, making her moan as she closed her eyes and leaned into the heavenly feel of his flesh against hers.

At a tap on the door, Hank groaned. "If that's my father—"

"Hello?" Dana called. "Are you guys decent?"

Hank swore softly under his breath and then, locking his gaze with Frankie's, grinned. "Come on in, Mom," he said as he grabbed Frankie, pulled her to him and kissed her hard on the mouth. Breaking off the kiss only after the door had opened, he said, "We are now, Mom."

## Chapter Thirteen

It was late by the time Dana left. She'd seemed in a talk-ative mood, and it was clear that she wanted to spend more time with her son. Frankie excused herself to go to bed. She hadn't been able to sleep, though. Her body ached with a need that surprised her. She hadn't felt this kind of desire in a very long time and definitely not this strong.

Trying to concentrate on something, anything else, she considered what she'd learned about Naomi Hill. Sweet, quiet, timid, scared of everything, a nondrinker who was honest as the day was long with only one de-sire in life—to get married and settle down.

Frankie frowned. Was her reason for giving Hank an ultimatum that night only because of that desire? Or was she running from something?

The thought wouldn't go away. Hours later, she heard Dana leave. She lay on her back, staring up at the ceil-ing, hardly breathing, wondering if Hank would come to her bed.

He didn't. She heard the creak of the bed in the other bedroom as he threw himself onto it. She smiled to herself hearing how restless he was. Like her, he was having trouble sleeping.

Frankie didn't remember dozing off until she awakened to daylight and the sound of rain pinging off the panes in her window. By the time she'd showered and dressed, determined to do what she had been hired to do, the rain had stopped and the sun had come out. Droplets hung from the pines, shimmering in the sunlight.

When she came out of the bedroom, she found that Hank was also up and dressed.

"I'm going to go talk to Tamara and then maybe go by the grocery store and talk to Roy," he said, not sounding happy about either prospect.

She nodded. He'd shaved and she missed the stubble from last night, but he was still drop-dead handsome. "I'd call you when I get back from seeing Butch Clark, but my phone…"

"Mine too. Why don't we meet back here and have lunch together and share whatever information we come up with? Be careful. I'm sure you haven't forgotten yesterday."

Not hardly. "See you before lunch." She could feel his gaze on her and knew their conversation wasn't over yet.

"About last night—"

"Did you have a nice visit with your mother?"

He grinned, acknowledging that he'd caught her attempt to steer the subject away from the two of them. "I did, but I wasn't referring to yet another interruption just when things were getting interesting. I was going to say, I didn't come to your bed last night not because I didn't want to. Just in case you were wondering. You say you want to keep this strictly professional, but should you change your mind…all you have to do is give me a sign."

She tried to swallow the lump in her throat. He was throwing this into her court. If she wanted him, she'd have to make the next move. Her skin tingled at the thought. "That's good to know," she said and headed for the door.

"No breakfast?" he said behind her. There was humor in his tone, as if he knew she needed to get away from him right now or she might cross that line.

"I'll get something down the road," she said over her shoulder without looking at him because he was right. The thought of stepping into his arms, kissing those lips, letting him take her places she could only imagine, was just too powerful. She turned up the hood on her jacket against the rain and ignored the cold as she kept walking.

HANK SWORE AS he watched Frankie leave. He would have loved to have spent this day in bed—with her. He almost wished he had gone to her bed last night.

As much as he wanted Frankie, he hadn't forgotten why they'd come back to the ranch, back to Big Sky, back to where Naomi had died. He would always love Naomi, he told himself. But for the first time in years, he felt ready to move on. Maybe he could once they'd found out the truth.

He saw his cell phone sitting in the bowl where he'd put it this morning and went to look for Frankie's. He found it beside the sink. It was still wet. He tried to open it. Nothing. Well, at least now she couldn't get those calls that she'd been ignoring.

Who was so insistent? Someone she didn't want to talk to. He'd seen her reaction each time she'd recognized the caller. She'd tensed up as if…as if afraid of the person on the other end of the line? Definitely a man, he thought, and wondered if anyone had ever tried to kill her before yesterday.

He could almost hear her say it went with the job.

But he'd felt her trembling in the water next to him after their escape from his pickup. She'd been as scared as he had been, so he doubted nearly dying went with the job. Although he had a bad feeling that someone *had* tried to kill her. Maybe the person who kept calling.

"Well, now he can't find you, just in case he's been tracking your phone," he said to the empty room.

Hank couldn't put it off any longer. He needed to get to the truth about Naomi. Confronting Tamara and Roy were at least places to start. He wasn't looking forward to it. He doubted they would change their stories, which would mean that he hadn't known Naomi.

He sighed, wishing he was curled up in bed with Frankie, but since that wasn't an option, he grabbed his jacket and headed out into the cool, damp summer morning.

RANDALL "BUTCH" CLARK was easy to find—in the back of his father's hardware store, signing in the most recent order. As the delivery driver pulled away, Butch turned and stopped as if surprised to see that he had company.

He was short, average-looking with curly sandy-blond hair and light brown eyes.

"Frankie," she said, holding out her hand as she closed the distance between them.

Butch hesitated. "If this is about a job, my dad does the hiring. I'm just—" He waved a hand as if he wasn't sure exactly what his title was.

"I'm not looking for a job. I'm here about Naomi."

*"Naomi?"* he repeated, both startled and suddenly nervous as he fiddled with the clipboard in his hands. "Is there something new with her that I don't know about?"

Frankie decided to cut to the chase. "I'm a private investigator looking into her death." If he asked for her credentials, she was screwed. Fortunately, he didn't.

His eyes widened in surprise. Or alarm? She couldn't be sure. "Why? It's been three years. I thought her death was ruled a suicide?" His voice broke.

She closed the distance between them, watching the man's eyes, seeing how badly he wanted to run. "You and I know it wasn't suicide, don't we, Butch?"

"I don't have any idea what you're talking about."

Frankie went on instinct based on Butch's reaction thus far. He was scared and he was hiding something. "You and Naomi were close." She saw him swallow as if he feared where she was headed. "So if anyone knew what was going on with her, it was you."

Butch didn't deny it. "Why are you asking about this now?"

"The marshal has reopened the case."

He took a step back, put down the clipboard on one

of the boxes stacked along the delivery ramp and wiped his palms on the thighs of his dirty work pants. "Look, I don't want to get involved."

"You're already involved, Butch. But I might be able to help you. No one needs to know about your…part in all this if—" he started to object but she rushed on "—you tell me what you know. The marshal didn't question you the first time, right?" She saw the answer. Hud hadn't known about the old boyfriend. "So there is no reason for your name to come up now, right?"

His eyes widened in alarm. "I didn't do *anything*."

"But Naomi did."

He looked down at his scuffed sneakers.

"Could we sit down?" she asked and didn't wait for an answer. There were three chairs around a folding card table that appeared to be used as a break room. Probably for the smokers since there was a full ashtray in the middle of the table along with several empty soda cans.

"Just tell me what you know and let me help you," she said. "I'm your best bet."

He pulled out a chair, turned it around and straddled it, leaning his chin on his arms as he looked at her with moist brown eyes. "I don't even know who you are or who you work for."

"Probably better that you don't if you want me to keep your name out of it, but—" She reached for her shoulder bag.

He quickly waved it off. "You're right. I don't want to know. But if you work for them, I had nothing to do with this. I told her not to keep the money. It was like she'd never seen a movie and known that they always come after the money."

Frankie did her best not to let her surprise show as she quickly asked, "Where did she find it?"

"She told me on the highway." His tone said he didn't believe her.

"Did she tell you how much money was in it?"

He looked away. "I told her not to count it. Not to touch it. To put it back where she found it and keep her mouth shut. But she saw there was a small fortune in the bag. She'd never seen that much money."

"What did she plan to do with it?"

Butch let out a bark of a laugh. "Buy a big house, marry that rancher she was dating, move down here in the valley, raise kids, go to soccer practice. She had it all worked out except..." He shook his head.

"Except?"

He looked at her as if she hadn't been listening. "The rancher didn't want to marry her, she thought someone was following her and she ended up dead."

Frankie caught on two things he'd said. Butch knew that the night of Naomi's death, Hank said he wasn't ready to get married. Someone was following her that night. "Did she tell the rancher about the money?"

"No way. She said he was too straitlaced. He'd want to turn it in to his father. He'd be too scared to keep it."

But timid little Naomi apparently wasn't. "You said someone was following her?" He glanced down, obviously just realizing what he'd said. "The night she died. That's when you talked to her."

He looked up but she shook her head in warning for

him not to lie. "She called the bar where I was having a drink with friends and told me that she thought she was being followed."

"What did you tell her to do?"

He rubbed a hand over his face. "I didn't know what to tell her. She sounded hysterical. I said give it back. Stop your car, give it to them. She said she couldn't, that she'd put some of the money down on a house and couldn't get it back."

"So then what did you tell her to do?"

"I thought that maybe if she explained the situation…"

Frankie groaned inside. If the money Naomi had found was what she thought it was, negotiating was out of the question. "So she pulled over and tried to bargain?"

He shrugged, his voice breaking when he spoke. "I don't know. The line went dead. I tried to call her back but there was no answer."

"Did she know who she'd taken the money from?" Frankie asked.

"If she did, she never said anything to me. I swear it." He rose from the chair. "Please, I thought this was over. I thought your people… Whoever you're working for. I thought they got most of their money back. At least, what was left." He frowned. "I thought it was over," he repeated.

Frankie got up from her chair. "As far as I'm concerned, it is over."

Relief made him slump and have to steady himself

on the back of the chair he'd abandoned. He let out a ragged breath and straightened. "So we're good?"

She nodded as a loud male voice called from inside the store.

"That's my father. I have to—" He was gone, running through the swinging doors and disappearing from sight.

Frankie went out the back way and walked around to the pickup Dana Savage had lent her. Climbing behind the wheel, she wished she had a cell phone so she could call Hank. Up the block she spotted the time on one of the banks. It was about forty minutes back to Big Sky. She'd tell Hank when she saw him. But at least now she knew the truth.

Naomi Hill had been murdered—just as he'd suspected. It didn't put them any closer, though, to knowing who'd killed her, but at least now they knew why.

Hank drove into Meadow Village after he left the ranch. Frankie had told him that Tamara worked at the Silver Spur Bar. But when he parked and went inside, he was told that it was her day off. He asked for her address and wrangled for a moment with the bartender before the man gave it over. Hank dropped a twenty-dollar bill on the bar as he left.

He knew the old cabins the bartender had told him about. But as he neared the row of four cabins, he spotted marshal office vehicles parked out front. Crime scene tape flapped in the wind.

Swearing, he pulled in and, getting out, started past the deputy stationed outside.

"Hold up," the deputy said. "No one goes inside. Marshal's orders."

"Tell him I need to see him," Hank said. He held up his hands. "Tell him his son is out here, Hank. Hank Savage. I'll stand right here until you get back and won't let anyone else get past. I promise."

The deputy disappeared inside and almost at once returned with Hud.

"What's going on?" Hank asked in a hushed voice as the two of them stepped over to the ranch pickup he'd driven into town.

"What are you doing here?"

"I came by to see Tamara Baker. Frankie had spoken to her about Naomi. I wanted to talk to her." Immediately he realized his mistake as he saw his father's eyes narrow. "Tamara said some things about Naomi that didn't seem right."

"Like what?"

He didn't really want to discuss this out here, let alone voice them at all, especially to his father. Also, the marshal hadn't answered his question. He pointed out both.

"Tamara's dead."

"Dead? Not—" He didn't have to say "murdered." He saw the answer in his father's expression.

"When I get through here, I think we'd better talk." With that, his father turned and went back inside as the coroner's van pulled up.

## Chapter Fourteen

Back at the ranch, Frankie went straight to the cabin to wait for Hank. She felt anxious. What she'd learned was more than disturbing. Naomi had apparently found the answer to her prayers—or so she thought. Where had she picked up the bag of money? It seemed doubtful that it had been tossed out beside the road.

At the sound of the door opening, she spun around and saw Hank's face. "What's happened?" she asked, feeling her pulse jump and her stomach drop.

"I went over to talk to Tamara Baker. She wasn't at the bar. I got directions to her cabin. My father was there along with a crime team and the coroner." He met her gaze. "She'd been murdered."

The news floored her. Stumbling back, she sat down hard on the sofa. The ramifications rocketed through her. She'd talked to Tamara and now she was dead. Swallowing down the lump in her throat, she said, "There's more. I'm pretty sure I know why Naomi was murdered."

Hank moved to a chair and sat down as if suddenly too weak to stand. "You talked to Butch."

"He said she found a bag of money."

*"What?"* he asked in disbelief.

"Drug money, I would imagine. Enough money that she put some of it down on a house in Bozeman for when the two of you got married."

He dropped his head into his hands. "This can't be true," he mumbled through his fingers.

"She called Butch that night at the bar where he was meeting his friends—"

"So this bastard knew about this the whole time?" Hank demanded as his head came up, his blue eyes flaring.

"She told him she was being followed. She was afraid it was them, whoever the money belonged to. She debated stopping and giving back what she had left with a promise to pay back the rest."

He groaned. "She was going to make a deal with a bunch of drug dealers?"

"Her phone went dead. He tried to call her back but there was no answer."

Hank shook his head. "She told him all of this? So he knew she was in trouble and he didn't do anything?"

Frankie knew that the tough part for Hank was that Naomi hadn't trusted him with her secret. It wasn't just that she'd been living a lie, the bonus at work, not telling him about getting fired, the drinking with Tamara, the close connection with her old boyfriend when she felt she was in trouble, and River Dean, the backup if things didn't work out with Hank.

It was a lot for the cowboy to take. She wondered how Naomi had planned to explain all this money she'd come into, including the house she was in the process of buying. Maybe an inheritance? Maybe Hank would have bought the explanation, except that he hadn't wanted to get married and move to Bozeman.

Naomi had been so naive that she'd thought the drug dealers wouldn't find out who'd taken their money? Especially if it had been a lot. A small fortune to Naomi might not have been that much to some people in the wealthy part of Big Sky. But the drug dealers would have wanted it back.

"I suspect, given what you just told me," Frankie said, "that Naomi also confided in Tamara."

Hank pushed to his feet, a hand raking through his hair as he walked to the window, his back to her. "I didn't know her at all." He sounded shocked. "I loved her so much and I had no idea who she really was."

"You loved the idea of her. You fell in love with what she wanted you to see. Eventually, you would have seen behind the facade. Hopefully, before it was too late to walk away unscathed."

HANK HEARD SOMETHING in her voice. Regret. He turned to study Frankie. "Is that what happened with this man who keeps calling you?" He didn't expect an answer. He thought of Naomi. "I'm not sure it was love—at least on her part. With love comes trust. She didn't trust me enough to tell me about the money."

"Your father is the marshal."

He let out a snort. "She really thought I'd go to my father with this?"

"Wouldn't you have?"

Hank laughed and shook his head. "I would have made her turn the money over to my father." He nodded. "It would have been the only smart thing to do and she would have hated me for it."

Frankie gave him a that's-why-she-didn't-tell-you shrug.

"Well, he has to know about all of this now. He probably has people he suspects are dealing drugs in the area. What are the chances that they killed Naomi and now Tamara?" His gaze came up to meet hers and his quickly softened. "You can't blame yourself."

"I talked to her and now she's dead. Who should I blame?"

"The man you said was sitting down the bar. He was the only witness when the two of you were talking, right?"

She nodded. "But she could have told someone after that."

He shook his head as all the ramifications began to pile up. "I knew she'd been murdered. I damn well knew it. But I would never have guessed..." He sighed. "When I saw my father at Tamara's cabin, I told him that you'd talked to Tamara about Naomi. I'm sorry. I slipped up."

"Don't you think it's time we tell your parents the truth? It's pretty obvious that we're investigating Naomi's death."

"Come on. Let's go." He headed for the door.

"Just like that?"

He shook his head. "My father could be here any moment. Let's go get some lunch. I don't want to be interrogated on an empty stomach."

They left the ranch with him driving the ranch pickup he'd borrowed that morning. "I know this out-of-the-way place." He turned onto the highway and headed south toward Yellowstone Park.

Lost in thought, he said little on the drive. He could see that Frankie was battling her own ghosts. He wondered again about the man in her life who kept calling. All his instincts told him that the man was dangerous.

As he neared the spot they would have lunch, he dragged himself out of his negative thoughts, determined to enjoy lunch with Frankie and put everything behind them for a while.

"My father and grandfather used to tell stories about driving down here in the dead of winter to get a piece of banana cream pie," he said as they turned into a place called the Cinnamon Lodge. "It used to be called Almart. Alma and Art owned it and she would save pieces of banana cream pie for them."

"That's a wonderful story," Frankie said, as if seeing that he wanted to talk about anything but Naomi. "Something smells good," she said as they got out and approached the log structure.

Hank figured she wasn't any more hungry than he was. But he'd needed to get out of the cabin, away from all of it, just for a little while. It wasn't until after they'd had lunch and were in the pickup again that he told her what he'd been thinking from the moment he saw the crime scene tape around Tamara's cabin.

"It's time for you to go back to Idaho. You can take one of the pickups and—"

"I'm not leaving," she said as he started the pickup's engine, backed out and pulled onto the highway.

"You don't understand. You're fired. I have no more use for your services."

FRANKIE LAUGHED AND dug her heels in. "You think you can get rid of me that easily?"

"I'll pay you the bonus I promised you as well as your per diem and—"

"Stop! You think I don't know what you're doing?"

He glanced over at her, worry knitting his brows. "It's too dangerous. I should have realized that after what happened yesterday with that truck. But now that we know what we're dealing with—"

"Exactly. What *we're* dealing with. I want to see this through. With you." Her last words broke with emotion.

Hank sighed and reached for her, pulling her over against him on the bench seat of the older-model pickup. She cuddled against him, finding herself close to tears. She couldn't quit this now. She couldn't quit Hank. "Frankie—"

She touched a finger to his lip. "I'm not leaving."

"Yesterday was a warning," he said. "I see that now. If we don't quit looking into Naomi's death—"

"Her *murder*," she said, drawing back enough to look at him. "Are you telling me that you can walk away now that you know the truth?" She could see that he hadn't thought about what he would do.

"We have no idea who they are. Unless my father can track down that truck and find the driver…"

"So you think that makes us safe? You think they

won't be worried about what we know, what we found out?"

"I don't want to think about it right now." He pulled her close again, resting his head against the top of hers for a moment as he drove.

She could hear the steady, strong thump of his heart as she rested her head against his chest. This man made her feel things she'd never felt before. Together there was a strength to them that made her feel safe and strong…and brazen.

"Then let's go back to the cabin and not think at all," she said, taking that unabashed step into the unknown as if she was invincible in his arms.

HANK MEET HER gaze and grinned as he slowed for the turnoff to the ranch. "Are you making a move on me, Miss Brewster?"

She sat up and started to answer when she looked out the windshield at the road ahead and suddenly froze. Following her gaze, he could see a large dark sedan parked on the edge of the road into the ranch. He looked over at Frankie as she moved out from under his arm to her side of the pickup. All the color had drained from her face.

"Frankie?" he asked as he made the turn into the ranch and drove slowly by the car. He could see a man sitting behind the wheel. Frankie, he noticed, hadn't looked. Because, he realized, she knew who it was.

"Frankie?" Her gaze was still locked straight ahead, her body coiled like a rattler about to strike.

"Stop," she said and reached for her door handle.

He kept going. "No way am I letting you face whatever that is back there alone."

She shot him a desperate look that scared him. "Damn it, Hank, this has nothing to do with you. Stop the pickup and let me out. *Now!*"

Frankie was right. He'd opened up his life to her, but hers had been off-limits to him from the get-go. Nothing had changed.

He gritted his teeth as he brought the pickup to a stop. Her door opened at once and she jumped out, slamming the door behind her as she started to walk back to where the car and driver waited.

Watching in the side mirror, he cursed under his breath as he remembered her frightened expression every time her cell phone had rung with a call from whoever the man had been. Hank would put his money on that same man now sitting in that car, waiting for her.

All his instincts told him that whoever this man was, he was trouble. Frankie could pretend he wasn't, but Hank knew better. Except that she'd made it abundantly clear she wanted to handle this herself.

With a curse, he shifted into gear and headed the pickup down the road toward the ranch. She didn't need his help. Didn't want it. The PI thought she could handle this herself. She probably could.

After only a few yards up the road, he slammed on the brakes. Like hell he was going to let her handle this on her own, whether she liked it or not.

Throwing the pickup in Reverse, he sped back up the road, coming to a dust-boiling stop in front of the car.

Frankie had almost reached the vehicle. He saw that

the driver had leaned over to throw the passenger-side door open for her to get in. The jackass wasn't even going to get out.

He could hear the man yelling at her to get in. Grabbing the tire iron from under the seat, Hank jumped out.

"She's not getting into that car with you," he said as he walked toward the driver's-side window. He could feel Frankie's angry gaze on him and heard her yell something at him, but it didn't stop him. "You have a problem with Frankie? I want to hear about it," he said, lifting the tire iron.

# Chapter Fifteen

The man behind the wheel of the car threw open his door and climbed out. He was as tall as Hank and just as broad across the shoulders. The man had bully written all over him from his belligerent attitude to the bulging muscles of his arms from hours spent at the gym. Hank heard Frankie cry, "J.J., don't!"

"Who the hell are you and what are you doing with my fiancée?" the man she'd called J.J. demanded.

Hank shot a look at Frankie across the hood of the man's car.

"She didn't mention that she's engaged to me?" J.J. said with obvious delight. "I see she's not wearing her ring either. But you haven't answered me. Who the hell are—" His words were drowned out by the sudden *whop* of a police siren as the marshal pulled in on the other side of Hank's pickup.

J.J. swore. "You bitch," he yelled, turning to glare at her. Frankie had stopped on the other side of his car. She looked small and vulnerable, but even from where he stood, Hank could see that she would still fight like a wild woman if it came to that. "You called the law on me?"

The man swung his big head in Hank's direction. "Or did you call the cops, you son of a…" He started to take a step toward Hank, who slapped the iron into his palm, almost daring him to attack.

J.J.'s gaze swung past him. Out of the corner of his eye, he saw his father standing in front of his patrol SUV. J.J. saw the marshal uniform as well, swore and hurriedly leaped back into his car. The engine revved and Hank had to step back as J.J. took off, tires throwing gravel before he hit the highway and sped away.

"What was that about?" Hud asked after he reached in to turn off the siren before walking over to his son.

Hank looked at Frankie, who was hugging herself and shaking her head. "It was nothing," he said. "Just some tourist passing through who wanted to give us a hard time."

His father grunted, clearly not believing a word of it. "I need to talk to the two of you. Your cabin. Now."

Hank nodded, his gaze still on Frankie. "We'll be right there."

J.J. DROVE AWAY, fuming. *She called the cops on me? Had she lost her mind? And that cowboy…* Hank Savage had no idea what he'd stepped into, but he was about to find out.

"The cowboy's name is Hank Savage. His father's the marshal of the resort town of Big Sky, Montana," his friend at the station told him after he'd managed to get the license plate number off one of the business surveillance cameras near Frankie's office. The camera had picked up not just the man's truck but a pretty good image of the cowboy himself going into Frankie's office and coming out again—with her. She'd gone down the block, gotten into her SUV and then followed the pickup.

"You recognize the cowboy?" his friend had asked.

"No. It must be a job." But she'd left her rig in her garage.

"Well, if it is a job, she went with him, from what you told me her neighbor said."

That was the part that floored him. Why would she take off with a man she didn't know? Unless she did know him. He thought of how the man had defended her. Hell, had she been seeing this cowboy behind his back?

He drove down the highway, checking his rearview mirror. The marshal hadn't come after him. That was something, anyway. But how dare his cowboy son threaten him with a tire iron. That cowboy was lucky his father came along when he did. He swore, wanting a piece of that man—and Frankie. He'd teach them both not to screw around with him.

He pulled into the movie theater parking lot and called his friend back in Lost Creek. After quickly filling him in, he said, "I'm going to kill her."

"Maybe you should come on back and let this cool down until—"

"No way. I don't know what's going on, but she's my fiancée."

Silence. Then, "J.J., she broke off the engagement. You can't force her to marry you."

"The hell I can't. Look, she's mad at me. I screwed up, got a little rough with her, but once we sit down and hash this out, she'll put the ring back on. I just can't have some cowboy get in the middle of this."

"Where'd she meet this guy?"

"That's just it. I have no idea. Why would she just leave with him unless she knew him before? The neighbor said she packed a small bag and left. If she'd been seeing this cowboy behind my back, I would have heard, wouldn't I?"

"It's probably just what you originally thought. A job."

He shook his head. "She was sitting all snuggled up next to him in the pickup. It's not a job. The bitch is—"

"Come back and let yourself cool down. If you don't, you might do something you're going to regret. You already have a couple strikes against you at work. You get in trouble down there—"

"Not yet. Don't worry. I'll be fine." He disconnected. Fine once he got his hands on Frankie. He sat for a moment until he came up with a plan. He'd stake out the ranch. The next time she left it, he'd follow her. But first he had to get rid of this car. He needed a nondescript rental, something she or the cowboy wouldn't suspect.

"I DIDN'T WANT you involved," Frankie said with rancor the moment they were in his pickup, headed back to the ranch. The marshal had waited and now followed them into the ranch property.

"You made that clear. None of my business, right?" He looked over at her, his eyes hard as ice chips. "It isn't like you and I mean anything to each other. Still just employer and employee. Why mention a fiancé?"

"I told you, I broke it off."

He continued as if he hadn't heard her. "It isn't like we were just heading up to our cabin to... What was it we were going to do, Frankie?"

She sighed and looked away. "J.J. and I were engaged. I called it off two months ago. He didn't take it well."

"So I gathered. Now he's still harassing you. Why haven't you gone to the authorities?"

"It's complicated. I don't have the best relationship with the local cops in Lost Creek."

"Because you're a private investigator?"

"Because J.J. is one of them. He's a cop."

"A cop?" Hank shook his head. He was driving so slowly, he knew it was probably making his father crazy. It was his own fault for insisting he follow them into the ranch. As if he thought they might make a run for it?

"How long did you date him?"

"Six months. He seemed like a nice guy. The engagement was too quick but he asked me at this awards banquet in front of all his friends and fellow officers. I... I foolishly said yes even though I wasn't ready. Even though I had reservations."

"He doesn't seem like the kind of guy who takes no for an answer." When she said nothing, he added, "So he put a ring on your finger and then he wasn't a nice guy anymore. Nor does he seem like a guy who gives up easily." Hank met her gaze.

She dragged hers away. "It's his male pride. All his buddies down at the force have been giving him a hard time about the broken engagement. It isn't as if his being unable to accept it has anything to do with love, trust me. He just refuses to let this go. I gave him back his ring and he broke into my house and left it on my dining room table. But this isn't your problem, okay? I'll handle it."

He shook his head. "He comes back, *I'll* handle it," he said. "I can see how terrified you are of him and for good reason. I asked you if he was dangerous. I know now that he is. That man's hurt you and next time he just might kill you. I'm not going to let that happen as long as you're—" their gazes met "—in my employ," he finished.

After parking next to his father's patrol SUV, he sat for a moment as if trying to calm down. He'd been afraid for her. She understood he'd been worried that she would have stupidly gotten into that car.

Through the windshield, she could see the marshal was standing next to his patrol SUV, arms crossed, a scowl on his face as he waited.

Beside her in the pickup cab, she could feel Hank's anger. "Right now I don't even know what to say to you. Would you have been foolish enough to climb into that car with that man?" He glanced over at her. "You make me want to shake some sense into you until your teeth rattle. Worse, you stubbornly thought you could handle a man like J.J. and didn't need or want my help."

She wanted to tell him that she'd been on her own for a long time. She wasn't used to asking for help, but he didn't give her a chance.

"I thought you trusted me," he said, his voice breaking with emotion as he parked in front of the house and climbed out.

FOR A MOMENT, Frankie leaned back against the seat, fighting tears. Hank had shot her a parting look before getting out and slamming the door behind him. It was filled with disappointment that wrenched at her heart. He'd thought she was smart. Smart wasn't getting involved with J.J. Whitaker. Worse was thinking she could handle this situation on her own. Hank was right. J.J. was dangerous. If he got her alone again, he would do more than hurt her, as angry as he was.

Wiping her eyes, she opened her door and followed the two men up the mountain to the cabin. She ached with a need to be in Hank's arms. J.J. had found her at the worst possible time. Had he been delayed a few hours, she would have been curled up in bed with Hank. Instead, Hank was furious at her, and with good reason.

She should have told him the truth way before this. J.J. was a loose cannon. What would have happened if the marshal hadn't come along when he did? She just hadn't thought the crazed cop would find her. Why hadn't she realized he would use any and every resource he had at his disposal to get to her? Especially if her nosy neighbor had told him that she'd left with some cowboy.

J.J. would have been jealous even if her relationship

with Hank were strictly business because he thought every man wanted what he had. With Hank acting the way he did…well, J.J. would be convinced she and Hank were lovers. They would have been, she thought as a sob bubbled up in her chest and made her ache.

Not that it would have solved anything. In fact, it would have complicated an already difficult situation. But now she was drowning in regret.

## Chapter Sixteen

The marshal and Hank were both waiting for her when she topped the hill at the cabin. Hank held the door open for her and his father. She walked past him, feeling his anger and his fear. She'd told him to let her handle it and yet he'd come back to save her. She loved him and wanted to smack him for it.

"Anyone else want a beer besides me?" Hank asked as he went straight to the kitchen. His father declined as he took a seat in the living area. Frankie could have used something stronger, but she declined a beer as well. She felt as if she needed to keep her wits about her as she sat down on the couch.

"You want to tell me what that was about on the highway?" Hud said quietly to Frankie since he'd already heard Hank's version.

"An old boyfriend who won't take no for an answer," she said. "He's a cop in Lost Creek, where I live. He tracked me here."

The marshal nodded. "He going to be a problem?"

She swallowed. "I hope not."

Hank came back into the room carrying a bottle of beer, half of it already gone. "If he comes back here—"

"You call me," Hud interrupted. "You call me and let me handle it. I mean it."

Hank said nothing, his face a mask of stubborn determination mixed with anger. She couldn't tell how much of it was anger at her for not telling him or wanting to handle it herself or being frustrated by the J.J. situation as well as the two of them and where they'd been headed earlier.

The marshal cleared his voice. "We found the truck that ran you off the road. It's an old one that's been parked up at an abandoned cabin. Lab techs are checking for prints, but they're not hopeful. Anyone who knew about the truck could have used it. I'm surprised the thing still runs. Anyway, the paint matched as well as the damage to the right side."

"So it was someone local," Hank said. He looked at Frankie and saw her relief that it hadn't had anything to do with her and J.J. The woman had so many secrets. He thought of Naomi and cursed under his breath. Except Naomi had been needy. Frankie was determined to handle everything herself. He shook his head at her and turned back to his father.

"That makes sense given what we've learned about Naomi's death," he said and looked to Frankie again to see if she wanted to be the one to tell him. She gave him a slight nod to continue.

She was on the couch, her legs curled under her with one of Hank's grandmother's quilts wrapped around her.

He could tell that her run-in with her former fiancé had rattled her more than she'd wanted him to see.

He was still angry and had a bad feeling that J.J. might come to the ranch next time looking for her. He'd obviously tracked her as far as the main entrance. How crazy was the cop? Wasn't it enough that they had drug dealers wanting to kill them?

"Naomi found a bag of money," Hank began and told his father what Frankie had found out about Naomi's final phone call to an old boyfriend saying she was being followed and asking him what she should do. Give what money she had left back? "And then apparently her phone went dead or she turned it off."

Hud swore under his breath. "Drug money?"

"That's the assumption."

"Did this old boyfriend, whose name I'm going to need, did he say where she'd found it?" He looked to Frankie. She shook her head. "And you knew nothing about this?" he said, turning back to Hank.

"Nothing." He chewed at his cheek for a moment, trying to hold back his hurt and anger, realizing that he was more angry at Naomi than Frankie, though both had kept things from him. He was aware of the distinction between the two. Naomi was his girlfriend, the woman he'd planned to marry. Frankie... He looked over at her. She was a hell of a lot more than his employee—that much he knew. "Apparently Naomi didn't trust me. Must be something about me that women don't trust."

Frankie groaned and shook her head. "Let's leave you and me out of this."

He saw his father following the conversation between them with interest for a moment before getting back to Naomi and the drug money.

"If she had told you, I hope you would have been smart enough to come to me. Wouldn't you?"

Hank nodded. "I certainly wouldn't have let her keep the money, which I'm sure is why she didn't tell me."

"So the two of you have been digging around in Naomi's death," Hud said after a moment. Hank glanced over at Frankie and considered telling his father about his arrangement with the PI. But he had a feeling his father already knew. Anyway, their arrangement was beside the point.

"Tamara must have at least suspected who the drug dealers were," Hank said.

"And contacted them to let them know that we were asking questions," the marshal said.

"Would explain how we ended up in the river."

"I'm pretty sure she was involved." They both looked over at Frankie, surprised that she'd spoken.

"You talked to Tamara," Hud said. "Did you get the feeling she knew more than she was telling you?"

"She hinted that Naomi was wilder than anyone knew, that she had secrets and lived a double life. But from what Hank had told me about her," Frankie continued, "I had the feeling Tamara was talking about herself."

"Well, whatever she knew, she is no longer talking," the marshal said. "And the two of you…" He took a breath and let it out. "I wish you'd been honest with me about what you were doing."

"You didn't believe that Naomi had been murdered," Hank pointed out, feeling his hackles rise a little.

"I know, and I'm sorry about that. You were right. I was wrong. But now you have to let me handle this. I need you both to promise that you're done investigating."

"I promise," Hank said, looking at Frankie.

"Fine," she said. "If that's what you want," she said to him, rather than the marshal.

"Do you have some suspects?" Hank asked.

"I hear things," his father said. "The problem is getting evidence to convict them. Are there drugs being distributed in Big Sky? Maybe even more than in other places in Montana just because of the amount of money here." He rose to leave. "I'm expecting you both to keep your promise. Otherwise, I'm going to lock you up. I'm tempted to anyway, just to keep you both safe. As much as I hate to say this, it might be a good idea for the two of you to go back home to Idaho. At least for a while."

Hank looked at Frankie. "We'll leave in the morning."

"After breakfast. Your mother will be upset enough, but at least have one more meal with her before you take off," Hud said and met Hank's gaze. "You might want to tell your mother the truth. I don't want her planning a wedding just yet."

Hank walked his father out. "Dad, that car earlier? It was Frankie's former fiancé. She broke up with him two months ago but he's continued to stalk her. He's a cop from Lost Creek."

"I'll keep an eye out for him."

"Thanks." He felt his father's gaze on him and seemed about to say something but must have changed his mind.

"See you at breakfast," Hud said, turned and left.

FRANKIE FELT AS if her heart would break. She felt ashamed. She should have known better with J.J. She'd ignored all the red flags. It made her more ashamed when she remembered how she'd given Hank grief for ignoring the obvious signs with Naomi. She prided herself on reading people, on seeing behind their masks, on using those skills to do her job.

But when it came to her own personal life? She'd failed miserably. It didn't matter that J.J. had hidden his real self from her. She still should have seen behind the facade. Now she couldn't get away from him. He must have tracked her phone. How else could he have found her? At least he hadn't tried to kill them in that old truck that forced them into the river. She could be thankful for that.

Throwing off the quilt, she headed for the shower, feeling dirty and sick to her stomach. She'd never wanted Hank to know about J.J., let alone have the two meet. After turning on the shower, she stepped under the warm spray and reached for the body gel to scrub away her shame and embarrassment.

Tomorrow she and Hank would go back to Idaho. She hated leaving anything unfinished. She'd at least found out why Naomi Hill had died. But she had no idea who might be behind the murder. As she tilted her face up to the water, she remembered the man sitting at the end of the bar the day she went to talk to Tamara. He'd been acting like he wasn't paying them any attention, but he'd probably been listening to their conversation. Also, Tamara had gone down the bar and the two had been whispering. What if he was—

The shower door opened, making her spin around in surprise, all thoughts suddenly gone as she looked into Hank's baby-blue eyes. "Mind if I join you?"

She stepped back and watched as he climbed in still dressed in everything but his boots. "You don't want to take off your clothes?"

"Not yet," he said as he closed the shower door behind them and turned to take her in. "Damn, woman, you are so beautiful."

"I'm so sorry that you had to find out about J.J.," she said, close to tears. "He's the big mistake of my life and I'm so ashamed for getting involved with such a loser."

He touched his finger to her lips and shook his head. "We all make mistakes. Look at me and Naomi. But you don't have to worry. I'm not going to let J.J. hurt you ever again. I promise."

"I don't want you—"

"Involved? Once I take off my clothes and get naked with you? We'll be in this together, you understand?"

She swallowed the lump in her throat, but could only nod.

He slowly began to unsnap his Western shirt.

"I think you'd better let me help you with that," she said, grabbing each side of the shirt and pulling. As the shirt fabric parted, revealing his muscled, tanned chest, she ached to touch him. As he drew her to him, she pushed her palms against the warmth of his flesh and leaned back for his kiss.

"Last chance," Hank said as he ended the kiss and reached for the buttons of his jeans. "There won't be any going back once these babies come off."

She laughed and pushed his hands away to unbutton his jeans and let them drop to the floor of the shower along with his underwear and his socks. She looked at his amazing body—and his obvious desire—and returned her gaze to his handsome face. "No going back," she said as she stepped into his arms again and molded her warm, wet body to his.

HANK KISSED HER passionately as he backed her up against the tiled wall of the shower, before his mouth dropped to her round, full breasts. Her nipples were dark and hard, the spray dripping off the tips temptingly. He bent his head to lick off a droplet before taking the erect nipple into his mouth and sucking it.

Frankie leaned her head back, arching her body against his mouth, a groan of pleasure escaping her lips. He took the other nipple in his mouth as his hand dropped down her belly and between her legs. He felt her go weak as his fingers found the spot that made her tremble. She clung to him as he made slow circles until she cried out and fell into his arms again.

He reached around to turn off the water and opened the shower door. After grabbing several large white bath towels from the hooks, he tied one around his waist and wrapped Frankie in the other. Sweeping her into his arms, he carried her toward his bedroom. His heart pounded. He meant what he'd told her. They were now in this together. No more secrets.

She looped her arms around his neck and leaned her face into the hollow of his shoulder as he kicked open the door to the bedroom, stalked in and, still holding her, kissed her, teasing her lips open with his tongue. The tip of her tongue met his and he moaned as he laid her on the bed.

She grabbed him and pulled him down with her. "I want you, Hank Savage," she said, the words like a blaze she'd just lit in his veins. "Oh, how I want you."

MUCH LATER THEY lay in each other's arms, Frankie feeling as if she was floating on a cloud. She couldn't remember ever feeling this happy, this content. But there was another emotion floating on the surface with her. She had trouble recognizing it for a moment because it was so new to her. Joy.

It made her feel as if everything was going to be all right. She usually wasn't so optimistic. She was too rational for that. But in Hank's arms, she believed in all the fairy tales. She even believed in true love, although she knew it was too early to be thinking this way. Look at the mistake she'd made with J.J. Six months hadn't been long enough to date him before getting engaged.

She looked over at Hank. And here she was curled up in bed with a man she'd only known for days.

"Are you all right?" he asked as she sat up to sit on the edge of the bed.

The reality of it had hit her hard. "I was just thinking this might be too fast."

He caressed her bare back. "I can understand why you're scared, but is that what your heart tells you?"

Gripping the sheet to her chest, she turned to look at him. She knew only too well what her heart was telling her. She just wasn't sure she could trust it right now.

Finding safer ground, she said, "I remembered something when I was in the shower—before you joined me. The man sitting at the bar. He was more than a regular. He and Tamara…they had a connection. I'm sure of it and it wasn't romantic. He had to overhear our conversation, which could mean…that if he was involved in the drug distribution and Tamara knew about it or was involved, he could have ordered the driver of that truck to either scare us or kill us."

"You're purposely avoiding the question."

Frankie gave him an impatient look. "Sandy blond, about your height, a little chunkier." That made him raise a brow. "You know what I mean."

Hank stopped her. "I know who you're talking about. I know exactly who you're talking about. I went to school with him. Darrel Sanders. He has a snow removal business in the winter. I have no idea what he does in the summer." He reached for his phone and realized the late hour. "I'd better wait and tell Dad at breakfast."

He drew her back onto the bed, turning her to spoon against her. "We can take all the time you want," he whispered into her ear, sending a shiver through her. "I'll wait."

She pressed her body against his in answer and felt his desire stir again. Chuckling, she turned in his arms to kiss him. He deepened the kiss and rolled her over until she was on top of him.

Frankie looked into his blue eyes and felt so much emotion that it hurt. Too fast or not, she was falling hard for this cowboy.

## Chapter Seventeen

Dana noticed right away that there was something different about her son and Frankie. She shot a look at Hud. He shrugged, but as he took his seat at the breakfast table, she saw him hide a knowing grin. She knew that grin.

"So, how are you two this morning?" she asked, looking first at her son, then Frankie.

"Great," they both said in unison and laughed.

She noticed that they were sitting closer together, and if she wasn't wrong, her son's hand was on Frankie's thigh. Whatever problems they'd been having, she was relieved to see that they'd moved on from them. At least for the time being. She feared that the ghost of Naomi was still hanging around.

"I made a special breakfast," she said. "Waffles, eggs, ham and bacon, orange juice and fresh fruit."

"Mom, you shouldn't have gone to all this trouble," Hank said, "but we appreciate it. I'm starved." He picked up the plate of waffles, pulled three onto his plate and passed the plate to Frankie.

"I can't remember the last time I had waffles," Frankie said and helped herself.

"Try the huckleberry syrup," he suggested. "It's my grandmother's recipe. Or there is chokecherry syrup, also my grandmother Mary's recipe." Dana had named her daughter after her.

She loved seeing her son and Frankie in such a good mood. She watched with a light heart as they helped themselves to everything she'd prepared. They both did have healthy appetites. She smiled over at Hud, remembering how he'd appreciated hers, back when she was that young.

She looked at the two lovebirds and wondered, though, if she'd really ever been that young. Nothing could spoil this moment, she thought, right before the phone rang.

Hud excused himself to answer it since it was probably marshal business.

Hank got up too, to follow his father into the other room.

Dana pushed the butter over to Frankie. "You look beautiful this morning. I love that shirt." It wasn't one of those baggy ones like she wore most of the time.

"Thank you." Frankie looked down at the shirt as if just realizing that she'd put it on that morning. When she looked up, her eyes clouded over.

"I'm sorry—was it something I said?"

"No, it's just that I love being here and—"

Hank came back into the room, followed by his father. Dana saw their expressions and said, "What's happened?"

Hud put a hand on his wife's shoulder. "It's just work, but Hank and Frankie are going back to Idaho today. They're leaving right after breakfast."

Dana shook her head as she felt her eyes burn with tears. "So soon?" she asked her son. "It feels like you just got here."

"It's for the best right now," Hank said. "We both have jobs to get back to, but don't worry. I'll be home again before you know it."

Her gaze went to Frankie as she recalled how close the young woman had been to tears just moments ago. Because she knew they were leaving? Or because she wouldn't be coming back?

"She'll be coming back too," Hank said quickly as if reading her expression. Her son sat back down at the table to finish his breakfast and gave Frankie a look that was so filled with love, Dana felt choked up.

"I certainly hope you'll both be back," she said, fighting tears.

"I have to go," her husband said as he leaned down to give her a kiss on the cheek. She reached back to grab his hand and squeeze it. She wished he would retire. There were days he left the house when she wasn't sure he would make it home alive again. It was a thought that filled her with fear. She couldn't wait for the days when the two of them would be here together on the ranch with their grandchildren and the phone wouldn't ring with marshal business.

"YOU TOLD YOUR dad about the man I saw at the bar?" Frankie asked as they left the ranch house.

"Darrel Sanders." He nodded as they walked up to the cabin to get their things.

She could tell that leaving here was hard on Hank. Probably because it was so hard on his mother. "Your mom is so sweet."

"Yeah, she is. Frankie, I know all this is new between us, but I have to be honest with you. Being here, it makes me wish I'd never left. I miss it."

She nodded. "I can see that."

"Not because of Naomi. Maybe in spite of her. I miss my family. I miss ranch work."

"There's no reason you shouldn't come back. This is your family legacy." Frankie could feel his gaze on her.

"You have to know that if, down the road, once you've had enough time to accept that we belong together..."

"What are you saying?" she asked, stopping on the trail to face him.

"That if my coming back here was a deal breaker with us, I would stay in Idaho and I would be fine at my job."

She shook her head. "I would never keep you from what you love or your family. But we still need to slow down. This is way too fast."

"Not for me, but I can see it is for you. Plus we still have to deal with your ex-fiancé. I get it. Like I told you, I'll wait." He leaned toward her, took her face in his big hands and kissed her. "Umm, you taste like huckleberries."

She saw the look in his eye and laughed. Why not? It wasn't as if they were in a hurry to get back to Idaho.

As Hank drove out of the ranch, he couldn't help looking back. Frankie noticed and reached over to put her hand on his thigh.

"You'll be back."

He nodded. "*We'll* be back."

She smiled and looked out her window. He realized she was looking in her side mirror.

His gaze went quickly to his rearview mirror. No sign of J.J. "Let's hope he gave up and went back to Idaho."

"I doubt it. But since that's where we're headed…"

"What are we going to do about him when we get back?"

"I've hesitated to get a restraining order because, one, I know it won't do any good, and, two, it will only infuriate him and make things worse."

He stole a look at her as he drove. He still couldn't believe this. He was crazy about her. She was all he'd thought about. But the J.J. situation scared him. They weren't out of the woods yet. Until J.J. was no longer a problem, he and Frankie couldn't move forward. "What other option is there?"

"Short of shooting him?" She brushed her hair back. This morning she'd tied back her long mane. Tendrils had escaped and hung in a frame around her face. She couldn't have looked more beautiful.

"I understand why he doesn't want to lose you. I feel the same way. But his methods are so desperate, so…"

"Insane?" She nodded. "Also his reasons. He wants me back to save face. If he loved me he wouldn't—" Her voice broke.

"I'm guessing he's been violent with you," he said as he drove away from Big Sky headed north.

She nodded without looking at him. "Please, I don't want to talk about him. It's a beautiful day and I don't want to spoil it."

It was. A crisp blue cloudless sky hung over the tall pines and rocky cliffs of the canyon. Beside them, the river flowed, a sun-kissed clear green. He felt her gaze on him.

"Are you all right with leaving? I mean, we came here to—"

"Because I was convinced Naomi was murdered. We have good reason now to believe it's true. It's up to my father now to find out the truth."

She nodded. "It feels unfinished."

He glanced over at her. "Once we knew what Naomi had gotten involved with, it was too dangerous to stay because I know you. You wouldn't stop looking. I couldn't let you do that. It was getting too dangerous. Not to mention my father would have locked us up if we continued to investigate it."

FRANKIE STARED AT him in surprise. "But you wouldn't have stayed and kept looking if I wasn't with you."

"I just told you. My father would have probably thrown me in jail is what would have happened."

"Hank—"

"There is no way I'm putting you in that kind of danger."

"That isn't your choice. This is what I do for a living."

"I've been meaning to ask you how you came to be a private eye."

She could see that he was changing the subject, but she answered anyway. "I had an uncle who was a private investigator. I started out working for him in his office. He took me on a few cases. I was pretty good at it. When he moved to Arizona and closed his office, I opened mine." She shrugged. "I kind of fell into it. Would I do it over? I don't know." She looked at him. "That day we went on the horseback ride up into the mountains?" He nodded. "I felt the kind of freedom I've always felt with my job. It was…exhilarating. If I could find a job that let me ride a horse every day…"

"As a rancher's wife, you could ride every day."

She'd been joking, wanting to change the subject. But now she stared at him and saw that he was completely serious. They hadn't even said that they loved each other and he was suggesting she become his wife.

But as she looked at him, she knew it in her heart. She did love him. She'd fallen for him, for his lifestyle, for his family. She'd fallen for the whole ball of wax and now he was offering it to her?

Frankie looked away. As she did, she saw the man stagger out into the highway. "Hank, look out!"

HANK HIT THE BRAKES. The pickup fishtailed wildly, but he got it stopped before he hit the man who'd dropped to his hands and knees in the middle of the highway.

He threw open his door, jumped out and rushed to the man gasping for breath, whose face was smeared with blood.

"Help me," the man said. "My car went off the road back in the mountains."

Hank reached down to help him up. Traffic had been light. What few drivers passed slowed down to look, but didn't stop.

"Here, let me help you to my pickup," he said as he half lifted the man to his feet. As they approached the passenger side, Frankie moved over to give him room to climb in with Hank's help.

After closing the door, Hank hurried around to slide behind the wheel. "I can take you to the hospital in Bozeman."

"That won't be necessary," the man said, no longer wheezing.

Hank shot a look at the man and felt his eyes widen as he saw the gun now pressed to Frankie's temple.

"Drive up the road," the man ordered. "I don't want to kill her, but I will."

# Chapter Eighteen

J.J. had parked down the road from the ranch turnoff. He'd been able to see anyone coming or going. Stakeouts were something he was good at because he required so little sleep. He was usually wired. Catching bad guys was his drug of choice.

Catching Frankie and straightening her up was enough motivation to keep him awake for days. His dedication paid off in spades this morning when he saw the pickup coming out of the ranch with both the cowboy and Frankie.

The pickup turned north and J.J. followed in the SUV he'd rented. It cost him a pretty penny to rent, but he would spare no expense to get Frankie back. As he drove, he admitted to himself that he'd made mistakes when it came to her. He'd put off the actual wedding, stringing her along for a while because while he liked the idea of having her all to himself, he wasn't ready to tie himself down.

He'd been happy knowing that no other man could have her as long as she was wearing his ring. So when she'd wanted to break up, he'd been caught flat-footed.

He'd thought it was because he hadn't mentioned setting a date for the wedding. But in that case, he would have expected her to start talking about making wedding plans or leaving bride magazines around or dropping hints and crying and giving him ultimatums.

Instead, she'd said she didn't want to marry him, that the engagement had been a mistake and that she wanted out. She'd handed him his ring. Hadn't even flung it at him in anger.

That was when he'd gotten scared that she was serious. No recriminations, no tears, just a simple "I don't want to marry you. I'm sorry."

It had hit him harder than he'd expected. He'd been relieved, and yet the thought of her just tossing him back like a fish that didn't quite meet her standards really pissed him off. He'd thought, *Like hell you're going to walk away from me.*

He'd gotten physical. But what guy wouldn't have under those conditions? That was when she stopped answering his calls, refused to see him, basically cut him off entirely. At first, he thought it was just a ploy to get him to the altar. Of course she wanted to marry him. He was a good-looking guy with a cool job. Didn't all women go for a man in uniform?

Since then he'd been trying to get her back every way he could think of. But it became clear quickly that she was serious. She wanted nothing more to do with him. That was when he got mad.

Now, as he followed the pickup north out of town, he considered what to do next. He had no idea where they were headed. But wherever they were going, they didn't seem to be in a hurry.

It was early enough that traffic was light, so he stayed back, figuring he couldn't miss them if they stopped anywhere in the canyon. Once out of it, he'd have to stay closer. After his all-night stakeout, he wasn't about to lose them now.

They were almost out of the canyon when he saw the pickup's brake lights come on. He quickly pulled over to see what was going on. There was no place for them to turn off, so what the—

That was when he saw the cowboy jump out and rush up the road. A few moments later, the cowboy returned and helped a man into the passenger side of the truck. The man appeared to be injured.

As the pickup pulled back onto the highway, so did J.J. This put a new wrinkle in things, he thought. When not far out of the canyon, the cowboy turned off before the town of Gallatin Gateway. Maybe they were taking the man to his house on what appeared to be the old road along the river. Still, it seemed strange.

J.J. followed at a distance, telling himself this might work out perfectly for him. When they dropped the man off, maybe that was when he'd make his move.

"WHAT IS THIS ABOUT?" Hank asked, afraid he knew only too well.

"You'll find out soon enough," the man said. "Right up here around the next corner, take the road to the left toward the mountains."

Hank couldn't believe he'd fallen for this. But in

Montana, you stopped to help people on the road. He hadn't given it a second thought, though he regretted that kindness now.

He shot a look at Frankie. She appeared calm, not in the least bit worried, while his heart was racing. The man had a gun to her head! He couldn't imagine anything worse, and then realized he could. At least Frankie wasn't standing on a ledge over the river, looking down at the rocks, knowing she was about to die.

He saw the turn ahead and slowed to take it, glancing into his rearview mirror. There was a vehicle way back on the road. No way to signal that they needed help.

They were on their own. He knew they would have to play it by ear. He would do whatever it took to keep Frankie safe—even if it meant taking a bullet himself.

He turned onto the road. As it wound back into the mountains, he told himself that it made no sense for the drug dealers to kidnap them, let alone kill them. They'd gotten away with murder for three years. If he and Frankie had uncovered evidence against them, they would have been behind bars by now.

So why take them? That was the part that made no sense. Running them off the road had been a warning to back off, but this…this terrified him. Maybe they were cleaning up loose ends, like with Tamara, since she obviously had known more than she'd told Frankie.

THE FIRST THING the marshal did when he left the ranch after breakfast was drive over to Darrel Sanders's house. He'd hoped to catch him before he got up. He remembered the boy Darrel had been as a classmate of Hank's. A nice-looking kid with a definite chip on his shoulder.

Darrel had moved into his mother's house after she died. It was a small house in a subdivision of other small houses away from Meadow Village.

But when he pulled up, he saw that Darrel's vehicle, an old panel van, was gone. He tried his number, let it ring until voice mail picked up before hanging up.

It made him nervous that Darrel wasn't around. The man worked in the winter but, as far as Hud could tell, did nothing in the summer to earn a living. The supposition was that he made so much with his snow removal business that he had summers off.

Hud sat for a moment, letting his patrol SUV idle in front of the house before he shut off the engine, got out and crossed the yard. He'd always gone by the book. But there was no way he could get a warrant based on what he had, which was simply suspicion.

At the house, he knocked and then tried the door. Locked. Going around the small house, he tried to look in the windows, but the curtains were pulled.

At the back, he stepped up onto the small porch. A row of firewood was stacked head high all along the back side of the house and down the fence, cutting off any view of most of the neighbors.

Hud tried the back door and, finding it locked, he put his shoulder into it. He wasn't as young as when he used to do this. The door held and his shoulder hurt like hell, but he tried again.

The lock gave and he opened the door and quickly stepped in, telling himself that he smelled smoke and thought he'd better check to make sure nothing was on fire inside. A lie, but one he would stand behind. The inside of the house wasn't as messy as he'd expected it to be. He'd wondered if Darrel had gone on the lam after Tamara's death, but if he'd packed up and taken off, there was no sign of it.

A pizza box sat in the middle of the table. He opened it and saw that several pieces were still inside. There were dishes in the sink and beer in the refrigerator. He had the feeling that Darrel hadn't gone far.

He thought about waiting for him, but after looking around and finding nothing of interest, he left by the way he'd come in, feeling guilty and at the same time vindicated.

He'd insisted before Hank left that he get a new cell phone before he left town. He tried his number now.

FRANKIE STARTED AS Hank's cell phone rang. She hadn't replaced her own, saying she'd take care of it once she got home. She wanted a new number, one that J.J. probably wouldn't have any trouble getting, though. That thought had come out of nowhere. A foolish thought to be worrying about J.J. when a stranger had a gun to her head.

Hank's cell rang again.

"Don't touch it," the man ordered, pressing the barrel of the gun harder against her temple and making her wince.

"It's probably my father, and if I don't answer it, he'll be worried and put a BOLO out on us."

The man swore. "Give me your phone." Hank dug it

out and handed it over. The man stared down at it for a moment and said, "Answer it. Tell him you're fine but can't talk because of the traffic and will call him later. Say anything more and the last thing your father will hear is this woman's brains being splattered all over you. Got it?"

"Got it." He took the phone back and did just as the man had told him before being ordered to hand the phone back.

Frankie watched the man pocket the phone. She hadn't been able to hear the other side of the conversation. But it appeared the marshal had accepted that Hank couldn't talk right now.

She took even breaths, letting herself be lulled by the rocking of the pickup as Hank drove deeper into the foothills. She knew better than to try to take the gun away from the man in these close quarters. She would wait and bide her time. She hoped Hank was on the same page. He appeared to be since he hadn't tried to get a message to his father.

They came over a rise and she saw a small cabin set back against rocks and pines. Several rigs were parked in front of it, including a panel van that she'd seen before. It took her a moment to remember where. In front of the Silver Spur Bar in Big Sky. Darrel Sanders's rig. So this was just as they suspected, about the drug money and Naomi's death.

"Park over there and then we're going to get out very carefully," the man said. "This gun has a hair trigger. If you try anything—"

"I get the picture," Hank said impatiently. "But now

this. If you shoot her, you'd better shoot me as quickly as possible because if you don't—"

"I get the picture," the man interrupted, and she saw him smile out of the corner of her eye.

Even knowing what this was about, she couldn't understand why they were being brought here. She didn't think it was to kill them, but she knew she could be wrong about that. The thought made her breath catch and her mouth go dry. She and Hank had just found each other. She had hardly let herself believe in this relationship. She didn't want it to be over so soon— and so tragically.

She'd said she needed time, but even after her bad experience with J.J., she knew in her heart that Hank was nothing like the cop. He was the kind of man who made a woman feel loved and protected. The kind of man who loved horses and wanted to make babies and raise a family.

Frankie felt tears burn her eyes as she let herself admit that she wanted that as well. Wanted to come back here to the ranch and raise their kids here. She wanted Hank.

The man opened his door and grabbed her with his free hand to pull her out of the pickup, the gun still pointed at her head. Hank had gotten out on the other side of the pickup and stood waiting, his gaze on the man as if hoping for an opportunity to get the gun away from him.

She willed Hank to look at her, and when he shifted his gaze, she smiled, hoping to reassure him that they were going to get through this. They had to. She'd seen

their future and she wasn't ready to give that up. If it
meant a fight…well, she was ready.

"WHAT A CHUMP," J.J. said as he looked after Hank and
Frankie. He couldn't believe how accommodating the
fool was. First he picked up a complete stranger from
the middle of the road and then what? Offered to drive
him home? And his home ended up being way down a
dirt road, back in the foothills?

J.J. had gone on past the turnoff when he'd seen the
pickup begin working its way back into the foothills.
After turning around, he'd found a place to park, pulled
his gun out of the glove box, checked to make sure it
was fully loaded, then stuck it in the waistband of his
jeans as he got out of the rental car.

It might be a hike back in to wherever the cowboy
had taken the man, but J.J. thought the area couldn't
be more perfect for what he had in mind. Even if they
dropped the man off and were headed back this way
before he reached the man's house on foot, he could
work with it.

Feeling as if Lady Luck had smiled on him, he
couldn't imagine a more perfect place to end this. Once
he explained things to the cowboy, he hoped that was
the end of any problem from him.

Frankie was his. Period. End of discussion. True,
right now she was giving him some trouble, but he
would try humbling himself, sweet-talking her, spoiling her, and if that didn't work then he'd have to get
physical. It wasn't something he wanted to do, but she
had to understand how things were going to be. She

couldn't embarrass him in front of his friends and his coworkers. She had to behave. No one respected a man who couldn't keep his woman under control.

Once they established the rules, hell, maybe he'd suggest they pick a wedding date. Marrying her might be the only way to keep her in line. If that was what he had to do, then he'd bite the bullet and get it over with. It wasn't like he had someone else he wanted to marry. There were some he wanted to get into bed, but he could do that easily enough after he was married to Frankie. She had to understand that he had his needs. Real men did.

J.J. was feeling good as he headed up the road. He'd gone a quarter mile when he realized that he couldn't hear the sound of a vehicle engine anymore. He came over a rise and saw why.

In the distance was a small cabin with four rigs parked in front of it, including the cowboy's pickup. What he didn't see was any sign of Frankie or the cowboy, though. Maybe the man they'd rescued had invited them in for something. A drink to pay them back for saving him?

Fine with J.J. He was in no hurry. He kept to the trees along the edge of the foothills until he was close enough to the cabin that he would see them when they came out.

Maybe he'd just hitch a ride with them when they left, he thought, feeling the weight of the gun pressing against his stomach. He pulled it out and sat down on a rock to wait, thinking about the future he and Frankie would have. Everything was going to be fine now. Like his boss had warned him, he just needed to get his life under control or he could be in trouble at work.

The memory made him grit his teeth. This was all Frankie's fault. But he would get the bitch in line—one way or the other.

THE MAN LED them into the cabin at gunpoint. Hank stepped through the door, Frankie and the man behind him, the gun still to Frankie's head. The cabin appeared larger on the inside than it had from outside. At a glance he took it all in as his mind raced for a way out of this that didn't get them both killed.

He saw a small kitchen against one wall, a bed and a half-dozen mismatched chairs around a table. Darrel was sitting in one of the chairs. A large man he didn't recognize was standing against the wall, looking tough. Hank didn't miss the holstered gun visible under the man's jacket.

He went on the defensive, determined not to let him see how worried he actually was. "What the hell, Darrel?"

His former classmate smiled. "Sit down, Hank. There's no reason to get all worked up. Les," he said to the man they'd picked up in the middle of the highway, "why don't you and Frankie sit over there." He pointed to the bed. "That way we can all see each other."

Hank hadn't moved. Darrel kicked out one of the chairs across the table from him. "Take a load off and let's talk."

"I can't imagine what we might have to talk about."

"Hank, we've known each other for too long to lie

to each other. So let's cut the bull. You know perfectly well why you're here. Sit."

Hank took the chair, turning it around to straddle the seat and rest his arms on the back. He'd be able to move faster this way—if he got the chance.

Darrel smiled, seeing what Hank was up to, but said, "Your father was by my house this morning looking for me and snooping around, I heard. I suspect it's your doing. Yours and your—" his gaze shifted to Frankie "—your lady friend's." He eyed Frankie with interest for a moment before turning back to Hank. "Picked yourself up a private eye, did you? Why would you do that?"

He considered several answers before he said, "I never believed that Naomi killed herself."

Darrel nodded with a grimace. "No, you never did."

"So I hired Ms. Brewster to help prove I was right."

"And did you?" He could feel the man's intense gaze on him.

"No. Suspecting is one thing. Proving is another. It's why Frankie… Ms. Brewster and I were leaving town." He didn't want Darrel thinking there was anything more between him and Frankie than employer and employee. He knew the man well enough to know he would use it against them.

Darrel raised a brow in obvious surprise. "Leaving? Giving up that easy? Just doesn't sound like you, Hank. Remember how you were when it came to competitive sports? You couldn't stand to let me win. So why give up now?" His former classmate seemed to consider it for a moment before his gaze swung to Frankie. "Things get a little too complicated for you?"

He saw no reason to lie. "They did. So we decided to put all of this behind us and go back to our lives in Idaho."

Darrel shifted his weight to lean across the table toward him. "I'm happy for you. Personally, I thought you were never going to get over Naomi, but apparently you've now found a woman who's made you forget her. Under normal circumstances, I'd wish you well. But here is the problem. I still want my money that your former girlfriend stole. I thought it was lost forever, but then you came back to the canyon and I figured, 'Hank's come back to pick up the money. He was in on it the whole time.' I actually admire you for waiting three years. I kept track of you and knew you hadn't spent it. For a while, I thought maybe Naomi hadn't even told you about it. So where is it? In your pickup? Trent, go take a look."

"Wait a minute," Frankie said, making them all turn to look at her. "Naomi didn't have the money on her that night, the night you killed her?"

# *Chapter Nineteen*

As J.J. had approached the cabin, he considered climbing in the back of the cowboy's pickup. From the hill where he sat, he could see that there appeared to be some old tarps in the back. He could hide, and when the time was right, he could pop up. *Surprise!*

The idea had its appeal. He just wasn't sure he could reach the pickup before they came out, and given the number of vehicles parked outside the cabin, he couldn't be sure how many people were inside.

The rock where he sat was far enough away that he could see the cowboy and Frankie when they came out, but they probably wouldn't notice him. It wouldn't take much for him to trot down to the road and stop them once they were out of sight of the cabin.

They seemed to have been in there for a while now, he thought, frowning. Maybe the man was more injured than he'd thought. What if they'd sent for an ambulance? Worse, the cops?

But as time passed with no sign of either, he was beginning to wonder what could be going on inside that cabin. Maybe he should get a little closer. The rock he was sitting on wasn't that comfortable anyway, he thought as he began to work his way down the hillside through the pines.

The front door of the cabin opened. He jumped back behind a pine, thinking it was about time they came out. But the man who emerged wasn't the cowboy. He was a big, tough-looking dude. Sunlight caught on the gun in the man's holster.

What the hell?

J.J. watched as the man went straight to the cowboy's pickup. It didn't take long to understand what was going on. The man was searching the truck. He obviously didn't find what he was looking for—even after going through their bags behind the seat. When he slammed the pickup door, he glanced at the tarps in the back and quickly climbed in to search there as well.

"Glad I wasn't under one of those tarps," J.J. said to himself as he watched the man finish his search and go back inside the cabin.

Something was definitely wrong and Frankie was in there. He considered what to do. No way was he busting in there, gun blazing. The way he saw it, all he could do was wait. Maybe if he heard screams from Frankie, he might have to change his mind.

Since the man had searched the pickup, it made sense that he wouldn't be looking in the back again. He continued down the hill, keeping his gun ready and his eyes focused on the cabin door.

Staying low, he made his way through the vehicles to the cowboy's pickup and leaped into the back, covering himself with the tarps to wait.

TRENT RETURNED MINUTES later from searching the truck. "Not there."

Frankie watched Darrel's jaw muscle bunch as the tension in the room became thick as smoke. But beside her, Les had released her arm and now merely sat with the gun pressed into the side of her head.

"I thought we were going to be straight with each other," Darrel said, clearly trying to contain his anger.

Frankie could see that Hank was getting angrier by the moment. "That was you the day at the river," Hank said. "That was you I saw running through the trees."

"I followed you thinking you were going for the money. Instead, you were doing what you always did, sitting and staring at that cliff. Three years, I've waited. When you came back after all this time, I thought it was finally to get the money."

Hank shook his head. "You had us forced off the road and into the river. You could have killed us."

"I doubted you would die, but at that point, you hadn't gone for the money and I was losing patience."

"When are you going to get it through your head?" Hank demanded. "We don't have your money. Now let us go."

"I don't think you realize your circumstances," Darrel shot back as he got to his feet and limped over to where Les had his gun to Frankie's head. He grabbed a handful of Frankie's dark hair in his fist as a switchblade suddenly appeared in his other hand. Frankie cried out in pain as he jerked hard on her hair, exposing her throat to the knife.

"I could cut her throat right now, and I will if you don't stop lying to me."

Hank leaped to his feet and took a step toward him. Behind him, Trent moved too quickly. She felt Darrel release her hair and turn.

"Don't!" Darrel yelled at Trent, but his command wasn't quick enough. The man had pulled his gun and now brought the barrel down hard on Hank's head.

Frankie screamed and jumped to her feet, only to be pulled back down by Les.

Darrel swore as Hank toppled to the floor. From where Les held her, she could see that his head was bleeding.

"Help him!" she cried.

Darrel, still swearing, limped over to him and checked for a pulse. "He's not dead." Hank moaned and struggled to sit up. "Get a towel for his head," he ordered. "Now!" Trent disappeared into the bathroom. "Everyone just calm down. I don't like things to get violent but I'm tired of being lied to. I want my money." He said the last through gritted teeth.

"Hank doesn't know where your money is," Frankie said, her voice breaking. She could see that he was dazed and bleeding, but alive. At least for now.

"Tie him up," Darrel ordered when Trent returned with the towel. He tossed the towel to Hank, who put it against the side of his head and flinched.

"Is that necessary?" Frankie demanded. "He's injured. He needs to go to the hospital, not be tied up." She got a warning side look from Darrel.

"You both brought this on yourselves," he said.

"Maybe you didn't know about the money, but obviously you do now. So stop lying. Since Hank and Naomi were going to get married and she had put money down on a house, don't tell me he doesn't know where she hid the rest of it."

Trent pulled out duct tape and, after helping Hank into a chair, bound him to it.

"I told you, I don't know," Hank mumbled and seemed to be fighting unconsciousness.

"I know who has your money," she said.

Hank's head came up. He shot her a pleading look. "Frankie—"

She turned her gaze on Darrel, who slowly swiveled around to look at her. "If you're lying, something much worse is going to happen to you. Do you understand?"

"Perfectly. But there's something I need to know first."

"You don't seem to be in a position to be making ultimatums," Darrel said, sounding almost amused.

"You're wrong. I'm the only person in this room who can get you your money." Darrel glanced at Hank. "He doesn't know," she said. "So if you didn't find the money on Naomi that night, then you're right—she hid it somewhere. But what I don't get is why you killed her before she told you where."

He seemed to consider whether to answer or not, and then swore. "One of my associates was handling it and made an error in judgment."

"That's what you call killing her?" Hank said through clenched teeth. She could see he was in pain from the head wound. "An error in judgment?"

"Tamara didn't kill her," Darrel said. "She took her up on the ledge to scare her since she knew Naomi was afraid of heights. All Naomi had to do was tell her where the money was. It wasn't in her vehicle. Nor her apartment, which had already been searched. We suspected it was hidden on the ranch, but we needed the location. Naomi refused to give it to her. Tamara argued with her. Naomi tried to push past her on the ledge to leave, making it clear that she was never going to tell. She took a misstep and fell to her death. Killing her was the last thing we wanted to do."

"Until you got the money," Frankie said. She could see that Hank was struggling to stay conscious, struggling with the news about Naomi.

"You both misjudge me," Darrel said. "Dead bodies complicate things. I prefer not to shed blood unless I have to. Unfortunately, some of my other associates are less reasonable." He rose unsteadily from his chair, and Frankie was reminded of his limp when he'd come into the bar.

Stepping back, he lifted his pant leg to expose a mass of red and purple scar tissue. When he spoke, there was fury in his voice. "You have no idea how much your former girlfriend has cost me, and not just in money and pain. I came close to getting my throat cut—and that would have been the faster and least painful in the long run, I realize now. My associates had much worse plans for me. I've been busting my ass for three years to pay them back. I've been waiting for you to return to town to collect the money after that foolish, stubborn woman took it and refused to tell us where she'd hidden it. Now," he said as he covered his injured leg again and slowly lowered himself into his chair.

He turned his attention to Frankie. "You say you know who has my money?"

She nodded. "One more question first, though," she said, making him groan. She knew she was trying his patience, but she also knew that she had leverage and she planned to use it. She had to use whatever she could to get them out of this. "How was Naomi able to steal the bag of money that she referred to as a small fortune? I would have thought you'd be watching it closer than that. Unless she was one of your associates."

Darrel laughed at that. "Hardly. She and Tamara had become friends. Naomi gave Tamara free groceries and even money out of the till sometimes when she came in and no one else was around." He swung his gaze back to Hank. "Your girlfriend was a shoplifter. Did you know that? She got her kicks by stealing. Tamara failed to mention that until later when my money went missing."

"So you didn't know who took it at first," Frankie said.

"No," Darrel admitted. "I waited to see who started spending."

Frankie thought of the house that Naomi had put a down payment on, hoping Hank would marry her. "How much money are we talking?" she asked.

Darrel shook his head.

"So you knew that Naomi had a larcenous streak and yet you left it lying around?"

Darrel gave her a warning look and then said, "I didn't leave it lying around. I'd brought the money to the bar that afternoon to meet someone. The person was running late and some men came into the bar. I didn't like their looks. I sensed trouble, so I hightailed it into the office. Unfortunately, I didn't have time to put the money into the safe. So I stuck it behind some liquor boxes. Two men jumped me as I walked out of the office. They didn't get far in their plan, but in the confusion of throwing them out of the place with some help from a couple of friends...the money disappeared."

"How did you know Naomi took it?"

He sighed. "It took a little while to figure it out. I had to go through a few possibilities first. In the end, Tamara and I both remembered Naomi being in the bar and disappearing when the trouble started. Tamara thought Naomi might have gone to the restroom before the fight broke out. My office is right across from the women's bathroom. When I heard she'd put money down on a house in Bozeman... Now, no more questions. Who has my money?"

Frankie thought of Randall "Butch" Clark. It hadn't taken much to get the truth out of him and that had worried her at the time. He'd seemed scared enough, but he had wanted her to believe that Naomi had the money on her that night. That she was thinking about stopping and giving the drug dealers what she had left.

But it seemed he'd lied about that. Still, she didn't want to get him killed. "I'm going to take you at your word that you're not into bloodshed," Frankie said, getting to her feet. Les leaped up as well as he tried to keep the gun on her and get a better grip on her. She didn't think he would shoot and knew she was taking a chance, but she'd bluffed her way this far. "Tell him to get that gun out of my face."

Darrel looked from her to Les. "Sit down, Les. I have a gun under the table. I can kill them both if necessary. You can put your piece away." He turned his gaze on her. "You have a lot of guts. He could have killed you just then before I could stop him."

She had a feeling that Les wasn't that quick-thinking, but kept it to herself. "Let me get this straight. Naomi didn't have the money on her that night, right?"

"I believe we already covered that."

"Tamara was following her that night, right? So what if she had the money and Tamara lied? She killed Naomi and kept the—"

"Tamara didn't have the money," Darrel said, talking over her. "Trust me, some of my more bloodthirsty associates talked to her about this at length before she…expired. She stuck to her story. Tamara took her up on the ledge to force her to tell what she did with it, but Naomi refused. Then the stupid woman slipped and fell."

HANK FELT AS if he was in a nightmare, one of his own devising. If he hadn't come back here, if he hadn't brought Frankie, if he'd just let Naomi go. His head ached and his vision blurred.

Frankie was scaring him, but he didn't know how to stop her—especially injured and bound to a chair.

"But if Naomi was being followed, how could she have dumped the money before she stopped or was pulled over?" Frankie asked.

Darrel shrugged. "You tell me."

"She'd already hidden the money," Frankie said, nodding as if to herself. "She called someone to tell the person where the money was in case something happened to her."

Frankie was right. Naomi had hidden the money and called the person she trusted—her old boyfriend, Butch. It was the only thing that made any sense. Naomi thought the money was safe. She didn't think the drug dealers would really kill her until they had it. If she hadn't slipped—

He felt Darrel's gaze on him. "That's exactly how I saw it. She hid the money and made a call to tell her lover where he could find it. How about it, Hank? Isn't that the way you see it?"

"Naomi didn't call Hank," Frankie said.

But Hank knew who Naomi had called—and so did Frankie. He looked at her and felt his heart drop. He could see what she was thinking, but wasn't sure how to head her off.

"Why wouldn't Naomi tell on that cliff?" Hank demanded, stalling for time, afraid that Frankie was only about to get herself in deeper. "That makes no sense." And yet he knew. He didn't even have to look at Frankie and see that she knew too. He felt his stomach drop.

"She wasn't giving up the money," Frankie said, sounding sad for the woman she'd been investigating and sad for him. "It meant that much to her."

He shook his head, unable to accept that he'd never really known Naomi. He knew that she'd always felt deprived and wanted desperately to have the life she dreamed of having. Still, he didn't want to believe that she would put money before her own life.

"That's crazy. She's standing on the edge of the ledge over the river and she'd rather die than give up the money?" he said.

No one said anything, but he saw that Darrel was staring at Frankie.

Hank felt as if he was on a runaway train with no way to stop it. No way to jump off either.

"I can get you your money," Frankie said to Darrel. "But you're going to have to let me leave."

"Frankie, no," Hank said, feeling dizzy. "You can't trust him." He let out a curse, feeling helpless and scared. "You can't expect him to stick by any deal, Frankie. He used to cheat at every sport I ever played with him."

Darrel shook his head at Hank but he was smiling. "I had to cheat. You were too good for me. But right now, I think I have the upper hand."

"Frankie—"

"Put some tape over his mouth," Darrel ordered, and Trent sprang to it.

Hank tried to put up a fight but it was useless. He felt weak even though he hadn't lost that much blood. He wondered if he had a concussion. Right now his only concern, though, was Frankie. He'd foolishly gotten to his feet, knowing that Trent was behind him. He hadn't expected the man to hit him. Neither had Darrel. Now he found himself duct-taped to a chair and gagged. And Frankie was about to make a deal that could get her killed.

SHE'D KNOWN HANK wasn't going to like this and would have tried to stop her if he could have. "Let me go get your money," she said again to Darrel.

"Do I look stupid? If I let you go, you'll hightail it straight to the authorities, and the next thing I know, there'll be a SWAT team outside my door."

"You have another option?" Frankie asked. "We can't tell you where the money is because we don't know. We didn't even know about it until recently. If you kill us, you'll never get the money and Hank's father will never stop looking for you. Stupid would be making your situation worse. Can't you see we're trying to help you figure this out?"

Darrel shook his head. "You make it sound like if you hand over the money, we all just walk away as if nothing ever happened. I just kidnapped the two of you."

"You are merely detaining us," Frankie said. "Until you get your money. Then you'll let us go. No harm, so to speak," she said, looking pointedly at Trent, "no foul. That's the deal."

"Trent goes with you."

She shook her head. "Not a chance. I go alone. It's the only way I have a chance of getting the person who took your money to admit the truth."

"How do I know you'll come back?"

"I'll come back. You have Hank."

"Good point," Darrel said. "I just wasn't sure you were that invested in him. If you don't come back, he dies. You call in the cops—"

"Save your breath. I'm not going to the authorities, but I need your word that he'll be safe until I get back," she said. "No more tough-guy stuff. The thing is, I don't know how long it will take me."

"You'd better not be playing me."

Frankie met Darrel's gaze. "You want your money. Hank and I want to get on with our lives." Her gaze went to Hank. He gave a small shake of his head and looked pointedly at Trent leaning against the wall again. Frankie knew this was dangerous, but she could see only one way out. Hank was already injured. She could imagine all of this going south quickly if she didn't do something. But what she was suggesting was a gamble, one she had no choice but to take.

"I'll give you until sundown."

Frankie shook her head. "I might need longer. Like I said, this could take a while."

Darrel shook his head. "Sundown or he's dead."

She wanted to argue but she could see she'd pushed the man as much as he was going to take. "Sundown, but promise me that I won't be followed. You need to trust me to handle this."

Darrel wagged his head. "You're asking a lot, sweetheart."

"It's Frankie. And I have a lot to lose," she said and looked at Hank. "There's one more thing that I need," she said to Darrel. "A gun."

# Chapter Twenty

All of her bravado gone, Frankie's hands were shaking as she climbed into the pickup. She laid the unloaded gun on the seat next to her. Darrel said he wasn't about to hand her a loaded gun.

"I'm taking one hell of a chance on you as it is," he'd said. "I give you a loaded gun…" He'd smiled as he'd shaken his head. "I'm betting a whole lot on you as it is, lady."

It was mutual, she thought now. She'd just gambled Hank's life on her suspicion of what had happened to the stolen drug money. What if she was wrong? Even if she was right, the money could be gone. Or Butch might refuse to give it to her. For all she knew, he could have gone on the lam after she'd talked to him at his father's hardware store.

Hank was depending on her. She drove toward Bozeman, checking behind her for a tail, trying not to speed for fear of being pulled over. She considered calling the marshal, but couldn't risk it. Not yet, anyway.

After parking behind the hardware store, she tucked the gun into her jeans and covered it with the shirt and jacket she'd put on earlier that morning. Taking a breath, she climbed out and entered the hardware store at the back through the delivery entrance. In the dim light of the empty area, she did her best to pull it together. Butch wouldn't be excited to see her to begin with. If he sensed how desperate she was, she feared he would run.

He wasn't in the office at the back. She started through the store, keeping an eye out for him. She was almost to the front when an employee asked if she needed help.

"I'm looking for Butch," she said, surprised that her voice sounded almost normal.

"He's on vacation and not expected back for a couple of weeks," the young man said.

Vacation? "It's urgent that I contact him. When did he leave?"

"I believe he planned to leave today."

"Could you give me his address? Maybe I can catch him if he hasn't left yet."

The young employee hesitated.

"Please. It's urgent."

"Well, I suppose it will be all right." He rattled off the address, and Frankie raced back the way she'd come.

Butch lived in a small house on the north side of town that, like most of Bozeman, had been completely remodeled. She wondered when and how much money it had cost. She prayed that he hadn't left yet and that he had been too scared to dip into the money.

As she parked on the street and got out, she noticed that the house looked deserted. The garage door was closed and there was a newspaper lying on the front step, unread. Her heart dropped to her feet as she walked toward the house, wondering what to do next.

That was when she heard a noise inside the house. As she approached the garage, she glanced into one of the small windows high on the door. Butch Clark was hurriedly packing for what looked like more than a two-week vacation.

HANK WATCHED DARREL, seeing him become more anxious and irritated with each passing hour. It hadn't been a surprise when the man had broken his word immediately, sending Trent after Frankie.

"Stay back. Don't let her spot you tailing her," Darrel had ordered. "She takes you to the money, you know what to do."

He'd felt his heart drop, afraid he knew exactly what Trent would do. All he could hope was that Frankie was as good at her job as he knew her to be and would spot the tail or be able to deal with Trent if she had to.

Darrel began pacing again. His pacing the cabin floor had turned out to be a godsend. He'd paid little attention to Hank as if he'd forgotten about him. Les had lain down on the bed and quickly gone to sleep.

Meanwhile, Hank had been working on the duct tape Trent had used to bind his wrists behind him to the chair. He'd found a rough spot on the wood where a screw was sticking out. He could feel the tape weakening as he sawed through layer after layer. It was tedious, but he had time, he kept telling himself. He had to be free when Frankie returned.

His head ached, but if he had a concussion it wasn't

a bad one. The dizziness had passed and he was feeling stronger by the moment.

When Darrel's cell phone rang, the man practically jumped out of his thin skin. Hank stopped what he was doing for a moment. He could hear the entire conversation at both ends since Trent was talking so loudly.

"What do you mean you lost her?" Darrel demanded.

"She was headed toward the north end of town but then suddenly veered off on a street. I stayed back like you said but then she was headed toward Main Street and she was gone."

Darrel swore. "You say she was headed toward the north side of town?"

"Yeah. I don't know why she suddenly—"

"She spotted a tail," he snapped. "Go back to the north side of town, where she was originally headed. Drive the streets until you find her. *Find her.*"

"Okay, I'll try, but    "

"Either you find her or you'd better keep going and hope I never find *you*. That clear enough for you?"

"I'll find her. I won't give up until I do."

J.J. WAS GETTING sick of lying in the back of the moving pickup under the tarps. He wasn't sure how much more of this he could take. But he had to know what Frankie was up to.

When she'd stopped the pickup the first time, she'd gotten out. He'd waited for a few moments and then taken a peek. He'd watched her go into the back of a hardware store before quickly covering up again. What was this about? None of it made any sense. She'd left the cowboy and gone shopping? Was it possible Hank Savage had known the man he'd picked up in the road? If so, then...

She'd come back sooner than he'd anticipated, the pickup door opening, closing, the engine starting and the truck moving again. Maybe she'd had to pick up something. An ax? A shovel? He'd shuddered at the thought.

The truck didn't go far before he felt something change. Frankie had been driving at a normal pace when suddenly she took off, turning this way and that. He had to hang on now or be tossed around the back of the pickup like a rag doll. What was going on?

When she finally slowed down and quit turning, she seemed to be backtracking. He'd been listening to the sounds around him. They'd been in traffic but now it had grown quieter. She brought the pickup to a stop. He heard her exit the truck. He listened, afraid to take a peek yet. He definitely had the feeling that they were in a residential part of town. He could hear the sound of someone using a leaf blower some distance away.

When he couldn't take the suspense any longer, he carefully rose and pushed back the edge of the tarp aside to peer out. What he saw shocked him. Frankie had pulled a gun and was now about to open someone's garage door. But before she could, the door suddenly began to rise with the sound of the mechanical engine pulling it up.

He heard an engine start up in the garage and saw Frankie step in front of the idling car, the gun raised to windshield level. "Stop, Butch!"

The car engine revved. Whoever was behind the wheel had backed the vehicle into the garage. For a fast getaway? The fool either had a death wish or was playing his luck. Either way, J.J. could see that Frankie was in trouble. The driver didn't seem afraid of the gun she was holding.

He threw back the tarp and jumped down to run at her, shoving her out of the way as the car came screaming out of the garage. He had drawn his own gun, but when he saw that the fool behind the wheel wasn't going to stop, he threw himself onto the hood and crashed into the windshield.

The driver hit his brakes hard. J.J. groped for something to hang on to but, failing, slid to the concrete, coming down hard. As he started to get up, he heard the engine rev again. He saw Frankie had the passenger-side door open and was screaming for the man behind the wheel to get out of the car.

He rolled to the side, but not quick enough. The door had caught him in the back of the head and the lights went out.

## Chapter Twenty-One

Butch rattled the handcuffs holding him restrained to the passenger-side door of his car. "How do I know you aren't going to kill me?" His voice squeaked—just as it had when she'd jumped into the car as he was trying to get away. She'd shoved the barrel of the gun into the side of his head and told him she was going to kill him if he didn't stop. He'd stopped.

"You don't." She'd grabbed the keys and forced him at gunpoint into the passenger seat to handcuff him to the door.

"Who was that back there?" Butch asked now as they drove away from his house.

"A cop." She glanced in the rearview mirror over the top of all Butch's belongings he'd loaded. So far no tail. Also no J.J. She'd checked for a pulse. He had still been breathing but wasn't conscious. She'd taken his cop gun. At least now she had real bullets and a vehicle that whoever Darrel had sent to follow her wouldn't know. Her tail would find the pickup at the house—if he found the house at all.

"*A cop?* You said you wouldn't go to the cops."

Frankie shook her head, keeping her attention on her driving. "I wanted to keep you out of it, Butch. Unfortunately, I had no idea just how deep you really were in all this. You lied to me, but for your sake and mine, you'd better not be lying to me now."

"I'm not." He sounded whiny. She could see why Naomi had dumped him. But he must have been the closest thing she had to a friend she could confide in.

"Why didn't you tell Naomi to give the money back right away?" she asked.

"I did. She wouldn't listen. She really thought she could get away with it."

Frankie shot him a look. "Kind of like you."

"Hey, what could I have done? They didn't know about me. I didn't know them. Naomi was dead. I knew where the money was hidden. So I waited to see what happened. Nothing happened. Until you showed up."

"You could have gone to the cops," she snapped. And then none of this would be happening. Hank wouldn't be in serious trouble back at the cabin and she wouldn't be racing out of town with two guns, one actually loaded, with a man handcuffed to the car and only a hope and a prayer that he wasn't lying to her.

She glanced over at Butch. He looked scared. That, she decided, was good. "I have to ask. Why did you wait to get the money?"

He turned to look out his side window. They'd passed Gallatin Gateway and were almost to Big Sky and Cardwell Ranch, where he swore Naomi had buried the money. "I had this crazy idea that they were watching the place where she buried it, you know, just waiting for me to show up so they could kill me like they did her."

Frankie thought about telling him what Darrel had said about Naomi's death. That was if he was telling the truth. Either way, Butch might have been able to save her—if he'd gone to the cops right away.

Nor did she point out that there was little chance Darrel would be watching the ranch 24/7 even if he knew where the money was buried.

She turned onto the dirt road into the ranch, her mind racing. What would she do when she found the money? Hank had been right. She couldn't trust Darrel to keep his word. He said she wouldn't be followed. A lie. Once she handed over the money…

As she drove into the ranch yard, Butch pointed in the direction of a stand of trees. The land dropped to a small creek. Frankie groaned inwardly. She just hoped that Naomi was smart enough to bury the money where the rising water didn't send it into the Gallatin River. It could be in the Gulf of Mexico by now otherwise.

"Tell me exactly where it is," she said as she brought the car to a stop at the edge of the incline to the creek.

"There's a statue or something, she said, near the water."

Frankie frowned. "A statue?" she asked as she looked down the hill and saw pine trees and a babbling brook but no statue.

"Maybe not a statue, but—"

"A birdbath," she said, spotting it in a stand of trees. She quickly put the keys in her pocket, opened the door and, grabbing the shovel she'd taken from his garage, got out. As she did, she glanced toward the house and saw no one. Maybe she would get lucky. She needed some luck right now.

It was a short walk down to a stand of trees on a rise above the creek. Someone had put a birdbath down here. Near it were two benches as if someone in the family came down here to watch the birds beside the river. Dana? She couldn't see the marshal sitting here patiently.

The birdbath, apparently made of solid concrete, proved to be heavier than it looked. She could have used Butch, but she didn't trust the man. She tried dislodging it and inching it over out of the way, wasting valuable minutes.

Finally, she just knocked it over, which took all her strength as it was. Then she began to dig. She wondered how Naomi had managed moving the birdbath and realized it had probably been her idea, the benches and the birdbath—after she'd buried the rest of the money.

The bag wasn't buried deep. Frankie pulled it out, sweating with the effort and the constant fear of what might be happening back at the cabin. The bag looked like one used by banks. It was large and heavy. She opened it just enough to see that it was stuffed with money, lots of money in large bills, and quickly closed it.

Leaving the shovel, she climbed back up the incline. As she topped it, she saw Dana standing by the side of the car.

WHEN J.J. CAME TO, he was lying on the grass with a monstrous headache. His gun was gone. So was

Frankie and the car and its driver. All she'd left behind was the cowboy's pickup.

J.J. limped into the house through the open garage door. The house felt deserted. He was moving painfully through the living room when he thought he heard a car door slam. Was it possible Frankie had come back? He couldn't believe she'd left him passed out on the concrete and hadn't even called an ambulance. But she'd managed to take his gun.

He pressed himself against a wall out of sight of the hallway as he heard footfalls in the garage. One person moving slowly, no doubt looking for him. Why had Frankie come back now? It didn't matter. He was ready for her.

He smiled to himself as he waited to pounce. She wouldn't know what hit her.

As a figure came around the corner, he lunged. He didn't realize his mistake until it was too late. The figure spun as if sensing him coming and caught him square in the face with his fist. As he took the blow, he realized that the figure was way too large to be Frankie, way too powerful and way too male.

"Who the hell are you?" he heard the man say as he crashed on the floor at the man's feet. Before he could answer, he heard the man pump a bullet into his gun. He rolled over, struggling to pull out his badge, when he heard the first shot echo through the room. The burn of the bullet searing through his flesh came an instant later.

He tried to get up, tried to get his badge out. The second shot hit him in the chest and knocked him back to the floor. As the big man moved closer, J.J. saw that it was the tough guy who'd searched the pickup earlier at the cabin.

"You've really screwed up now," J.J. managed to say as he felt his life's blood seeping from him. "You just killed a cop."

"I'D LIKE TO tell you that this isn't what it looks like," Frankie said as she approached Dana. She saw that the woman had her cell phone clutched in her hand and knew at once that she'd already called the marshal.

"I thought you and Hank had gone back to Idaho," Dana said. Her voice trembled as her gaze took in the weapon Frankie had stuck in the waist of her jeans. Her shirt and jacket had come up during her battle with the birdbath.

"How long before Hud gets here?" Frankie asked.

"Where's Hank?" the older woman asked. She sounded as scared as Frankie felt.

"He's in trouble. I need to get back to him, Dana. I'm a private investigator. It's too long a story to get into right now. I need to leave before Hud gets here."

Dana shook her head, tears in her eyes. "I knew something was wrong. But I hoped..." Inside the car, Butch began to yell for Dana to help him. "That man is handcuffed and you have a...gun."

Frankie knew she couldn't stand here arguing. She started past Dana when she heard the sound of a siren. Moments later she saw the flashing lights as the SUV topped a rise and came blaring into the ranch yard.

She let out a shaky breath and felt tears burn her

eyes. There was still time before sundown. But that
would mean talking her way out of this, and right now,
covered in mud, holding a bag of even dirtier drug
money, she wasn't sure she had the words. All she knew
was that she had to convince the marshal before sundown.

HUD SHUT OFF the siren. As he climbed out, he took
in the scene. The man handcuffed in the car tried to
slide down out of sight. Dana stepped to Hud, and he
put his arm around her before he turned his attention
to the young woman his son had fallen in love with.
"Frankie?"

She held out the bag. "It's the drug money. They
have Hank. If I don't give the money to them by sundown…" Her voice broke.

He nodded and stepped to her to take the money.
"And that?" he asked, tilting his head toward the man
in the car.

"It's Butch Clark, Naomi's old boyfriend. He's
known where the money was buried all these years."

Hud nodded and glanced at his watch. "We have a
little time. Whatever's happened, we will deal with it.
You say they have Hank." She nodded. "Tell me everything," he said as he walked her toward the house.

"What about him?" Dana asked behind them.

"He's fine where he is for the time being," Hud said
without a backward glance. Inside the house, Frankie
quickly cleaned up at the kitchen sink as she told him
about the man stumbling out onto the highway, being

taken to the cabin, the demand for the money and Hank being injured.

Dana gasped at that point, her eyes filling with tears, but she held it together. Hud had to hand it to her—she was a strong woman and always had been. Her son was injured and being held by drug dealers. It scared the hell out of him, but Dana fortunately wasn't one to panic in a crisis. He appreciated that right now.

"Okay," he said when Frankie finished. "You say Darrel gave you an unloaded gun." He picked up the Glock he'd taken from her. "This one is loaded."

She nodded. "J.J. must have followed us. He was hiding in the back of the pickup. He tried to stop Butch when Butch was attempting to flee. He was hit by the car, but he was alive the last time I saw him."

Hud studied the woman, amazed by her resilience as well as her bravery. "You don't think Darrel will let the two of you go when you take him the money, right?"

She shook her head. "He doesn't want to kill us, but…"

"What will you do?" Dana asked her husband.

"The first thing is read Butch Clark his rights and get him locked up in my jail so he's not a problem." Hud pulled out his phone and called a deputy to come handle it. As he hung up, he looked at Frankie. "I need to take you back to Hank's pickup. There's time before sundown. Then you drive back to the cabin with the bag of money."

"Where will you be?" Dana asked.

"In the back of the pickup. I'll need to grab a few

things and have Bozeman backup standing by." He got to his feet. "Let's go get Hank."

HANK WATCHED DARREL pace the cabin floor and worked surreptitiously at the thick tape binding his wrists behind him to the chair. He'd made a point of acting like he was still dizzy and weak from the blow, mumbling to himself incoherently until Darrel had removed the duct tape.

"Water," Hank had mouthed. "Please."

Darrel had gotten him some, holding it to his lips so he could take a few gulps. "She'll be back," Hank said when he took the water away. "With the money." And that was the part that terrified him the most, because he had no doubt that his former classmate would go back on his word. No way were he and Frankie walking out of here alive. "She does what she says she's going to do."

Darrel had started pacing again. Hank saw him looking out the window where the sun was dropping toward the horizon at a pace that had them both worried. Now the man turned to look at him and laughed. "You sure about that? If I were her, I'd take the money and go as far away from here as I possibly could."

"That's you. Frankie isn't like that." But right now, he wished she was. At least she would be safe. He'd gotten her into this. He deserved what he got. But Frankie… He couldn't bear to think of her being hurt, let alone—

"You'd better be right." Darrel sounded sad, as if he would be sorry for killing him. "I hate the way this whole thing spiraled out of control, and all because of that girlfriend of yours."

Hank couldn't argue with that. "I fell in love with a woman I didn't know. She hid so much from me, including stealing your money."

"And you think you know this one?" Darrel scoffed at that. "All women are alike. You really haven't learned anything since high school, have you. They will double-cross you every time. I knew this one—" He stopped talking to turn and look out the window again. He'd heard what Hank had.

The sound of his pickup's engine could be heard as the truck approached the cabin. Frankie had come back with the money. And before sundown.

"I've got to hand it to you, Hank. This woman really is something. If she's got the money, then I'd say this one is a keeper."

"Keep your promise. Let us go. We want nothing to do with any of this and you know it."

"Yeah, I hear you," Darrel said, actually sounding as if he regretted what was going to happen next. "We're going to have to talk about that." He stepped over to the bed and kicked the end of it. Les stirred from a deep sleep. "Wake up. We've got company. Go out and make sure she's alone."

"Me? Why do I have to—"

Darrel cuffed the man on the head. "Go!"

Les stumbled from the bed, clearly still half-asleep, and headed for the door. Darrel stood at the window, his back to him. Hank worked feverishly at the tape. Just a little more. He felt it give.

FRANKIE DID AS Hud had told her and parked next to the
panel van, out of sight of the cabin. She stayed in the
pickup, sitting behind the wheel, after she'd turned off
the engine, waiting.

She desperately wanted to see Hank. She had to
know that he was all right. But the marshal had assured her—Hank was safer if they did things his way.

She wasn't going to argue. She was thankful that she
wasn't facing this completely alone. Because she had
a bad feeling that once she got out of the pickup with
the money, both she and Hank were as good as dead.

Les frowned as he saw where she was parking. He
walked around the front of the vehicles to stop in front
of the pickup. "Get out!" he ordered, still frowning. He
looked as if he'd just woken up, which made her heart
race. What had Darrel done with Hank after she'd left
that he'd let Les sleep?

When she didn't get out, he stepped up to try the
door and, finding it locked, glanced back at the cabin
before he began to fumble for his gun. That was when
Hud rose and coldcocked him with the butt end of a
shotgun. The man dropped between the pickup and
panel van without a sound.

As the marshal hopped down out of sight of the
cabin windows, Frankie opened her door.

"Leave the bag with the money here," Hud said as
he cuffed and gagged Les before rolling his body under
the pickup. "Go into the cabin to check on Hank. When
Darrel asks, tell him that Les took it from you. I need
to know how many men are in there."

She nodded and whispered, "Trent was following

me. I don't see his vehicle, so I don't think he's back yet. It should just be Darrel."

"Let's hope," Hud said and motioned for her to go before Darrel got suspicious.

Frankie headed for the cabin, praying with each step that Hank was all right. As she pushed open the door, the first thing she saw was Darrel. He had a gun in his hand, pointed at her heart. Her gaze leaped past him to Hank. She saw pleasure flash in his blue eyes at seeing her, then concern. He was still in the chair, but he seemed to feel better than the last time she'd seen him.

"Where's my money?" Darrel demanded, already sounding furious as if he'd worked himself up in the time she'd been gone. The door was open behind her, but he was blocking her from going to Hank.

"Les has it. He took it from me." She could see that he didn't believe her. She described the bag. "I didn't touch the money, but the bag is heavy, and when I looked inside... I think all but the five grand she used for a down payment on the house is in there. Or at least enough to get you out of hot water. Now let us go."

Darrel shook his head, still blocking her from going to Hank, and yelled, "Les!" Not hearing an answer, he yelled again. "Bring the money in here."

She looked past him and saw Hank slowly pull his wrists free from behind him. He shook them out as if he'd lost all feeling in his arms after all this time of being taped to the chair. She gave a small shake of her head for him not to move.

"Les is probably out there counting the money," Frankie said, hoping the man would step outside, where the marshal was waiting. "Or has already taken off with the bag."

"On foot?" Darrel demanded and grabbed her as they both heard the scrape of chair legs on the floor.

HANK MOVED QUICKLY. Darrel was right about one thing. He'd always been better at sports than his classmate. Fortunately, that athletic prowess benefited him now when he needed it the most.

As Darrel turned, there was a moment of surprise, a hesitation that cost him. He was about to put the barrel of the gun to Frankie's head when Hank hit him in the side of his head with his fist and grabbed the gun. Darrel staggered from the blow but didn't go down. His grip on Frankie seemed to be the only thing holding him up.

Hank twisted the gun from the man's hand. The two grappled with it for a moment before Darrel let out a cry of pain. Frankie shoved him off her and pulled the Glock from behind her to point it at the drug dealer as he went down. She looked over at Hank, who stood beside her, the gun in his hand pointed at Darrel's heart as well.

Behind them Frankie heard the marshal say, "Well, look at the two of you. It appears you didn't even need my help." There was a smile in his voice as well as relief as he reached for his phone to let the cops know that he'd take that backup now. "I have two perps who need to be taken to jail. Also going to need a medic as well," he said, looking at the dried blood on his son's temple. "And I'm going to need a ride back to Big Sky."

"We could have given you a ride," Hank said after his father cuffed Darrel and read him his rights. Frankie could hear sirens in the distance. She leaned against Hank, his arm around her. She told herself that all she needed was a hot shower and she'd stop shaking.

"I thought you two might like some time together. But I guess you know this means you can't leave for Idaho for a while," the marshal said.

Hank glanced at her. "I think we're good with that."

FRANKIE HELPED HERSELF to another stack of silver-dollar-sized pancakes, slathered on butter and then drowned them in chokecherry syrup. She couldn't remember ever being this hungry.

So much had happened and in such a short time. She would have worried about that before Hank. She was no longer worried about it happening too fast. Instead, she was ready for the future in a way she'd never been before. She felt free, everything looking brighter, even before she'd heard the news about J.J.

Trent had been arrested and confessed everything, including killing the cop. He'd said it was self-defense, that J.J. had been reaching for his gun. But the Glock hadn't been found on the cop—or at the scene—because Frankie had taken it.

After hearing what all the cops had against him, including assaulting Hank and dealing drugs, along with killing an unarmed cop, Trent decided to make a deal for a lesser sentence for what he knew about the drug ring and Darrel's part in it.

Frankie could feel Dana watching her eat and

smiling. "So you're a private investigator," she said. "Sounds dangerous. I was thinking that if you were to get married and have babies..."

Swallowing the bite in her mouth, Frankie grinned at her. "Hank hasn't asked me to marry him and you're talking babies."

"He'll ask. I've never seen my son happier."

Frankie thought about the hot shower she'd stepped into last night after they'd returned to their cabin. Hank had joined her, sans his clothes this time. Their love-making had been so passionate under the warm spray that she felt her cheeks heat at the memory even now.

"He makes me happy too," she said and took an-other bite of pancake.

"I can tell," Dana said with a secret smile. "You're glowing this morning. If it wasn't too early, I'd think you were pregnant."

Frankie almost choked on her bite of pancake. True, last night in the shower they hadn't used protection, but pregnant? She swallowed.

"Would that be so awful?" Dana asked.

She thought about it for one whole instant and smiled. "Not at all." The thought of her child growing up on this ranch made her happy. She and Hank had talked about the future last night after their shower. He'd asked how she'd feel about living on the ranch, if she would still want to work as a private investigator, if she wanted children, how she felt about dogs and cats and horses.

She'd laughed as she'd listened to his questions and

grinned. "I'd love living on this ranch, I'd probably want to be involved in ranching with you rather than continue working as an investigator, I do want children, and I love dogs, cats and horses. After that horseback ride with you, I'm hooked."

"Was it the horseback ride or me that got you hooked?" he'd asked with a grin.

"By the way, where *is* my son?" Dana asked, interrupting her thoughts.

Frankie helped herself to a slice of ham and just a couple more pancakes. "He went to say goodbye to Naomi."

HANK PARKED IN the pines beside the Gallatin River as he'd done so many times before. This time he was anxious to reach the water. He climbed out and wound his way through the tall pines. A breeze swayed the tops of the boughs, whispering. The sound of the river grew louder. He could feel the sun as it fingered its way through the pines. He breathed in the scent of pine and water as if smelling it for the first time.

Ahead, he got his first glimpse of the cliff. It was dark and ominous-looking, shadowed this morning until the sun rose high enough to turn it a golden hue.

It seemed strange to make this trek after everything that had happened. He wasn't sure he could ever forgive Naomi for what she did. He and Frankie had almost gotten killed because of a bag full of money. He still couldn't believe that she'd died protecting it.

He broke out of the pines and stood for a moment at

the edge of the trees. The breeze was stronger here. It rippled the moving surface of the river and ruffled his hair at his neck. He took off his Stetson and turned his face up to the breeze, letting it do what it would with his normally tousled dark hair. He couldn't help but think of Frankie's fingers in the wet strands last night as she pulled him down to her mouth. The memory of the two of them laughing and making love in the shower made him smile for a moment before he dropped down to the edge of the river.

He listened to the gentle roar of the water as it rushed over the rocks and pooled at his feet. The breeze lifted his hair as he looked up. The ledge was a dark line cut across the rock surface. For three years it had lured him back here, looking for answers. Now he knew it all.

He thought of Naomi standing on that ledge that night with Tamara. He'd always thought of her as help-less, defenseless, fragile and delicate. He'd always felt he had to protect her—even her memory. He could al-most see her teetering on that ledge. Would they have let her live if she'd given them the money? They would never know. But he knew now that she was willing to die rather than give it up.

Hank hated what that said about her. He thought of her mother working all those years to support herself and her daughter. Was that what had made Naomi think she had to steal? Or was it a sickness that had started with shoplifting and had gotten away from her?

Naomi's mother had made a life for herself with a man who loved her. Lillian would survive this since he suspected she knew her daughter much better than he ever had.

He waited to feel Naomi's spirit, to see a ghostly flash of her. He expected to feel her presence as he had so many times before. He'd always thought she was waiting here for him, pleading with him to find her killer.

Now he felt nothing but the summer breeze coming off the cool surface of the river. He stared at the ledge through the sunlight, but felt nothing. Naomi was gone—if she'd ever really been here.

As he settled his Stetson back on his head, he realized it was true. Naomi's ghost had been banished for good. He felt lighter. Freer. The cliff no longer held him prisoner. Neither did Naomi.

"Goodbye," he said, glancing once more at the cliff before he started back to the pickup. He realized that he could walk away without ever looking back, without ever coming back. It felt good. *He* felt good. He couldn't wait to get to Frankie. They were leaving today, but they would return.

He drove toward the ranch, excited about life for the first time in three years. He couldn't wait to see Frankie. But first there was something he had to do.

HUD LOOKED UP to find his son standing in the doorway of his office. "Is everything all right?" he asked, immediately concerned. Hank had an odd look on his face.

"I need to ask a favor."

He and Hank hadn't talked much since everything had happened. His son's statement about what had transpired at the cabin had filled in a lot of the blanks. He'd wondered how Hank had taken the news about Naomi and if he would finally be able to put the past behind him—with Frankie's help.

"Name it. If there's something I can do…"

Hank came into his office and closed the door behind him. His son seemed nervous. That, he realized, was what he'd been picking up on the moment he saw him standing in the doorway. He'd never seen him nervous. Angry, yes. But not like this. He realized that whatever his son had to ask him, it was serious.

"When I asked you for Grandmother's ring—"

Hud swore. He'd forgotten the day that his son had come to him and asked for his grandmother's ring. Since he was a little boy, Hank had been told that his grandmother Cardwell's ring would go to Mary, but that his grandmother Savage's ring was his for the day that he met the love of his life and asked her to marry him.

But when Hank had asked for it, saying he was going to marry Naomi no matter what anyone thought because they were all wrong about her, Hud had turned him down.

"I'm sorry, son. I can't let you give Naomi the ring." He and Dana had discussed it numerous times in the days before Hank had come to him. They'd seen that Naomi was pushing marriage and could tell that their son wasn't ready. Add to that Naomi's…problems, as Dana referred to them.

"She's a thief," Hud had said. "Not just that. You

know she's pressing Hank to leave the ranch to work for her stepfather."

"Maybe it's what he wants."

Hud remembered being so angry with his wife that he'd gotten out of bed and pulled on his jeans, had left. He and Dana seldom argued. But that night he hadn't been able to take any more. He'd driven up to Hebgen Lake to see his father, Brick, an old-time lawman. Hud had named one of his twin son's after his father; the other one after Dana's father, Angus.

He and his father had often been at odds, and yet that night, the old lawman was who he'd gone to for help. It was the same year that Brick had passed away. He remembered waking him up that night. Why he chose his father was a mystery since the two of them had spent years at odds.

But Brick had given him good advice. "Stick to your guns. He's your son. You know him. He won't love you for it. Quite the contrary." He'd seen the gleam in his old man's eyes and known that he was talking about the two of them and the years they'd spent knocking heads. "You're doing him a real disservice if you just give in to keep the peace."

He'd stayed the night, driven back the next morning and told Dana that he wasn't giving Hank the ring if he asked for it again. She'd been furious with him, but he'd stuck to his guns, even though it had cost him dearly both with his wife and his son. He'd never known if Hank would have married Naomi anyway if she'd lived.

"When you'd asked for my mother's ring, I thought

you were making a mistake," Hud said now. "I didn't want you giving the ring to the wrong woman and later regretting it when you met the love of your life."

Hank shook his head. "It was your decision since my grandmother apparently put you in charge of it."

"Actually, it was your grandpa Brick," he said.

"Did he also advise you to not give it to me?" Hank asked.

Hud wanted to be as honest with him as possible. "Your mother and I argued about it. I had to leave, so I drove up to your grandfather's place and asked him what I should do."

Hank's eyes widened. "You actually asked your father for advice?"

"It happens," Hud said and smiled. "Admittedly, it took years before I found myself doing that."

With a grin, his son said, "It's hard for me to admit that you were right."

"I understand."

"But I'm back. I want to give Grandmother's ring to Frankie, and I'm not taking no for an answer this time. Rightfully, it's my ring to do—"

"I totally agree." Hud reached into the drawer where he'd put the ring after meeting Frankie.

"You have it here?"

"I had a feeling you'd want it," he said.

Hank shook his head as he took the small velvet box. "I will never understand you."

"Probably not." He watched his son lift the tiny lid and saw Hank's eyes light up as he stared down at the diamond engagement ring.

"Do you think she'll like it?" The nervousness was back.

"She'll love it because she loves you."

FALL WAS IN the air that late day in August. The seasons changed at will in Montana and even more so in the canyon so close to the mountains. One day would feel like summer, the next fall, and in the blink of an eye snow would begin.

Dried leaves rustled on the aspens as Frankie rode her horse out of the pines and into the wide meadow. She breathed in the crisp, clean air, reined in her horse and dismounted at the edge of the mountain to wait for Hank. He'd been acting strange all day. She knew it had to be because they would be leaving here—at least temporarily.

Last night they'd lain in bed, wrapped up in each other after making love, and talked about the future.

"Are you sure you'd be happy at the ranch? Because if not, we could—"

She'd kissed him to stop the words. "Hank, I love the ranch. I can't imagine living anywhere more...magical."

He'd eyed her suspiciously. "You aren't just saying that because you're crazy in love with me."

"I am crazy in love with you, but no, I wouldn't lie to you." He'd told her that the ghost of Naomi was gone, but she wondered. He still thought that because Naomi could never be happy at the ranch, neither could any other woman. She knew it would take time for him to realize that she was nothing like Naomi.

"Look at your mother, Hank. She loves this ranch

just like her mother did. Isn't that why your grandmother left it to her, passing on the legacy? And all the
women your uncles are married to. They're all happy
living here," she continued. "Isn't it possible I'm more
like your mother than…?" She wouldn't say "Naomi."
"Than some other woman might be?"

He'd nodded and smiled as he kissed her. "I feel so
lucky. I keep wanting to pinch myself. I guess that's
why it's so hard for me to believe this is real. I never
dreamed…" He kissed her again. "That I could be this
happy."

Now, as he rode up beside her, his Stetson hiding
much of his handsome face, she felt almost afraid. He'd
been so quiet all morning and it wasn't like him to hang
back on his horse the way he had. As she watched him
slowly ride toward her, her heart fluttered. She was
crazy in love with this man, just as she had told him.
And yet maybe this was too fast for both of them.

She thought of J.J. and quickly pushed it away. Hank
wasn't J.J. Whatever was going on with Hank—

At a sound in the pines, she looked past Hank to see
Hud and Dana come riding out of the trees. Behind
them were Mary and Chase, and behind them were
Stacy and the rest of the family.

Frankie blinked. "What?"

Hank looked up and grinned. "I am terrible at keeping secrets, and this one was killing me this morning,"
he said as he dismounted and took her in his arms. "I
hope you don't mind."

Mind that he'd invited his entire family on their
horseback ride? She felt confused, and yet as every-

one rode toward them, they were all smiling. One of the uncles brought up the rear with a huge bunch of helium balloons.

"Hank?" she asked. He only hugged her tightly. She could see the emotion in his face and felt her heart take off like a wild horse in a thunderstorm. "Hank?" she repeated as they all began to dismount. His uncle was handing out the balloons. "I think you'd better tell me what's going on."

The family had formed a circle around them and seemed to be waiting, just like Frankie. Hank turned to her, taking both of her hands in his.

"I know this is fast, but if I've learned anything, it's that when things are right, they're right," Hank said and cleared his voice. "You are the most amazing woman I've ever met. You're smart, talented, independent to a fault, stubborn as the day is long, courageous—way too courageous, I might add—determined and…beautiful and loving and everything I could want in one unique woman."

She tried to swallow around the lump in her throat. "Thank you, I think."

A murmur of laughter rose from the group gathered.

"You saved my life in so many ways," Hank continued. "I can never thank you enough for that. And you've brought just joy to my life when I never thought I'd ever feel again. Frankie…" He seemed at a loss for words.

"Come on. Get on with it," someone yelled at the back of the group, followed by another burst of laughter.

Hank laughed with them. "They all know that I'm like my father, a man of few words." Yet another burst of laughter. "But if I forget to tell you all of these things in the future, I wanted to be sure and say them today. I love you, Francesca 'Frankie' Brewster, with all my heart."

She watched him drop to one knee to the applause of the group.

He looked up at her, his blue eyes filled with love. She felt her own eyes fill with tears as he asked, "Will you do me the honor of marrying me?"

The tears overflowed and cascaded down her cheeks as she nodded, overwhelmed by all of this.

He reached into his pocket and pulled out a small velvet box. "This ring was my grandmother Savage's." He took it out, held her left hand and slipped it on her finger.

She gazed down at it. "It's beautiful," she said as he got to his feet. Looking into his handsome face, she whispered, "I love you," and threw her arms around him.

As the two of them turned, his family let out a cheer and released the balloons. Frankie looked up toward the heavens as dozens of colorful balloons took flight up into Montana's big sky. She'd never seen a more beautiful sight because of what they all represented.

Hank hugged her and then everyone else was hugging her, the meadow full of love and congratulations. "This is only the beginning," he said with a laugh. "You always wanted a big family. Well, you're going to have one now."

"I never dreamed…" she said and couldn't finish. How could she have dreamed that one day she'd meet a cowboy and he'd take her home and give her a family?

\* \* \* \* \*

# COWBOY'S REDEMPTION

This one is for Stelly, who even at four loves stories where the heroine gets to help save herself.

# *Chapter One*

Running blindly through the darkness, Lola didn't see the tree limb until it struck her in the face. It clawed at her cheek, digging into a spot under her right eye as she flung it away with her arm. She had to stifle the cry of pain that rose in her throat for fear she would be heard. As she ran, she felt warm blood run down to the corner of her lips. The taste of it mingled with the salt of her tears, but she didn't slow, couldn't. She could hear them behind her.

She pushed harder, knowing that, being men, they had the advantage, especially the way she was dressed. Her long skirt caught on something. She heard the fabric rend, not for the first time. She felt as if it was her heart being ripped out with it.

Her only choice was to escape. But at what price? She'd been forced to leave behind the one person who mattered most. Her thundering heart ached at the thought, but she knew that this was the only way. If she could get help...

"She's over here!" came a cry from behind her. "This way!"

She wiped away the warm blood as she crashed through the brush and trees. Her legs ached and she didn't know how much longer she could keep going. Fatigue was draining her. If they caught her this time…

She tripped on a tree root, stumbled and almost plunged headlong down the mountainside. Her shoulder slammed into a tree trunk. She veered off it like a pinball, but she kept pushing herself forward because the alternative was worse than death.

They were closer now. She could feel one of them breathing down her neck. She didn't dare look back. To look back would be to admit defeat. If she could just reach the road before they caught up to her…

Suddenly the trees opened up. She burst out of the darkness of the pines onto the blacktop of a narrow two-lane highway. The glare of headlights blinded her an instant before the shriek of rubber on the dark pavement filled the night air.

## Chapter Two

Major Colt McCloud felt the big bird shake as he brought the helicopter low over the bleak landscape. He was back in Afghanistan behind the controls of a UH-60 Black Hawk. The throb of the rotating blades was drowned out by the sound of mortar fire. It grew louder and louder, taking on a consistent pounding that warned him something was very wrong.

He dragged himself awake, but the dream followed him. Blinking in the darkness, he didn't know where he was for a moment. Everything looked alien and surreal. As the dream began to fade, he recognized his bedroom at the ranch.

He'd left behind the sound of the chopper and the mortar fire, but the pounding had intensified. With a start, he realized what he was hearing.

Someone was at the door.

He glanced at the clock on his bedside table. It was after three in the morning. Throwing his legs over the side of the bed, he grabbed his jeans, pulling them on as he fought to put the dream behind him and hurry to the door.

A half dozen possibilities flashed in his mind as he moved quickly through the house. It still felt strange to be back here after years of traveling the world as an Army helicopter pilot. After his fiancée dumped him, he'd planned to make a career out of the military, but then his father had died, leaving him a working ranch that either had to be run or sold.

He'd taken a hundred-and-twenty-day leave in between assignments so he could come home to take care of the ranch. His father had been the one who'd loved ranching, not Colt. That's why there was a for-sale sign out on the road into the ranch.

Colt reached the front door and, frowning at the incessant knocking at this hour of the morning, threw it open.

He blinked at the disheveled woman standing there before she turned to motion to the driver of the car idling nearby. The engine roared and a car full of what appeared to be partying teenagers took off in a cloud of dust.

Colt flipped on the porch light as the woman turned back to him and he got his first good look at her and her scratched, blood-streaked face. For a moment he didn't recognize her, and then it all came back in a rush. Standing there was a woman he'd never thought he'd see again.

"Lola?" He couldn't even be sure that was her real name. But somehow it fit her, so maybe at least that part of her story had been true. "What happened to you?"

"I had nowhere else to go." Her words came out in a

rush. "I was so worried that you wouldn't be here." She burst into tears and slumped as if physically exhausted.

He caught her, swung her up into his arms and carried her into the house, kicking the door closed behind him. His mind raced as he tried to imagine what could have happened to bring her to his door in Gilt Edge, Montana, in the middle of the night and in this condition.

"Sit here," he said as he carried her in and set her down in a kitchen chair before going for the first-aid kit. When he returned, he was momentarily taken aback by the memory of this woman the first time he'd met her. She wasn't beautiful in the classic sense. But she was striking, from her wide violet eyes fringed with pale lashes to the silk of her long blond hair. She had looked like an angel, especially in the long white dress she'd been wearing that night.

That was over a year ago and he hadn't seen her since. Nor had he expected to since they'd met initially several hundred miles from the ranch. But whatever had struck him about her hadn't faded. There was something flawless about her—even as scraped up and bruised as she was. It made him furious at whoever was responsible for this.

"Can you tell me what happened?" he asked as he began to clean the cuts.

"I... I..." Her throat seemed to close on a sob.

"It's okay, don't try to talk." He felt her trembling and could see that she was fighting tears. "This cut under your eye is deep."

She said nothing, looking as if it was all she could

do to keep her eyes open. He took in her torn and filthy dress. It was long, like the white one he'd first seen her in, but faded. It reminded him of something his grandmother might have worn to do housework in. She was also thinner than he remembered.

As he gently cleaned her wounds, he could see dark circles under her eyes, and her long braided hair was in disarray with bits of twigs and leaves stuck in it.

The night he'd met her, her plaited hair had been pinned up at the nape of her neck—until he'd released it, the blond silk dropping to the center of her back.

He finished his doctoring, put away the first-aid kit, and wondered how far she'd come to find him and what she had been through to get here. When he returned to the kitchen, he found her standing at the back window, staring out. As she turned, he saw the fear in her eyes—and the exhaustion.

Colt desperately wanted to know what had happened to her and how she'd ended up on his doorstep. He hadn't even thought that she'd known his name. "Have you had anything to eat?"

"Not in the past forty-eight hours or so," she said, squinting at the clock on the wall as if not sure what day it was. "And not all that much before that."

He'd been meaning to get into Gilt Edge and buy some groceries. "Sit and I'll see what I can scare up," he said as he opened the refrigerator. Seeing only one egg left, he said, "How do you feel about pancakes? I have chokecherry syrup."

She nodded and attempted a smile. She looked skittish as a newborn calf. Worse, he sensed that she was having second thoughts about coming here.

She licked her cracked lips. "I have to tell you. I have to explain—"

"It's okay. You're safe here." But safe from what, he wondered? "There's no hurry. Let's get you taken care of first." He'd feed her and get her settled down.

He motioned her into a chair at the kitchen table. He could tell that she must hurt all over by the way she moved. As much as he wanted to know what had happened, he thought she needed food more than anything else at this moment.

"While I make the pancakes, would you like a hot shower? The guest room is down the hall to the left. I can find you some clothes. They'll be too large for you, but maybe they will be more comfortable."

Tears welled in her eyes. He saw her swallow before she nodded. As she started to get to her feet, he noticed her grimace in pain.

"Wait."

She froze.

"I don't know how to say this delicately, but if someone assaulted you—"

"I wasn't raped."

He nodded, hoping that was true, because a shower would destroy important evidence. "Okay, so the injuries were…"

"From running for my life." With that she limped out of the kitchen.

He had the pancake batter made and the griddle heating when he heard the shower come on. He stopped to listen to the running water, remembering this woman in a hotel shower with him months ago.

That night he'd bumped into her coming out of the hotel bar. He'd seen that she was upset. She'd told him that she needed his help, that there was someone after her. She'd given him the impression she was running from an old boyfriend. He'd been happy to help. Now he wondered if that was still the case. She said she was running for her life—just as she had the first time they'd met.

But that had been in Billings. This was Gilt Edge, Montana, hundreds of miles away. Didn't seem likely she would still be running from the same boyfriend. But whoever was chasing her, she'd come to him for help.

He couldn't turn her away any more than he'd been able to in that hotel hallway in Billings last year.

LOLA PULLED OUT her braid, discarding the debris stuck in it, then climbed into the steaming shower. She stood under the hot spray, leaned against the smooth, cool tile wall of the shower and closed her eyes. She felt weak from hunger, lack of sleep and constant fear. She couldn't remember the last time she'd slept through the night.

Exhaustion pulled at her. It took all of her energy to wash herself. Her body felt alien to her, her skin chafed from the rough fabric of the long dresses she'd been wearing for months. Stumbling from the shower, she wrapped her hair in one of the guest towels. It felt good to free her hair from the braid that had been wound at the nape of her neck.

As she pulled down another clean towel from the bathroom rack, she put it to her face and sniffed its freshness. Tears burned her eyes. It had been so long since she'd had even the smallest creature comforts like good soap, shampoo and clean towels that smelled like this, let alone unlimited hot water.

When she opened the bathroom door, she saw that Colt had left her a sweatshirt and sweatpants on the guest-room bed. She dried and tugged them on, pulling the drawstring tight around her waist. He was right, the clothes were too big, but they felt heavenly.

She took the towels back to the bathroom to hang them and considered her dirty clothing on the floor. The hem of the worn ankle-length coarse cotton dress was torn and filthy with dirt and grime. The long sleeves were just as bad except they were soiled with her blood. The black utilitarian shoes were scuffed, the heels worn unevenly since she'd inherited them well used.

She wadded up the dress and shoved it into the bathroom wastebasket before putting the shoes on top of it, all the time feeling as if she was committing a sin. Then again, she'd already done that, hadn't she.

Downstairs, she stepped into the kitchen to see Colt slip three more pancakes onto the stack he already had on the plate.

He turned as if sensing her in the doorway and she was reminded of the first time she'd seen him. All she'd noticed that night was his Army uniform—before he'd turned and she'd seen his face.

That he was handsome hadn't even registered. What she'd seen was a kind face. She'd been desperate and

Colt McCloud had suddenly appeared as if it had been meant to be. Just as he'd been here tonight, she thought.

"Last time I saw you, you were on leave and talking about staying in the military," she said as he pulled out a kitchen chair for her and she sat down. "I was afraid that you had and that—" her voice broke as she met his gaze "—you wouldn't be here."

"I'm on leave now. My father died."

"I'm sorry."

He set down the plate of pancakes. "Dig in."

Always the gentleman, she thought as he joined her at the table. "I made a bunch. There's fresh sweet butter. If you don't like chokecherry syrup—"

"I love it." She slid several of the lightly browned cakes onto her plate. The aroma that rose from them made her stomach growl loudly. She slathered them with butter and covered them with syrup. The first bite was so delicious that she actually moaned, making him smile.

"I was going to ask how they are," he said with a laugh, "but I guess I don't have to."

She devoured the pancakes before helping herself to more. They ate in a companionable silence that didn't surprise her any more than Colt making her pancakes in the middle of the night or opening his door to her, no questions asked. It was as if it was something he did all the time. Maybe it was, she thought, remembering the first night they'd met.

He hadn't hesitated when she'd told him she needed his help. She'd looked into his blue eyes and known she could trust him. He'd been so sweet and caring that she'd almost told him the truth. But she'd stopped herself. Because she didn't think he would believe her? Or because she didn't want to involve him? Or because, at that point, she thought she could still handle things on her own?

Unfortunately, she no longer had the option of keeping the truth from him.

"I'm sure you have a lot of questions," she said, after swallowing her last bite of pancake and wiping her mouth with her napkin. The food had helped, but her body ached all over and fatigue had weakened her. "You had to be surprised to see me again, especially with me showing up at your door in the middle of the night looking like I do."

"I didn't even know you knew my last name."

"After that night in Billings... Before I left your hotel room, while you were still sleeping, I looked in your wallet."

"You planned to take my money?" He'd had over four hundred dollars in there. He'd been headed home to his fiancée, he'd told her. But the fiancée, who was supposed to pick him up at the airport, had called instead with crushing news. Not only was she not picking him up, she was in love with one of his best friends, someone he'd known since grade school.

He'd been thinking he just might rent a car and drive home to confront the two of them, he'd told Lola later. But, ultimately, he'd booked a flight for the next morning to where he was stationed and, with time to kill, had taken a taxi to a hotel, paid for a room and headed for the hotel bar. Two drinks later, he'd run into Lola as he'd headed from the bar to the men's room. Lola had saved him from getting stinking drunk that night. Also from driving to Gilt Edge to confront his ex-fiancée and his ex-friend.

"I hate to admit that I thought about taking your money," she said. "I could have used it."

"You should have taken it then."

She smiled at him and shook her head. "You were so kind to me, so tender…" Her cheeks heated as she held his gaze and remembered being naked in his arms. "I'm sure I gave you the wrong impression of me that night. It wasn't like me to…with a complete stranger." She bit her lower lip and felt tears well in her eyes again.

"There is nothing wrong with the impression you left with me. As a matter of fact, I've thought of you often." He smiled. It was a great smile. "Every time I heard one of those songs that we'd danced to in my hotel room that night—" his gaze warmed to a Caribbean blue "—I thought of you."

She looked away to swallow the lump that had formed in her throat before she could speak again. "It wasn't an old boyfriend I was running from that night. I let you believe that because I doubted you'd have believed the truth. I did need your help, though, because right before I collided with you in that hallway, I'd seen one of them in the hotel. I knew it was just a matter of time before they found me and took me back."

"Took you back?"

"I wasn't a fugitive from the law or some mental institution," she said quickly. "It's worse than that."

He narrowed his gaze with concern. "What could be worse than that?"

"The Society of Lasting Serenity."

## Chapter Three

"The fringe religious cult that relocated to the mountains about five years ago?" Colt asked, unable to keep the shock from his voice.

She nodded.

He couldn't have been more stunned if she'd said she had escaped from prison. "When did you join that?"

"I didn't. My parents were some of the founding members when the group began in California. I was in Europe at university when they joined. I'd heard from my father that SLS had relocated to Montana. A few years after that, I received word that the leader, Jonas Emanuel, needed to see me. My mother was ill." Her voice broke. "Before I could get back here, my mother and father both died, within hours of each other, and had been buried on the compound. According to Jonas, they had one dying wish." Her laugh could have cut glass. "They wanted to see me married. Once I was on the SLS compound, I learned that, according to Jonas, they had promised me to him."

"That's crazy." He still couldn't get his head around this.

"Jonas is delusional but also dangerous."

"So you were running from him that night I met you?"

She nodded. "But, unfortunately, when I left the hotel the next morning, two of the 'sisters' were waiting for me and forced me to go back to the compound."

"And tonight?" he asked as he pushed his plate away.

Lola met his gaze. "I escaped. I'd been locked up there since I last saw you within miles of here at the Montana SLS compound."

Colt let out a curse. "You've been held there all this time against your will? Why didn't you—"

"Escape sooner?" She sounded near tears as she held his gaze.

He saw something in those beautiful eyes that made his stomach drop.

Her voice caught as she said, "I had originally gone there to get my parents' remains because I don't believe they died of natural causes. I'd gotten a letter from my father right before I heard from Jonas. He wanted out of SLS, but my mother refused. My father said he feared the hold Jonas had on her and needed my help because she wasn't well."

"What are you saying?"

"I think they were murdered, but I can't prove it without their bodies, and Jonas has refused to release them. Legally, there isn't much I can do since my parents had signed over everything to him—even their daughter."

Murder? He'd heard about the fifty-two-year-old charismatic leader of the cult living in the mountains outside of town, but he couldn't imagine the things Lola was telling him. "He can't expect you to marry him."

"Jonas was convinced that I would fall for him if I spent enough time at the compound, so he kept me there. At first, he told me it would take time to have my parents' remains exhumed and moved. Later I realized there was no way he was letting their remains go anywhere even if he could convince me to marry him, which was never going to happen."

Maybe it was the late hour, but he was having trouble making sense of this. "So after you met me…"

"I was more determined to free both my parents and myself from Jonas forever. I wasn't back at the compound long though, when I realized I was pregnant. Jonas realized it, too. I became a prisoner of SLS until the birth. Then Jonas had the baby taken away and had me locked up. I had to escape to get help for my daughter."

"Your daughter?"

She met his gaze. "That's why I'm here… She's *our* daughter," she said, her voice suddenly choked with tears. "Jonas took the baby girl that you and I made the first night we met."

COLT STARED AT HER, too shocked to speak for a moment. *What the hell?* "Are you trying to tell me—"

"I had your child but I couldn't contact you. Jonas kept me under guard, locked away. I had no way to get a message out. If any of the sisters tried to help me, they were severely punished."

He couldn't believe what he was hearing. "Wait. You had the baby at the compound?"

She nodded. "One of the members is a midwife. She delivered a healthy girl, but then Jonas had the child taken away almost at once. I got to hold her only for a few moments and only because Sister Amelia let me. She was harshly reprimanded for it. I got to look into her precious face. She has this adorable tiny heart-shaped birthmark on her left thigh and my blond hair. Just fuzz really." Tears filled her eyes again.

Colt ran a hand over his face before he looked at her again. "I'm having a hard time believing any of this."

"I know. If Jonas had let me leave with my daughter, I wouldn't have ever troubled you with any of this," she said.

"You would never have told me about the baby?" He hadn't meant to make it sound like an accusation. He'd expected her to be offended.

Instead, when she spoke, he saw only sympathy in her gaze. "When I met you, you were on leave and going back the next day. You were talking about staying in the Army. Your fiancée had just broken up with you."

"You don't have to remind me."

"What you and I shared that night…" She met his gaze. "I'll never forget it, but I wasn't fool enough to think that it might lead to anything. The only reason I'm here now is that I need help to get our daughter away from that…man."

"Don't I have a right to know if I have a child?"

"Of course. But I wouldn't be asking anything of

you—if Jonas hadn't taken our daughter. I'm more than capable of taking care of her and myself."

"What I don't understand is why Jonas wants to keep a baby that isn't his."

She didn't seem surprised by his skepticism, but when he looked into her eyes, he saw pain darken all that beautiful blue. "I can understand why you wouldn't believe she's yours."

"I didn't say that."

"You didn't have to." She got to her feet, grabbing the table to steady herself. "I shouldn't have come here, but I didn't know where else to go."

"Hold on," he said, pushing back his chair and coming around the table to take her shoulders in his hands. She felt small, fragile, and yet he saw a strength in her that belied her slim frame. "You have to admit this is quite the story."

"That's why I didn't tell you the night we met about the cult or the problems I was having getting my parents' remains out. I still thought I could handle it myself. Also I doubt you would have believed it." Her smile hurt him soul deep. "I wouldn't have believed it and I've lived through all of this."

He was doing his best to keep an open mind. He wasn't a man who jumped to quick conclusions. He took his time to make decisions based on the knowledge he was able to acquire. It had kept him alive all these years as an Army helicopter pilot.

"So what you're telling me is that the leader of SLS has taken your baby to force you to marry him? If he's so dangerous, why wouldn't he have just—"

"Forced me? He tried to…join with me, as he put it. He's still limping from the attempt. And equally determined that I will come to him. Now that I've shamed him…he will never let me have my baby unless I completely surrender to him in front of the whole congregation."

"Don't you mean *our* baby?"

Lola gave him an impatient look. Tears filled her eyes as she swayed a little as if having trouble staying upright after everything she'd been through.

He felt a stab of guilt. He'd been putting her through an interrogation when clearly she was exhausted. It was bad enough that she was scraped, cut and bruised, but he could see that her real injuries were more than skin deep.

"You're dead on your feet," he said. "There isn't anything we can do tonight. Get some rest. Tomorrow…"

A tear broke loose and cascaded down her cheek. He caught it with his thumb and gently wiped it away before she let him lead her to the guest bedroom where she'd showered earlier. His mind was racing. If any of this was true…

"Don't worry. We'll figure this out," Colt said as he pulled back the covers. "Just get some sleep." He knew he wouldn't be able to sleep a wink.

Could he really have a daughter? A daughter now being held by a crackpot cult leader? A man who, according to Lola, was much more dangerous than anyone knew?

Lola climbed into the bed, still wearing his too-large

sweats. He tucked her in, seeing that she could barely keep her eyes open.

"Dayton." At his puzzled look, she added, "That's my last name." They'd shared only first names the night they met. But that night neither of them had been themselves. She'd been running scared, and he'd been wallowing in self-pity over losing the woman he'd thought he was going to marry and live with the rest of his life.

"Lola Dayton," he repeated, and smiled down at her. "Pretty name."

He moved to the door and switched off the light.

"I named our daughter Grace," she said from out of the darkness. "Do you remember telling me that you always loved that name?"

He turned in the doorway to look back at her, too choked up to speak for a moment. "It was my grandmother's name."

LOLA THOUGHT SHE wouldn't be able to sleep. Her body felt leaden as she'd sunk under the covers. She could still feel the rough skin of Colt's thumb pad against her cheek and reached up to touch the spot. She hadn't been wrong about him. Not that first night. Not tonight.

She closed her eyes and felt herself careening off that mountain, running for her life, running for Grace's life. She was safe, she reminded herself. But Grace…

The sisters were taking good care of Grace, she told herself. Jonas wouldn't let anything happen to the baby. At least she prayed that he wouldn't hurt Grace to punish her even more.

The thought had her heart pounding until she realized the only power Jonas had over her was the baby. He wouldn't hurt Grace. He needed that child if he ever hoped to get what he wanted. And what he wanted was Lola. She'd seen it in his eyes. A voracious need that he thought only she could fill.

If he ever got his hands on her again… Well, she knew there would be no saving herself from him.

COLT KICKED OFF his boots and lay down on the bed fully dressed. Sleep was out of the question. If half of what Lola had told him was true… Was it possible they'd made a baby that night? They hadn't used protection. He hadn't had anything. Nor had she. It wasn't like him to take a chance like that.

But there was something so wholesome, so innocent, so guileless…

Rolling to his side, he closed his eyes. The memory was almost painful. The sweet scent of her body as she lay with her back to him naked on the bed. The warmth of his palm as he slowly ran it from her side down into the saddle of her slim waist to the rise of her hip and her perfectly rounded buttocks. The catch of her breath as he pulled her into him and cupped one full breast. The tender moan from her lips as he rolled her over to look into those violet eyes.

Groaning, Colt shifted to his back again to stare up at the dark ceiling. That night he'd lost himself in that delectable woman. He'd buried all feelings for his former fiancée into her. He'd found salvation in her body, in her arms, in her tentative touch, in her soft, sweet kisses.

He closed his eyes, again remembering the feel of

her in his arms as they'd danced in his hotel room. The slow sway, their bodies joined, their movements more sensuous than even the act of love. He'd given her a little piece of his heart that night and had not even realized it.

Swinging his legs over the bed, he knew he'd never get any rest until he checked on her. Earlier, he'd gotten the feeling that she wanted to run—rather than tell him what had brought her to his door. She hadn't wanted to involve him, wouldn't have if Jonas didn't have her baby.

That much he believed. But why hadn't she told him what she was running from the night they'd first met? Maybe he could have helped her.

He moved quietly down the hallway, half-afraid he would open the bedroom door only to find her gone and all of this like his dream about being back in Afghanistan.

After easing open the door, he waited for his eyes to adjust to the blackness in the room. Her blond hair lay like a fan across her pillow. Her peaceful face made her appear angelic. He found himself smiling as he stared down at the sleeping Lola. He couldn't help wondering about their daughter. She would be three months old now. Did she resemble her mother? He hoped so.

The thought shook him because he realized how much he wanted to believe her. A daughter. He really could have a daughter? A baby with Lola? He shook his head. What were the chances that their union would bring a child into this world? And yet he and Lola had done more than make love that night. They'd connected in a way he and Julia never had.

The thought of Julia, though, made him recoil. Look how wrong he'd been about her. How wrong he'd been about his own mother. Could he trust his judgment when it came to women? Doubtful.

He stepped out of the room, closing the door softly behind him. Tomorrow, he told himself, he would know the truth. He'd get the sheriff to go with them up to the compound and settle this once and for all.

Colt walked out onto the porch to stare up at the starry sky. The air was crisp and cold, snow still capping the highest peaks around town. He knew this all could be true. Normally, he would never have had intercourse with a woman he didn't know without protection. But that night, he and Lola hadn't just had sex. They'd made love, two lost souls who'd given each other comfort in a world that had hurt them.

He'd been heartbroken over Julia and his friend Wyatt. Being in Lola's arms had saved him. If their lovemaking had resulted in a baby…a little girl…

Yes, what was he going to do? Besides go up to that compound and get the baby for Lola? He tried to imagine himself as a father to an infant. What a joke. He couldn't have been in a worse place in his life to take on a wife and a child.

He looked across the ranch. All his life he'd felt tied down to this land. That his father had tried to chain him to it still infuriated him—and at the same time made him feel guilty. His father had had such a connection to the land, one that Colt had never felt. He'd loved being a cowboy, but ranching was more about trying to make a living off the land. He'd watched his father struggle for years. Why would the old man think he would want this? Why hadn't his father sold the place, done something fun with the money before he'd died?

Instead, he'd left it all to Colt—lock, stock and barrel, making the place feel like a noose around his neck.

"It's yours," the probate attorney had said. "Do whatever you want with the ranch."

"You mean I can sell it?"

"After three months. That's all your father stipulated. That you live on the ranch for three months full-time, and then if you still don't want to ranch, you can liquidate all of your father's holdings."

Colt took a deep breath and let it out. "Sorry, Dad. If you think even three *years* on this land is going to change anything, you are dead wrong." He'd put in his three months and more waiting for an offer on the place.

When his leave was up, he was heading back to the Army and his real job. At least that had been the plan before he'd found Lola standing on his doorstep. Now he didn't know what to think. All he knew was that he had to fly. He didn't want to ranch. Once the place sold, there would be nothing holding him here.

He thought about Lola asleep back in the house. If this baby was his, he'd take responsibility, but he couldn't make any promises—not when he didn't even know where he would be living when he came home on leave.

Up by the road, he could see the for-sale sign by the gate into the ranch. With luck, the ranch would sell soon. In the meantime, he had to get Lola's baby back for her. His baby.

He pushed open the door and headed for his bed-room. Everything was going to work out. Once Lola understood what he needed to do, what he had to do…

He lay down on the bed fully clothed again and closed his eyes, knowing there was no chance of sleep. But hours later, he woke with a start, surprised to find sunlight streaming in through the window. As he rose, still dressed, he worried that he would find Lola gone, just as she had been that morning in Billings.

The thought had his heart pounding as he padded down to the guest room. The door was partially ajar. What if none of it had been true? What if she'd real-ized he would see through all of it and had taken off?

He pressed his fingertips against the warm wood and pushed gently until he could see into the dim light of the room. She lay wrapped in one of his mother's quilts, her long blond hair splayed across the pillow. He eased the door closed, surprised how relieved he was. Maybe he wasn't a good judge of character when it came in women—Julia a case in point—but he wanted to be-lieve Lola was different. It surprised him how *much* he wanted to believe it.

LOLA WOKE TO the smell of frying bacon. Her stomach growled. She sat up with a start, momentarily confused as to where she was. Not on the hard cot at the com-pound. Not locked in the claustrophobia-inducing tiny cabin with little heat. And certainly not waking to the wonderful scent of frying bacon at that awful prison.

Her memory of the events came back to her in a rush. What surprised her the most was that she'd slept.

It had been so long that she hadn't been allowed to sleep through the night without being awakened as part of the brainwashing treatment. Or when the sisters had come to take her breast milk for the baby. She knew the only reason, other than exhaustion, she'd slept last night was knowing that she was safe. If Colt hadn't been there, though…

She refused to think about that as she got up. Her escape had cost her. She hurt all over. The scratches on her face and the sore muscles were painful. But far worse was the ache in her heart. She'd had to leave Grace behind.

Still dressed in the sweatshirt and sweatpants and barefoot, she followed the smell of frying bacon to the kitchen. Colt had music playing and was singing softly to a country music song. She had to smile, remembering how much he'd liked to dance.

That memory brought a rush of heat to her cheeks. She'd told herself that she hadn't been in her right mind that night, but seeing Colt again, she knew that was a lie. He'd liberated that woman from the darkness she'd been living in. He'd brought out a part of her she hadn't known existed.

He seemed to sense her in the doorway and turned, instantly smiling. "I hope you don't mind pancakes again. There was batter left over. I haven't been to the store. But I did find some bacon in the freezer."

"It's making my stomach growl. Is there anything I can do to help?"

"Nope, just bring your appetite." He motioned for

her to take a seat. "I made a lot. I don't know about you, but I'm hungry."

She sat down at the table and watched him expertly flip pancakes and load up a plate with bacon.

As he set everything on the table and took a chair, he met her gaze. "How are you feeling?"

"Better. I slept well." For that he couldn't imagine how thankful she was. "On the compound, they would wake me every few hours to chant over me."

"Sounds like brainwashing," Colt said, his jaw tightening.

"Jonas calls it rehabilitation."

He pushed the bacon and pancakes toward her. "Eat while it's hot. We'll deal with everything else once we've eaten."

She looked into his handsome face, remembered being in his arms and felt a flood of guilt. If there was any other way of saving Grace, she wouldn't have involved him in this. But he had been involved since that night in Billings when she'd asked for his help and he hadn't hesitated. He just hadn't known then that what he was getting involved in was more than dangerous.

Once Jonas knew that Colt was the father of her baby… She shuddered at the thought of what she was about to do to this wonderful man.

## Chapter Four

Colt picked at his food. He'd lied about being hungry. Just the smell of it turned his stomach. But he watched Lola wolf down hers as if she hadn't eaten in months. He suspected she hadn't eaten much. She was definitely thinner than she'd been that night in Billings a year ago.

But if anything, she was even more striking, with her pale skin and those incredible eyes. He was glad to see her hair down. It fell in a waterfall of gold down her back. He was reminded again how she'd looked the first time he'd seen her—and when he'd opened the door last night.

"I've been thinking about what we should do first," Colt said as he moved his food around the plate. "We need to start by getting you some clothing that fits," he said as if all they had to worry about was a shopping trip. "Then I think we should go by the sheriff's office."

"There is somewhere we have to go first," she said, looking up from cutting off a bite of pancake dripping with the red syrup. "I know you don't trust me. It's all right. I wouldn't trust me, either. But don't worry, you will." She smiled. She had a slight gap between her two front teeth that made her smile adorable. That and the innocence in her lightly freckled face had sucked him in from the first.

He'd been vulnerable that night. He'd been a broken man and Lola had been more than a temptation. The fact that she'd sworn he was saving her that night hadn't hurt, either.

He thought about the way she'd looked last night when he'd found her on his doorstep. She still had a scratch across one cheek and a cut under her right eye. It made her look like a tomboy.

"You have to admit, the story you told me last night was a little hard to believe."

"I know. That's why you have to let me prove it to you."

He eyed her suspiciously. "And how do you plan to do that?"

"Do you know a doctor in town who can examine me?"

His pulse jumped. "I thought you said—"

"Not for that. Or for my mental proficiency." Her gaze locked with his. "I need you to know that I had a baby three months ago. A doctor should be able to tell." He started to argue, but she stopped him. "This is where we need to start before we go to the sheriff."

He wanted to argue that this wasn't necessary, but they both knew it was. If a doctor said she'd never given birth and none of this was real, then it would be over.

No harm done. Except the idea of him and Lola having a baby together would always linger, he realized.

"I used to go to a family doctor here in town. If he's still practicing…"

Dr. Hubert Gray was a large man with a drooping gray mustache and matching bushy eyebrows over piercing blue eyes.

Colt explained what they wanted.

Dr. Gray narrowed his gaze for a moment, taking them both in. "Well, then, why don't you step into the examination room with my nurse, Sara. She'll get you ready while I visit with Colt here."

The moment Lola and Sara left the room, the doctor leaned back in his office chair. "Let me get this straight. You aren't even sure there is a child?"

"Lola says there is. Unfortunately, the baby isn't here."

The doctor nodded. "You realize this won't prove that the child is yours—just that she has given birth before."

Colt nodded. "I know this is unusual."

"Nothing surprises me. By the way, I was sorry to hear about your father. Damn cancer. Only thing that could stop him from ranching."

"Yes, he loved it."

"Tell me about flying helicopters. You know I have my pilot's license, but I've never flown a chopper."

Colt told him what he loved about it. "There is nothing like being able to hover in the air, being able to put it down in places—" he shook his head "—that seem impossible."

"I can tell that you love what you do, but did I hear you're ranching again?"

"Temporarily."

A buzz sounded and Dr. Gray rose. "This shouldn't take long. Sit tight."

True to his word, the doctor returned minutes later. Colt looked up expectantly. "Well?" he asked as Dr. Gray took his seat again behind his desk. Colt realized that his emotions were all over the place. He didn't know what he was hoping to hear.

Did he really want to believe that Lola had given birth to their child to have it stolen by some crazy cult leader? Wouldn't it be better if Lola had lied for whatever reason after becoming obsessed with him following their one-night stand?

"You wanted to know if she has recently given birth?" the doctor asked.

"Has she?" He held his breath, telling himself even if she had, it didn't mean that any of the rest of it was true.

"Since she gave me permission to provide you with this information, I'd say she gave birth in the past three months."

Just as she'd said. He glanced at the floor, not sure if he was relieved or not. He felt like a heel for having even a glimmer of doubt. But Lola was right. He'd had to know before he went any further with this. It wasn't like he really knew this woman. He'd simply shared one night of intimacy all those months ago.

There was a tap at the door. The nurse stuck her head in to say that the doctor had another patient waiting. Behind the nurse, he saw Lola in the hallway. She looked as if she'd been crying. He quickly rose. "Thank you, Doc," he said over his shoulder as he hurried to Lola, taking both of her hands in his. "I'm sorry. I'm so sorry. You didn't have to do this."

Her smile was sad but sweet as she shook her head. "I just got upset because Dr. Gray is so kind. I wish he'd delivered Grace instead of…" She shook her head. "Not that any of that matters now."

"It's time we went to the sheriff," he said as he led her out of the building. She seemed to hesitate, though, as they reached his pickup. "What?"

"Just that the sheriff isn't going to be able to do anything—and that's if he believes you."

"He'll believe me. I know him," he said as he opened the pickup door for her. "I went to school with his sister Lillie and her twin brother, Darby. Darby's a good friend. Both Lillie and Darby are new parents. As for the sheriff—Flint Cahill is as down-to-earth as anyone I know and I'm sure he's familiar with The Society of Lasting Serenity. Sheriff Cahill is also the only way we can get on church property—and off—without any trouble."

She still looked worried. "You don't know Jonas. He'll be furious that I went to the law. He'll also deny everything."

"We'll see about that." He went around the truck and slid behind the wheel. As he started the engine, he looked over at her and saw how anxious she was. "Lola, the man has taken our daughter, right?" She nodded. "Then I don't give a damn how furious he is, okay?"

"You don't know how he is."

"No, but I'm going to find out. Don't worry. I'm going to get to the bottom of this, one way or the other."

She looked scared, but said, "I trust you with my life. And Grace's."

Grace. Their child. He still couldn't imagine them having a baby together—let alone that some cult leader had her and refused to give her up to her own mother.

Common sense told him there had to be more to the story—and that's what worried him as he drove to the sheriff's department. Sheriff Cahill would sort it out, he told himself. As he'd said, he liked and trusted Flint. Going up to the compound with the levelheaded sheriff made the most sense.

Because if what Lola was telling him was true, they weren't leaving there without Grace.

SHERIFF FLINT CAHILL was a nice-looking man with thick dark hair and gray eyes. He ushered them right into his office, offered them a chair and something to drink. They took chairs, but declined a beverage.

"So what is this about?" the sheriff asked after they were all seated, the office door closed behind them.

Colt could see that Lola liked the sheriff from the moment she met him. There was something about him that exuded confidence, as well as honesty and integrity. She told him everything she had Colt. When she finished, though, Colt couldn't tell from Flint's expression what he was thinking.

The sheriff looked at him, his gray eyes narrowing. "I'm assuming you wouldn't have brought Ms. Dayton here if you didn't believe her story."

"I know this is unusual." He glanced over at her. Her scrapes and scratches were healing, and she looked good in the clothes they'd bought her. Still, he saw that she kept rubbing her hand on her thighs as if not believing she was back in denim.

At the store, he'd wanted to buy her more clothing, but she'd insisted she didn't need more than a couple pairs of jeans, two shirts, several undergarments and hiking shoes and socks. She'd promised to pay him back once she could get to her own money. Jonas had taken her purse with her cash and credit cards. Her money was in a California bank account. Once she had Grace, she said she would see about getting money wired up to her so she could pay him back.

Colt wasn't about to take her money, but he hadn't argued. The one thing he'd learned quickly about Lola was that she didn't expect or want anything from him— except help getting her baby from Jonas. That, she'd said, would be more than enough since it could get them both killed.

At the time, he'd thought she was exaggerating. Now he wasn't so sure.

"I believe her," Colt told the sheriff. "What do you know about The Society of Lasting Serenity?"

"Just that they were California based but moved up here about five years ago. They keep to themselves. I believe their numbers have dropped some. Probably our Montana winters."

"You're having trouble believing that Jonas Emanuel would steal Lola's child," Colt said.

Flint sighed. "No offense but, yes, I am." He turned

to Lola. "You say your only connection to the group was through your parents before their deaths and your return to the States?"

"Yes, they became involved after I left for college. I thought it was a passing phase, a sign of them not being able to accept their only child had left the nest."

"You never visited them at the California compound?" the sheriff asked.

"No, I got a teaching job right out of college in the Virgin Islands."

Flint frowned. "You didn't visit your parents before you left?"

Lola looked away. "By then we were…estranged. I didn't agree with some of the things they were being taught in what I felt was a fringe cult."

"So why would your parents promise you to Jonas Emanuel?" the sheriff asked.

She let out a bitter laugh. "To *save* me. My mother believed that I needed Jonas's teaching. Otherwise, I was doomed to live a wasted life chasing foolish dreams and, of course, ending up with the wrong man."

"They wanted you to marry Jonas." Flint frowned. "Isn't he a little old for you?"

"He's fifty-two. I'm thirty-two. So it's not unheard-of."

The sheriff looked over at Colt, who was going to be thirty-three soon. Young for a major in the Army, he knew.

"I doubt my parents took age into consideration," Lola said. "One of the teachings at the SLS is that everyone is ageless. My parents, like the other members, were brainwashed."

"So you went to the compound after you were notified that your parents had died," the sheriff said.

"I questioned them both dying especially since earlier I'd received a letter from my father saying he wanted out but was having a hard time convincing my mother to leave SLS," she said. "Also I wanted to have them buried together in California, next to my older sister, who was stillborn. My parents were both in their forties when they had me. By then, they didn't believe they would ever conceive again."

"So you had their bodies—"

"Jonas refused to release them. He said they would be buried as they had wished—on the side of the mountain at the compound. I went up there determined to find out how it was that they had died within hours of each other. I also wanted to make him understand that I would get a lawyer if I had to—or go to the authorities."

"That's when you learned that you'd been promised to him?" the sheriff asked.

"Yes, as ridiculous as it sounds. When I refused, I was held there against my will until I managed to get away. I'd stolen aboard a van driven by two of the sisters, as they call them. That's when I met Colt."

"Why didn't you go to the police then?" Flint asked.

"I planned to the next morning. I'd gone into the back of the hotel when I saw one of the sisters coming in the front. I ducked down a hallway and literally collided with Colt. I asked for his help and he sneaked me up to his room."

The sheriff looked at Colt. "And the two of you hit it off. She didn't tell you what she was running from?"

"No, but it was clear she was scared. I thought it was an old boyfriend."

Flint nodded and looked to Lola again. "You didn't trust him enough to ask for his help the next morning?"

"I didn't want to involve him. By then I knew what Jonas was capable of. This flock does whatever he tells them. The few who disobey are punished. One woman brought me extra food. I heard her being beaten the next morning by her own so-called sisters. When I had my daughter, they took her away almost at once. I could hear her crying, but I didn't get to see her again. The women would come in and take my breast milk, but they said she was now Jonas's child. He called her his angel. I knew I had only one choice. Escape and try to find Colt. I couldn't fight Jonas and his followers alone. And Jonas made it clear. The only way I could see my baby and be with her was if I married him and gave my life to The Society of Lasting Serenity."

Flint pushed back his chair and rose to his feet. "I think it's time I visited the compound and met this Jonas Emanuel."

# Chapter Five

Colt followed the sheriff's SUV out of town toward the Judith Mountains. The mountains began just east of town and rose to the northeast for twenty miles. In most places they were only about ten miles wide with low peaks broken by stream drainages. But there were a number of peaks including the highest one, Judith Peak, at more than six thousand feet.

It was rugged country. Back in the 1950s the US Air Force had operated a radar station on top of the peak. The SLS had bought state land on an adjacent mountaintop in an isolated area with few roads in or out. Because it was considered a church, the SLS had rights that even the sheriff couldn't do anything about.

So Colt was nervous enough, but nothing compared to Lola. In the pickup seat next to him, he could feel her getting more agitated the closer they got to the SLS compound. He reached over to take her hand. It was ice-cold.

"It's going to be all right," he tried to assure her—and himself. If what she'd told him was true, then Jonas would have to hand over the baby. "Jonas will cooperate with a lawman."

She didn't look any more convinced than he felt. He'd dealt with religious fanatics for a while now and knew that nothing could stop them if they thought they were in the right.

"Jonas seems so nice, so truthful, so caring," she said. "He's fooled so many people. My parents weren't stupid. He caught them in his web with his talk of a better world." She shook her head. "But he is pure evil. I hate to even think what he might have done to my parents."

"You really think he killed them."

"Or convinced my mother to kill herself and my father."

Colt knew that wouldn't be a first when it came to cult mania.

"Clearly the sheriff wasn't called when they died. Jonas runs SLS like it's his own private country. He told me that his religious philosophy requires the bodies to be untouched and put into the ground quickly. Apparently in Montana, a religious group can bury a body on their property without embalming if it is done within so many hours."

The road climbed higher up the mountain. Ahead, the sheriff slowed. Colt could see that an iron gate blocked them from going any farther. Flint stopped, put down his window and pushed a button on what appeared to be an intercom next to the gate. Colt whirred down his window. He heard a tinny-sounding voice tell him that someone would be right down to let them in.

A few minutes later, an older man drove up in a Jeep. He spoke for a few moments with the sheriff before opening the gate. As Colt drove through, he felt the man's steely gaze on him. Clearly the SLS didn't like visitors. The man who'd opened the gate was wearing a gun under his jacket. Colt had caught sight of the butt end of it when the man got out of his rig to open the gate.

As they passed, he noticed something else interesting. The man recognized Lola. Just the sight of her made the man nervous.

LOLA FELT HER body begin to vibrate inside. She thought she might throw up. The memories of being imprisoned here for so long made her itch. She fought the need to claw her skin, remembering the horrible feel of the cheap cloth dresses she was forced to wear, the taste of the tea the sisters forced down her throat, the horrible chanting that nearly drove her insane. That wasn't all they'd forced on her once they'd quit coming for her breast milk. There'd been the pills that Sister Rebecca had forced down her throat.

She felt a shiver and hugged herself against the memories, telling herself she was safe with Colt and the sheriff. But the closer they got to the compound, the more plagued she was with fear. She doubted either Colt or the sheriff knew who they were dealing with. Jonas had gotten this far in life by fooling people. He was an expert at it. At the thought of what lies he would tell, her blood ran cold even though the pickup cab felt unbearably hot.

"Are you all right?" Colt asked, sounding worried as he glanced over at her.

She nodded and felt a bead of perspiration run down between her shoulder blades. She wanted to scratch her arm, feeling as if something was crawling across it, but feared once she started she wouldn't be able to stop.

Just driving up here brought everything back, as if all the crazy they'd been feeding her might finally sink in and she'd be a zombie like the other "sisters." Isn't that what Jonas had hoped? Wasn't that why he was just waiting for her return? He knew she'd be back for Grace. She couldn't bear to think what he had planned for her.

By the time they reached the headquarters and main building of the SLS, there was a welcome group waiting for them. Lola recognized Sister Rebecca, the woman Jonas got to do most of his dirty work. Sister Amelia was there, as well, but she kept her head down as if unable to look at her.

Lola felt bad that she'd gotten the woman in trouble. She could still hear Amelia's cries from the beating she'd received for giving her extra food. She could well imagine what had happened to the guards after she'd escaped. Jonas would know that she hadn't been taking her pills with the tea. Sister Amelia would be blamed, but there had been nothing Lola could do about that.

Flint parked his patrol SUV in front of the main building. Colt parked next to him. Lola felt her body refuse to move as Colt opened his door. She stared at the two women standing like sentinels in front of them and fought to take her next breath.

"Would you feel better staying out here in the truck?" Colt asked.

She wiped perspiration from her lip with the back of her hand. How could she possibly explain what it was like being back here, knowing what they had done to her, what they might do again if Colt didn't believe her and help her?

Terrified of facing Jonas again, she thought of her baby girl and reached for her door handle.

COLT WONDERED IF bringing Lola back here wasn't a mistake. She looked terrified one moment and like a sleepwalker the next. What had they done to her? He couldn't even imagine, given what she'd told him about her treatment. They'd taken her baby, kept her locked up, hadn't let her sleep. He worried that was just the tip of the iceberg, though.

One of the two women, who were dressed in long simple white sheaths with their hair in braided buns, stepped forward to greet them.

"I'm Sister Rebecca. How may we help you?" Appearing to be the older of the two, the woman's face had a blankness to it that some might have taken for serenity. But there was something else in the eyes. A wariness. A hardness.

"We're here to see Jonas Emanuel," the sheriff said.

"Let me see if he's available," she said, and turned to go back inside.

Colt started to say something about Jonas making himself available, but Flint stopped him. "Let's keep this as civilized as we can—at least to start."

The second woman stood at the foot of the porch steps, her fingers entwined and her face down, clearly standing guard.

A few moments later, Sister Rebecca came out again. "Brother Emanuel will see you now." She motioned them up the porch steps as the other woman drifted off toward a building in the pines where some women were washing clothes and hanging them on a string of clotheslines.

"Seems awfully cold to be hanging wash outside this time of year," Colt commented. Spring in Montana often meant the temperature never rose over forty in the mountains.

Sister Rebecca smiled as if amused. "We believe in hard work. It toughens a person up so a little cold weather doesn't bother us."

He thought about saying something about how she wasn't the one hanging clothes today in the cool weather on the mountaintop, but he followed the sheriff's lead and kept his mouth shut.

As Sister Rebecca led them toward the back of the huge building, Colt noticed the layout. In this communal living part of the structure, straight-backed wooden chairs were lined up like soldiers at long wooden tables. Behind the dining area, he could hear kitchen workers and the banging of pots and pans. An aroma arose that reminded him of school cafeterias.

What struck him was the lack of conversation coming from the kitchen, let alone any music. There was a utilitarian feeling about the building and everything in it—the workers included. They could have been robots for the lack of liveliness in the place.

Sister Rebecca tapped at a large wooden door. A cheerful voice on the other side said, "Come in." She opened the door and stood back to let them enter a room that was warm and cozy compared to the other part of the building.

A sandy-haired man, who Colt knew was fifty-two, had been sitting behind a large oak desk. But now he pushed back his office chair and rose, surprising Colt by not just his size, but how fit he was. He had boyish good looks, lively pale blue eyes and a wide, straight-toothed smile. He looked much younger than his age.

The leader came around his desk to shake hands with the sheriff and Colt. "Jonas Emanuel," he said. "Welcome." His gaze slid to Lola. When he spoke her name it was with obvious affection. "Lola," Jonas said, looking pained to see her scratched face before returning his gaze to Colt and the sheriff.

"We need to ask you a few questions," Sheriff Cahill said, introducing himself and Colt. "You already know Ms. Dayton."

"Please have a seat," Jonas said graciously, offering them one of the chairs circled around the warm blaze going in the rock fireplace to one side of the office area. Colt thought again of the women hanging wet clothes outside. "Can I get you anything to drink?"

They all declined. Jonas took a chair so he was facing them and crossed his legs to hold one knee in his hands. Colt noticed that he was limping before he sat down.

"How long have you known Ms. Dayton?" Flint asked.

"Her parents were founding members. Lola's been a member for the past couple of years," Jonas said.

"That's not true," she cried. "You know I'm not a member, would never be a member."

Colt could see that she was even more agitated than she'd been in the truck on the way up. She sat on the edge of her chair and looked ready to run again. "Just give me my baby," she said, her voice breaking. "I want to see my baby." She turned in her chair. Sister Rebecca stood at the door, fingers entwined, head down, standing sentry. "My baby. Tell her to get my baby."

Colt reached over and took her hand. Jonas noticed but said nothing.

"As you can see, Ms. Dayton is quite upset. She claims that you are holding her child here on the property," the sheriff said.

Jonas nodded without looking at Lola. "Perhaps we should speak in private. Lola? Why don't you go with Sister Rebecca? She can make you some tea."

"I don't want any of your so-called tea," Lola snapped. "I want my child."

"It's all right," Flint said. "Go ahead and leave with her. We need to talk to Jonas. We won't be long."

Lola looked as if she might argue, but when her gaze fell on Colt, he nodded, indicating that she should leave. "I'll be right here if you need me." Again he could feel Jonas's gaze on him.

After Sister Rebecca left with Lola, the leader sighed

deeply. "I'm afraid Lola is a very troubled woman. I'm not sure what she's told you—"

"That you're keeping her baby from her," Colt said.

He nodded sadly. "Lola came to us after her parents died. She'd lost her teaching job, been fired. That loss and the loss of her parents… We tried to help her since she had no one else. I'm sure she's told you that her parents were important members of our community here. On her mother's death bed, she made me promise that I would look after Lola."

"She didn't promise Lola to you as your wife?" Colt asked, and got a disapproving look from the sheriff.

"Of course not." Jonas looked shocked by the accusation. "I had hoped Lola would stay with us. Her parents took so much peace in living among us, but Lola left."

"I understand she ran away some months ago," Flint said.

"A year ago," Colt added.

Again Jonas looked surprised. "Is that what she told you?" He shook his head. "I foolishly suggested that maybe time away from the compound would be good for her. Several of the sisters were making a trip to Billings for supplies. I talked Lola into going along. Once there, though, she apparently became turned around while shopping and got lost. In her state of mind, that was very traumatic. Fortunately, the sisters found her, but not until the next morning. She was confused and hysterical. They brought her back here where we nursed her back to health and discovered that while she'd been lost in Billings, she'd been assaulted."

Colt started to object, but the sheriff cut him off. "She was pregnant? Did she say who the father was?"

Jonas shook his head. "She didn't seem to know." The man looked right at Colt, his blue eyes giving nothing away.

"Where is the baby now?" Flint asked.

"I'm afraid the infant was stillborn. A little boy. Which made it all the more traumatic and heartbreaking for her since we all knew that she had her heart set on having a baby girl. I'm not sure if you know this, but her mother had a daughter before Lola who was stillborn. I'm sure that could have played a part in what happened. When Lola was told that her own child had been stillborn, she had a complete breakdown and became convinced that we had stolen her daughter."

"Then you won't mind if we have a look around," the sheriff said.

"Not at all." He rose to his feet, and the sheriff and Colt followed. "I'm so glad Lola's been found. We've been taking care of her since her breakdown. Unfortunately, the other night she overpowered one of her sisters and, hysterical again, took off running into the woods. We looked for her for hours. I was going to call your office if we didn't hear from her by this afternoon. When she left, she forgot her pills. I was afraid she'd have another psychotic event with no one there to help her."

"Don't you mean when Lola *escaped* here?" Colt asked.

Jonas shook his head as if trying to be patient. "Escaped?" He chuckled. "Do you see razor wire fences around the compound? Why would she need to escape? We believe in free will here at Serenity. Lola can come and go as she pleases. She knows that. But when she's in one of her states…"

"What kind of medication is she on?" the sheriff asked.

"I have it right here," Jonas reached into his pocket. "I had Sister Rebecca bring it to me when I heard that you were at the gate. I was so glad that she had come back for it. I believe Dr. Reese said it's what they give patients with schizophrenia. I suppose she didn't mention to you that she'd been taking the medication. It helps with the anxiety attacks, as well as the hallucinations."

"Dr. Reese?" Flint asked.

"Ben Reese. He's our local physician, one of the best in the country and one of our members," Jonas said.

"I'd like to see where the baby was buried," Colt said.

"Of course. But let's start with the tour the sheriff requested."

Colt memorized the layout of the buildings as Jonas led them from building to building. Everywhere they went, there were people working, both men and women, but definitely there were more women on the compound than men. He saw no women with babies as most of the women were older.

"Our cemetery is just down here," Jonas said. Colt followed Jonas and the sheriff down a narrow dirt path that wound through the trees to open in a meadow. Wooden crosses marked the few graves, the names of the deceased printed on metal plaques.

He spotted a relatively fresh grave and felt his heart drop. It was a small plot of dark earth. What if Jonas was telling the truth? What if Lola had had a son? *His* son? And the infant was buried under that cold ground?

"It is always so difficult to lose a child," Jonas was saying. "We buried him next to Lola's parents. We thought that would give her comfort. If not now, later when she's…better. We're waiting for her to name him before we put up the cross."

"I think I've seen enough," Sheriff Cahill said, and looked at Colt.

Colt didn't know what to think. On the surface, it all seemed so…reasonable.

"Sister Rebecca took Lola to the kitchen," Jonas said. "Lunch will be ready soon. I believe we're having a nice vegetable soup today. You're welcome to join us. Some of the sisters are better cooks than others. I can attest that the ones cooking today are our best."

"Thank you, but I need to get back to Gilt Edge," Flint said. "What about you, Colt?"

He knew the sheriff wasn't asking just about lunch or returning to town. "I'll see what Lola wants to do," he said, after taking a last look at the small unmarked grave before heading back toward the main building.

"If Lola is determined not to stay with us, I just hope she'll get the help she needs," Colt heard Jonas tell the sheriff. "I'm worried about her, especially after your visit. Clearly she isn't herself."

LOLA SHOVED AWAY the cup of tea Sister Rebecca had tried to get her to drink. She'd seen Colt and the sheriff go out to search the complex with Jonas. "I know you hid her the moment the sheriff punched the intercom at the gate. Please…" Her voice broke. "I just want to see her so I know she's all right."

Sister Rebecca reached over to pat her hand—and shove the tea closer with her other hand.

Lola jerked her hand back. "You can't keep her. She's mine." Tears burned her eyes. "Keeping a baby from her mother…"

"You aren't taking your medication, are you? It makes you like this. You really should take it so you're more calm."

"Brain-dead, you mean. Half-comatose, so I'm easy to manipulate. If you keep me drugged up, I won't cause any trouble, right?"

"You wouldn't have left here if you'd been taking your medication." Sister Rebecca shook her head. "You know we were only trying to help you. I should have been the one giving you your medication instead of Sister Amelia. She let you get away with not taking it and look what's happened to you, you poor dear."

Lola scoffed. "As if you care. And Sister Amelia didn't know anything about what I was doing," she said quickly, fearing that the next beating Amelia got could kill her. "I was hiding them under my tongue until she turned away."

The woman nodded. "Well, should you end up staying here, we won't let that happen again, will we."

"I'm not staying here."

Sister Rebecca said nothing as the front door opened and Colt came in. Through the open doorway, Lola could see Jonas and the sheriff standing out by the patrol SUV. She could tell that Jonas had convinced the sheriff that she was crazy.

Standing up too quickly, Lola knocked over her chair. It clattered to the floor. Dizzy, she had to hang on to the table for a moment. When the light-headedness passed and she could let go, she started for the door. But not before she realized Colt had seen her having trouble standing.

She swept past him, determined not to let the sheriff leave. Her baby was hidden somewhere in the complex. Jonas had had one of his followers hide her. The sheriff had to find her. Lola had to convince him—

At the sound of a baby crying, she stumbled to an abrupt stop. "Do you hear that?" she called down to the sheriff from the top of the porch steps. "It's my baby crying." He looked up in surprise. So did Jonas. Both seemed to stop to listen.

For a moment, Lola thought that she had imagined it. Fear curdled her stomach. She felt Colt's hand on her shoulder as he reached for her. She could see that they believed Jonas. Her eyes filled with tears of frustration and pain.

And then she heard it again. A baby began to squall loudly. The sound was coming from the laundry. She shrugged off Colt's hand and ran down the steps. Jonas reached for her, but she managed to sweep past him. Grace. It was her baby crying for her. She knew that cry. She'd heard it in the middle of the night when the sisters had come for her breast milk. Somehow Grace had known she was here.

"Lola, don't," Jonas called after her. "Sister Rebecca, help Lola. She's going to hurt herself."

She could hear running footsteps behind her, but she was almost to the laundry-room door. Sister Rebecca had set off an alarm. As Lola burst into the room, a half dozen women were already looking in her direction. Lola paid them no mind. She ran toward the woman holding the baby.

Inside this room with the washers and dryers going, though she could barely hear the baby crying, all Lola could think about was getting to the woman before they hid Grace away again. Reaching the woman, she heard the infant let out a fresh squall as if the mother had pinched the poor thing.

Lola grabbed for the baby, but the woman swung around so all she got was a handful of dress cloth from the woman's shoulder.

"Lola, stop." It was the sheriff's voice as he stepped between her and the woman with the child. "May I see your baby?" he said to the woman.

# Chapter Six

Colt watched the woman with the infant look at Jonas standing in the doorway. The leader nodded that she should let the sheriff look. Colt held his breath as the woman turned so they could see the baby she held. The infant had stopped crying and now looked at them with big blue eyes fringed with tear-jeweled lashes.

"Grace?" Lola whispered as she tried to see the baby.

"May I?" the sheriff asked, and held out his arms.

After getting Jonas's permission, the woman released the baby to Flint. He carefully pulled back the knitted blanket the infant was wrapped in. Colt found himself holding his breath.

The sheriff peeked under the gown the baby wore. Colt knew he was looking for the small heart-shaped birthmark that Lola had told him about. He checked under the baby's diaper. His shoulders fell a little as he looked up at Lola and shook his head. "It's a little boy."

"No," Lola cried. "I heard my baby. This isn't the baby I heard crying. It can't be. Sister Rebecca pulled the alarm. She warned them to hide my baby." She looked from the sheriff to Colt and back again before bursting into tears.

Colt stepped to her and pulled her into his arms. She cried against his chest as he looked past her to the sheriff. He'd watched the whole thing play out, holding his breath. The baby the sheriff had taken from the woman was adorable and about the right age. Was it possible Lola was wrong about the sex of the infant she'd given birth to? Maybe the baby hadn't died.

But Lola had been so sure it was a little girl. She'd convinced him. And there was the tiny heart birthmark that Lola had seen on their daughter. But what if she was wrong and Jonas was telling the truth about all of it?

Now he felt sick. He thought of the small grave next to Lola's parents'. He felt such a sense of loss that it made him ache inside. He pulled Lola tighter to him, feeling her heart breaking along with his own.

As the sheriff spoke again with Jonas, Colt led Lola out of the laundry and down the path toward his pickup.

"I heard her," she said between sobs. "The first baby I heard. It was Grace. I know her cry. A mother knows her baby's cry. Sister Rebecca pulled the alarm to warn them so they could hide her again." She began to cry again as he led her to the truck and opened the passenger-side door for her. "Please, Colt, we can't leave without our baby."

He tried to think of what to say, but his throat had closed with all the emotions he was feeling, an incredible sense of loss and regret. It broke his heart to see Lola like this.

Lola met his gaze with a look that felt like an arrow

to his chest before she climbed into the pickup. As he closed the passenger-side door, the sheriff walked over. "You all right?" Flint asked.

All Colt could do was nod. He wasn't sure he would ever be all right.

"I think we're done here," the sheriff said. "If you want to take it further..."

He shook his head. "Thanks for your help," he managed to get out before walking around to the driver's side of his pickup. As he slid behind the wheel, he saw that Lola had dried her tears and was now sitting ramrod straight in her seat with that same look of surrender that tore at him.

He started the engine, unable to look at her.

"You don't believe me. You believe..." She stopped and he looked over at her. She was staring straight ahead. He followed her gaze to where Jonas was standing on the porch of the main building. There was both sympathy and pity in the man's gaze. "He's lying." But Lola said it with little conviction as Colt started the pickup and headed off the compound.

Lola closed her eyes and leaned back against the pickup as they headed down the mountain road. What had she expected? That Jonas would just hand over Grace? She'd been such a fool. Worse, she feared that they'd made things worse for Grace—not to mention the way Colt had looked at her. Leaving them alone with Jonas had been the wrong thing to do. She knew what that man was like. Of course the sheriff would believe anything the leader told him. But Colt?

"What did Jonas tell you?" She had to ask as she squeezed her eyes shut tighter, unable to look at him. "That I'm crazy?"

"He said your baby died. That it was a little boy. He showed me the grave."

She let out a muffled cry and opened her eyes. Staring straight ahead at the narrow dirt road that wound down the mountain, she said, "Is that what convinced you I was lying?"

"Why didn't you tell me you were on prescription medication?" Colt asked.

She let out a bark of a laugh. "Of course, my *medication*. What did he tell you it was for?"

"He hinted it was for schizophrenia and that after your breakdown—"

"Right—my breakdown. What else?"

He glanced over at her. "He said you were fired from your teaching job."

Tears blurred her eyes. She bit her lower lip and drew blood. "That at least is true. I resisted the advances of the school principal. When some materials in my classroom went missing, I was fired. Three days later, I heard that my parents had died. Perfect timing," she said sarcastically. "I'm not a thief. I wouldn't give in, so she did what she said she would, she fired me, claiming I stole the materials. It was my word against hers—even though it wasn't the first time something like that had happened involving her. I had planned to fight it once I took care of getting my parents remains returned to the California cemetery. So what else did Jonas tell you about me?"

"That you're a troubled young woman."

"I am that," she agreed. "Given everything that has been done to me, I think that is understandable." Ahead she could see Brother Elmer waiting at the gate for them. Elmer was her father's age. When she'd first arrived at the compound, she'd asked him what had happened to her parents and Elmer had been too terrified to talk to her. She'd only had that one opportunity. Since then Elmer had kept his distance—just like the rest of them.

"Stop up here, please," Lola said, even though the gate was standing open.

Colt said nothing and did as she asked.

She put down the truck window as Colt pulled alongside the man. Elmer met her gaze for a moment before he dropped his head and stared at his feet. "Elmer, you know I'm not crazy. Help me, please," she pleaded. "You were my father's friend. Tell this man the truth about what really goes on back there in the compound."

Elmer continued to focus on the ground.

"Okay, just tell me this," she said, her voice cracking with emotion. "Is Grace all right? Are they taking good care of her?" She didn't expect an answer. She knew the cost of going against Jonas. Everyone did. If she was right and Jonas had had her parents killed...

Elmer raised his head slowly. As he did, he grabbed hold of the side of the truck, curling his fingers over the open window frame. His fingers brushed her arm. His gaze rose to meet hers. He gave one quick nod and removed his hands.

"You should move on now so I can close this gate, Sister Lola."

COLT BLINKED, TELLING himself he hadn't just seen that. His heart beat like a war drum. He swore under his breath. He'd seen the man's short, quick nod. He'd seen the compassion in Elmer's eyes.

Jonas Emanuel was a liar.

Colt wasn't sure who he was more angry with, Jonas or himself. He'd bought into the man's bull. He'd *believed* him. But the man had been damned convincing. The grave. The pills. The crying baby that wasn't Grace.

Shifting the pickup into gear, he felt as if he'd been punched in the gut numerous times. He kept seeing that tiny grave, kept imagining his son, their son, lying in a homemade coffin under it—just as he kept seeing Lola sobbing hysterically in his arms after hearing what she thought was her baby crying.

"Lola."

"Please, just leave me alone," she said as she closed her window and tucked herself into the corner of the pickup seat as he pulled away, the gate closing behind him. When he looked over at her a few miles down the road, he saw that anger and frustration had given way to emotional exhaustion. With the sun streaming in the window, she'd fallen asleep.

Colt was thankful for the time alone. He replayed everything Lola had said, along with what Jonas had told him. He hadn't known what to believe because the man was that persuasive. Jonas had convinced the sheriff— and Flint Cahill was a shrewd lawman.

But as he looked over at the woman sleeping in his pickup, he felt his heart ache in ways he'd never experienced before. He would slay dragons for this woman. He wanted to turn around and go back and…

He couldn't let his emotions get the best of him. He never had before. But this woman had drawn him from the moment he'd met her. He thought about the fear he'd seen in her eyes that first night. There'd been no confusion, though. If anything, they'd both wanted to escape from the world that night and lose themselves in each other. And they had. He remembered her naked in his arms and felt a pull stronger than gravity.

Would he have believed her if she'd told him on that first night what was going on? Probably not. Look how easily he'd let Jonas fool him. Colt was still furious with himself. He would never again question anything she told him.

Glancing in the rearview mirror, he wasn't surprised to see that they were being followed. Everything she'd told him had been true.

So where was the child he and Lola had conceived? He couldn't bear the thought of Grace being in Jonas's hands. But he also knew that they couldn't go back there until they had a plan.

As he slowed on the outskirts of Gilt Edge, Lola stirred. She shot him a glance as she sat up.

"Before we go back to the ranch, I thought we'd get something to eat," he said, keeping his eye on the large dark SUV a couple of car lengths behind them.

"There is no reason to take me back to the ranch. You can just pull over anywhere and let me out."

"I'm not going to do that."

"I can understand why you don't want to help me, but I'm not leaving town until—"

"You get Grace back."

She stared at him. "Are you mocking me?"

"Not at all," he said, and looked over at her. "I'm sorry. I should have believed you. But I do now."

Tears welled in her eyes and spilled down her cheeks. "You believe me about Grace?"

"I do. I saw that armed guard who let us through the gate. I saw him nod when you asked him about Grace."

She wiped at her tears. "Is that what changed your mind?"

"That and a lot of other things, once I had time to think about it. That first night, you were scared and running from something, but you weren't confused. Nor do I think you were confused the next morning. You checked my wallet to see who I was. You considered taking the four hundred dollars in it, but decided not to. Those were not the actions of a troubled, mentally unstable woman. Also, we're being followed."

Lola glanced in her side mirror. "How long has that vehicle been back there?"

"Since we left the compound."

She seemed to consider that. "Why follow us? If they wanted to know where you lived…"

"I think they are more interested in you than me, but I guess we'll find out soon enough. That's the other thing that made me believe you once I was away from Jonas's hocus-pocus disappearing-baby act. I saw guards armed with concealed weapons around the perimeter of the compound. While there might not be any razor wire and a high fence, that place is secure as Fort Knox."

"So how are we going to find Grace and get her out of there?"

"I don't know. I haven't worked that out yet."

She looked at him as if afraid of this change in his attitude. "The sheriff believes Jonas."

"I don't blame Flint. Jonas is quite convincing. He certainly had me going."

Lola let out a bitter laugh. "How do you think he got so many people to follow him to Montana? To give him all their money, to convince them that to find peace, they needed to give up everything—especially their minds and free will."

"Why wasn't he able to brainwash you?" he asked as he glanced in the rearview mirror. Their tail was still back there.

"I don't know. The meditation, the chanting, the affirmations on the path to peace and happiness? I blocked them out, thinking about anything else. Also, I didn't buy into any of it. I was surprised my father did. It's one reason I didn't see them for so many years. My father wrote me and I spoke with my mother some on the phone, but there was no way I was going to visit them on the compound and they never left except to move to Montana with SLS."

"How was it your father was one of the founding members if it wasn't like him to buy into Jonas's propaganda?"

"My father would have done anything to make my mother happy. That's why he didn't leave after he quit believing in Jonas. He wouldn't have left her there alone. I'm sure he finally saw what my mother couldn't. That Jonas was a fraud. I feel terrible for those lost years."

"The man at the gate…"

"Elmer? He and my father were friends. It's possible that, like my father, he has doubts about SLS and Jonas. Also, not everyone is easily brainwashed into believing everything Jonas says. They might believe he has a right to my child because he says so. But that doesn't mean some aren't sympathetic to a mother losing her baby, our baby, to Jonas."

"I still don't understand how Jonas thinks he can get away with this."

"Because he has."

He glanced over at her, seeing that she was right. Jonas did rule that compound like it was his own country, and because his society was considered a church, he was protected.

"He has Grace," she said. "He knows I can't live without her. Except he's wrong if he thinks I'll let him keep my child, let alone that I would ever be his wife."

Colt glanced over at her. "So he knows we'll be back."

# Chapter Seven

Lola looked out the side window as the road skirted Gilt Edge. Her heart beat so loudly that she thought for sure Colt would be able to hear it. Tears stung her eyes, but this time they were tears of relief.

*Colt believed her.*

The liberation made her weak. She'd seen his face earlier in the laundry when the baby had turned out not to be hers. She'd seen the heart-wrenching sympathy in his gaze, as well as the pain. He'd been so sure at the moment that she was everything Jonas had told him. A mentally unstable woman who couldn't accept the death of the baby she'd carried for nine months. *His* baby.

But Colt had seen the truth. He'd seen Elmer's slight nod, and when he looked at everything, he knew she was telling the truth.

She wiped at her tears, determined not to give in to the need to cry her heart out. They still didn't have Grace. Her stomach ached with a need to hold her baby. Jonas had Grace and that alone terrified her. Would he hurt the baby to get back at her?

No. He'd fooled the sheriff. He would feel safe and

superior. He would simply wait, knowing, as Colt said, that they'd be back. Or at least she would. Jonas thought he'd fooled Colt, too.

She tried to assure herself that Jonas wouldn't hurt Grace just to spite her. The baby was his only hope of getting Lola back to the compound. She'd looked into Jonas's eyes as they'd left. He hadn't given up on her being his wife. He would need Grace if he had any hope of making that happen.

At least that must be his thinking, she told herself. It would be a cold day in hell before she would ever succumb to the man. And only then so she could get close enough to kill him.

"Do you think Jonas knows I'm Grace's father?" Colt asked, dragging her out of her dark thoughts. "He looked me right in the eye and told me that you swore you didn't know who the father was."

"I did. I was afraid he'd come after you. Or send some of his men to hurt you—if not kill you. He was quite upset to realize I was pregnant. I told him I didn't know your name. You were just someone who'd helped me."

"Helped himself to you. Isn't that what Jonas thought?"

She shrugged. "He was so angry with me. I'm not sure when he decided he wanted my baby. Our baby."

"Well, he can't have her."

"We will get her back, won't we?"

He reached over and took her hand.

"I mean, if you dig up the grave and prove that—"

"Lola, that would take time and be very iffy. First

off, that is probably what Jonas is expecting us to do. Second, even if we had proof that your baby didn't die, I'm not sure we could get a judge to send up an army to search the place for Grace."

"Then what do we do?" She felt close to tears again.

"The problem is that it is hard for the authorities to get involved in these types of pseudo-religious groups, especially when, according to Jonas, you're a member—and so were your parents. It's your word against Jonas's. So I'm afraid we're on our own. But that's not a bad thing." He smiled at her. "I'll do everything in my power and then some to bring Grace home to you."

She smiled and squeezed his hand, knowing that she could depend on Colt.

COLT PULLED UP in front of the Stagecoach Saloon on the outskirts of Gilt Edge. The large dark SUV that had been following them drove on past. He tried to see the driver, but the windows were tinted too dark. The license plate was covered with mud, no accident either, he figured.

But it didn't matter. He knew exactly where it had come from.

"The sheriff's brother and sister own this place," Colt said as he parked and turned off the engine. "They serve some of the best food in the area. I thought we'd have something to eat and talk. It shouldn't be that busy this time of the day."

Lola's stomach growled in answer, making him smile. "I thought I would never eat after Grace was taken from me. But soon I realized that I needed my strength if I had any hope of getting her back. Not that I was given much food on the compound."

They got out, Lola slowing to admire the place. "I love this stone building."

"It was one of the original stagecoach stops along here. Lillie Cahill bought it with her brother Darby, to preserve it." He pushed open the door and Lola stepped in.

"Something smells wonderful," she whispered to Colt as they made their way to an out-of-the-way table by the window. All this time eating nothing but the swill that had come out of the compound kitchen had left her ravenous.

There were a few regulars at the bar but other than that, the place was empty. A man who resembled the sheriff came over to take their orders. He had Flint's dark hair and gray eyes and was equally good-looking. "Major McCloud," the young man said, grinning at Colt.

"Just Colt, thank you."

"I heard you were back. Welcome home. Again, so sorry about your father."

"Thanks, Darby." All of the Cahills had been at the funeral. Colt's father would have liked that. He'd always respected their father, Ely Cahill, even though a lot of people in this town considered him a nut. "This is my friend Lola."

Darby turned to Lola and said, "Nice to meet you."

"Congrats on the marriage and fatherhood. How's your family?" Colt asked, since that's what small-town people did. Everyone knew everyone else. He was sure

Darby had heard about Julia and Wyatt since they'd all gone to school together.

"Fine. Lillie's married and now has a son, TC. She married Trask Beaumont. If you're sticking around for a while, you'll have to meet Mariah and my son, Daniel. Don't know if Flint mentioned it, but his wife, Maggie... Yep. Expecting."

Colt laughed. "Must be somethin' in the water. Which reminds me. Ely still kickin'?"

Darby laughed. "Hasn't changed a bit. Still spends most of his time up in the mountains when he's not hanging around the missile silo." He sighed. "So what can I get you?"

"What's cooking today? Something smells delicious."

"Our cook, Billie Dee, whipped up one of her down-home Texas recipes. Today it's shrimp gumbo. Gotta warn ya, she's determined to add some spice in our lives and convert us Montanans."

"I'll have that," Lola and Colt said in unison, making Darby chuckle.

"Two coming up. What can I get you to drink?"

Colt looked at Lola. "Two colas?" She nodded and Darby went off to place their order.

"What was that about... Ely?"

"The Cahill patriarch. Famous in these parts because back in 1967, he swore he was abducted by aliens next to the missile silo on their ranch." Colt explained how the government had asked for two-acre plots around the area for defense back in the 1950s. "You might have seen that metal fence out in one of my pastures? There might be a live missile in it. No one but the government knows for sure."

"The missile silos on your property would be scary enough, but aliens?"

He laughed and nodded. "What makes Ely's story interesting to me is that night in 1967 the Air Force detected a flying-saucer type aircraft in the area. Lots of people saw it, including my father."

"So it's possible Ely is telling he truth as he knows it," she said, wide-eyed.

He shrugged. "I guess we'll never know for certain, but Ely swears it's true."

Darby brought their colas, and they sat in companionable silence for a few minutes.

"It feels so strange to be in a place like this," Lola said. "It's so…normal. I haven't had normal in way too long."

"How long had you been held at the compound before I met you in Billings?"

"Almost a month. The first week or so I was trying to get my parents' remains released to a mortuary in Gilt Edge. Jonas had been kind enough to offer me a place to stay until I could make arrangements. I didn't realize that he was lying to me until I tried to leave and realized there were armed guards keeping me there. At least I wasn't locked up in a cabin that time. I had the run of the place, or I would never have gotten away in the back of the van when the sisters drove to Billings."

And Colt would never have met her. They would never have made love and conceived Grace, Colt thought. Funny how things worked out.

Darby put some background music on the jukebox. The sun coming in the window gave the place a golden glow. Colt had been here a few times when he was home on leave. He was happy for Lillie and Darby for making a go of the place.

"How did you manage to get away this last time?" he asked.

"I'd been hiding my pills under my tongue until Sister Amelia left my cabin. I would spit them out and poke them into a hole I'd found in the cabin wall. The night I escaped, I pretended to be sick and managed to distract Sister Rebecca. When she wasn't looking, I hid the fork that was on my tray. She didn't notice that it was missing when she took my tray and left. I used the fork to pick the lock on the window and went out that way."

Darby returned a few moments later, accompanied by a large woman with a Southern accent carrying two steaming bowls of shrimp gumbo.

"Billie Dee, meet Colt McCloud," Darby said as he joined them. "Colt and I go way back. He's an Army helicopter pilot who's finally returned home—at least for a while, and this is his friend Lola."

"Pleased to meet you," the woman with the Texas accent said. "Hope you like my gumbo."

"I know we will," Colt said, and took a bite.

"Not too spicy for you?" the cook asked with a laugh.

"As long as it doesn't melt the spoon, it's not too spicy for me," Colt said, and looked to Lola.

She had tasted the gumbo and was smiling. "It's perfect."

Billie Dee looked pleased. "Enjoy."

Darby refilled their colas and gave them pieces of Billie Dee's Texas chocolate sheet cake to convey both "welcome home" and "glad to meet you."

Left alone again, Colt asked, "How are you doing?"

Lola realized that she felt better than she had in a long time. Just having food in her stomach made her feel stronger and more able to hold off the fear and frustration. She needed her baby.

But Colt believed her, and that made all the difference in the world. That felt like a huge hurdle given how convincing Jonas could be. Even more so, she was glad that she hadn't been wrong about Colt. They'd only been together that one night, but she hadn't forgotten his kindness, his tenderness, his protectiveness. Just having someone she could depend on… Her heart swelled as she looked over at him. "We're going to get Grace back, aren't we?"

JONAS STOOD AT the window of his cabin. He'd had his cabin built on the side of the mountain so he could look down on the compound. For a man who'd started with nothing, he'd done all right. He often wished his father was still alive to see it.

"Look, you sanctimonious old son of a bitch. You, who so lacked faith that I would accomplish anything in my life. You, who died so poor that your congregation had to scrape up money to have you buried behind the church you'd served all those years. You, who always managed to cut me down as if you couldn't stand it that I might do better than you. Well, I did!"

Thinking about his father made his pulse rise dangerously. He had to be careful not to get upset. Stress made his condition worse. So much worse that some of his followers had started to notice.

He stepped over to the small table where he kept his medication. He swallowed a pill and waited for it to work. He tried not to think about the father who had kicked him out at sixteen. But it wasn't his old man who was causing the problem this time. It was Lola.

"Lola." Just saying her name churned up a warring mix of emotions that had been raging inside him for some time. Over the years, a variety of willing women had come to his bed in the night. He'd turned none of them away, but nor had he wanted any of them to keep for himself. Until Lola.

Her mother had shown him a photograph of her daughter back when Maxine and her husband, Ted, had joined SLS. The Society was just getting on its feet in those days. The Daytons' money had gone a long way to start things rolling.

Jonas had especially liked Maxine, since he knew she was the one calling the shots. Ted would do anything for his wife. And had. All Jonas had to do was steer Maxine in whatever direction he wanted her to go and Ted would come along as a willing participant. If only they were all that easy to manage, he thought now with a sigh.

The photo of Lola had caught him off guard. There was a sweetness, a purity in that young face, but it was what he saw in her eyes. A fire. A passion banked in those mesmerizing violet eyes that had made him want to be the one to release it.

He'd done everything he could to get the Daytons to bring Lola to the California ranch. But the foolish girl had taken off right after high school to attend a college abroad. She'd wanted to become a teacher. Jonas had groaned when Maxine told him, and he'd conveyed his thoughts.

*I think she could be anything she wants to be with my help. I really want to help her meet her potential. Lola is destined to do so much more than teach. She and I could lead the world to a better place. She might be the one person who could bring peace to the world.*

Maxine had loved it, but Lola hadn't been having any of it. Right after college she'd headed for the Virgin Islands to teach sixth-grade geography at a private school down there. What a waste, he'd thought, not just for Lola but for himself. He had imagined what he could do with a woman like that warming his bed at night. They could run SLS together. Lola would bring in the men. He'd bring in the women. They could build an empire and live like royalty.

He'd known that Ted wasn't happy after the move to Montana. Jonas had heard him trying to get Maxine to leave. That was the first time that Jonas had realized that Ted had held out on him. Ted hadn't bought into SLS either mentally or financially. He hadn't turned over all his money. He'd set some aside for Lola, and no small amount, either.

Ted's dissatisfaction and attempts to get Maxine to leave hadn't fitted into Jonas's plan. He suddenly realized there was only one way to get Lola to come to him. Maxine and Ted would have to die—and soon.

Getting Maxine to sign a paper of her intentions to persuade Lola to marry him had taken only one private session with her. Maxine had bought into SLS hook, line and sinker. If she wanted to save her daughter… He'd promised to give Lola the kind of life her mother had only dreamed of. Then he'd had Ted and Maxine disposed of and, just as he'd planned, Lola flew to Montana, bringing all that fire inside her.

But he'd underestimated her. She was nothing like her mother. He'd thought that his charm, his wit, his sincerity would work on the daughter the way it had on her mother. That was where he'd made his first mistake, he thought now as he watched dusk settle over the compound.

There'd been a series of other mistakes that had led to her getting pregnant by another man. That was a blow he still reeled from. But it hadn't changed his determination to have Lola, one way or another. Not even some Army pilot/rancher could stop him. No, he had the one thing that Lola wanted more than life.

She would be back. And this time, she wouldn't be leaving here again.

# Chapter Eight

After shrimp gumbo at the Stagecoach Saloon, Colt took them to the grocery store. He and Lola grabbed a cart and began to fill it with food. He loved her enthusiasm. After being locked up and nearly starved for so long, she was like a kid in a candy store.

"Do you like this?" she would ask as she picked up one item after another.

"Get whatever sounds good to you."

She scampered around, quickly filling the cart with food she obviously hadn't had for a while as he grabbed the basics: milk, bread, eggs, butter, bacon and syrup.

"I suspect you can live on pancakes," she said, eyeing what he'd added to the cart.

He'd only grinned, realizing that he'd never enjoyed grocery shopping as much as he had with her today. They felt almost like an old married couple as they left the store. He found himself smiling at Lola as she tore into a bag of potato chips before they even reached the pickup. He unloaded their haul and had started to replace the cart in the rack when he heard someone call his name.

"Colt?"

He froze at the sound of Julia's voice. Somehow he'd managed not to cross paths with her since he'd been back in town, but only because he'd shopped either very early or very late. He'd picked a bad day to run out of groceries, he thought now with a grimace.

"Colt?"

Lola set her potato chip bag in the back of the pickup bed and walked over to join him. He could feel her looking from him to Julia, wondering why he wasn't responding. With a silent curse, he turned to face the woman he'd been ready to marry a year ago.

Julia looked exactly the same. Her dark hair was shorter, making her brown eyes seem even darker. She looked good, slim and perfect in a dress and heels. Julia always liked to dress up—even to go to the grocery store. Gold glittered at her ears, her neck and, of course, on her ring finger, along with the sizable diamond resting there. The one he'd bought hadn't been nearly as large.

He swore under his breath. As many times as he'd imagined what it would be like running into her again, he'd never imaged this. Lola was watching the two of them as if enjoying a tennis match.

Colt had hoped that he wouldn't feel anything, given what Julia had done to him. But he'd believed in this woman, believed they would share the rest of their lives; otherwise, he would never have asked her to marry him. It had taken him almost three years to pop the question. He'd wanted to be sure. What a fool he'd been.

"I heard you were back," Julia said, and glanced from

him to Lola beside him. "I was so sorry to hear about your father. I was at the funeral…"

He'd seen her and managed to avoid her.

"How are you?" she asked, sounding as if she cared.

As if sensing who this woman was and what she'd meant to him, Lola reached over and took his hand, squeezing it gently.

"I'm good," he said, squeezing back. "And you?"

"Fine." She looked again at his companion, her gaze going to their clasped hands.

"I heard you've put the ranch up for sale." Julia hesitated. She brushed a lock of her hair back from her forehead, looking not quite as confident. "Does this mean you're going back into the military?" His joining the Army's flight program had been a bone of contention between them.

He shook his head, as if what he planned to do was any of her business.

"I was just wondering," she said, no doubt seeing him clenching his teeth. "I was hoping that if you were staying around Gilt Edge we could…" Again she hesitated. "Maybe we could have a cup of coffee sometime and just talk."

Just talk the way they had before she'd had an affair with Wyatt? Or talk the way they had when she hadn't shown up at the airport to give him a ride home?

"Our last conversation…" Julia looked again at Lola for a moment. "It went so badly. I'd left you messages. I had no way of knowing you hadn't gotten them or the letter I sent."

"You were clear enough on the phone the last time

we talked," he said, wishing she would just say whatever it was she needed to say so he didn't have to keep standing there. He could tell that she was waiting for him to introduce her to Lola, but his heart was beating too hard. Julia and Wyatt had hurt him badly. Her and one of his friends? Equal amounts of anger and regret had him shaking inside.

But he didn't want to get into an argument here in the grocery store parking lot in front of Lola. He didn't want Julia to know just how much she and Wyatt had hurt him. And he feared that if he started in on her, he wouldn't be able to stop until all of his grief and rage and hurt came pouring out.

"I'm glad you're home." Julia looked from him to Lola again and forced a weak smile. "It was good to see you. If you change your mind about that cup of coffee…" She stood for a moment, looking awkward and unsure, something new for Julia, he thought. And he realized that she needed him to tell her it was okay, what she'd done. That he forgave her. That he wanted her and Wyatt to be happy. Julia was struggling with the guilt.

That alone should have made him feel better, he thought as she turned and left them standing there. Instead, he felt as if he'd been ambushed by a speeding freight train.

"I'm sorry," Lola said as she let go of his hand.

He couldn't speak so merely nodded as he took the cart to the rack and quickly returned to the pickup. Lola grabbed her potato chips out of the back and joined him in the cab. He'd expected her to be full of questions.

Instead, she buckled up, holding the bag of potato

chips as if she'd lost her appetite, and quietly let him process what had just happened. He was thankful to her for that. And for taking his hand back there.

"Thanks," he said, after he got the truck going and drove out of the parking lot.

"It was the first time you've seen her since...since the breakup." It wasn't a question, but he answered it anyway.

"I've managed to avoid her. Just my luck..." He shook his head.

"I can see how painful it is."

"I'm more angry than hurt."

Lola looked out the side window. "Betrayal is always painful." She hugged herself.

He glanced over at her, thinking what a strong, determined woman she was. Not the kind who would give up when things got a little tough.

"Julia turned out not to be the woman I thought she was," he said. "I'm better off without her."

Lola said nothing, no doubt sensing that no matter what he said, he wasn't completely over his former fiancée or what she had put him through.

It made him angry that his heart hadn't let go of the hurt. The anger he didn't mind living with for a while.

WHAT WOULD LOLA do now? That was the question Jonas knew he should be asking himself as he stepped back inside his warm, elegantly furnished cabin.

She must think him a complete fool. Her great escape. He let out a bark of a laugh. Did she really think she could have gotten away unless he'd let her? Sure, he'd had his men chase her with instructions to make sure that she got away.

He'd known she would run straight to the father of her baby. As if he hadn't known she was lying about not knowing who she'd lain with. He scoffed at the idea. Sister Rebecca had seen her with a man near the hotel bar that night. Unfortunately, Lola and the man had disappeared on the elevator too quickly.

But Rebecca had managed to get the information. Major Colt McCloud. An Army helicopter pilot. Jonas would ask what she could see in a man like that, but he wasn't that stupid. The man was good-looking, part cowboy, part flight jockey. He had just inherited a large ranch.

Not that Jonas had been certain Colt McCloud was the man who'd knocked Lola up. No, he hadn't known that until today when the man had shown up with Lola and the sheriff.

Lola was too bound up from her conservative up-bringing to go to bed with just anyone. So she'd seen something beyond Colt McCloud's good looks. Jonas swore under his breath as he moved to the fireplace to throw on another log. Just the thought of the cowboy pilot made his blood boil. How dare the man come up here making demands.

Jonas thought he might have convinced Colt that Lola was unstable and not to be believed. She'd certainly played into his plan perfectly when she'd lost it in the laundry room. But he couldn't be sure about Colt. The man was probably smitten with Lola and would want to believe her.

At least the sheriff wouldn't be returning. He'd been sufficiently convinced. Law enforcement always backed off when it came to churches. Just like the government did. He smiled at the thought of how he'd been able to build The Society of Lasting Serenity without anyone looking over his shoulder.

Until now.

"You could return the baby," Sister Rebecca had dared to say to him before the dust had even settled earlier today. "You know she'll be back if you don't."

"Mind your place," he'd snapped. He'd seen how jealous the older woman was of Lola. He suspected she'd been mean to her, cutting her rations, possibly even being physically abusive to her. He hadn't stopped it, wanting Sister Rebecca's loyalty.

But now he wondered how much longer he might be able to count on Rebecca. Once Lola was back—and she would be back—Sister Rebecca might have to be taken down a notch or two. Then again, maybe it was time to retire her. Not that she would ever be allowed to leave. She knew too much.

Strange how a valuable asset could so quickly become a liability.

As soon as he had Lola… Yes, he would dispose of Sister Rebecca. It would be almost like a wedding gift for his new wife. Not that he would tell Lola what had really happened to the older woman. Let her believe he'd given Rebecca a golden parachute and sent her off to some island to bask in the sun for the rest of her days.

He stared into the flames as the log he'd added began to crackle and spark. If he was Colt McCloud, what would he do? Jonas smiled to himself, then picked up the phone. "We're going to need more guards tonight, especially around the cemetery."

AFTER RUNNING INTO JULIA, Colt had known it was just a matter of time before he and Wyatt crossed paths. He'd promised himself that when it happened, when he finally did see his traitorous, former good friend, he would keep his cool. He wasn't going to lose his temper. If Wyatt wanted Julia, a woman who would betray her fiancé while he was fighting a war oceans away, then she was all his.

He'd visualized seeing both of them, but even in his imagination, he hadn't known what he would do. He'd told himself that he would tell them both off, make them feel even more guilty, if possible, hurt them the way they had hurt him.

But look what had happened when he'd seen Julia. He'd been boiling inside, his heart pounding, anger and hurt a potent mixture. And he'd said none of what he'd planned. Instead, he hadn't wanted them to know how much they'd hurt him. Or even how angry he still was.

After seeing Julia, it made him wonder when it could happen with Wyatt. How would Wyatt react? He just hoped Lola wouldn't have to witness it again. Colt thought that Wyatt must be dreading the day when they would come face-to-face again as much as he was. Colt hoped he'd given Wyatt a few sleepless nights worrying about it. Because, in a town the size of Gilt Edge, a meeting had to happen.

But Colt was sorry that it had to happen at this moment as he stopped to get gas on the way out of town. Lola had gone inside the convenience mart to use the ladies' room.

As he stood filling the pickup with gas, Wyatt drove up, pulling to a pump two away from him.

Colt froze, his heart in this throat, as he watched Wyatt get out of his pickup and step to the fuel pump. He thought about staying where he was, pretending he never saw him. But that was way too cowardly. Anyway, he wanted to get this over with.

He finished fueling his truck and walked down the line of gas pumps. Wyatt looked up and saw him and seemed to freeze. They'd grown up together, hung out with many of the same friends since grade school. It was only after college that Colt, needing to do something more with his life, had enlisted in the Army helicopter program.

Wyatt had tried to talk him out of it. "Why do you need to go so far away? You're going to get yourself killed and for what?"

Colt hadn't been able to explain it to him. So he'd left to fly and fight while Wyatt had stayed on his family ranch and stolen Julia.

He took a step toward the man he'd thought he'd known better than himself. As he did, he wondered what he would come out of his mouth or if he would be able to speak. His pulse thundered in his ears as he advanced on his former friend.

"Colt." Wyatt was a big, strong cowboy. He put up both hands in surrender but held his ground. "Colt, whatever you're thinking—"

Colt hit him hard enough to drive him back a couple of steps. Wyatt banged into the side of his pickup.

"I don't want to fight you," Wyatt said as one large hand went to his bleeding nose.

"That's good," Colt said. "Since you'd probably take me." He knew that might be true since Wyatt had a few inches on him and a good twenty pounds, but as angry as he was, he'd fight like hell.

His hands were balled into fists, but he didn't hit him again. Wyatt's bleeding nose looked broken. Colt was reminded of the time Wyatt had taken on the school bully, a kid twice his size back then. His former friend was tough and had never backed down from a fight in all the time Colt had known him.

He took a step back, hating that he was remembering the years of their friendship. His eyes burned with tears, but damned if he was going to cry. Looking at Wyatt, he realized that losing Julia had hurt; losing someone he'd considered a close friend, though, had ripped out his heart.

He turned on his heel and walked back to his pickup before he made a complete fool of himself. His knuckles hurt, but nothing like his heart as he listened to Wyatt get into his truck and drive away.

LOLA HAD SEEN everything from the front window of the convenience store when she'd come back from the restroom. The "fight" had ended quickly enough.

She didn't have to ask who the man had been.

Wyatt Enderlin. When she'd asked Colt about him, he'd said they'd been friends. "It's a small town. We make friends for life here." She could imagine how much Wyatt's betrayal hurt Colt.

She pushed open the door and walked out to Colt's truck, climbing in without a word. Out of the corner of her eye, Lola saw him rub his skinned and swollen knuckles before he climbed behind the wheel.

It wasn't until they were in the pickup headed toward the ranch that Colt said, "You saw?"

She hesitated, forcing him to look over at her. "I wanted you to hit him again."

He smiled sadly at that. "I hadn't planned to even hit him once."

"Do you feel better or worse?"

Chuckling, he said, "Better and worse."

"Well, you got that out of the way."

"Right, I got to see them both on the same day. Lucky me." He drove in silence for a few minutes. "Wyatt and I were like brothers at one point growing up. I'd always wanted a brother..." He shook his head.

"He was your friend."

"*Was* being the key word here. My other friends like Darby Cahill never would have done that."

"Which hurts worse?" she finally asked.

Colt shot her a glance before turning back to his driving. "Wyatt."

"Maybe one day—"

"I don't think so. Being in the military you learn which men you can trust in battle. Those are the men you want watching your back. Wyatt, as it turned out, isn't one of them."

"I'm sorry." She let the words hang in the air for a moment. "Do you believe in fate?"

They were almost at the turnoff to the ranch. Ahead she could see the for-sale sign. They hadn't talked about it. She doubted they would because she already knew from the first time they'd met how Colt felt about flying the big birds in the military.

"Fate?" he asked, glancing at her for a moment before he slowed for the turn.

"Maybe it was fate that has brought us all to this point in our lives."

FATE? LOLA COULDN'T be serious. If his fate was having his fiancée hook up with his good friend behind his back, then he'd say he was one unlucky bastard. He said as much to Lola.

"I was thinking more about the way we met."

Instantly he hated having rained on her parade like that.

"If Julia hadn't broken up with you and had met you at the airport like she was supposed to, then you wouldn't have been in that hotel that night and I wouldn't have…"

Would some other man have saved her? Or taken advantage of a young woman who was obviously inexperienced and desperate? The thought made him sick to his stomach, but he wouldn't have known because he would never have laid eyes on Lola Dayton.

Nor would he be worrying about how to get their baby away from a madman at an armed and dangerous cult compound at the top of a mountain, he thought as he parked in front of the house at the ranch and shut off the engine.

But as he looked over at Lola, the anger he'd been feeling ebbed away. "You're right," he said, softening his tone as he reached over and squeezed her hand. "It definitely was fate that brought us together." Damn fickle fate, he thought, realizing with growing concern how much Lola was getting to him.

He put Julia, Wyatt and the past out of his mind and concentrated on what to do next. He knew what he was going to have to do. It went against his military training. A man didn't go in alone with no backup. Nor did he take matters into his own hands. He went through proper channels.

But there was no way the sheriff was going to be able to get a warrant to have whatever was buried on the church grounds exhumed—even if Colt could talk Flint into doing it. Jonas would fight it and drag out the process. Meanwhile, that madman had their baby. Baby Grace, the daughter he had yet to lay eyes on.

After helping put the groceries away, he went into the ranch office. The maps were in a file—right where his father had kept them. He found the one he needed and spread it out on the desk.

"We need proof that Jonas is lying," Lola said from the open doorway.

"Proof won't do us any good. We need to find Grace and get her out of there."

"But that grave. If you dig it up—"

Colt shuddered at the thought. "That's exactly what Jonas will expect me to do." He recalled a shortage of manpower on the compound. But a woman could be just as deadly with a gun, he reminded himself. "While they're busy guarding the cemetery, I'll find Grace."

"I'm going with you," she said, stepping into the small office.

He shook his head, hating how intimate it felt with her in here. "It's going to be hard enough for me to get onto the grounds—and away again—without being caught."

"Exactly. They will expect you and will have doubled the guards. You're going to need me."

He started to argue, but she cut him off. "I have lived there all this time. I know the weakest spots along the perimeter. I also know the guards. And, maybe more important, I know where to look for Grace."

Admittedly, she made a good argument. "Lola, if we are both caught, no one will know we're up there. If Jonas is as dangerous as you think he is, we'll end up in the cemetery."

"If one of us is caught, then the other can distract them while whoever has Grace gets away."

He hated that her argument made sense, more sense than him trying to find Grace on his own. "Can you draw a map of the place?"

She nodded.

"Good. We leave at midnight."

LOLA HADN'T DARED HOPE, but as she watched Colt studying the web of old logging roads around the mountain compound on the map, she let herself believe they could succeed. They would get in, find Grace and slip back out with her. Once she had Grace in her arms, no way would she let anyone rip her out again. Especially Jonas.

"I'll need paper and a pen," she said as she leaned over the desk. Their gazes met for a moment, his gaze deepening. She felt goose bumps ripple over her skin. Heat rushed to her center. Then he quickly looked away and began searching for what she needed.

She drew a map of the compound buildings, marking those that were used for housing. "I know you got a tour, but I thought this would help. As you can see there are two women's dorms, one for the women with babies. There is only the one men's dorm on the opposite side the main building."

"What's this?" Colt asked as he moved to her side to point at a large cabin away from the others and at the top of her diagram.

"Jonas's. He likes to look down on his followers."

"And this one at the bottom right?" His fingers brushed hers.

A shiver ran the length of her spine. She felt her nipples harden to pebbles under her top. "That's the storage room, shop and health center." Her voice cracked with emotion.

"And this one bottom left?" There was no doubt. He'd purposely brushed against her as he pointed to the only other structure. The bare skin of his arm was warm. His touch sent more shivers rippling through her. Her nipples ached inside her bra.

"Laundry." She turned enough to meet his eyes. What she saw made her molten inside. His gaze was dark with desire as his fingers trailed up her arm to brush against the side of her breast.

*WHAT THE HELL are you doing?* As if he could stop himself. He looked into Lola's beautiful violet gaze and knew he was lost. He wanted her. Needed her. Thought he would die if he didn't have her right now. This had been building inside him all day, he realized. Maybe since the first time he'd met her.

"Colt?" she breathed, and shuddered as his fingers brushed over the hard tip of her nipple. She moaned softly, her head going back to expose her slim silken neck.

He bent to kiss her throat, nipping at the pale skin, and felt her shiver before trailing kisses down into the hollow between her breasts. "Yes, Lola?" he asked, his muffled voice as filled with emotion as hers had been.

When she didn't answer, he raised his head to look into her eyes. He held her gaze, seeing the answer in all that lovely blue.

Cupping her other breast, he backed her up against the office wall and dropped his mouth to hers. Her lips parted and he took the invitation to let his tongue explore her as his free hand found the waistband of her jeans and slipped inside.

She let out a gasp as he found the sweet cleft between her legs. "Colt." This time it was a plea. She was wet. He began to stroke her, drawing back to look into her eyes. Her head was back and her mouth open. Tiny sounds escaped her lips as he slowly stroked, until he could feel her quiver against his fingers and finally cry out.

Withdrawing his hand, he swung her up into his arms and strode to his bedroom. He didn't want to think about later tonight when they would go up the mountain. Nor did he want to think about the future or even why he was doing this right now.

All he knew was that he wanted her more than his next breath. The only thing on his mind was making love to this woman who had captivated him from the first time he'd laid eyes on her.

## Chapter Nine

Just before midnight, Lola and Colt loaded into his pickup and headed toward the SLS encampment. Colt had programmed his phone with the latest GPS information and had mapped out their best route up the mountain.

They'd both dressed in dark clothing. Lola had borrowed one of his black T-shirts. Her blond hair was pulled up under one of his black caps.

Earlier, after making love several times, they'd showered together, then sat down again with the map. His plan was to approach this like a battle.

Lola had showed him on her diagram what she thought was the best way in—and out again. The layout of the compound was star shaped, with the large main building at its center. It was where everyone ate, met for church and meetings, and where Jonas had his office.

From it, the other buildings formed the points of a star. At the top was Jonas's cabin, on the left center were the women's two dorms and on the right, the men's dorm. At the bottom was the laundry to the left and the health center, shop and storage building to the right.

"Once we grab Grace, someone will sound the alarm. Everyone will get a weapon and go to the edge of the property."

"The SLS is sounding less and less like a church by the moment," Colt had said.

"If the intruder or escapee is caught, a second signal will sound announcing the all clear," she'd said.

Colt had studied her for a moment. He couldn't help thinking of her earlier, naked in his arms. He wondered if he could ever get enough of this woman. "You're sure about this?"

She'd smiled, nodding. She really did have an amazing smile. "Whichever one of us has Grace gets out if the alarm goes off. Whoever doesn't have her distracts the guards to give them a chance to escape."

"Who will have Grace?" he'd asked.

"I guess it will depend on who finds her first. Once we approach the housing part, someone is bound to see us."

Colt would have preferred a more comprehensive plan. "You must have some idea where they are keeping Grace."

"Normally, she would be in the second women's dorm where the other babies are kept," she'd said. "But Jonas will know that I haven't given up. He might have ordered that Grace be kept in the other women's dorm."

"Where were they keeping you before you escaped?"

She'd drawn in a tiny box. "That's the cabin. It serves as the jail."

"And you could hear Grace crying when they came to pump your breast milk?" She'd nodded. "You're thinking they had our baby in this dorm, the farthest one to the west and closest to the cabin where you were being kept. I'll take that one, then head east to the second women's dorm if I don't see you. They won't expect us to come in from different directions."

"We'll meet up there. Or if the alarm goes off, just try to meet back at the pickup"

Now, as the road climbed up the mountain, he looked over at Lola. She appeared calm. Her expression was one of determination. She was going after her baby. *Their* baby. Her last thought was her own safety.

His heart ached at the thought of their lovemaking. He couldn't let anything happen to this woman. Grace needed her. He needed her, he thought and pushed the thought away. What he needed was to get himself, Lola and their baby out of that compound alive tonight. Later he'd think about what he needed, what he wanted, what the hell he was going to do once Lola and Grace were safe.

The night was thankfully dark. Low clouds hunkered just over the tops of the tall ebony pines. No stars, let alone the moon, shone through. Colt thought they couldn't have picked a better night.

Still, he was anxious. So much was riding on this and he felt they were going in blind. What he did know had him both worried and scared. If Jonas or any of his followers caught them…

He couldn't let himself go down that trail of thought. If they wanted to get Grace out of there, they had no choice but to sneak in like thieves, find her and take her. Isn't that what Jonas had done?

LOLA HAD BEEN lost in thought when Colt pulled the pickup over, cut the engine and doused the lights. She'd been thinking about the ocean and the time she'd almost drowned.

Her father had saved her, plucking her from the depths and carrying her to the beach. She remembered lying on the warm sand staring up at the sky and gasping for breath as her father wept in relief over her.

She had no idea why that particular memory had surfaced now. Anything to keep her mind off what was about to happen once they reached the compound. She'd learned to let her mind wander during Jonas's attempts to brainwash her. She would think of anything but what was happening—just like now.

With the headlights off, they were pitched into blackness. She listened to the tick, tick, tick of the cooling engine, her heart a hammer in her chest.

"You ready?" he asked, his voice low and soft.

She nodded and locked gazes with him. Colt looked as if there was something he wanted to say. She'd seen that same look earlier after they'd made love.

Earlier, she'd put a finger to his lips. She hadn't wanted him to say the words that he thought he needed to say. Colt was an honorable man, but she couldn't let him say things that he'd later regret. Nor had she been able to bear the thought of him pouring his soul out to her at that moment. Just as now.

There was too much riding on what they were about to do. Emotions were high and had been since she'd appeared at his door in the middle of the night. There was no need to say anything then or now, though she understood his need. She too wanted to open her heart to him because both of them knew how dangerous this mission was. Neither of them might get out of this alive.

Just as he started to speak, she opened her door and stepped into the darkness. She gulped the cold spring-night air and fought her fear for Colt and their daughter, a gut-wrenching fear that made her eyes burn with tears.

COLT SAT FOR a moment alone in the cab of the dark pickup. What had he been about to say? He shook his head. Lola had cut him off—just as she had earlier.

He sighed, wondering at this woman.

Then he got out, and the two of them headed through the dark pines for the hike to the compound.

They moved as silently as they could once their eyes adjusted to the darkness under the towering pines. A breeze stirred the boughs high above them, making the pines sigh.

Colt led the way until they were almost to the SLS property. The whole time, he'd been acutely aware of Lola behind him.

Now he stopped and motioned her forward. They stood inches apart for a long moment, listening.

Lola had suggested entering the property on the opposite side of the cemetery and the farthest away from any main road up to the mountaintop.

The main road was gated, so Jonas wouldn't be expecting them to come that way. That was also the most visible, so they'd opted for this approach.

But now it was time to separate. Colt could feel the tension in the air, as well as the tension between them.

Lola had made it clear that she didn't want any words of undying love. But, after everything they'd shared, he felt the need to say something, do something.

He drew her close, looked into her violet eyes and kissed her.

"What was that?" she demanded in a whisper. "It felt like a goodbye kiss."

He shook his head and leaned close to whisper, "A promise to see you soon." As he drew back, he saw her smile. "Good luck," he whispered, and turned and headed in the opposite direction, his heart in his throat. If things didn't go well, he didn't want his last memory to be of her standing in the darkness, looking up at him with those big blue eyes and him not doing a damned thing.

Now he thought of her slightly gap-toothed smile and held it close to his heart for luck. Ahead he saw the no-trespassing sign and knew a guard wasn't far away.

LOLA TOUCHED HER tongue to her lower lip as she made her way through the pines. Just the thought of Colt's kiss made her heart beat a little faster. If she'd been falling for him before that moment, well, she'd just fallen a little further. She warned herself that this wasn't any way to go into a relationship.

Her mother would have called it "going in the back door." Maxine would not have approved of Lola having a baby out of wedlock when she could have married Jonas and given Grace a father.

But Grace did have a father. A fine father. Lola just didn't see them becoming a family. She shook the thought from her head and tried to concentrate. Getting Grace back, that was all that mattered.

She hadn't gone far when she saw a faint light bobbing through the trees ahead of her.

Ducking down, she watched as Elmer made his way along the edge of the property. She waited until he was well past her before she rose and sneaked onto the compound. The only lights were the ones outside the buildings that illuminated parts of the grounds.

Lola edged along the pines until she reached the edge of the men's dorm. Only one light shone at the front. She moved cautiously along the back, keeping to the dark shadows next to the building and being careful not to step on anything that might make a sound.

She had no desire to wake anyone, though she thought the men's dorm was probably fairly empty. All of the men would be on guard duty tonight and maybe even some of the women.

Elmer would be turning back soon on his guard circuit. If she hurried, she should be able to reach the closest women's dorm and slip inside the nursery before he started back this way.

Before the first time she'd escaped, she'd had the run of the place, including the one women's dorm, where she'd stayed with the sisters. She'd even helped with the babies a few times. Because of that, she knew where to find the main nursery.

"If I find her first, how will I know her?" Colt had asked.

She'd smiled and said, "You'll know her and she'll know you."

"No, seriously."

"There were two babies born in the past six months that I know of. The boy we saw in the laundry and Grace."

At the end of the men's dorm, Lola stopped to listen. She heard nothing on the breeze. The distance between her and the women's dorms was a good dozen yards—all of them in the glow of the men's dorm light.

She looked for any movement in the darkness beyond. Seeing none, she sprinted the distance and dropped back into the shadows. Her heart pounded as she waited to see if she'd been spotted by one of the guards. The only one she'd seen was Elmer, but she knew there were others stationed around the compound, more than usual, just as she'd told Colt.

As she caught her breath, she thought of Colt and wondered where he was. Saying a silent prayer for his safety, she crept along the edge of the building to the door to the main nursery and grasping the knob, turned it.

COLT RECOGNIZED THE guard as one he'd seen here yesterday. The man looked tired and bored as he moved along the edge of the property and fiddled with the handgun holstered at his hip.

The guard had only gone a few feet when he stepped into the shadows and suddenly drew his weapon like an Old West gunfighter. He took the stance for a moment, pointing the gun into the darkness ahead of him and then holstered his weapon again as he moved on to practice his fast draw a few yards later.

Colt had been startled for a moment when the guard had suddenly drawn his weapon. He'd been more than a little relieved to see that the man's gun was pointing only at some imaginary person in the dark.

He slipped behind the man, closing the distance from the dense pines to the edge of the closest women's dorm. Stopping to listen, he heard a sound that froze him in place.

A low growl followed by another. This part of the country had its share of bear from black bear to grizzly. But the low growling sound he'd just heard wasn't coming from the darkness, he realized. Instead, it floated out of the open window on the back side of the women's dorm. Someone was snoring loudly.

It gave him good cover as he moved cautiously along the dark side of the building. Only a dim light shone inside. Staying as far back as possible, he peered in. The large room was filled with bunk beds like a military barrack. He recognized the woman in the closest lower bunk. Sister Alexa, a woman Colt had met in passing the day Jonas gave him the tour.

She let out a snort and stirred. He saw her eyes flicker and he froze. She blinked for a moment before her eyes fluttered shut and her snoring resumed.

Colt ducked away from the window and made his way down to the end that Lola said could house a second nursery. The outside light high over the front door of the main building cast a circle of golden light.

He watched from the dark shadows at the edge of the light. He'd only seen two guards so far, one on the way in and another crossing the complex, before he'd made his way to the far end of the building where he would find the nursery.

From where he stood, he could see toward the cemetery where Lola's parents were buried. He wondered about the small mound of fresh dirt next to them. Was something buried under there?

Jonas seemed like a man who didn't take chances. At the very least, he would have buried a small wooden casket. Colt remembered seeing the shop on his tour of the complex. Followers made wooden crosses in the shop that they sold when they went into town to raise money for the poor, Lola had told him. She said she doubted the poor ever saw a dime of it.

"I think it's Jonas's way of keeping them busy and making a little extra cash. The crosses are crude, but I think people feel sorry for the followers and give them money."

He thought now about the small casket he'd seen in one corner of the shop during his tour and swallowed hard. What if Jonas had filled the casket under that mound of dirt since their visit?

The thought made his stomach roil. He pressed his back against the side of the women's dorm and waited for the guard he'd seen earlier to cross again.

From inside the women's dorm, he heard a baby begin to cry. His heart lodged in his throat. Grace?

LOLA TURNED THE knob slowly. The door creaked open an inch, then another. A small night-light shone from one corner of the room, illuminating four small cribs. In one of the cribs, a baby whimpered.

She looked toward the doorway into the sleeping room with its bunk beds. She could hear someone snoring softly, heard the rustle of covers and then silence.

Her heart pounded as she slipped through the door and into the nursery. The first two cribs were empty. She moved to the third one. The baby in it was small. A newborn. Sister Caroline's baby, she realized. Caroline had been due when Lola had run away from the compound that night.

She stepped to the last crib, looked down at the sleeping baby and felt her heart begin to pound.

COLT STOOD AGAINST the wall in the darkness outside the nursery. Inside, he heard the sound of footfalls as someone awakened in the dorm and headed for the nursery.

A few moments later, he heard a woman talking soothingly. The baby quit crying. He could hear the woman humming a tune to the child, but he didn't recognize the song.

Then again, he knew no children's songs. He tried to imagine himself getting up in the middle of the night to calm his crying infant and couldn't. It was so far from what he'd been doing for the last eleven years.

What kind of father would he make when he didn't even know a song he could sing a child? Or could even imagine himself doing something like that? In all his years he'd never held a baby. He'd be afraid he would drop it with his big clumsy hands.

He could see the woman's shadow as she'd come into the room and now watched her swaying with the infant in her arms, singing softly, willing the baby back to sleep. Was the baby Grace?

He waited, staying to the dark shadow of the building as, in the distance, he saw the guard come back from making his rounds. The man was headed for the men's dorm. Change of shift? He hadn't anticipated that and realized he should have.

Where he was standing, the man would have to pass right by him. Colt had no chance of going undetected. Nor could he move away from the building without being seen.

Inside the nursery, he saw the shadow of the woman move. The singing continued as she seemed to lay the infant back into its crib. The man was getting closer now. His head was down. He looked tired, bored, ready to call it a night.

Where was his replacement? For all Colt knew, there could be another guard headed from the opposite direction.

He realized the music had stopped inside the nursery. Reaching over, he tried the door. The knob turned in his hand.

He had no choice. He could stay where he was and be seen by the guard, or he could chance slipping into the nursery and coming face-to-face with the woman tending the baby.

He slipped into the nursery to find it empty except for four cribs lined up against one wall. As the door closed behind him, he heard voices outside. Two men. And then silence.

Colt waited a few more seconds before he approached the cribs and saw that all but one of the cribs was empty.

He moved quietly to the crib being used and looked down at the sleeping baby. The infant lay on its back, eyes closed. He carefully reached in and pulled up the homemade shift the baby wore.

FOR A MOMENT, Lola couldn't move or breathe. Her heart swelled to bursting as she looked down at the precious sleeping baby. She would have recognized her baby anywhere, but still, with trembling fingers, she lifted the hem of the infant's gown.

There on Grace's chubby little left thigh was the tiny heart-shaped birthmark. A sob rose in her throat. She desperately wanted to lift her daughter from the crib. For so long she'd yearned to hold her baby in her arms.

She tried to get control of her emotions, knowing that once she picked up Grace, she would have to move fast. With luck, Grace wouldn't cry. But being startled out of sleep she might, and it would set off an alarm that would awaken the women in the dorm, if not the whole complex.

Lola wiped at the warm tears on her cheeks as she stared at her daughter. Grace was beautiful, from her tiny bow-shaped mouth to her chubby cheeks. As if sensing her standing over the crib, Grace's eyes fluttered and she kicked with both legs.

Lola grabbed two of the baby blankets stacked next to the cribs. Reaching down, she hurriedly lifted her daughter. Grace started, her eyes coming wide-open in alarm.

Quickly wrapping her infant in the blankets, Lola turned toward the door and felt a hand drop to her shoulder.

# Chapter Ten

Lola had been in midstep when the hand dropped to her shoulder. The fingers tightened, forcing her to stop. She turned, terrified of who she would find standing behind her.

Sister Amelia put a finger to her lips before Lola could speak. Their gazes locked for what seemed an eternity. Neither looked away until Grace stirred in Lola's arms.

"Go," Amelia whispered, and pushed her toward the door. From back in the dorm came the sound of footfalls. "Go!"

Lola stumbled out the door, Grace wrapped in a blanket and clutched to her chest. Behind her, she heard Sister Amelia say something to the woman who'd awakened. Then the door closed behind her and she was standing out in the dark of the building.

*Run!* The thought rippled through her, igniting her fight-or-flight impulse. She had Grace. If she could get her off the compound…

From the dark, she heard a sound. A whisper of movement. A dark shadow emerged and she saw it was one of the guards. She recognized him by the arrogant way he moved. Brother Zack. She'd seen the way the former military man looked at her when he thought no one was watching. She'd heard that he'd been drummed out of the service but could only guess for what. He'd struck fear in her the nights when she knew he was the guard working outside the cabin where she was being held.

If Sister Rebecca hadn't been in charge of her "rehabilitation" and had sisters coming every hour or so to chant over her, Lola feared what Brother Zack might have done.

Now she watched him move through the darkness, her heart in her throat. Had he seen her? He appeared to be headed right for her. From inside the baby blankets, Grace whimpered.

COLT CHECKED THE BABY. No heart-shaped birthmark on either chubby leg. The moment he lifted the thin gown, the baby began to kick. Its eyes came open. Colt froze, afraid to breathe. The baby's gaze became more unfocused. Its eyes slowly closed.

He took a breath and let it out slowly. Grace wasn't here. He stepped toward the door. The floor creaked under his boot. He froze again, listening. With a glance over his shoulder, he stepped to the door, pushed it open a few inches and slipped outside.

The dark night felt like a shroud over the complex. Only circles of golden light from the outside lamps illuminated a few spots around the complex. He waited for his eyes to adjust, keeping himself tucked back against the shadow of the building. Nothing seemed to move but the pine boughs in the breeze.

Off in the distance, an owl hooted, then the night fell silent again. He had no idea how long he'd been inside the nursery or where the guards might be now.

On the way in, he'd thought they'd been changing shifts. That meant the new ones might be more alert, having just started. He thought of Lola. She'd gone to the other women's dorm. Had she found Grace?

His fear was that Jonas would want the baby closer to him, knowing Lola wouldn't give up. But wouldn't he want one of the sisters watching over her? Jonas didn't seem like a hands-on father figure. Colt wondered if he, himself, was. He could only hope that Lola had already found Grace.

He looked around, but saw no one. It appeared that most of the guards were out by the cemetery. Jonas had thought Lola would try to get evidence to take to the sheriff. He had thought no one believed her—not even Colt. Maybe especially Colt.

He spotted one of the guards moving slowly through the pines out on the perimeter. He wanted desperately to go look for Lola, but they'd agreed that the best plan would be for them to meet at the pickup. That way if one of them was caught, the other could go for help rather than walk into a trap that would snare them both.

As soon as the guard was out of sight, Colt crossed between the buildings and worked his way along the dark side of the second women's dorm.

He reached the end of the building and looked to the

expanse of open land he would have to cross to reach the dark safety of the pines.

As he started to take a step, he heard a sound behind him and spun around to come face-to-face with Lola. One glance at her expression told him that the bundle in her arms was Grace.

She took a step toward him, smiling, tears in her eyes, and suddenly the night came alive with the shrill scream of an alarm.

Lola felt Grace start at the horrible sound. From inside the blankets, the baby began to cry. Lola tore the blankets from the crying baby and thrust Grace's wriggling small body at Colt. "Take her and go!" she cried. "Go! I'll distract them." She could see that he wanted to argue. "Please."

He grabbed the now-screaming baby and, turning toward the pines, ran.

Lola felt a fist close on her heart as she looked down at the empty blanket in her hand. She didn't have time for regrets. She'd gotten to see her daughter, hold her for a few priceless minutes, but now she had to move, and she knew the best way to make the alarm stop.

Grabbing up several large stones lying along the side of the building's foundation, she quickly wrapped them in the baby blankets, then hugged the bundle against her chest. It wouldn't fool anyone who got too close, but it might work long enough to get her where she needed to go.

Turning, she hurried back toward the center of the

compound. She desperately needed to distract the guards and give Colt a chance to escape with Grace.

SLS members poured out of the dorms in their nightwear. She half ran toward Jonas's cabin, screaming at the top of her lungs. Guards came running from all directions.

Zack saw her and charged her. He would have taken her down, but Jonas had come out of his cabin. Seeing what was happening, he shut off the alarm with his cell phone.

"Leave her alone, Brother Zack!" he yelled down. "Don't hurt the baby."

Zack stopped just inches from her. She could see his disappointment. He hadn't cared if he hurt the baby. He had been looking forward to getting his hands on her.

"Bring her to me," Jonas ordered.

Zack reached for her, but she jerked back her arm. One of the rocks shifted and she had to grip her bundle harder.

"Never mind, Brother Zack," Jonas called down. "Lola, I know you don't want to hurt the baby. Come up to my cabin. I promise I won't hurt you or the child."

As if she believed a word out of his mouth. But she walked slowly up the hill, holding the bundle of rocks protectively against her breast.

She listened to make sure that none of the guards had stumbled across Colt and Grace. But there'd been no more activity at the edge of the complex, no shouts, no gunshots. Jonas had sounded the all clear siren. His followers were slowly wandering back to either their beds or their guard duty.

Before she reached the steps to the cabin, Jonas told Zack to leave only a few guards on duty. The rest, he said, could go to bed for what was left of the night.

Clearly he thought that the danger was over and that Lola had acted alone.

She stopped at the bottom of the porch steps and looked up at Jonas. He had a self-satisfied look on his face. He thought he'd won. He thought he had her and he had Grace.

"How did you get here?" Jonas asked suddenly, looking past her.

"I stole his pickup."

"Colt McCloud's? I thought he was your hero?" he mocked.

"Some hero," she said. "But that doesn't surprise you, does it? You knew he'd believe you and not me."

Jonas almost looked sorry for her. "The man's a fool."

She hugged the bundle tighter.

"You should come in. It's cold out here," he said. "Is the baby all right?"

She knew he had to be wondering how Grace had been able to sleep through all of the racket. He had to be getting suspicious.

"She is so sweet," Lola said, glancing down for a moment to peel back of the edge of the blanket so only she could see what was inside. She smiled down at the rock. "She really is an angel." She wanted to give Colt as much time as possible to get away with Grace, but she knew she couldn't keep standing out here or Jonas was going to become suspicious.

"As I've said all along," he agreed as she mounted the steps. He reached for the baby, but she turned to the side, holding the bundle away from him.

"Please, let me hold her just a little longer." Tears filled her eyes at just the thought of the few minutes she'd had Grace in her arms and the thought that they might be all she was going to get.

Jonas relented. "Of course, hold her all you want. There is no reason you should be separated from your child. If you stay here, you will have her all the time. Imagine what your life could be like here with me."

"I have." She hoped she kept the sarcasm out of the voice as she moved to the middle of the room, giving herself a little elbow room.

"We could travel. Europe, the Caribbean, anywhere your heart desired. We could take Angel with us."

"Her name is Grace."

He ignored that as he started to close the door. He froze and cocked his head, taking in the bundle in her arms again. "It really is amazing she slept through all of that noise," he said again.

"She knows she's with her mother now. She knows she's safe."

Jonas looked out the still-open doorway as if suddenly not so sure about being alone with her. She saw Zack watching them.

Lola knew she had no choice. Zack was watching, expecting trouble, and Jonas was getting suspicious. She had no choice.

"Europe? I love Europe," she said, and saw Jonas relax a little. He waved Zack away and closed the door.

She looked around, remembering the last time she'd been brought here. Jonas had told her that he would make her his wife—one way or another. He'd tried to kiss her and she'd kicked him hard enough in the shin to get away and, apparently, given him a permanent limp.

Behind her, she heard him lock the door and limp toward her.

# Chapter Eleven

Colt reached the pickup. All the way, he'd hoped that he would find Lola waiting for him even though he knew there was little chance of that.

Still, he was disappointed when he got there to find he was alone. Grace had quit crying not long after they'd left the compound. He was grateful for that since he was sure it had helped him get away.

He opened the passenger-side door, the dome light coming on as he laid the bundle Lola had given him on the seat to get his first look at his daughter.

A pair of big blue eyes stared up at him. He lost his heart in that moment. He touched the perfect little cheek, soft as downy feathers. She did resemble Lola, but he thought he could see himself a little in her, too.

"Hi, Grace," he whispered, his voice breaking. Tears welled in his eyes. He swallowed the lump in this throat. He had the baby, but what now?

He turned off the dome light, realizing that if someone had followed him, they would be able to see him through the pines. He stared into the darkness, willing Lola to appear.

He had to assume that Jonas had her by now. He'd heard the alarm go off and then another signal, which he'd assumed must be the all clear. Why would Jonas sound it unless he'd thought there was nothing more to fear?

Which meant he had Lola. She'd sacrificed herself to save her daughter. Their daughter.

He looked toward the dark trees, silently pleading for that not to be the case. He needed her. Grace needed her.

They had Lola. He couldn't leave without her. But he couldn't go back for her with the baby for fear of getting caught.

Nor could he stay there much longer. If Jonas suspected she hadn't come alone...

"What are we going to do, Grace?" he asked as he wrapped her in his coat and watched her fall back to sleep.

WITH HER BACK to Jonas, Lola reached into the baby blanket with her free hand and slowly turned to face him.

"What really happened to my parents?"

He had been moving toward her but stopped. "They were getting old, confused toward the end. Your mother came down with the flu. It turned into pneumonia. Your father stayed by her side. She was getting better and then she just...died."

She nodded, knowing that it happened at her mother's age, and not believing a word of it. "And my father?"

"I think he died of grief. You had to know how he was with your mother. I don't think he could live without her."

That too happened with people her parents' age who had been married as long as they had. "You didn't have them killed?" She said it softly so he wouldn't think it was an accusation. It wasn't like she expected the truth.

"Lola." There was that disappointing sound in his voice again. He took a step toward her. "Why must you always think the worst of me? Your parents believed in me."

Well, at least her mother had—until he'd had her killed, Lola thought. She wondered if he'd done it himself and realized how silly that was. Of course, he hadn't. Her heart went out to her parents. She couldn't bear thinking about their last moments.

"I took care of your baby for you. I wouldn't hurt a hair on that sweet thing's head. Or on yours. Let me see her." He was close now, and she feared he would make a grab for the baby.

She loosened her hold on the baby blanket bundle a little and faced him, her hand closing tightly around the rock inside.

"Thank you for taking care of her," she said, letting her voice fill with emotion.

"I will take care of you, too—if you give me a chance." He was getting too near—within reaching distance.

She took a step toward him, closing the distance between them as she pretended to hold out the baby for him to take. She had to be close. She had to make it count. It was her only hope of getting out of here and being with Grace.

As Jonas opened his arms for the baby, she pulled out the rock and swung it at his head. He managed to deflect the blow partially with his hand—just enough to knock the rock from her hold.

But she'd swung hard enough that the rock kept going. It caught him in the temple. He stumbled back. She pulled out the second rock, dropping the baby blankets, as she swung again.

This time, he didn't get a chance to raise an arm. The rock connected with the side of his head. His blood splattered on the rock, on her hand. He stood for a moment, looking stunned, then he went down hard on the wood floor.

Lola didn't waste any time. For all she knew he could be out cold—or only momentarily stunned and soon sounding the alarm so the whole cult would be on her heels.

She ran just as she had before. Only this time, she wasn't leaving her baby behind.

Colt had never had trouble making a decision under duress. He'd been forced to make quick ones flying a chopper in Afghanistan. But one thing he'd never done was leave a man behind.

He couldn't this time, either. He'd purposely not taken a weapon into the compound earlier. They'd needed to get Grace out clean, and that meant not killing anyone—even if it meant getting themselves killed.

Now he took the weapons he would need. He was changing the rules—just as he was sure Jonas was. Wrapped in his coat, he laid Grace down on the floorboard of the pickup. She would be plenty warm enough—as long as he came back in a reasonable amount of time.

Locking the pickup door, he turned back toward the woods and the SLS compound. He wasn't leaving without Lola. And this time, he was armed and ready to fight his way in and out of the place if he had to.

LOLA FELT A sense of déjà vu as she ran through the woods. Her pulse hammered in her ears, her breath coming out in gasps. And yet she listened for the sound of the alarm that would alert the SLS members to fill the woods. Jonas would not let her get away if he had to run her to ground himself.

If he was able.

She had no idea how badly he'd been hurt. Or if he was already hot on her heels.

She crashed through the darkness, shoving away pine boughs that whipped her face and body. Colt had said how important it was for them get in and out of the compound without causing any more harm than was necessary.

"We're the trespassers," he'd told her. "We're the ones who will get thrown in jail if we fail tonight. We need to get in there and out as clean as possible."

She thought about the blood on the rock and could

see something staining her right hand as she ran. Jonas's blood. She hadn't gotten out clean. She might have killed him. A cry escaped her lips as her ankle turned under her and she fell hard.

She struggled to get up as she hurriedly wiped the blood on the dried pine needles she'd fallen into. But the moment she put pressure on her ankle, she knew she wasn't going far. She didn't think it was broken, but she also couldn't put any weight on it without excruciating pain.

Grace. Colt. She had to get to them. They would have left by now, but she couldn't stay here. She couldn't let Jonas or one of his sheep find her. If Jonas was still alive. The thought that she might have killed him made her shudder. It had been one thing to wish him dead, to think she could kill him to save her daughter, but to actually know that she might have killed the man…

She crawled over to a pine tree and used the trunk to get to her feet. As she started to take a step, she saw a figure suddenly appear out of the blackness of the trees.

Lola felt a sob rise in her throat. She'd never been so glad to see anyone in her life. Colt. He seemed just as overwhelmed with joy to see her. She'd thought he would have left—as per their plan. But he couldn't leave her.

Another sob rose as he ran to her, grabbed her and pulled her to him, holding her so tightly she could hardly breath. "Lola," he kept saying against her hair. "Lola."

She couldn't speak. Her throat had closed as she

fought to hold back the tears of relief. As he let go, she stepped down on her bad ankle and let out a cry of pain.

"You're hurt. What is it?" he asked, his voice filled with concern.

"My ankle. I'm not sure I can walk."

He swung her up in his arms and carried her through the trees to the truck. She hadn't realized how close she was to where they'd parked it earlier.

She looked around, suddenly scared. "Grace? Where's Grace?"

He unlocked the passenger side of the pickup, opened the door and picked up a bundle wrapped in his coat. She heard a sound come from within the bundle as Colt helped her into the pickup and put Grace into her arms. The tears came now, a floodgate opening. No longer could she hold back.

Tears streaming down her face, she turned back the edge of Colt's coat, which was wrapped around the infant. "Grace," she said as Colt slid behind the wheel, started the truck and headed off the mountain.

Lola held her baby, watching her daughter's sweet face in the faint light as Grace fell back asleep. She thought she could stare into that face forever. For so long she'd feared she'd never see her again, never hold her. She wiped at her tears and looked over at Colt. He smiled and she could see the emotion in his face.

"Have you met your daughter?" she asked.

"I have," he said, his voice sounding rough. "We got acquainted while we were waiting for you, until I couldn't wait any longer and had to come looking for you."

"I'm so thankful you did."

"Let's go home," he said, his voice breaking.

Tears filled her eyes again as she looked from him to their daughter. She pulled Grace close as they left the mountain and headed toward the ranch. Home.

## Chapter Twelve

Jonas came to, lying on his back in a pool of his own blood. His hand went to the side of his head and came away sticky. He stared for a few moments at his fingers, the tips bright red, before he tried to sit up.

His head swam, forcing him to remain where he was. He couldn't remember what had happened. Had he fallen? He'd been meaning to have one of the brothers fix that rug to keep the corner from turning up.

But from where he lay, he could see that the rug wasn't to blame. Not twelve inches from him sat a rock the size of a cantaloupe. A dark stain covered one side of it. Nearby was a baby blanket and another rock of similar size.

Memory flooded him along with a cold, deadly rage. The pain in his skull was nothing compared to the open wound of Lola's betrayal. His heart felt as if it had been ripped out of his chest.

He thought of those moments when she'd been holding what he thought was her infant in her arms. They'd been talking and she had made it sound as if she was weakening toward him. His heart had soared with hope that she was finally coming around. He had so much to offer her. Had she finally realized that she'd be a fool to turn him down?

He'd been so happy for those moments when he'd thought things were going to work out with her and even the baby. That other man's baby, but a baby Jonas was willing to raise as his own as long as Lola became his wife and submitted to him.

The shock when she'd pulled the rock from the baby blankets was still painfully fresh. It had taken him a moment, his arms outstretched as he'd reached to take her and the infant to his bosom. The shock, the disappointment, the disbelief had slowed his movements, letting the rock get past his defenses and stun him just long enough that she was able to pull out the second rock and hit him much harder.

He closed his eyes now. He was in so much pain, but a thought wriggled its way through. His eyelids flew open. His mind felt perfectly clear, making him aware of the quiet. He recalled the alert alarm going off. When Lola had come to him with the baby... Yes, he recalled. He'd sounded the all clear signal.

Why hadn't there been another alert? He had to assume that Lola had gotten away. Gotten away with the baby. If she'd been caught, she would have been brought to him by now. And if Sister Rebecca had checked the crib and found the baby missing...

For a moment, he thought the alarm must have sounded while he'd been unconscious. But if that was true, then Brother Zack would have come to check on him and found him lying here, bleeding to death.

Two things suddenly became crystal clear. Even through the excruciating pain, he saw now that Lola couldn't have acted alone. She would have had help to get the baby off the compound. And her showing up at his door with what he thought was the baby was only a diversion.

He let out a bitter laugh. As persuasive as he'd been, it was just as he'd feared. He hadn't convinced Colt Mc-Cloud that the woman was unbalanced, that their baby boy had died, that he should leave Lola while he could.

Apparently, she'd been more convincing than he had been. He grimaced at the thought. Admittedly, he had to give her credit—her plan had worked. Or had it been Colt McCloud's plan? He closed his eyes, cursing the man to hell. Colt was a dead man.

But so was he, he realized, if he didn't get help. He was still bleeding and even more light-headed. He felt around for his cell phone to activate the alarm.

He had to turn his head to find it. The pain was so intense that he almost passed out. He closed his hand around the phone and, leaving bloody fingerprints, hit the button to activate the alarm.

His hand holding the phone dropped to his side as the air filled with the shrill cry of the alert. Any moment Brother Zack would come bursting through the door. He could always depend on Zack.

Unlike someone else, he thought, remembering his second realization. If he was right, Colt had taken the baby while Lola had pretended to be acting alone. The alarm had sounded and she had known that she couldn't get away. So she'd come up to Jonas's cabin with the rocks in the baby blankets.

But wouldn't someone have checked the baby's crib? And then wouldn't Sister Rebecca, who was responsible for the infant, have realized the baby was gone and summoned help? Pulled the alarm again?

As Brother Zack burst through the front door and rushed to him, Jonas felt the steel blade of betrayal cut even deeper. One of his flock had betrayed him.

# Chapter Thirteen

Colt woke to find Lola and the baby sleeping peacefully next to him. He felt his heart do a bump in his chest. The sight filled him with a sense of joy. A sense that all was right in the world.

Last night on the way down the mountain he'd felt like they were a family. It was a strange feeling for a man who'd been so independent for so long. They'd been exhausted, Lola barely able to walk on her ankle. He'd gotten them both inside the house and safe as quickly as he could.

With Grace sleeping in the middle of his big bed, he'd taken a look at Lola's ankle. Not broken, but definitely sprained badly. He'd wrapped it, both of them simply looking at each other and smiling. They'd done it. They'd gotten Grace back.

He had questions, but they could wait. Or maybe he never had to know what had happened back at the compound. He told himself it was over. They had Grace. That was all the proof they needed against Jonas should he try to take either the baby or Lola back.

They'd gone to bed, Grace curled between them, and fallen asleep instantly.

At the sound of a vehicle, Colt wondered who would be coming by so early in the morning as he slipped out of bed and quickly dressed.

Someone was knocking at his front door by the time he reached it. He peered out, worried for a moment that he'd find Jonas Emanuel standing on his front step.

"Sheriff," Colt said as he opened the door.

"A moment of your time," Flint said.

Colt stepped back to let the sheriff enter the house. Flint glanced around, clearly looking for something.

He'd been wondering how Jonas was going to handle this. He'd thought Jonas wouldn't call in the sheriff about the events of last night. He still didn't think he would. But this was definitely not a social call.

"What can I help you with, Sheriff?"

Flint turned to give him his full attention. "Jonas reported a break-in at the SLS compound last night. I was wondering if you knew anything about that."

"Was anything taken?"

Flint smiled. "Apparently not. But Jonas was injured when he tried to apprehend one of the intruders."

That was news. Colt thought of Lola just down the hall still in bed with Grace. Last night when he was wrapping her ankle, he'd seen what looked like blood on her sleeve. But he hadn't want to ask what she'd had to go through to get away.

"He see who did it?" Colt asked.

"Apparently not," Flint said again.

Just then the sound of a baby crying could be heard down the hall toward the bedroom.

Flint froze.

"So nothing was taken," Colt said. "Jonas's injuries…"

"Aren't life-threatening at this point," Flint said as Lola limped down the hall from the bedroom, the baby in her arms.

Lola spotted the sheriff and stopped, her gaze flying to Colt. She looked worried until Colt said, "You remember Lola. And this is our daughter, Grace."

Colt moved to her to take the baby. He stepped to the sheriff, turning back the blanket his daughter was nestled in.

Every time he saw her sweet face his heart swelled to overflowing. She was so precious. Having never changed a diaper in his life, he'd learned quickly last night.

Now he lifted the cotton gown she'd been wearing when Lola had taken her from the crib last night at SLS to expose the tiny heart-shaped birthmark.

"Our baby girl," Colt said. "We'll be going to the doctor later today to have her checked over—and a DNA test done, in case you were wondering."

Flint nodded solemnly, and Colt handed Grace back to Lola. As she limped into the kitchen with the baby, the sheriff said, "I'm not going to ask, but I hope you know what you're doing."

"That little girl belongs with her mother."

The sheriff met his gaze. "And her father?"

"I'm her father."

Flint sighed. "I was at the hospital this morning taking Jonas's statement. He isn't filing assault charges because he says he doesn't know who attacked him. I see Lola is limping."

Colt said nothing.

"You sure this is over?" the sheriff asked.

"It is as far as I'm concerned."

Flint nodded. "Not sure Jonas feels that way. Got the impression he's a man who is used to getting what he wants."

Colt couldn't have agreed more. "He can't have Lola and Grace, but I don't want any trouble."

The sheriff shook his head at that. "I'm afraid it won't be your choice."

He knew a warning when he heard one. Not that he had to be told that Jonas was dangerous. "He's brainwashed those people, taken their money and keeps them up on that mountain like prisoners."

Flint nodded. "A choice each of them made."

"Except for the children up there."

"You think I like any of what I saw on that mountain?" Flint swore. "But you also know there is nothing I can do about it. That's private property up there. Jonas has every right to keep trespassers off. Not to mention it is church property, holy ground under the law."

"I have no intention of going up there."

"I wish I thought it was that simple." The sheriff had taken off his Stetson when he'd come into the house, and now he settled his hat back on his head. Turning, he started for the door. "You know my number," he said over his shoulder. "I'll come as quickly as I can. But I fear even that could be too late."

"Thanks for stopping by, Sheriff."

At the door, Flint turned to look back at him. Lola had come out of the kitchen carrying the baby. She was smiling down at Grace, cooing softly.

Flint's expression softened and Colt remembered that Darby had mentioned the sheriff's wife was pregnant. "Have a good day," Flint said, and left.

JONAS LISTENED TO the doctor tell him how lucky he was. He had a monster headache and hated being flat on his back in the hospital when he had things that needed to be done —and quickly.

"You lost a lot of blood," the doctor was saying. "If your…friend hadn't gotten you here when he did…"

"Yes, it is fortunate that Brother Zack found me when he did," Jonas said. He didn't need the doctor telling him how lucky he was. He was very aware. But a man made his own luck. He'd learned that when he'd left home to find his own way in life.

Not that he discounted what nature had given him—a handsome, honest-looking face, mesmerizing blue eyes and snake-oil-salesman charm. But he was the one who'd taken those gifts and used them to the best of his ability. Not that they always worked. Lola, a case in point. They'd worked enough, though, that he was a very rich man and, until recently, he would have said he had very loyal followers who saw to his every need. What more could a man ask for?

"You're going to have a headache for a while, but

fortunately, you suffered only a minor concussion. A fall like that could have killed a man half your age. Like I said, lucky."

"Lucky," Jonas repeated. "Yes, Doctor, I was. So when can I be released?"

"Your laceration is healing quite nicely, but that bandage needs to be changed regularly so I'd prefer you stay in the hospital at least another day, maybe longer."

That was not what he wanted to hear. "One of the sisters could change my bandage for me. Really, I would be much more comfortable in my own home. I have plenty of people to look after me."

The doctor wavered. Jonas knew that the hospital staff would be much more comfortable with him gone, as well. A half dozen of the brothers and some of the SLS sisters had been coming and going since his "accident." He'd seen the way the hospital staff looked at them, the men in their black pants and white shirts, the woman in their long shapeless white dresses.

"I'd prefer you stay another day at least. I'll give instructions to one of your…sisters for after that. We'll see how you're doing tomorrow."

"I'm feeling so much better. I promise that when you release me, I will rest and take care of myself." His head ached more than he had let the doctor know. He didn't want any medication that would make his brain fuzzy. He needed his wits about him now more than ever.

"Like I said, we'll see how you are tomorrow," the doctor said, eyeing him suspiciously. The man knew Jonas couldn't be feeling that good, not with his head almost bashed in. He also knew the doctor had to be questioning how he could have hurt himself like this in a fall.

Jonas just wished he would go away and leave him alone.

"I need to ask you about these pills you've been taking," the doctor said, clearly not leaving yet. "One of your church members told me they were for a bad heart, but that's not the medication you're taking."

"No, it's not for a heart ailment," Jonas had to admit. "I'd prefer my flock not worry about my health, Doctor."

"If you're suffering from memory loss at your age, then we need to run some tests and see—"

"I have early-onset Alzheimer's," Jonas interrupted.

The doctor blinked.

"It is in the beginning stages, thus the pills I'm taking. I can assure you that I'm being well taken care of."

The doctor seemed at a loss for words.

"I believe Brother Zack is waiting in the hall," Jonas said to the doctor. "Would you ask him to step in here? I need to talk to him."

Realizing he was excused, the doctor left. A few moments later, Zack stuck his head in the door.

Jonas motioned him in. "Close the door. Have you seen Sister Rebecca?"

"Not since last night."

"Who was on duty at the second nursery last night?" he asked.

Zack frowned. "Sister Alexa." His eyes widened as he realized what the leader was really asking. "Sister Rebecca was taking care of the…special baby."

The angel. That's what Jonas had told his flock. That he'd had a vision and Lola's baby was a chosen one.

"Sister Rebecca." Jonas nodded and closed his eyes for a moment. He'd known it, but had needed Zack to verify his suspicions. Rebecca had been with him since the beginning. If there was anyone he knew he could trust, could depend on, it was her. He slowly opened his eyes and stared up at the pale green ceiling.

Zack stood at the end of the bed, waiting. Rebecca and Zack had never gotten along. Jonas blamed it on simple jealousy. Both were in the top positions at SLS. He knew how much Zack was going to enjoy the task he was about to give him.

"Go back to the complex," Jonas told him. "I want Sister Rebecca—" if she was still there "—restrained. Use the cabin where Sister Lola stayed. Guard it yourself." He finally looked at Zack, who nodded, a malicious glint in his gaze even as he fought not to smile.

"I'll take care of it."

AFTER THE SHERIFF LEFT, Colt stepped to Lola and Grace and pulled them close. He knew the sheriff was worried and with good reason. Jonas was an egomaniac who enjoyed having power over other people. He ran his "church" like a fiefdom. He would be incensed to have lost Lola and the baby, but there was really nothing he could do. At least not legally. Once the DNA results came back, once they had proof that Grace was Colt's daughter...

He tried to put it out of his head. Jonas was in the

hospital. He'd lied to the sheriff. It was over. Hopefully, the man would move on with some other obsession.

Colt cooked them breakfast while Lola fed Grace. He loved watching them together. It made his heart expand to near bursting.

Their day was quickly planned. First the DNA tests, then shopping for baby things. Never in his life had Colt thought about buying baby things, but now he realized he was excited. He wanted Grace to have whatever she needed.

At the doctor's office DNA samples were taken, then Colt took Lola and Grace to the small-box store on the edge of town. He was amazed at all the things a baby needed. Not just clothing and a car seat, but bottles and formula, baby food, diapers and wipes.

"How did babies survive before all of these things were on the market?" he joked, then insisted they get a changing table.

"It's too much," Lola said at one point.

"It's all good," he'd said, wanting only the best for his daughter. At the back of his mind, like a tiny devil perched on his shoulder, a voice was saying, "What are you doing? You are going back on assignment soon."

He shoved the thought aside, telling himself that he'd cross that bridge when he got there. He still had time. But time for what? There hadn't been any offers on the ranch. It was another thought that he pushed aside. Instead, he concentrated on Lola and Grace, enjoying being with them. Enjoying pretending at least for a while that they were a family.

He didn't even need the DNA test. That was all

Lola. "We need it for Jonas should he ever try to take Grace again," she'd said. "Also, I don't want you to have doubts."

"I don't have any doubts."

She'd given him a dubious look. "I want it settled. Not that I will ever ask anything of you. And I will pay you back for all the baby things you bought. I called this morning and am having some money wired to me."

"That isn't necessary."

But she said nothing, a stubborn tilt to her chin. He hadn't argued.

Instead, he took them back to the Stagecoach Saloon where, the moment they walked in, he knew that Billie Dee was cooking up her famous Texas chili.

Lillie Cahill Beaumont just happened to be there visiting her brother, along with Darby and his wife, Mariah. They oohed and aahed over Grace and Lola did the same with their babies.

By the time they got home, Colt was ready for a nap, too. After Lola put Grace down, she came into the bedroom and curled up against him. He held her close, breathing in the scent of her. He'd never been more happy.

# Chapter Fourteen

The next day, Jonas couldn't wait for the doctor to stop by so he could hopefully get out of the hospital. He knew that Zack was taking care of things on the complex, but he worried. He still couldn't believe that Rebecca would betray him. It shook the stable foundation that he'd built this life on. Never would he have suspected her of deceiving him.

When the doctor finally came by, he hadn't wanted to send Jonas home yet. It took a lot of lying to get the doctor to finally release him. It was late in the day before he finally got his discharge papers.

Elmer picked him up at the hospital and drove him to the compound. He liked Elmer, though he'd seen the man's faith in their work here fading. He and Lola's father had been friends. Jonas suspected Elmer only stayed because he had nowhere else to go. But that was all right. Jonas still thought that when the chips were down, he could depend on Elmer.

Once at the compound, Zack was waiting, Excusing Elmer, Jonas let Zack help him inside. He was weak and his head ached, but he was home. He had things that needed to be taken care of and had been going crazy in the hospital.

Three of the sisters entered his cabin, fussed over him until he couldn't take it any longer and sent them scurrying. The pain in his head was better. It was another pain that was riding him like a dark cloak on his shoulders.

As soon as he was settled, Jonas asked Zack to bring him Sister Rebecca. "She's still detained in the small cabin, right?"

"She is," Zack said.

"How is her…attitude?"

"Subdued."

Jonas almost laughed since it didn't seem like a word Zack would ever have used. "Subdued? Is she on anything?"

"No, but I've had the sisters chanting over her every few hours. I thought it was something you would have done yourself had you been here."

He was both touched and annoyed by Zack taking this step without his permission. But he needed Zack more than ever now so he let it go. "You did well. Thank you."

Zack beamed and Jonas saw something in the man's eyes that gave him pause. Zack wanted to lead SLS. The man actually thought he had what it took to do it. The realization was almost laughable.

"Bring Sister Rebecca to me," he said, and closed his eyes, his head pounding like a bass drum. He wondered if he shouldn't have put this off until he was feeling better.

Zack hurried out, leaving him peacefully alone with his thoughts. Lola had made a fool out of him by sleeping with Colt McCloud. To add to his embarrassment, she'd gotten pregnant. That child should have been his.

Instead, he'd put aside his hurt, his fury, his embarrassment and offered to raise the baby as his own. Still, she'd turned him down. How could she have humiliated him even more?

He let out a bark of a laugh. What had she done? She'd almost killed him—after giving him hope that she was weakening. The latter hurt the most. Offering hope was a poisonous pill that he'd swallowed in one big gulp. And now even his flock was turning against him.

Was he losing his mind faster than he'd thought? Could he trust his judgment?

He started at the knock on the door, forgetting for a moment that he'd been expecting it. "Come in."

The moment Rebecca walked through the door, he could see the guilt written all over her face. Brother Zack stood directly behind her. He started to step into the cabin, and Jonas could tell Zack thought he was going to get to watch this.

"That will be all, Zack."

The man looked surprised and then disappointed. But it was the flicker of anger he saw in Zack's eyes that caused concern.

Jonas watched his right-hand man slowly close the door, but he could tell he'd be standing outside hoping to hear whatever was going on. Was Zack now becoming a problem, too?

He saw Sister Rebecca quickly take him in. In her gaze

shone concern and something even more disturbing—
sympathy, if not pity. His head was still bandaged, dark
stitches under the dressing, but his headaches were getting better. Stuck in the hospital, he'd had plenty of time
to think over the past two days.

It was bad enough to be betrayed by Lola, even worse
by Sister Rebecca, because he'd come to depend on
her. She had to have known that Lola's baby had gone
missing. It would have been the first thing she would
have checked. Seeing the baby missing, she should have
come to him.

He was anxious to talk to her, but as he looked at
her standing there, he felt a loss of words for a moment.
He kept telling himself that he was wrong. Sister Rebecca had been with him for years. She wouldn't betray him. Couldn't. He'd always thought she was half
in love with him.

Which was probably why she hadn't come to him
to let him know the baby wasn't in her crib. Even if
she'd seen Lola with that bundle in her arms entering
his cabin, she should have come to him. If she had, his
head wouldn't be killing him right now. But he suspected Rebecca had wanted to be shed of Lola and the
baby he was so determined to make his.

Since Zack had locked up Rebecca, she would know
she was in trouble. He wondered what story she would
tell him and how much of it he could believe?

COLT ALMOST CHANGED his mind. Things had been going
so well that he didn't want or need the interruption.
He enjoyed being with Lola and Grace. If he said so

himself, he'd become proficient at diaper changes and getting chubby little limbs into onesies. He liked the middle-of-the-night feedings, holding Grace and watching her take her bottle. Her bright blue eyes watched him equally.

"I'm your daddy," he'd whispered last night, and felt a lump rise in his throat.

So when Julia had called and said it was important that they meet and talk, he hadn't been interested.

"If this is about you needing me to forgive you—"

"No. It's not that," she'd said quickly. "I doubt you can ever forgive me. I know how badly I hurt you."

Did she? The news had blindsided him. Hell, he'd been expecting her to pick him up at the airport—not break up with him to be with one of his friends. He still couldn't get his head around how that had gone down. No warning at all. He'd thought Wyatt hadn't even liked Julia. He knew that Darby didn't think she was right for him. Not that Darby had ever said anything. But Colt had been able to tell.

He could laugh now. He used to think that Darby just had his expectations set too high. But then Colt had met Mariah and realized that his friend had just been holding out for the real thing. Darby had done well.

"Julia, I can't see what meeting you for coffee could possibly—" It had been Lola who'd insisted he meet with Julia. She'd walked in while he was on the phone. As if gifted with ESP, she'd motioned to him that he should go.

"Fine," he'd said into the phone. "When and where?" He had just wanted to get it over with.

Now he drove past the coffee shop, telling himself that there was nothing Julia could say that would change anything. But she'd sounded…strange on the phone. He suspected something was up. Did he care, though?

He circled the block, saw a parking space and pulled his pickup in to it. For a moment he sat behind the wheel debating what he was about to do. And why had Lola been all for him seeing his ex? Was she worried that he wasn't over Julia? Or was she hoping to hook the two of them up again?

He'd heard her on the phone calling a car dealership to order a vehicle. "You don't have to do that. You can use my pickup whenever you want."

"I need my own car, but thank you," she'd said.

He thought of the discussion they'd had after he'd hung up from Julia.

"I knew that was Julia on the phone," Lola had said. "I wasn't eavesdropping. You talk to her in a certain way." She'd shrugged.

"A certain way?"

"I can't describe it, but you owe her nothing."

"Then why should I meet with her?"

"Because it won't be over until you tell her how you feel," Lola had said.

He had laughed. She made life seem so simple, and yet could her life have been any more complicated when he'd met her? "Okay, I'll meet with her with your blessing."

"You don't need my blessing."

He stepped to her and, taking her shoulders in his

hands, pulled her close. "All I care about is you and Grace. You have to know that."

"So you'll talk to her. You'll be honest. You'll see if there is anything there that you might have missed. Or that you want back."

He'd wanted to argue the point, but she'd put a finger to his lips.

"You should go. She'll be waiting."

Let her wait, he thought now as he glanced at his watch. Let her think he wasn't coming—look how she'd treated him at the Billings airport.

Then, just wanting to be done with this, he climbed out and walked down to the coffee shop. It was midafternoon. Only a few tables were taken. Julia had chosen one at the back. Where no one would see the two of them together and report back to Wyatt?

As he pushed open the door, he saw her frowning down at her phone. Checking the time? Or reading a text from Wyatt?

She looked up as if sensing him and motioned him over. "I got you a coffee—just the way you like it."

Except he'd never liked his coffee that way. Julia had come out to the ranch when they'd first started dating with some caramel-mocha concoction. When he'd taken a sip, he'd had to force a smile and pretend he'd liked it. His mistake.

"It's good, huh. I thought you'd like it. You always have the same boring coffee. I thought we'd shake things up a bit," she'd said. And from then on, she'd decided that was the way he liked his coffee.

"Thanks," he said now, without sitting down, "But

I never liked my coffee that way. I'll get my own." He moved to the counter and ordered a cup of black coffee before returning to the table.

She looked sullen, pouting like she used to when he'd displeased her—which was often enough that he knew this look too well.

"So what is it you want?" he asked as he sat down but didn't settle in. He didn't plan to stay long and was regretting coming here, no matter what Lola had said. He couldn't see how this could help anything.

Julia let out a nervous laugh. "This is not the way I saw this going."

"Oh?"

She seemed to regroup, drawing in a long breath, sitting up a little straighter. He was suddenly aware that she'd dressed up. He caught a hint of the perfume she used to wear when they were together because he'd commented one time that he liked it. He frowned as he realized she hadn't been wearing it the day they'd accidentally run into each other.

"What's going on, Julia?"

She looked away for a moment, biting down on the corner of her lower lip as if nervous. He used to think it was cute.

"I've made a terrible mistake. I didn't mean to blurt it out like that, but I can tell you're still angry and have no patience with me. Otherwise, you wouldn't have been so late, you would have drunk the coffee I ordered you and you wouldn't be looking at me as if you hated me."

He wasn't going to try to straighten her up on any of that. "Mistake?"

Julia looked at him as if she thought no one would be that daft. "Wyatt. I was just so lonely, and it looked as if you were never going to quit the military and come home…"

"How did you two get together? I always thought Wyatt didn't like you."

She mugged a face at him. "You don't need to be cruel."

"I'm serious. He never had a good word to say about you. Or was he just trying to keep his feelings for you from me?"

"I have no idea. And I don't care. He probably didn't like me. Maybe that's why we aren't together anymore."

Colt realized he wasn't surprised. Julia hadn't gotten him to the altar. He remembered that had been the case with an earlier boyfriend, too. Looked like there was a pattern there, he thought but kept it to himself.

"That's too bad."

"I can tell that you're really broken up over it."

After the initial shock had worn off, he'd actually thought Julia and Wyatt wouldn't last. Julia was beautiful in a classic way, but definitely high maintenance. He could see that clearly after being around Lola. As for Wyatt, well, he'd never had a serious girlfriend. He'd always preferred playing the field, as he called it.

"I'm sincerely sorry it didn't work out. Is that all?"

"Colt, stop being so mean." She sounded close to tears. She glanced around to make sure no one had heard her. "I feel so bad about what I did to you."

"You shouldn't." He realized he meant it. For a while,

he'd hoped she choked on the guilt daily. Now he didn't feel vindictive. He realized he no longer cared.

"I know how hurt you must be."

"I was hurt, Julia. That was one crushing blow you delivered, but I've moved on."

"With that woman you were with the other day? Are you in love with her?"

Now there was the question, wasn't it? "It's complicated."

"It doesn't have to be." She reached across the table and covered his hand.

He pulled his free. "Are you suggesting what I think you are?"

She looked at him as if to say, *No one can be this dense.* "I want you back. I'll do anything." She definitely sounded desperate.

Colt had played with this exact scheme in his mind on those long nights in the desert after she'd dumped him. It had been like a salve that made him feel better. Julia begging to come back to him. Him loving every minute of it before he turned her down flat.

Now it made him feel uncomfortable because he no longer wanted to hurt her. If anything, he felt indifferent and wondered what he'd ever seen in this woman. He couldn't help comparing her to Lola. Julia came up way short.

"Julia, you and I are never getting back together. Truthfully, I doubt we would have made it to the altar."

"How can you say that?" she demanded. "You asked me to marry you."

"I did. But I didn't realize then how wrong we were

for each other. I overlooked things, thinking they would change once we were married. Now I know better. I'm sure it was the same for you. Otherwise, how could you have fallen so quickly in love with another man?"

She seemed at a loss for words.

"So I imagine we both would have realized we weren't right for each other before we made a huge mistake."

Julia stared at him as if looking at a stranger. "I don't believe this."

Had she expected him to take her back at the snap of her fingers? The flutter of her eyelashes? She really hadn't known him. Even if he'd never met Lola, he wouldn't have taken Julia back. She'd proved the kind of woman she was—not the kind a man could ever trust.

Colt got to his feet. "You should try to work things out with Wyatt. Now that I think about it, you two belong together."

Her eyes widened, then narrowed dangerously. "Do you realize what you're throwing away? And for what? That…that…woman I saw you with the other day?" She made a distasteful face.

"Easy, Julia," he said, lowering his voice. "You really don't want to say anything about the mother of my child."

*"What?"* she sputtered.

"Lola and I have a beautiful daughter together."

Openmouthed, she stared at him. "Lola? That's not possible. You can't have known her long enough to… Are you going to *marry* her?"

"I haven't asked her yet, but you know me. I like to

take my time. Also, I'm a little gun-shy after my last engagement."

Julia pushed to her feet. He'd never seen her so angry. It made him want to laugh because he realized, with no small amount of relief, that had he married her, he would have seen her like this a lot.

The one thing he did know was that he was completely over her. No hard feelings. No need for retribution. No need to ever see this woman again.

"This never happened," she said with a flip of her head. "You hear me? You're right. Wyatt and I are perfect together. We're going to get married and be happy."

He smiled. "So you and Wyatt aren't broken up." He let out a bark of a laugh. "Good to see that you haven't changed. Give Wyatt my regards."

Julia stormed out. Colt finished his coffee and threw away the cups Julia had left behind. He smiled as he headed for the door. He couldn't wait to get home to Lola and Grace.

## Chapter Fifteen

Lola saw the change in Colt the moment he walked in the door. It was as if a weight had been lifted off his shoulders. He was smiling and seemed…happy.

"I guess I don't need to ask how it went." Her heart had been pounding ever since Julia's phone call. A woman knows. Julia wanted more than Colt's forgiveness. A woman like that would try to hold on to him, to keep him in the wings—if she didn't already want him back.

Colt met her gaze. "She wants me back."

It felt as if a fist had closed around her heart, but she fought not to let him see her pain. "That must seem like a dream come true."

He laughed. "I'll admit at one time it would have been. But no," he said with a shake of his head as he stepped to her. "It would never have happened even if I hadn't met you. But now that I have…" He leaned down to kiss her softly on the mouth. As he drew back, he saw that she was frowning.

"I don't want you giving up the woman you love because of me and Grace," she said quickly. "I told you. We can take care of ourselves."

"That wasn't what I meant." His blue-eyed gaze locked with hers and she felt a bolt of heat shoot to her core. "Julia is the last person on earth that I want."

She swallowed. "But you asked her to marry you."

"I did." He chuckled. "And I have no idea why I did. Honestly, I feel as if I dodged a bullet. But I don't want to talk about her. I want you," he said as he drew her close again. "Is Grace sleeping?"

While he'd been gone, Lola had practiced what she was going to say to him. But when she looked up into his blue gaze and saw the desire burning there, it ignited the blaze inside her.

She told herself that they could have a serious talk later. There was time. Colt was in such a good mood, she didn't want to bring him down. She cared too much about him. But that was the problem, wasn't it? She was falling in love with him. And that was why she and Grace had to leave before Colt did something stupid like ask her to stay.

LATER, AFTER MAKING LOVE and falling into a sated sleep, Colt heard Grace wake up from her nap and slipped out of bed to go see to her. "Hi, sweetheart," he said as he picked her up and carried her over to the changing table. As he changed her, he talked to her, telling her how pretty and sweet she was.

She was Lola in miniature, from her pert nose to her bow-shaped mouth to her violet eyes. And yet, he saw some of himself in the baby—and knew it might be only because he wanted it to be true. They hadn't gotten the DNA results, not that he was worried.

What bothered him was how much he wanted to see himself in Grace. How much he wanted to tell her about all the things he'd teach her as she grew up. What he wanted to do was talk about the future with Grace—and Lola.

Getting Lola's baby back was one thing, but seeing himself in this equation? He would have said the last thing he needed was a family. He was selling the ranch and going back into the service. That had been his plan and he'd always had a plan.

Now he felt rudderless and aloft, not knowing if he was up or down. What would he do if not go back to flying choppers for the Army? Ranch?

He stared into Grace's adorable face, feeling his heart ache at the thought of being away from her. He picked her up, holding her as he felt his heart pounding next to hers. Fatherhood had always been so far off in the future. But now here it was looking back at him with so much trust… He thought of his own father, his parents' disastrous marriage, how disconnected he'd felt from both of them.

He knew nothing about being a father or a husband. A part of him felt guilty for asking Julia to marry him. True, he'd put her off for years. It had come down to break up or marry her. He'd thought it was what he'd wanted.

Now, though, he knew his heart hadn't been in it. What he'd told Julia earlier had been true. He doubted they would have made it to the altar. After he'd put that diamond—she'd picked it out herself—on her finger, all she'd talked about was the big wedding they would have, the big house, the big life.

He'd let her talk, not really taking her seriously. He should have, though.

While Lola… Well, she was different. Her heart was so filled with love for their child that she'd risked her life numerous times. He'd never met anyone like her. And Grace… She smiled and cooed up at him, her gaze meeting his, and he felt her steal another piece of his heart if she hadn't already taken it all.

"Does she need changing?" Lola asked from the doorway.

"All taken care of. She just smiled at me."

Lola laughed. "I saw that." She'd been watching from the doorway, he realized. He wondered how long she'd been there. She was wearing one of his shirts and, he'd bet, nothing under it. She couldn't have looked sexier.

His cell phone rang. Lola moved to him to take the baby.

After pulling out his phone, Colt felt a start when he saw that it was Margaret Barnes, his Realtor, calling. He'd forgotten about her, about listing the ranch. All that seemed like ages ago.

"Hello?" he said as he headed out of the nursery.

"Colt, I have some good news for you. I have a buyer for your ranch."

For a moment he couldn't speak. He looked back at Lola and Grace from the doorway. Lola was rocking the baby in her arms, smiling down at her, and Grace was cooing and smiling up at her mother—just as she had done moments before with her father.

"Colt, are you there?"

"Yes." He saw Lola look up as if she heard something in his voice.

"You said to find a buyer as quickly as I could. If you have some time today, stop by my office. I can get the paperwork all ready. The buyer is fine with your asking price and would like to take possession as soon as possible."

He felt as if the earth was crumbling under his feet. Yes, he'd told her to find a buyer and as quickly as possible. But that had been before. Before Lola had shown up at his door in the middle of the night. Before he'd known about Grace.

"What is it?" Lola asked, seeing his distress as she joined him in the living room. "Bad news?"

He stood holding his phone after disconnecting. "That was the Realtor."

Lola hadn't asked about the for-sale sign on the road into the ranch and he hadn't brought it up. But Lola knew what his plans had been months ago. The night they'd met he'd told her he was going to accept another Army assignment rather than resign his commission, like he'd been planning before that night, to marry Julia.

"Does she have a buyer for the ranch?" Lola asked, giving nothing away.

He wasn't sure what kind of reaction he'd been expecting. His gaze went to Grace in her arms. He felt his heart breaking. Lately, his only concern had been protecting Lola, getting Grace back and making sure that horrible Jonas didn't have either of them.

He hadn't thought about the future. Hadn't let himself. "I think we should talk about—" His phone rang again. He checked it, hoping it was the Realtor calling again. He'd tell her he needed more time.

It was the doctor calling. He glanced at Lola and then picked up. "Doc?" he said into the phone.

"Your test results are back. You're welcome to come by and I would be happy to explain anything you didn't understand about DNA testing."

"Let's just cut to the chase, Doc."

Silence hung on the other end of the line for a long few moments. "The infant is a match for both Lola and you, Colt."

"Thanks, Doc." He looked to Lola, who didn't appear all that interested. Because she'd known all along.

"Are you all right?" she asked.

He nodded, but he wasn't. Grace had fallen back to sleep in her arms. Had there ever been a more beautiful, ethereal-looking child? No wonder Jonas had wanted her. Wanted her and Lola.

If he looked like a man in pain, he was. Lola and the baby had taken his already topsy-turvy life and given it a tailspin. All he'd wanted just days ago was to get out of this town, out of this state, out from under the ranch his father had left him and the responsibility that came with it.

Now, though, he no longer wanted to run. He wanted to plant roots. He wanted to make them a family. "I think we should get married." The words were out and he wasn't sorry to hear them. But he should have done something romantic, not just blurted them out like that.

To his surprise, Lola smiled at him. "That's sweet, but…it's too early, isn't it?"

Too early? Like in the morning or—

"We hardly know each other."

"I'd say we know each other quite well," he said as he picked up the tail end of his shirt she was wearing.

She laughed and playfully slapped his hand away as she headed for the spare room that they'd made into a makeshift nursery. "You know what I mean."

He followed her and watched as she put Grace down in the crib. "We have a daughter."

"Yes, we do. But we can't get married just for Grace. You know that wouldn't work."

"But neither can I let the two of you walk out that door," he said.

"Colt, that door will soon be someone else's."

She had a point.

"I won't sell the ranch."

She gave him a pointed look. "I owe you my life and Grace's. But I also owe you something else. Freedom. Grace and I can take care of ourselves now. Jonas is no longer a problem. He isn't going to bother us, not after the sheriff saw our daughter and knows that Jonas lied about keeping her from me. My parents set aside money for me should I ever need it and I saved the money I made teaching. Grace and I will be fine."

"But *I* won't be fine."

She looked at him, sympathy in her gaze.

"Lola, I need you. I need you and our daughter. I want us to be a family."

Tears welled in her eyes as she tried to pass him. "Colt."

He took her in his arms. "I know we haven't known each other long. But the night we met, we connected in a way that neither of us had before, right?" She nodded, though reluctantly it seemed. "And we've been through more than any couple can ever imagine, and yet we worked together and pulled it off against incredible odds. If any two people can make this work, it's you and me."

She smiled sweetly, but he could tell she wasn't convinced. "We're good together, I won't deny that. But, Colt, you don't want to ranch. You admitted that to me the first night we met. Now you're talking about keeping the ranch just to make a home for me and Grace? No, Colt. You would grow to resent us for tying you down. I see how your eyes light up when you talk about flying helicopters. That's what you love. That's where you need to be."

He wanted to argue, but he couldn't. She'd listened to him. She knew him better than even he knew himself. "Still—"

"No," she said as she moved down the hallway to the room that they now shared. She began to pick up her clothing. "This is best and we both know it."

It didn't feel like the best thing to do. He'd come to look forward to seeing Lola's face each morning, hear her singing to the baby at night and spending his days with the two of them.

"Promise you won't leave just yet," he said, panicking at the sight of her getting her things ready.

She stopped and looked at him. "I'll stay until the ranch closes so you can spend as much time with Grace as possible. But then we have to go."

"It isn't just Grace I want to spend time with," he said as he drew her close. He kissed her and told himself he'd figure out something. He had to. Because he couldn't bear the thought of either of them walking out of his life.

JONAS STUDIED THE woman before him, letting her wait. Sister Rebecca was what was known as a handsome woman. She stood almost six feet tall with straight brown hair cut chin-length. Close to his own age, she wasn't pretty, never had been. If anything, she was nondescript. You could pass her on the street and not see her.

That was one reason she'd worked out so well all these years. She didn't look dangerous. A person hardly noticed her. Until it was too late.

Studying her, Jonas admitted that he'd come to care very deeply for her. He had depended on her. Her betrayal cut him deeper even than Lola's. Fury gripped him like fingers around his throat.

Along with guilt, he saw something else in her face now. She knew that he knew what she'd done.

"Rebecca?"

She raised her gaze slowly. The moment she met his eyes, her face seemed to crumble. She rushed to him to fall to her knees in front of his chair. "Forgive me, Father," she said, head bowed. "Please forgive me."

He didn't speak for a moment, couldn't. "For almost getting me killed or for letting Lola get away with the baby?"

She raised her head again. While pleas for forgiveness had streamed from her mouth, there was no sign of regret in her eyes.

"You stupid, foolish woman," he said with disgust, and pushed her away.

She fell back, landing hard. He watched as she slowly got to her feet. Her dark eyes were hard, her smile brittle. Defiance burned behind her gaze, a blaze that he saw had been burning for some time. Why hadn't he seen it? Because he'd been so consumed with Lola for so long.

"I have done whatever you've asked of me for years," she said, anger making her words sharp as knives hurled at him.

"As you should, as one of my followers," he snapped.

She let out a humorous laugh that sent a chill up his spine. "I wasn't just one of your followers."

He felt for his phone and realized he'd left it over on the table, out of his reach. Zack had said he would be right outside the door. But would he be able to get in quickly enough if Rebecca attacked? Jonas knew he wasn't strong enough to fight her off. Rebecca probably knew it, too.

"Many times you were wrong, but still I did what you asked without question," she continued as she moved closer and closer until she was standing over him. "All these years, I've followed you, looked up to you, trusted that you were doing what was best for our community, best for me."

He swallowed, afraid he'd created a monster. If he was being honest, and now seemed like a good time for it, he'd let her think that one day the two of them would run SLS. He'd trusted her above all others, even Zack.

"You didn't sound the alarm when you found the crib empty," he said, trying to regain control and get the conversation back on safer ground.

She shook her head. "No, when I found Sister Amelia standing next to the empty crib, I told her to go back to bed and let me handle it. I thought about sounding the alarm, but then I didn't. In truth? I was overjoyed to see the brat gone, along with her mother."

"That wasn't your decision to make."

She smiled at that. "You would destroy everything for that woman? You would take her bastard and raise it as your own? I thought of you as a god, but now I see that you are nothing but a man with a man's weaknesses."

The truth pierced his heart and he instantly recoiled. "You will not speak to me like this or there will be serious consequences."

A chuckle seemed to rise deep in her, coming out on a rugged breath. "Will you have the sisters chant more over me? You've already locked me up. Or…" Her gaze was hard as the stone Lola had used to try to bash his head in. "Will you have me killed? It wouldn't be the first time you've had a follower killed, would it?"

The threat was clear in her gaze, in her words. Rebecca knew too much. She could never leave this compound alive, and they both knew it.

He grabbed for his phone, but she reached it first. She held the phone away from him, stepping back, daring him to try to take it from her.

"This is ridiculous, Sister Rebecca. You would throw away everything we have worked so hard for out of simple jealousy?"

She raised a brow, but when she spoke her voice betrayed how close she was to tears again. This was breaking her heart as much as his own. "I know you. After all these years, I know you better than you know yourself. You'll go after her and that baby. You'll have her one way or another even if it means destroying everything."

He stared at her, hearing the truth in her words and realizing that he'd let her get too close. She *did* know him.

She looked down at the phone in her hand, then up at him. She pushed the alarm. The air on the mountaintop filled with the scream of the siren.

When Zack burst through the door, she threw Jonas his phone and, with one final look, turned and let Zack take her roughly by the arm and lead her back to her prison.

She wouldn't be locked up there long, Jonas thought. He owed her that at least, he thought as he sounded the all clear signal. But things weren't all right at all and he feared they never would be again.

## Chapter Sixteen

Colt had been worried that the sheriff was right, that Jonas wasn't going to take what had happened lying down. Hearing that Jonas had been released from the hospital, he'd almost been expecting a visit from the SLS leader.

He'd been ready, a shotgun beside the door. But the day had passed without incident and so had the next and the next.

The days seemed to fly by since he'd signed the ranch papers and deposited a partial down payment from the buyer. He'd kept busy selling off the cattle and planning the auction for the farm equipment. He tried not to think about the liquidation of his father's legacy, telling himself his old man knew how much he hated ranching. It was his own fault for leaving Colt the ranch.

He was in the barn when he heard footfalls behind him and turned to see Lola. "So the buyer doesn't want any of this?" she asked.

"No, I believe he plans to subdivide the property. It won't be a ranch at all anymore."

"And the house?"

"Demo it and put in a rental probably."

Lola said nothing, but when he saw her looking out the barn door toward the mountains, there was a wistfulness to her he couldn't ignore.

"I'm not leaving Montana. This will always be my home. I'm just not ranching. With what I got from the sale, I can do anything I want." But that was it. He didn't know what he wanted. His heart pulled him one way, then another.

"How long has your family owned this property?" she asked.

"My great-grandfather homesteaded it," he said. "I know it must sound disrespectful of me to sell it."

She shook her head. "It's yours to do with whatever you want, right?"

"Yes." He didn't bother to tell her that the three-month stipulation his father had put on it was over. "You were right. I'm not a rancher. I have no interest."

"But you're a cowboy."

He laughed. "That I will always be. I'm as at home on a horse as I am behind the controls of a helicopter. Ranching is a different animal altogether. Most ranchers now lease their land and let someone else worry about the critters, the drought, the price of hay. Few of them move cattle on horseback. They ride four-wheelers. Everyone seems to think ranching is romantic." He laughed at that. "It's the most boring job I've ever done in my life."

"That's why you're selling," she said with a smile. "It's the right thing."

He hadn't needed her permission, but he was thankful for it. As much as he denied it, there was guilt over selling something his father had fought for years to keep.

Nor had he contacted the Army about his next assignment, putting that off, as well. He still had plenty of leave, so there was time.

He'd also put off his Realtor about when the new owners could take possession. It sounded as if they hoped to raze the house as soon as he moved out.

He knew he couldn't keep avoiding giving a firm date and time, but once that happened Lola and Grace would be gone.

"Where will you go?" he asked Lola.

"Probably back to California. At least for a while." The car she'd ordered had come, and she'd been able to get to her funds and make sure Jonas couldn't access them. She'd had to get a new driver's license since Jonas had taken her purse with hers inside, along with her passport and checkbook and credit cards.

Colt had heard her on the phone taking care of all that. No wonder he could feel the days slipping away until not only this ranch and the house he'd grown up in were gone, but also Lola and the baby. He worried that once he went back to the Army, this would feel like nothing more than a dream.

Yet, he knew that he would ache for Lola and Grace the rest of his life—if he let them get away. He'd always see their faces and yearn for them.

He'd never felt so confused in his life. What would he do if not go back to the Army? He was almost thirty-three. He couldn't retire even if he wanted to, which he didn't. He wanted to fly. But he couldn't ask Lola and Grace to wait for him for the next two to five years. He couldn't bear the thought of her worrying about him, or the worst happening and him never making it back.

His cell phone rang. Margaret again. "I'd better take this," he said to Lola. As she walked back toward the house, he picked up. "Margaret, I might have changed my mind."

Silence. "It's too late for that and you know it. Colt, what is this about?"

*A woman and a child. The rest of my life. Regrets.*

"If you're having second thoughts about selling the ranch—"

"I'm not. I just need a little more time to get off the property."

More silence. "I'll see what I can do but, Colt, they are getting very impatient. I need to tell these buyers something concrete. I can't keep putting them off or they are going to change their minds or fine you, which they can under the contract you signed." She sounded angry. He couldn't blame her.

As he looked out at the land, he had a thought. "I'll be in first thing in the morning."

"What does that mean?" she asked after a moment.

"I have an idea."

She groaned. "Could you be a touch more specific?"

"I'm selling the ranch, but there's something I need."

"Okay," she said slowly. "Why don't we sit down with them in the morning, if you're sure you won't change your mind."

He pocketed his phone and watched Lola as she

slipped in the back door of the house. Taking off his Stetson, he wiped the sweat from his brow with his sleeve. "Do something," he said to himself. "Do something before it's too late."

"SHE'S STAYING ON the ranch with Colt McCloud," Zack told Jonas later that afternoon.

"Is the baby with them?"

"I've had the place watched as you ordered. They took the baby into town the next morning, bought baby clothes and supplies, and returned to the ranch."

So they were settling in. They thought it was over. "What kind of security?"

"No security system on the house. But I would imagine he has guns and knows how to use them since he's a major in the Army."

"I'm sure he does." That's why they would strike when the cowboy least expected it. He looked past Zack toward the main building below him on the hill. "You led church this morning?"

He nodded.

"What is the mood?"

Zack seemed to consider that. "Quite a few of them are upset over Sister Rebecca."

He'd suspected as much. "I'll lead the service tonight." Zack didn't appear to think that was going to make a difference. Jonas thought about the things that Rebecca had said and ground his teeth. He still had a headache, and while his wound was healing, it was a constant reminder of what Lola had done to him. Worse, she'd bewitched him, put a spell on him as if sent by the devil to bring him down.

Did he really want her back, or did he just want to retaliate? Did it matter in the long run? His memory was getting worse. The pills didn't seem to be working. He couldn't be sure how long he had until he was a blubbering old fool locked up in some rest home.

He shook his head. He wasn't going out that way. "I don't want Lola or the baby injured."

"What about McCloud?"

"Kill him and dispose of his body. I know the perfect place. If possible, leave no evidence that we were there."

COLT LEFT THE barn headed for the house, suddenly excited that his idea just might be the perfect plan. "Lola?" he cried as he burst through the back door.

"Colt?" She was standing in the kitchen wearing an apron that had belonged to his mother. He hadn't seen it in years. She must have found it in a drawer he and his father had obviously never bothered to look in.

"What?" she asked, seeing the way he was looking at her.

"You look so cute in that apron, that's all." He stepped to her. "I'm selling the ranch."

"I know."

"You were right. I'd make a terrible rancher, always did. This was my father's dream, not mine. I'm a helicopter pilot."

She nodded. "I thought we already knew this. So you're going to take the commission the Army is offering you."

"No."

She tilted her head. "No?"

"No," he said, smiling. "For years, my friend Tommy and I have talked about starting our own helicopter service here in the state. We're good at what we do. With the money from the ranch, I can invest in the birds we'll need."

"That sounds right up your alley. But are you sure?"

He nodded. "Come here." He put his arm around her waist and ushered her over to the window. "Look out there. See that."

"Yes? That mountainside?"

"Imagine a house in that grove of aspens and pines. The view from there is incredible. Now imagine an office down by the road and a helipad. The office would be just a hop, skip and a jump from the house. We'd have everything we need for Grace and any other children we have."

LOLA SMILED AT HIM, caught up in his enthusiasm. "Isn't that land part of the ranch?"

He grinned. "I'm going to buy it back."

"Aren't you being a little impulsive?"

"Not at all. I've been thinking about this for years." He seemed to see what she meant and turned her to face him. "And I've been thinking about being with you since that first night. With you and Grace here... Lola, I've fallen for you and Grace..." He shook his head. "It was love at first sight even before I knew for certain that Grace was mine. I want you to stay. I want us to be a family."

"Colt, do you know what you're saying?" But it was

what he wasn't saying that had her stomach in knots. She knew he wanted her and Grace, but she wouldn't let herself go into a loveless marriage just to give her daughter a home.

She said as much to him.

He stared at her. "Damn it, Lola, I love you."

She blinked in surprise. All their lovemaking, their quiet times together, those moments with Grace. She'd waited to hear those words. Well, maybe not the "damn it, Lola" part. But definitely the "I love you" part. Her heart had assured her that he loved her and Grace. And yet, she wouldn't let herself believe it was true until he finally told her.

"I love you," he repeated as if they were the most honest words he'd ever spoken. "I've only said those words twice to a woman. With Julia, it was over two years before I said them. I don't think it was a coincidence that I held off. With you… I've been wanting to say them for days now."

"Oh, Colt, I've been waiting to hear them. I love you, too."

He reached into his pocket and pulled out a small velvet box.

Lola gave a small gasp.

"This ring was handed down from my great-great-grandmother to my great-grandmother to my grandmother. When my grandmother gave it to me, she made me promise only to give it to a woman who was my equal." He opened the box.

She looked down at a beautiful thick gold band circled in diamonds. "Oh, Colt." Her gaze went to his. "I don't understand. Julia—"

"I didn't give it to her."

"Why?"

He shrugged. "I don't know. It didn't seem…right for her. She picked out one she liked uptown."

Her heart went out to him. Julia had hurt him badly in so many ways, only proving how wrong she was for him almost from the start.

"Now I realize that I was saving this ring so I could live up to the promise I made my grandmother," he said. "I want you to wear it." He dropped to one knee. "Will you marry me, Lola Dayton, and be my wife and the mother to my children?"

She smiled through the burn of tears. "Yes."

He slipped the ring on her finger. It fit perfectly. "Now what is the chance of that?" he said to her, only making her cry and laugh at the same time.

Swinging her up into his arms, he spun her around and set her down gently. "For the first time in so long, I am excited about the future."

She could see that he'd been dragged down by the ranch, Julia and the past, as well as his need to do what he did so well—fly.

Colt kissed her softly on the mouth. She felt heat rush through her and, cupping his face in her hands, kissed him with the passion the man evoked in her.

He swung her up in his arms again, only this time he didn't put her down until they reached the bedroom.

THAT EVENING, JONAS held church in the main building. He'd gathered them all together to give them the news.

He could feel the tension in the air. There'd been a time when he'd stood up here and felt as if he really was a god sent to this earth to lead desperate people looking for at least peace, if not salvation.

As he looked over his flock, though, all he felt was sad. His father used to say that all good things end. In this case, the preacher was right.

"Brothers and sisters. I have some sad news. As you know, Sister Rebecca has chosen to leave us. It is with a heavy heart that I had to let her go." He wondered how many of them knew the truth. Too many of them probably. He was glad he'd had Zack bury her far away from the compound.

"But that isn't the only news. I have decided that it is time to leave Montana." His words were followed by a murmur of concern that spread through his congregation. "As many of you know, I'm in poor health. My heart... I'm going to have to step down as your leader."

The murmurs rose. One woman called out, "What's to become of us?"

He'd bilked them out of all their money. A lot of them were old enough now that they would have a hard time getting a job. He didn't need this crowd turning on him as Sister Rebecca had.

"Brother Zack will be taking those who want to go to property I've purchased in Arizona. It's farmable land, so you can maintain a life there. Each of you will be given a check to help with your expenses."

The murmur in the main building grew louder. "If you have any questions, please give those to Brother Zack. I trust him to make sure that each and every one of you will be taken care of." That quieted them down, either because they were assured or because they knew how Zack had taken care of other parishioners who'd became troublesome.

"It is with a heavy heart that I must step down, but I know that you all will be fine. You will leave tomorrow. Go with Godspeed." He turned and walked away, anxious to get back to his cabin and pack. The sale of his property would be enough to pay off his followers—not that he would be around to hear any complaints after tonight.

He rang for Zack. Since he'd told Zack of his plan, the man had been more than excited. Jonas had recognized that frenzied look in Zack's eyes. He'd seen it in his own. Zack would be Father Zack. God help his followers.

"I need you to pick about six brothers and a few sisters for a special mission," he told Zack. It would be one of their last missions under him.

Zack nodded, clearly understanding that he needed to pick those who would still kill for their leader.

"Make sure one of them is Brother Elmer."

"Are you sure? I mean—"

"Already questioning my authority?" he asked with a chuckle.

"No, of course not."

"Good. I have my reasons."

"I'll get right on it," Zack said, and left him alone.

Jonas looked around the cabin. He'd had such hopes when he'd moved his flock to Montana. He couldn't get maudlin now. He had to think about his future. He stepped to the safe he had hidden in the wall, opened it and took out the large case he kept there full of cash and his passport. Next to it was Lola's purse.

He took that out, as well, and thumbed through it even though he knew exactly what was in it since he'd often looked through it. He liked touching her things. He found her passport. Good, it was up-to-date. He'd deal with getting the baby out of the country when it came time.

After putting Lola's passport beside his own into his case, he closed the safe. There was nothing keeping him here after tonight. He would have everything he'd ever dreamed of, including a small fortune waiting in foreign banks across the world.

He thought of his father, wishing he could see him now. "Go ahead, say it. You were right about me, you arrogant old sanctimonious fool. I was your worst nightmare and so much more. But you haven't seen anything yet."

# Chapter Seventeen

Colt woke to the sound of both outside doors bursting open. The sudden noise woke the baby. Grace began to cry in the room down the hall. Lola stirred next to him and Colt, realizing what was happening, grabbed for his gun in the nightstand next to him.

Moments before he had lain in bed, with Lola beside him.

They were on him before he could draw the gun. They swept into the room, both men and women. Colt fought off the first couple of men, but a blow to the back of his head sent him to the floor and then they were on him, binding his hands behind him, gagging him, trussing his ankles and dragging him out of the house.

He tried to see Lola, but there was a group of women around her, helping her dress. In the baby's room, he heard Grace quiet and knew they had her, as well.

The strike had been so swift, so organized, that Colt realized he'd underestimated Zack—the only ex-military man in SLS. Clearly he had more experience at these kinds of maneuvers than Colt had thought.

Still stunned from the blow to his head, he was half carried, half dragged to a waiting van.

"Take care of him, Brother Elmer," he heard Zack say, the threat clear in the man's tone. Zack must have known that Brother Elmer was a weak link. "Brother Carl will go with you to make sure the job is done properly."

The van door slammed. Elmer started the engine and pulled away. The whole operation had taken less than ten minutes.

"DON'T HURT HIM!" Lola had cried as Colt was being dragged from the bedroom. Three women blocked her way to keep her from going after the men.

"Dress!" Sister Caroline ordered.

"My baby?"

"Grace will be safe as long as you do what we ask," Sister Amelia said. But there was something in Amelia's tone, a sadness that said not even she believed it.

Lola had no choice. They had Colt. They had Grace. She dressed quickly in a blouse and jeans, pulled on her sneakers and let the women lead her outside to a waiting van.

Sister Shelly was already in the van and holding Grace.

"Let me hold her," Lola said, steel in her voice.

The women looked at one another.

"Give the baby to Lola," Sister Amelia said and Shelly complied.

She sat holding the now-fussing Grace as the van pulled away. "Where are they taking Colt?"

No one answered. Her heart fell. Hadn't she feared that Jonas would retaliate? He'd be humiliated and would have to strike back. Isn't that what the sheriff had warned them about?

But what could he hope to achieve by this? The sheriff would know who took them. The first place Flint Cahill would look was the compound.

She remembered something she'd overheard while a prisoner at SLS. Some of the women had been worried that Jonas wasn't himself, that his memory seemed to be failing him. He often called them by the wrong names, got lost in the middle of a sermon. They questioned in hushed voices if it was his heart or something else, since they'd seem him taking pills for it.

"What is going on?" Lola asked, sensing something different about the group of women.

"We're leaving Montana," Sister Amelia said, and the other sisters tried to hush her. "She'll know soon enough," Amelia argued. "Father Jonas announced it earlier. He's selling the land here. Some are going to a new home in Arizona. Others…" Her voice broke. "I don't know where they're going."

Lola realized that their leader wasn't here. "Where is Sister Rebecca?" The question was met with silence. "Amelia?"

"She's gone."

"Everyone is leaving," Sister Shelly said, sounding near tears. "Father Jonas… He's letting Brother Zack lead the group in Arizona. He will be Father Zack now."

Lola couldn't believe what she was hearing as the van reached the highway and headed toward the compound. "He's putting Zack in charge?" She knew that the women in this van must feel the same way she did about Zack. "Did Jonas say what he is planning to do?"

Silence. Lola hugged Grace to her, her fear mounting with each passing mile as the van turned onto the road up to the mountain. Lola saw no other taillights ahead. No headlights behind them. Where had they taken Colt?

COLT COULDN'T SEE OUT, but he could tell that Elmer and Carl weren't taking him to the compound. He had a pretty good idea what their orders had been when Zack had told Elmer to take care of him.

He was furious with himself. He'd thought Jonas would have no choice but to give up. He should have known better. He should have taken more precautions. Against so many, he knew he and Lola hadn't stood a chance.

When they'd gone to the compound and rescued Grace, he'd thought this could be settled without bloodshed. It was why he hadn't taken a gun to the compound the first time that night. He didn't want to kill one of Jonas's sheep. They were just following orders, though blindly, true enough. But he hadn't wanted trouble with the law.

Now, though, he saw there was no way out of this. Jonas had taken Lola and Grace. Nothing was going to stop him. He was going to end this once and for all no matter whom he had to kill.

Colt rolled to his side. They'd bound his wrists with plastic ties. He worked to slip his hands under him. If he could get a foot into the cuffs, he knew he could break free.

As he did, he watched the men in the front seat. Neither turned around to check on him. He got the feeling they didn't like being awakened in the middle of the night for this any more than Colt had. And now they had been ordered to kill someone. They had to be questioning Jonas and the SLS. He already knew that Brother Elmer had a weak spot for Lola and her baby.

He managed to get his hands past his butt. He lay on his back, catching his breath for a moment before he pushed himself up. Once he had his hands in front of him…

The van slowed. Elmer shifted down and turned onto a bumpy road that jarred every muscle in Colt's body. Colt caught a glimpse of something out the back window and realized where they were taking him. The old gravel pits outside of Gilt Edge. He caught the scent of the water through the partially opened windows up front. It was the perfect place to dump a body. Weighted down, there was a good chance the remains would never be found.

He felt his heart pound as he worked to free his wrists. The plastic restraints popped—but not louder than the rattle of the van on the rough road. Colt went to work on the ones binding his ankles.

As the van came to a stop, he resumed his original position, his hands behind him, feet together as he lay on his side facing the door.

Both men got out. He waited, wondering if either

of them was armed or if the plan had been simply to drown him.

The van door opened noisily. "Can you get him out?" Elmer asked his companion.

Carl grunted but reached for him.

Colt swung his feet around and kicked the man in the chest, sending Carl sprawling in the dirt. He followed with a quick jab to Elmer's jaw. The older man stumbled and sat down hard on the ground.

So far, Colt hadn't seen a weapon, but as he jumped out, he saw Carl fumbling for something behind him. The man came up with a pistol. Right away, Colt saw that he wasn't comfortable using it. But that didn't mean that Carl wouldn't get lucky and blow Colt's head off.

He rushed around the back of the van to the driver's side. Grabbing open the door, he leaped in and started the van. As he threw the engine into Reverse, he saw Carl trying to get a clear shot. Elmer had stumbled to his feet and was blocking Carl's way—either accidentally or on purpose.

Colt didn't try to figure out which as he hit the gas. The van shot back. He cranked the wheel hard, swinging the back end toward the two men.

Carl got off two shots. One bullet shattered the back window of the van. The other took out Colt's side window, showering him with glass, and just missing his head before burying itself in the passenger-side door.

Elmer had parked the van close to the edge of the gravel pit, no doubt to make unloading his body easier.

As Colt swung the van at the two men, they tried to move out of the way. But Elmer was old and lost his footing. He was the first to go tumbling down the steep embankment and splash into the cold, clear water.

Carl had been busy trying to hit his target with the gun so he was caught unaware when the back of the van hit him and knocked him backward into the gravel pit. He let out a yell as he fell, the sound dying off in a loud splash.

Colt shifted into first gear and tore off down the bumpy road, thankful to be alive. He hoped both men could swim. If so, they had a long swim across the pit to where they would be able to climb out.

If either of their cell phones still worked after that, they might be able to warn Jonas. Not that it would matter.

Colt sped toward his house to get what he needed. This time he was taking weapons—and no prisoners.

FOR LOLA, WALKING into Jonas's cabin with the bundle in her arms felt a little like déjà vu. Only this time, there was a precious sleeping baby instead of rocks in her arms. As she entered, propelled by Brother Zack, she told herself that she would die protecting her daughter. Did Jonas know that, as well?

"Leave her," Jonas ordered. Zack started to argue, but one look at their leader and he left, saying he would be right outside the door if he was needed. The sisters scattered, and the door closed, leaving Lola and Grace alone with Jonas.

He still had a bandage on the side of his head, but she knew better than to think his injury might slow him down.

"You are a very difficult woman."

"Only when someone tries to force me into doing something I don't want to do or they take my child from me."

He glanced at the bundle in her arms. "May I see her?"

Lola didn't move. "What do you hope to get out of this?" she demanded.

"I thought I was clear from the beginning. I want you. It's what your parents wanted—"

"I don't believe that. I heard from my father before he…died. He wanted out of SLS. He was trying to convince my mother to leave. I believe that's why you killed them both."

Jonas shook his head. "Are we back to that?"

"You're a fraud. This is no church. And you are no god. All this is only about your ego. It's a bad joke."

"Are you purposely trying to rile me?"

"I thought maybe it was time you heard the truth from someone instead of Sister Rebecca telling you how wonderful you are."

"Sister Rebecca is no longer with us."

"So I heard. Did you kill her yourself or make one of your sheep do it?" She knew he could not let Rebecca simply walk away. She'd been with him from the beginning. She'd done things for him, knew things.

"Why do you torment me? I cared about Rebecca."

"And yet you had her killed. I don't like the way you care about people."

At the sound of vehicles and activity on the mountain below them, Lola moved cautiously to the window, careful not to turn her back on Jonas.

She frowned as she saw everyone appearing to be packing up and moving. Fear coursed through her. "What's going on? I thought they weren't leaving until tomorrow?"

"Our time in Montana has come to an end. We are abandoning our church here."

What Amelia had told her was true. "So they're scurrying away like rats fleeing a sinking ship. You're really going to let them go?"

"All good things must end."

She thought of Colt as she had on the ride to the compound. Something told her that he hadn't been brought here. "Where is Colt?"

Jonas shook his head. "As I said, all good things must end."

Tears burned her eyes. "If you hurt him—"

'What will you do? Kill me? They will put you in prison, take away your baby. No, it is time you realized that you have never been in control. You are mine. You will always be mine. I will go to any lengths, including having Grace taken away so you never see her again if that's what it takes to keep you with me."

Fear turned her blood to ice as she looked into his eyes and understood he wasn't bluffing.

"You have only one choice. Come with me willingly and Grace will join us once we are settled."

*No*, she screamed silently. She didn't trust this man. But she also knew she couldn't keep someone like Zack from ripping Grace from her arms. Just as she knew that Jonas wasn't making an empty threat. She'd known this man was dangerous, but she hadn't realized how much he was willing to give up to have her—and Grace.

"You have only a few minutes to make up your mind, Lola." He had his phone in his hand. "Once I push this button, Zack will take Grace. If you ever want to see her again, you will agree to go with me."

"Where?" She knew she was stalling, fighting to find a way out of this. Colt. If he was dead, did she care what happened to her as long as she had his baby with her?

"Europe, South America. I haven't decided yet. Somewhere far away from all this. I have money. We will live well. We will be a family."

She thought of the family Colt had promised her and felt the ring on her finger.

Jonas's gaze went to her left hand. His face contorted in anger. "Take that off. Take that off now!"

## Chapter Eighteen

Colt dialed the number quickly, knowing he had no choice even if he ended up behind bars. It would be worth it as long as Lola and Grace were safe from Jonas Emanuel once and for all.

"I need to borrow a helicopter," he said, the moment his friend answered.

"Mind if I ask what for?" Tommy Garrett asked, sounding like a man dragged from sleep in the wee hours of the morning. Tommy worked as a helicopter mechanic outside of Great Falls. Colt had served with him in Afghanistan and trusted the man with his life— and Lola's and Grace's.

"A madman has the woman I love and my baby daughter."

There was a beat of silence before Tommy said, "You planning to do this alone?"

"Better that way. I'll leave you out of it."

"Like hell. Tell me where you are. Outside my shop I have a Bell UH-1 Huey that needs its shakedown. The old workhorse is being used to fight forest fires. I'm on my way."

Colt knew the Huey could do up to 120 mph. But a safe cruising speed for helicopters was around a hundred. Without having to deal with traffic, road speeds or winding highways, the response time in a helicopter was considerably faster than anything on the ground. It was one reason Colt loved flying them.

So he wasn't surprised when Tommy landed in the pasture next to Colt's house thirty minutes later. The sun was coming up, chasing away the last of the dark. He could make out the mountains in the distance. Within a matter of minutes, they would be at the compound. He tried not think about what they would find.

"How much trouble is this going to get you in?" Colt asked his friend as he loaded the weapons in the back and climbed into the left seat, the crew chief seat.

"You just worry about what happens when we put this bird down," Tommy said in the adjacent seat at the controls.

As they headed for the mountaintop in the distance, Colt told him everything that had happened from that moment in the hotel in Billings to earlier that night.

When he finished, Tommy said, "So this woman is the one?"

For a moment, Colt could only nod around the lump in this throat. "I've never met anyone like her."

"Apparently this cult leader hasn't, either. Tell me you have a plan." He swore when Colt didn't answer right away.

"There will be armed guards who are under the control of the cult leader, Jonas Emanuel. But we don't have time to sneak up on them. You don't have to land. Just get close enough to the ground that I can jump," Colt said as he began to strap on one of the weapons he'd brought. "Did I mention that these people are like zombies?"

"Great, you know how I love zombies. Except you can't kill zombies."

"These are religious zealots. I suspect they will be as hard to kill as zombies."

"This just keeps getting better and better," Tommy joked.

Colt looked over at him. "Thank you."

"Thank me after we get out with this woman you've fallen in love with and your daughter." He shook his head. "You never did anything like normal people."

"No, I never did. There's the road that goes up to the compound."

Tommy swooped down, skimming just over the tops of the pines, and Colt saw something he hadn't expected.

"What the hell?" As they got closer to the mountain, Colt spotted the line of vans coming off the mountain. He felt a chill. "Something's going on. Fly closer to those vehicles," he said to Tommy, who immediately dipped down.

Inside the vans, he saw the faces of Jonas followers. There were a dozen vans. As each passed, he saw the pale faces, the fear in their eyes.

"Where do you think they're going?" Tommy asked.

"I have no idea. Leaving for good, from the looks of

it. What is Jonas up to? Are these people decoys or are they really clearing out?" He thought of Lola and the baby. How crazy was Jonas? Would he kill them and then kill himself, determined that Colt would never have either of them?

"Up there," Colt said, pointing to the mountain-top. Tommy swung the helicopter in the direction he pointed. Within a few minutes, the buildings came into sight. Colt didn't see any guards. He didn't see anyone. The place looked deserted. Had everyone left?

Not everyone, he noticed. There was a large black SUV sitting in front of Jonas's cabin.

"Think you can put her into that clearing in front of the cabin?"

"Seriously?" Tommy said. "You forget who you're talking to. Give me a dime and I can set her down on it." Colt chuckled because he knew it was true.

LOLA LOOKED DOWN at the antique ring that Colt had put on her finger. She swore she would never take it off. It felt so right on her finger. Colt felt so right.

Jonas moved faster than she thought he could after his injury. He grabbed the baby from her arms and shoved her. She fell back, coming down hard on the floor. "I told you to take if off. Now!"

"Give me Grace."

"Her name is Angel, and if you don't do what I say this moment…"

Lola pulled off the ring. She knew it was silly. Colt was probably dead. She'd lost so much. What did a ring matter at this point? The one thing she couldn't lose was Grace, and yet she felt as if she already had in more ways than one. Jonas had them captive. He could do whatever he wanted with Grace. Just as he could do whatever he wanted with her now.

"Happy?" she asked, still clutching the ring in her fist.

"Throw it away." He pointed toward the fireplace and the cold ashes filling it.

She hesitated again.

"Do as I say!" Jonas bellowed at her, waking up Grace. The baby began to cry.

Lola tossed the ring toward the fireplace. It was a lazy, bad throw, one that made Jonas's already furious face cloud over even more. The ring missed the fireplace opening, pinged off the rock and rolled under the couch. She looked at Jonas. If he really did have a bad heart, she realized his agitation right now could kill him. She doubted she would get that lucky, though.

He seemed to be trying to calm down. Grace kept crying and she could tell it was getting on his nerves.

She got to her feet. "Let me have her. She'll quit crying for me."

He shook his head. "I'm not sure I can trust you," he said slowly.

Colt was gone. The ring was gone. But Jonas had something much more precious. He had Grace. But Lola wasn't giving up.

"How do I know I can trust *you*?" she said.

The question surprised him. He'd expected her to cower, to promise him anything. She knew better than to do that. Jonas was surrounded by people who bowed down to him. Lola never had and maybe that's why he was so determined to have her.

She approached him. "You hurt my baby and I will kill you. I'll cut your throat in your sleep. Or push you down a flight of stairs. Or poison your food. It might take me a while to get the opportunity, but believe me, I will do it."

He chuckled as his gaze met hers. "I do believe you. I've always loved your spirit. Your mother told me what a headstrong young woman you were. She wasn't wrong."

It hurt to have him mention her mother. Was it possible that Jonas could get away with the murders he'd committed? She feared it was. She thought of Colt and felt a sob rise in her throat. She forced it back down. She couldn't show weakness, not now, especially not for Colt. She had to think about Grace.

"We seem to be at an impasse," Jonas said. "What do you suggest we do?"

"I suggest you give me my baby and let me leave here."

He shook his head. "Not happening. Neither you or your baby will be leaving here—except with me."

"So what are you waiting for?" she demanded.

Jonas chuckled as he tilted his head as if to listen. "We're waiting for Colt. I just have a feeling he will somehow manage to try to save you one more time."

Lola listened as her heart thumped against her rib cage. Colt? He was alive? She thought she heard what sounded like a helicopter headed this way.

"I believe that's him now."

COLT FOUGHT THE bad feeling that had settled in the pit of his stomach. Jonas was playing hardball this time. He wasn't going to let Lola and Grace go—not without a fight to the death. That's if they were still alive.

"Change of plans," he said to Tommy. He felt as if time was running out for Lola and Grace. "Put us down and wait for me," he said, fear making his voice sound strained as he passed Tommy a handgun. "I hope you won't have to use this. It appears that the guards have left, but I've already underestimated Jonas once and I don't want to do it again. I'm hoping this won't take long."

As Colt started to jump out, Tommy grabbed his sleeve. "Be careful."

Colt nodded. "You, too."

"I'll be here. Good luck."

Colt knew that if there was anyone he wanted on his side in a war it was Tommy Garrett—and this was war. These soldiers would die for their leader. They were just as devoted to dying for their cause as the ones he'd fought in Afghanistan.

The moment the chopper touched the ground, he leaped out and ran up the mountainside to where a large black SUV sat, the engine running and Brother Zack behind the wheel. Behind him, he heard Tommy shut down the engine. The rotors began to slow.

Colt looked around. The only person he'd seen so far was Zack, but that didn't mean that another of the guards hadn't stayed behind.

As he approached the SUV, he could hear the bass coming from the stereo. Closer, he saw that Zack had on headphones and was rockin' out. He must have had the stereo cranked, which explained why he hadn't heard the helicopter land. Nor had he heard him approach.

Colt yanked open the door. A surprised Zack turned. Colt grabbed him by his shirt and hauled him out. Unfortunately, Zack was carrying and he went for his gun. Zack was strong and combat trained. But Colt was fighting for Lola's and Grace's lives.

Colt managed to get hold of the man's arm, twisting it to the point of snapping as they struggled for the weapon. When the shot went off, it was muffled— just like Zack's grunt. Blood blossomed on the front of Zack's white shirt. The gun dropped, falling under the SUV.

As the man slumped, Colt shoved him back inside the vehicle, shut off the stereo and slammed the door before turning to Jonas's cabin. He'd seen suitcases in the back of the SUV and suspected the sheep weren't the only ones fleeing.

Colt pulled his holstered gun and climbed the steps. He had another gun stuck in the back of his jeans under his jacket. He always liked to be prepared— especially against someone like Jonas Emanuel.

He could still hear the sweep of the helicopter's rotors as they continued to slow. The wooden porch floor creaked under his boots. He braced himself and reached for the doorknob.

Before he could turn it, Lola opened the door. Her face had lost all its color. Her violet eyes appeared huge. He could see that she'd been crying. The sight froze him in place for moment. What had Jonas done to her? To Grace?

"Where is Jonas?" Colt asked quietly. Suddenly there wasn't a sound, not even a meadowlark from the grass or a breeze moaning in the pines. The eerie quiet sent a chill up his spine. "Lola?" The word came in a whisper.

"I'm leaving with Jonas," she said.

"Like hell." He could see that Jonas had put the fear into her and used Grace to do it. He'd never wanted to strangle anyone with his bare hands more than he did the cult leader at this moment.

"Please, it's what I want." Her words said one thing; her blue eyes pleaded with him to save Grace.

He pushed past her to find Jonas sitting in a chair just yards away. He was holding Grace in such a way that it stopped Colt cold.

JONAS RELISHED THE expression on Colt's handsome face. It almost made everything worth what he was going to have to give up. The cowboy thought he could just bust in here and take Lola and the baby? Not this time.

"Lola is going with me and so is her baby," he said as he turned the baby so she was facing her biological father and dangling from his fingers. He wanted Colt to see the baby's face and realize what he would be risking if he didn't back off.

"I don't think so," Colt said, but without much conviction. Jonas was ready to throw the baby against the rock fireplace if Colt took another step. The cowboy wasn't stupid. He'd figured that out right away. But he'd been stupid enough to come up here again. The man should have been dead.

Idly, Jonas wondered what had gone wrong at the gravel pit. He'd known he couldn't depend on Elmer, but he was disposable. Brother Carl had inspired more faith that he would get the job done. Jonas had assumed that Carl would have to kill both Elmer and Colt. Clearly, the job had been too much for him.

"Has he hurt you?" Colt asked Lola.

She shook her head.

Jonas was touched by the cowboy's concern, but quickly getting bored with all this. "Elmer and Carl?" he asked, curious.

"Swimming, that is, if either of them knows how," Colt answered.

"And Brother Zack?"

"No longer listening to music in your big SUV."

So he couldn't depend on Zack to come to his rescue. Another surprise. Everyone was letting him down. Just as well that he was packing it all in. He'd grown tired of the squabbling among the sisters and the backbiting of the brothers. Human nature really was malicious.

Still, he would miss Zack. And now who would lead his people to the promised land of Arizona? He chuckled to himself since he didn't own any land in Arizona. But they wouldn't know that until they got there, would they?

He saw the cowboy shoot a look at Lola. She was standing off to Colt's left as if she didn't know what to do. He could see the tension in her face. She wasn't being so smart-mouthed now, was she? As much as he was enjoying this, he didn't have to ask what she was hoping would happen here.

But, this time, she'd been outplayed. The cowboy was going to lose. It was simply a matter of how much he would have to lose before this was over. Did he realize that he wasn't getting out of here alive? At this point, Jonas wasn't sure he cared if Lola and the baby survived either, though he still wanted the woman, and damned if he wouldn't have her—dead or alive. The thought didn't even surprise him. His father used to say that one day he would reach rock bottom. Was this it?

"Why would you want a woman who doesn't love you?" Colt asked conversationally, as if they were old friends discussing the weather—and took a step closer.

"Because I can have her. I can have anything I want, and I want her. The baby is optional. I guess that's up to you."

"How's that?"

"You can't reach me before I hurl your baby into the rock fireplace. But if you try, I will, and then we will only be talking about Lola. The thing is, I don't think she will love you anymore, not after you got her baby killed," Jonas said. "Want to take a chance on that? Take another step…"

COLT COULD SEE that Jonas's arms were tiring from holding Grace up the way he was. He was using the baby like a shield. There was no way Colt could get a shot off with Jonas sitting and the baby out in front of him. Nor could he chance that, as he fired, Jonas wouldn't throw Grace into the rocks.

One glance at Lola and he knew that what they both feared was a real possibility—Jonas could drop the baby at any moment. Or, worse, throw Grace against the rock fireplace as he was threatening.

"Colt, I'll go with him. It's the only way," Lola pleaded as she stepped to him, grabbing his arm.

It was a strange thing for her to do and for a moment he didn't understand. Then he felt her reach behind him to the pistol he had at his back. She must have seen the bulk of it under his shirt. She freed the gun and dropped her hands to her sides, keeping turned so Jonas couldn't see what she held. Then she began to cry.

"You heard her," Jonas said. "Leave before someone gets hurt. Before you get hurt." His arms were shaking visibly. "If you care anything about this child…"

Jonas knew Colt wasn't leaving without Lola and Grace. Saying he could walk away was all bluff. Did he have a weapon handy? Colt suspected so.

Lola was still halfway facing him so she could keep the gun in her hand hidden. Colt feared what she planned to do, but he could feel time running out. Jonas was losing patience. Worse, his arms were shaking now. He couldn't hold the baby much longer—and he couldn't back down. Wouldn't.

"Tell him, Jonas," she cried, suddenly running toward the cult leader and dropping to her knees only feet from him after sticking the gun in the waist of her jeans. "Tell him I'm going with you, and that it's true and to leave."

The cult leader hadn't expected her to do that. For a moment, it looked as if he was going to throw the baby.

Before he could, Lola grabbed for Grace with her left hand. At the same time, she pulled the pistol from behind her with her right. She had hold of Grace's chubby little leg and wasn't letting go.

Everything happened fast after that. Colt, seeing what Lola had planned, took the shot the moment Lola managed to pull the baby down and away from Jonas's smug face. Colt had always been an expert shot. Even during the most stressful situations.

He missed. Jonas had fallen forward just enough that the shot went over his head and lodged in the back of the chair. Before he could fire again, he heard Lola fire. She'd taken the shot from the floor, shooting under Grace to hit the man low in the stomach. He saw Jonas release Grace as he grabbed for his bleeding belly.

Lola dropped the gun and pulled Grace into her arms. They were both crying. As Colt rushed to the cult leader, his gun leveled at the man's head, Lola scrambled away from Jonas with Grace tucked in her arms.

Jonas was holding his stomach with one hand and fumbling for something in the chair with the other. Colt was aiming to shoot, to finish Jonas, when he saw that it wasn't a gun the cult leader was going for. It was the man's phone.

He watched Jonas punch at the screen, his bloody fingers slippery, his hands shaking. It took a moment for the alert to sound. Jonas seemed to wait, one bloody hand on his stomach, the other on his phone. He stared at the front door, expecting it to come flying open as one of the guards burst in.

Seconds passed, then several minutes. Nothing

happened. Jonas looked wild-eyed at the door as if he couldn't believe it.

"They've all left," Colt said. "There is no one to help you."

Jonas looked down at his phone. With trembling fingers he made several attempts to key in 9-1-1 and finally gave up. "You have to call an ambulance. It's the humane thing to do."

"This from the man who was about to kill my baby daughter?"

"You would let me bleed to death?"

Colt looked over at Lola, huddled in the corner with Grace. Their gazes met. He pulled out his own phone and keyed in 9-1-1. He asked to speak to the sheriff.

When he was connected with Flint, he said, "You were right. Jonas hit us in the middle of the night. He sent two men to kill me. I left them in the old gravel pits. He took Lola and Grace, but they are both safe now. Unfortunately, one of his guards tried to shoot me. He's dead outside here on the compound and Jonas is wounded, so you'll need an ambulance and a—" He was going to say *coroner*, but before he could get the word out, the front door of the cabin banged open.

He spun around in time to see Zack bleeding and barely able to stand, but the man could still shoot. He fired the weapon in his hand in a barrage of bullets before Colt could pull the trigger.

LOLA SCREAMED. GRACE WAILED. It happened so fast. She'd thought it was all over. Finally. She'd thought they were finally safe. And so had Colt. He hadn't expected Zack to be alive—let alone come in shooting— any more than she had.

Colt threw himself in Grace's and her direction. As he did, he brought up the weapon he'd been holding on Jonas. The air filled with the loud reports of gunfire.

Lola laid her body over Grace's to protect her, knowing that Colt had thrown himself toward them to do the same. It took her a few moments to realize that the firing had stopped. She peeked out, terrified that she would find Colt lying dead at her feet.

Colt lay on his side, his back to her. She put Grace down long enough to reach for him. He was holding his leg, blood oozing out from between his fingers. He looked up at her.

"Are you and Grace—"

"We're fine. But you're bleeding," Lola cried.

"It's just a flesh wound," Colt said. "Don't worry about me. As long as you and Grace are all right…" He grimaced as he tried to get to his feet.

In the doorway, Zack lay crumpled on the floor. Lola couldn't tell if he was breathing or not. Her gaze swung to Jonas. He had tumbled out of his chair. He wasn't breathing, given that the top of his head was missing. She looked away quickly.

Grace's wailing was the only sound in the room. She rushed to her. As she did, she saw Colt's cell phone on the floor and picked it up. The sheriff was still there.

"We need an ambulance. Colt is wounded. Zack and Jonas are dead."

"Tommy," Colt said, trying to get to his feet. "He would have seen Zack heading for the cabin…" He limped to the door and pushed it open. Beyond it, he saw Tommy slumped over the controls of the helicopter. "There isn't time to wait for an ambulance. Tell the sheriff we'll be at the hospital."

As she related to the sheriff what Colt had said, she hurried to the couch. Squatting down, she fished her ring from under it. Her gentle toss of it hadn't hurt the ring or the diamonds. She slipped it on her finger, feeling as if now she could face anything again. Then, holding Grace in her arms, she ran after Colt to the helicopter sitting like a big dark bird in the middle of the compound.

COLT IGNORED THE pain as he ran to the helicopter. When he reached Tommy, he hurriedly felt for a pulse. For a moment, he thought his friend was dead, and yet he didn't see any blood. He found a pulse and felt a wave of relief. He'd dragged his friend into this. The last thing he wanted to do was get him killed.

On closer inspection, he could see a bump the size of a goose egg on Tommy's head. He figured Zack must have ambushed him before coming up to the cabin to finish things.

"Is he...?" Lola asked from behind him. She held a crying Grace in her arms and was trying to soothe her.

"He's alive, but we need to get him to the hospital. Come around the other side and climb in the back with Grace." Colt helped them in and then slid into the seat and took over the controls. He started up the motor. The rotors began to turn and then spin. A few minutes later, he lifted off and headed for Gilt Edge.

The helicopter swept over the tops of the pines and out of the mountains. Colt glanced over at Tommy. He seemed to be coming around. In the back, Lola had calmed Grace down and she now slept in her mother's arms.

He told himself that all was right with the world. Lola and Grace were safe. Tommy was going to make it. But he was feeling the effects of his blood loss as he saw the hospital's helipad in the distance. He'd never lost a bird. He told himself he wasn't going to lose this one—especially with the precious cargo he was carrying.

Colt set the chopper down and turned off the engine. After that, everything became a blur. He knew he'd lost a lot of blood and was light-headed, but it wasn't until he'd shut down the chopper and tried to get out that he realized how weak he was.

The last thing he remembered was seeing hospital staff rushing toward the helicopter pushing two gurneys.

# Chapter Nineteen

Colt woke to find Lola and Grace beside his bed. He tried to sit up, but Lola gently pushed him back down.

"Tommy is fine," she told him as if knowing exactly what he needed to hear. "A mild concussion. The doctor is having a terrible time keeping him in bed. We're all fine now."

Colt relaxed back on the pillows and smiled. "I was so worried. But everyone's all right?"

She nodded. "I was worried about you." She pushed a lock of hair back from his forehead and looked into his eyes. "You lost so much blood, but the doctor says you're going to be fine."

He glanced over at the IV attached to his arm. "I remember flying the chopper to the hospital but not much after that." He took her hand and squeezed it. "How is Grace?"

"Sleeping." Lola pointed to the bassinet the nurses had brought in for her. "I refused to leave until I knew you were all right." They'd also brought in a cot for Lola, he saw. "I've just been going back and forth from your room to Tommy's."

Colt smiled, took her hand and squeezed it. "I almost lost you. Again."

"But you saved me. Again. Aren't you getting tired of it?"

He shook his head. "Never." He glanced down at the ring on her finger. When he'd come into the cabin, he'd seen her rubbing the spot on her left hand where it had been. He hadn't been surprised Jonas hadn't liked seeing the ring on her finger. "When are you going to marry me?"

"You name the day. But right now you're in the middle of selling your ranch and holding an auction, and the doctor isn't going to let you out of here for a while. The bullet missed bone, but your leg is going to take some time to heal. Also, I believe you missed your appointment with your Realtor."

Colt grimaced. "Margaret. She is going to be furious."

"I called her. Apparently, ending up in the hospital bought you some time."

"I need to talk to Tommy, but I want to talk to him about my plan for the future, for *our* future."

The hospital-room door opened and Sheriff Flint Cahill stuck his head in. "Our patient awake? I hate to interrupt, but I need to talk to Colt if he's up to it."

Colt pulled Lola down for a kiss. "I'll talk to the sheriff. You can leave Grace. If she wakes up, I'll take care of her."

She nodded. "I know you will." She said hello to the sheriff. "I'll just be down the hall."

Flint took off his Stetson and pulled up a chair. "I've

already spoken with Tom Garrett and Lola. I have their statements, but I need yours. I have two dead men up on the mountain, two suffering from dehydration and two more in the hospital. Elmer and Carl have been picked up. They both said they were the ones who almost got killed, not you." He pulled out his notebook and pen. "Said you knocked them into the gravel pit."

Colt nodded. "After they took me from my house in the middle of the night, tied me up and planned to kill me and dump me in the pit. They probably didn't mention that."

"Actually, Elmer confessed this morning. They're both behind bars." The sheriff sighed. "Just give me the basics. You'll have to come down to the office when you're released."

Colt related everything from the time he was awakened by the cult members breaking into the house until he landed the helicopter at the hospital.

"It would have been nice if you'd given me a call," Flint said.

"Jonas would have killed them. He was so close to hurting Grace…" His voice broke. "If Lola hadn't acted when she did…"

"Jonas had one bullet in him from a gun registered to you, but all the others were from a gun registered to Jonas himself. We found it next to Zack's body. Why would Zack kill his own leader?"

Colt shook his head. "He came in firing. When I jumped out of the way, he kept firing…"

"He's the one who wounded you?"

"Yes. And the one who knocked out Tommy, but he might have already told you that."

"Actually," the sheriff said. "He didn't see who or what hit him."

"Zack was the only guard left. Everyone else vacated the property."

"Lola said that most of them were headed to Arizona, where Jonas had promised them a place to live, but we can't find any property owned by him or SLS," Flint said. "We did, though, find a variety of places where he has stashed their money, a lot of it. I would imagine there'll be lawsuits against his estate."

"Lola thinks he murdered her parents. They're buried on the compound."

The sheriff raked a hand through his hair. "We saw that there is a new grave in the woods. We were able to contact a couple of SLS followers who didn't make it any farther than town. They said they think he killed Sister Rebecca and that she is buried in the new grave." He shook his head. "He had me fooled."

"Me, too. For a while," Colt admitted.

Grace began to whimper next to his bed.

The sheriff put away his notebook and pen as he rose. "I'll let you see to your daughter." He tipped his Stetson as he left.

THE STORY HIT the local paper the next day. SLS members were spilling their guts about what had gone on up at the compound. A half dozen had already filed lawsuits against the fortune Jonas had amassed.

The article made Colt and Tommy sound like heroes.

Colt figured that was Lola's doing since she'd told him she'd been interviewed by a reporter. She'd said she was anxious for her story—and that of her parents—to get out.

"Maybe it will keep other people from getting taken in by men like Jonas," she'd said. "He caught my parents at a vulnerable time in their lives. But if they could be fooled, then anyone can."

Lola picked him up after the doctor released him from the hospital.

He sat in the passenger seat of the SUV she'd had delivered to his house. The woman was damned independent, but he liked that about her. Grace grinned at him from the car seat as they drove out to the ranch. Drove home. Well, home for a while anyway. All he'd been able to think about was getting back to that old ranch house that had felt like a prison before Lola. Now it felt like home.

Not that he was going to get sentimental and hang on to the house. Or the ranch. He wanted a new start for his little family.

They'd been home for a while when Tommy stopped by the house to see how he was doing before taking his helicopter home.

"You've met Lola," Colt said.

Tommy nodded.

"We got to know each other while we were waiting on you to get well. I had to thank him for all he did in helping us." She turned to the man from where she was making cookies in the kitchen. "We owe you. If you can stick around for twelve minutes, I will have a batch of chocolate chip cookies coming out of the oven. It's not much, given what you did for us."

"I'm just glad you're all right," Tommy said, looking bashful. "Anyway, I owe your husband. He saved my life. I'd do anything for him. I got to tell you, I think our boy Colt has done good this time," his friend said, grinning at Lola, then Colt. "You got yourself a good one," he said with a wink. "So what's this plan you wanted to talk to me about?"

"You're not mad at me for almost getting you killed?" Colt asked.

Tommy looked embarrassed. "I let some cult member sneak up on me."

"Zack was ex-military."

"That makes me feel a little better, but let's keep it to ourselves, okay? So what's up?" he asked as he took the chair he was offered at the kitchen table. Lola checked the cookies. Grace was watching her from her carrier on the counter. Colt liked watching Lola cook. He just liked watching her and marveling at how lucky he'd gotten.

"Colt?" Tommy said, grinning as he drew his attention again.

He laughed, then got serious. "Remember all the times we talked about starting our own helicopter service?" Colt and Tommy had spent hours at night in Afghanistan planning what they would do when they got out of the Army. Only Colt had stayed in, so their dream of owning their own flight company had been put off indefinitely.

"You still thinking about it?" Tommy asked.

"I know you're doing great with your repair business. I know you might not be interested in starting a company with me, but I've sold the ranch. I have money to invest. You don't have to answer right now. Take a few days to—"

"I don't need a few days. Absolutely," his friend said. "Where were you thinking of headquartering it?"

"There's a piece of land close by I'd like to build a house on. Right down the road from it would be the ideal place for the office, with lots of room for the shops and landing any number of birds."

Tommy laughed. "You really have been thinking about this." He glanced past Colt to Lola, who was busy taking the cookies out of the oven. "What about the military?" he asked, his gaze shifting back to Colt.

"I've decided not to take the upcoming assignment and resign my commission. I'm getting married. I have a family now. I don't want to be away from them."

"I get it," Tommy said as he took the warm cookie Lola offered him. "How soon?"

"I can make an offer on the land and we can get construction going on the shops and hangers—"

"How long before you get married?" Tommy asked with a laugh and took a bite of the cookie, before complimenting Lola.

"In three weeks. That was something else I needed to talk to you about," Colt said. "I need a best man."

LOLA WANTED TO pinch herself. She couldn't believe she was getting married. She'd never been so happy. She was glad they'd put off the wedding for a few weeks. There'd been a lot of questions about everything that had happened up on the mountain. The investigation, though, had finally ended.

It had taken a while for the bodies of her parents and Sister Rebecca to be exhumed. Just as she'd suspected, autopsies revealed that both of her parents had been poisoned. So had Rebecca. Lola made arrangements to have their remains flown to California and reinterred in the plots next to her sister's.

"You have nothing to feel guilty about," Colt had assured her.

"But if I'd come straight home after university and tried to get them out of that place—"

"You know it wouldn't have done any good. They were determined that you join them, right?"

She'd nodded. "But if I'd come right home when I got my father's letter, maybe I could have—"

"You know how Jonas operated. It wouldn't have made a difference. You said yourself that your mother adored Jonas. You couldn't have gotten her to leave and your father wouldn't have left without her, right?"

She'd known he was right. Still, she hated that she hadn't been able to save them. She was just grateful to Colt. If it hadn't been for him…

Lola looked down at her sleeping daughter. Yes, if it hadn't been for him there would have been no Grace.

COLT WANDERED THROUGH the days afterward, more content than he had ever been. He and Lola went horseback riding. She took to it so well that she made him promise he would teach Grace when she was old enough.

"I'll teach all of the kids."

"All of the kids?" she'd asked with one raised eyebrow.

He'd smiled as he'd pulled her to him. "Tell me you wouldn't mind having a couple more."

"You want a son."

"I want whatever you give me," he'd said, nuzzling her neck and making her laugh. "I'll be taking all girls if that's what you've got for me."

Lola had kissed him, promising to give him as many children as he wanted.

"And I'll teach them all to fly. Which reminds me, anytime you want to go for a ride… The helicopters will be coming in right after the wedding."

The new owners of the ranch had allowed Colt to stay on with his family until he was able to get a mobile home put on the land he'd bought back from them. "We'll live in it until the house is finished, then maybe use it for the office until the office building is done."

Lola seemed as excited as he was about the business they were starting with Tommy. She kept busy with her new friends Lillie and Mariah. They were actually talking playdates for the kids.

He ran into Wyatt a couple more times in town. He hadn't wanted to slug him. Actually, he'd wanted to thank him. The thought had made him laugh.

Also, Colt hadn't been that surprised when Julia called. He almost hadn't answered. "Hello?"

"Colt, it's Julia. I saw your engagement announcement in the newspaper not long after that story came out. What a story."

He didn't know what to say.

"Wyatt and I are over. I know you don't care, but I wanted you to hear it from me first."

"I'm sorry." He really was. He no longer had any ill will toward either of them and said as much.

"I won't bother you again. I'm actually leaving town. But I had to ask you something..." She seemed to hesitate. "It's amazing what you did for this Lola woman. You really put up a fight to save her and the baby."

He waited, wondering where she was going with this.

"Why..." Her voice broke. "Why didn't you put up a fight for me?"

It had never crossed his mind to try to keep Julia from marrying Wyatt. She was right. He hadn't put up a fight. He'd been hurt, he'd been angry, but he hadn't made some grandiose effort like riding a horse into the church to stop the wedding—if it had ever gone that far.

"I hope you find what you're looking for," he said, because there wasn't anything else he could say.

"And I hope you're unhappy as hell." She disconnected.

He looked over at Lola and laughed.

"Julia," she said.

"Yep, she called to say she liked the article."

Lola smiled. "You're a terrible liar."

"She's leaving town."

"Really?" She didn't seem unhappy to hear that.

"She wished us well."

"Now I know you're lying," she said as he pulled her close.

THE WEDDING TOOK PLACE in a field of flowers surrounded by the four mountain ranges. Colt had purchased the property just days before. He'd had to scramble to get everything moved in for the ceremony.

What had started as a small wedding had grown, as old and new friends wanted to be a part of it.

"Lola, I know this isn't what we planned," Colt had apologized. They'd agreed to a small wedding, and somehow it had gone awry.

She had laughed. "I love that all these people care about you and want to be there. They're becoming my friends, as well." Lillie and Mariah had given her a baby shower, the three becoming instant friends.

He kissed her. "I just want it to be the best day of your life."

"That day was when I met you."

Colt couldn't believe how many people had helped to make the day special. Calls came in from around the world from men he'd served with. A dozen of them flew in for the ceremony. The guest list had continued to grow right up until the wedding.

"Let us cater it for you," Lillie and Mariah had suggested. "Darby insists. And the Stagecoach Saloon is all yours for the reception, if it rains."

Lola had hugged her new friends, eyes glistening and Colt thought he couldn't be more blessed. Lola had accepted their kind offer and added, "Only if the two of you will agree to be my matrons of honor."

So much had been going on that the weeks leading up to the wedding had flown by. Colt wished his father was alive to see this—his only son changing diapers, getting up for middle-of-the-night feedings, bathing the baby in the kitchen sink, and all the while loving every minute of it.

Tommy always chuckled when he came by and caught Colt being a father. "If the guys could see you now," he'd joked. But Colt had seen his friend's wistful looks. He hoped Tommy found someone he could love as much as Colt loved Lola.

She'd continued to amaze him, taking everything in her stride as the ranch auction was held and the sale of the ranch continued. She'd had her things shipped from where they'd been in storage and helped him start packing up what he planned to keep at the house.

He'd felt overwhelmed sometimes, but Lola was always cool and calm. He often thought of that woman he'd met in Billings—and the one he'd found on his doorstep in the middle of the night. Often he didn't feel he was good enough for her. But then she would find him, put her arms around him and rest her head on his shoulder, and he would breathe in the scent of her and know that this was meant to be.

Like standing here now in a field of flowers next to Lola with all their friends and the preacher ready to marry them. If this was a dream, he didn't want to wake up.

LOLA COULDN'T BELIEVE all the people who had come into her life because of Colt. She looked over at him. He was so handsome in his Western suit and boots. He was looking at her, his blue eyes shining. He smiled as the preacher said, "Do you take this woman—"

"I sure do," he said, and everyone laughed.

Lola hardly remembered the rest of the ceremony. She felt so blissfully happy that she wasn't even sure her feet had touched the ground all day.

But she remembered the kiss. Colt had pulled her to him, taking his time as he looked into her eyes. "I love you, Lola," he'd whispered.

She'd nodded through her tears and then he'd kissed her. The crowd had broken into applause. Cowboy hats and Army caps had been thrown into the air. Somewhere beyond the crowd, a band began to play.

Lillie hugged her before handing her Grace. Lola looked up from the infant she held in her arms, her eyes full of tears. Colt put his arm around both of them as they took their first steps as Mr. and Mrs. Colt McCloud.

\* \* \* \* \*

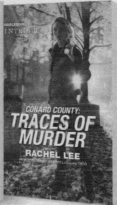

Lena Love kicked a rock out from underneath her foot, then bent down and tightened the twill shoelaces on her brown leather hiking boots.

The crime scene investigator, who doubled as a forensic science technician, stood back up and eyed Los Angeles's Cucamonga Wilderness trail. Sharp-edged stones and ragged shards of bark covered the rugged, winding terrain.

"Watch your step," she uttered to herself before continuing along the path of her latest crime scene.

Lena squinted as she focused on the trail. Heavy foliage loomed overhead, blocking out the sun's brilliant rays. She pulled out her flashlight, hoping its bright beam would help uncover potential evidence.

An ominous wave of vulnerability swept through her chest at the sight of the vast San Gabriel Mountains. She spun around slowly, feeling small while eyeing the infinite views of the forest, desert and snowy mountainous peaks.

The wild surroundings left her with a lingering sense of defenselessness. Lena tightened the belt on her tan suede blazer. She hoped it would give her some semblance of security.

It didn't.

Lena wondered if the latest victim had felt that same vulnerability on the night she'd been brutally murdered.

"Come on, Grace Mitchell," Lena said aloud, as if the dead woman could hear her. "Talk to me. Tell me what happened to you. *Show* me what happened to you."

A gust of wind whipped Lena's bone-straight bob across her slender face. She tucked her hair behind her ears and stooped down, aiming the flashlight toward the majestic oak tree where Grace's body had been found.

Lena envisioned spotting droplets of blood, a cigarette butt, the tip of a latex glove…*anything* that would help identify the killer.

This was her second visit to the crime scene. The thought of showing up to the station without any viable evidence yet again caused an agonizing pang of dread to shoot up her spine.

Grace was the fifth victim of a criminal whom Lena had labeled an organized serial killer. He appeared to have a type. Young, slender brunette women. Their bodies had all been found in heavily wooded areas. Each victim's hands were meticulously tied behind their backs with a three-strand twisted rope. They'd been strangled to death. And the amount of evidence left at each scene was practically nonexistent.

But the killer's signature mark was always there. And it was a sinister one.

*Look for*
**The Heart-Shaped Murders** *by Denise N. Wheatley,*
*available June 2022 wherever*
*Harlequin Intrigue books and ebooks are sold.*

Harlequin.com

# Get 4 FREE REWARDS!

### We'll send you 2 FREE Books plus 2 FREE Mystery Gifts.

FREE Value Over $20

Both the **Harlequin Intrigue®** and **Harlequin® Romantic Suspense** series feature compelling novels filled with heart-racing action-packed romance that will keep you on the edge of your seat.

# *Love Harlequin romance?*

## DISCOVER.

Be the first to find out about promotions, news and exclusive content!

**f** Facebook.com/HarlequinBooks

**🐦** Twitter.com/HarlequinBooks

**⊡** Instagram.com/HarlequinBooks

**P** Pinterest.com/HarlequinBooks

**You Tube** YouTube.com/HarlequinBooks

ReaderService.com

## EXPLORE.

Sign up for the Harlequin e-newsletter and download a free book from any series at **TryHarlequin.com**

## CONNECT.

Join our Harlequin community to share your thoughts and connect with other romance readers!
**Facebook.com/groups/HarlequinConnection**

**HARLEQUIN**

*Heartfelt or thrilling, passionate or uplifting—Harlequin is more than just happily-ever-after.*

With twelve different series to choose from and new books available every month, you are sure to find stories that will move you, uplift you, inspire and delight you.